Her ten super[...] [...]e
that one of the [...] [...]h
mys[...]

THE REIGNING QUEEN OF MYSTERY!

MARTHA GRIMES

"ONE OF THE ESTABLISHED MASTERS OF
THE GENRE."

—*Newsweek*

"STYLISH AND WITTY—FRESH TRIBUTE TO
THE CLASSICAL BRITISH WHODUNIT."

—*San Francisco Chronicle*

"READ ANY ONE [OF HER NOVELS] AND
YOU'LL WANT TO READ THEM ALL."

—*Chicago Tribune*

"A CLASS ACT . . . SHE WRITES WITH
CHARM, AUTHORITY, AND IRONIC WIT."

—*Kirkus Reviews*

"FIRST-RATE . . . A MASTER AT DELIVER-
ING THE SIGNIFICANT DETAIL."

—*Booklist*

"IF JANE AUSTEN WERE ALIVE AND WELL
AND WRITING MYSTERY STORIES TODAY,
SHE'D BE MARTHA GRIMES."

—*The Hartford Courant*

*The Orlando Sentinel

By Martha Grimes

THE MAN WITH A LOAD OF MISCHIEF
THE OLD FOX DECEIV'D
THE ANODYNE NECKLACE
THE DIRTY DUCK
JERUSALEM INN
HELP THE POOR STRUGGLER
THE DEER LEAP
I AM THE ONLY RUNNING FOOTMAN
THE FIVE BELLS AND BLADEBONE
THE OLD SILENT

THE OLD FOX
DECEIV'D

Martha Grimes

A DELL BOOK

Published by
Dell Publishing
a division of
Bantam Doubleday Dell Publishing Group, Inc.
666 Fifth Avenue
New York, New York 10103

To my brother Bill

ISBN: 0-440-16747-7

Reprinted by arrangement with Little, Brown and Company, Inc.

Printed in the United States of America

Published simultaneously in Canada

Two previous Dell Editions

February 1991

19   18   17   16   15   14   13   12   11   10

RAD

· I ·

Night
at the Angel Steps

1.

SHE came out of the fog, her face painted half-white, half-black, walking down Grape Lane. It was early January and the sea-roke drove in from the east, turning the cobbled street into a smoky tunnel that curved down to the water. The bay was open to the full force of gales, and the scythelike curve of Grape Lane acted as a conduit for the winds from the sea. Far off the fog siren known as the Whitby Bull gave its four mournful blasts.

The wind billowed her black cape, which settled again round her ankles in an eddying wave. She wore a white satin shirt and white satin trousers stuffed into high-heeled black boots. The click of the heels on the wet stones was the only sound except for the dry *gah-gah* of the gulls. One strutted on a ledge above her, pecking at the windows. To avoid the wind she clung to the fronts of the tiny houses. She looked up alleyways that seemed to end in cul-de-sacs, but from which steps like hidden springs curled down to other passages. The narrow street came right up to the cottage doors and black iron bootscrapers. She stopped for a moment beneath the dim streetlamp when someone passed her on the other side of the lane. But in this fog, no one was recognizable. She could see the pub at the end of the lane by the breakwater, its windows glowing mistily like opals in the dark.

When she came to the iron gates of the Angel steps, she stopped. The wide stair was on her left and connected Grape Lane and Scroop Street above with Our Lady of the Veil, the church at the top of the village. She unlatched the gates and walked up, a long walk to a small landing where a bench served as a resting place. Someone was sitting there.

The woman in black and white took a step back and down, startled. She opened her mouth to speak. The figure had risen, two arms coming out suddenly as if jerked by strings — out, up and down. Struck again and again, the woman finally fell like a puppet and was kept from rolling down the steps only because the other one grabbed at her cape. Her body lay collapsed, sprawling, head down the steps. The other person turned and stepped over her, almost casually, and walked down the Angel steps back to Grape Lane, keeping close to the wall so as not to step in the blood.

It was Twelfth Night.

2.

"Certain kinds of people have *always* got away with murder!" Adrian Rees slammed his glass on the bar. He had been extolling the virtues of Russian literature and Raskolnikov.

No one in the Old Fox Deceiv'd was especially interested.

Adrian tapped his empty glass with his finger. "Another, Kitty me love."

"Don't 'Kitty-me-love' me, and you'll not be gettin' another until I see your money." Kitty Meechem wiped the counter where he'd banged the mug, sending his neighbor's beer over the sides of his glass like sea spray. "Drunk as a lord."

"Drunk is it? Ah, Kitty me gurhl . . ." His tone was wheedling as he reached out a hand towards Kitty's light brown locks, a hand she slapped away. "You'd not even stand one of your own countrymen?"

"Har! And yer no more Irish than me ginger cat."

The cat in question was curled up on a scrap of rug before the blazing hearth. It was always there, like a plaster ornament. Adrian wondered when it was ever up and around enough to get the cuts and scratches it sported. "Looks lazy enough to be Irish," said Adrian.

"Would you listen to the man? Him who spends his days dabbin' and daubin' and paintin' women without a stitch on." That comment earned a few sniggers up and down the line at the bar. "That cat does more an honest day's work than many I know."

Adrian leaned across the counter and stage-whispered: "Kitty, I'll tell all Rackmoor you posed for me in the nude!"

Titters to the left, giggles to the right from Billy Sims and Corky Fishpool. Imperturbable and rocklike, Kitty merely kept swabbing down the bar. "I'll have none a yer darty paintings and none a yer darty mouth. But" — she knifed the foam from a couple of glasses of dark beer — "only yer darty money. Or will I be seein' any this night a tall a tall?"

Adrian looked hopefully from Billy to Corky, both of whom immediately struck up fresh conversations with those beside them. No buyers. Not for his paintings, either, which was why he had no money.

"You should be worrying about the state of your souls, not your purses!"

Corky Fishpool looked at him and picked his teeth. Adrian returned to the tale of Raskolnikov: "He came back to the conniving old woman again and again to pawn his few belongings . . . tight she was." (And here he leveled a glance at Kitty Meechem, who ignored him.) "Then one day he crept up the stairs . . ." Adrian's fingers walked slowly towards Billy Sims's glass, which was quickly pulled out of reach. "And when he got inside and her back was turned — VROOM! He let her have it." He noticed he had drawn a few more listeners, coming up to stand behind him. But no one offered to buy. Not even Homer could get a drink out of this lot.

"What'd t'fool do that fer, it's daft, fer a bit a money as 'e got." This came from Corky's cousin, Ben Fishpool, a humorless, literal man, a beefy fisherman with a face like a slab off the cliffside, and a dragon tattooed on his forearm. He kept his own pewter mug hanging above the bar. He drank by holding it finger in handle, thumb on rim, as if making sure no one would wrest it away.

"Because he wanted to understand the nature of guilt, something you swillers of ale would not appreciate." Adrian reached for a pickled egg in a bowl and Kitty slapped his hand away.

"Summat daft, 'e be," mumbled Ben, not satisfied with that explanation.

"Guilt, redemption, sin! That's what it's all about." Adrian twirled round and addressed the room at large. The air was almost fruity with the pungent smoke of many tobaccos. Smoke hung suspended over the tables as if the sea-fret had crept in, penetrated the walls, slid under the door and across the sills. Adrian thought it should have been a grand place to talk about guilt and sin; the expressions of those still hanging on till closing time seemed fairly to dote on life's being a trial. Any burst of laughter was soon quelled, as if the offender had caught himself having a giggle in a graveyard.

"Raskolnikov wanted to show that certain kinds of people could do murder and not suffer for it." No one seemed to be listening.

"And don't you go wheedlin' money out a Bertie," said Kitty, as if she hadn't heard a word about sin, guilt nor Raskolnikov. "I seen you do that only this last week. Shameful, it is." She flicked the bar-towel in his direction. "A grown man gettin' beer money from a wee bairn, a pore, pore, motherless lad."

Adrian hooted. "Bertie? A 'pore, pore motherless lad'? Christ, he charges more interest than the banks. I think Arnold keeps the books." Even behind those thick glasses, the kid had eyes like rivets. He'd have a confession out of Raskolnikov inside of two minutes.

"And you needn't go sayin' nasty things about Arnold, neither. I've seen Arnold walk down wee paths along these cliffs, no wider'n a wee snake. While *you* can't even walk a straight line up to the High."

"Ha ha ha," said Adrian, unable to outtalk Kitty, as usual, or think of a witty reply. His eye fell on Percy Blythe's glass

of bitter. Percy Blythe's sharp little eyes screwed up and he
put his two hands quickly over the glass. Then he went back
to his reading.

"Philistines! You none of you understand sin and guilt!"

"That and fifty pence'll buy you a pint," said Kitty.
"TIME, GENTLEMEN, PLEASE!"

The door slapped shut behind him and Adrian buckled
up the oilskin over his blue guernsey and pulled his knitted
cap down over his ears. January in Rackmoor was hell.

The Old Fox Deceiv'd was so near the water that waves
once washed its outer walls. At one time, high waves had
swept the bow of a ship straight through it. Finally, a seawall had been erected. The front of the pub faced the little
cove where tiny boats slapped about in the water. From the
north toward Whitby came the mournful dirge of the
Whitby Bull.

Four narrow streets converged here: Lead Street, the
High, Grape Lane and Winkle Alley. The High was the
only one of them wide enough for a car, if any intrepid
driver felt like daring the incredible angle of descent from
the top of the village. It was on the High that Adrian lived,
near the other end where the street dog-legged before con-
tinuing its gravity-defying ascent. He decided to walk along
Grape Lane, though; it was not quite so steep and there
were fewer booby traps of broken cobbles. Behind him as
he walked he could still hear the regulars in the Fox hanging on until the quarter-hour closing. Philistines.

He heard her before he saw her.

Just as he was passing the Angel steps, he heard the tiny
hammer-taps of the high heels. She came out of the fog on
the other side of Grape Lane, walking towards the Angel
steps and the sea. The wind whipped her black cape round
her white trousers. Adrian thought he was proof against
any odd sight in Rackmoor, yet he shrank back a bit against

the cold stone of a cottage. For the barest moment she stopped in the arc of one of the few lamps and he took her in.

When Adrian wanted to remember something — the scattered pattern of colored leaves; the lay of the moonlight; the fold of velvet across an arm — he didn't have to look twice. The shutter of his eye snapped it, fixed it in his memory, filed it for future reference. He had always thought that he would make one hell of a police witness.

In those few seconds beneath the lamp she was painted in his memory: the black cape, white satin shirt and pants, black boots, black cap on her head. But it was the face that was memorable. As if a line had been drawn absolutely evenly down the bridge of her nose, the left side was painted white, the right side black. And a small, black mask completed the weird, checkerboard look.

She walked on quickly toward the Angel steps and the sea, the high heels drumming back into the fog. He stood staring into nothing for a few seconds.

Then he remembered it was Twelfth Night.

3.

"Shall I be Mother?"

Bertie Makepiece held the stoneware teapot aloft. It was very late to be up making tea, but with no school tomorrow, Bertie felt he could indulge himself; he'd been peckish ever since their evening meal. He was wearing an apron much too large so he had secured it with the tie running round his chest and under his arms. Now he stood with teapot poised over cup and waited patiently for Arnold's answer.

None was forthcoming from the occupant of the other chair. One might have felt, though, looking into Arnold's earnest eyes, that his failure to respond was not because he was a dog, but because, No, he really didn't want to be Mother.

Arnold was a Staffordshire terrier the color of a Yorkshire pudding or a fine, dry sherry. The unnervingly steady look of his dark eyes might have made one think he was not a dog at all, but someone doing an impersonation, zipped up in a dog suit. He was a quiet dog; seldom did he bark. It was as if he had decided one couldn't make it through life on mouth alone. The other village dogs followed him, but respectfully, at a distance. Arnold was a dog's dog. Whenever he snuffled along walks and through alleyways, he always gave the impression of being onto something big.

"Did you hear something, Arnold?"

Arnold had nearly finished the milk in his bowl — laced with a bit of tea — and sat up, ears pricked.

Bertie slid off his chair and padded over to the window. Their cottage on Scroop Street was wedged between two others: one belonged to some summer people and the other to old Mrs. Fishpool who put out scraps for Arnold which he took up the alley and buried in the dustbin.

The Makepiece cottage was near the Angel steps. The hardier parishoners trudged up them every Sunday to Our Lady. Looking out and down, Bertie could see nothing through the fog except the ghostly outlines of peaked roofs and chimney pots below.

There was a tapping above him on the window of his bedroom. Bertie jumped. A herring gull, maybe, or a fulmar: *ag-ag-aror*, it seemed to be chuckling, as if it had a joke on the village. They were always doing that, waking him in the morning sometimes, coming like visitors to knock at the door. Gulls and terns — bloody old birds acted like they owned the place.

Arnold was standing behind him, waiting to go out. "Well, hop it, then, Arnold." Bertie opened the door and Arnold slipped through like a shadow. Bertie called after him, "Mind you're back soon."

The dog stopped and looked back at Bertie; probably, he understood. Bertie stood there awhile, looking out at the moving mist. What he had heard had sounded like a scream. The birds were always screaming.

One scream sounded pretty much like another in Rackmoor.

4.

It was the Wakeman who found her.

Billy Sims had continued his evening revels with Corky Fishpool long after the closing of the Fox, visiting first one crony, then another in Lead Street and Winkle Alley. It was a night of celebration, after all.

Now, with his tricornered hat and fawn tunic on backwards, he decided to gain his own small cottage in Psalter's Lane, beside Our Lady, by walking up the Angel steps, although he knew they were unlit and unsafe in the winter darkness. With his horn tucked under his arm, he weaved upwards.

His foot struck something. Something unyielding and yet soft, not stone. He had no torch, but he did have matches. He struck one.

The match spurted up and he saw the upside-down and blood-covered face, the limbs going off in impossible directions, making the black-and-white figure look like a huge doll.

Billy Sims nearly took a dive down the steps. When he remembered that it was Twelfth Night, and that this was but some mummer who had strayed from a party, it only served to turn the nightmare real.

5.

Detective Inspector Ian Harkins of the Pitlochary C.I.D. was furious. The first really meaty case to come his way and the Chief Constable wanted to throw it to somebody from C.I. in London. *Over my dead body*, thought Harkins, grinning a little at his own gallows humor. Harkins had the face to go with it, sunken-eyed and skeletal.

His knuckles whitened on the telephone. "I see no reason for calling London. I'm not even there yet and you're talking about Scotland Yard. Kindly give me a chance." There was a certain acidity in his *kindly*.

Superintendent Bates reluctantly allowed him twenty-four hours. It sounded like the kind of case that might turn up complications; Leeds would not be happy.

Harkins finished dressing. For Ian Harkins, this was not a matter of dragging on unmatched socks and unpressed suit. He did it in front of a cheval mirror. He had a tailor in Jermyn Street and a rich aunt in Belgravia who doted on him, although she questioned his strange predilection for the frozen North and talked about his work as if it were a sometime hobby which had suddenly become addictive.

It wasn't a hobby; Harkins was an excellent policeman. His mind was shrewd, incisive, uncluttered by sentiment.

Harkins adjusted the belt on a camel's-hair coat, specially lined against the Yorkshire winter, and drew on gloves of a leather so fine they nearly melted on his hands. It was true he was an excellent policeman, but he was damned if he'd go about looking like one.

But a C.I.D. man is not supposed to waste time in dalliance over his clothes. To make up for it he hopped into his Lotus Elan, drove it up to ninety, and almost hoped some idiot patrolman would try to stop him on the fifteen miles of icy road to Rackmoor and the coast.

"Been bashed about pretty smartly, hasn't she?"

Detective Constable Derek Smithies grimaced. The description seemed much more appropriate to a rugby game than a bloody murder.

Ian Harkins got up from where he had been kneeling and adjusted the coat round his shoulders. His emaciated face made him look ten years older than he was. To make up for the skeletal look — cheekbones as prominent as small wings — he wore a long, full mustache. He had removed his beautiful, butter-leather gloves to examine the body. He drew them on again like a surgeon.

From the station in Pitlochary, a town five times the size of Rackmoor, but still with only a small police force, Inspector Harkins had called in half-a-dozen men, including a local doctor and the constable scratching down notes behind him. The Scene of Crimes man had already been and gone. A fingerprint expert was yet to come, a man who had the reputation for being able to lift stuff off the wings of flies. The pathologist got up, grunted, wiped his hands.

"Well?" said Harkins, shoving a thin, hand-rolled Cuban cigar back in his mouth.

The doctor shrugged. "I don't know. It looks like somebody took a pitchfork to her."

Harkins looked at him. "A rather unwieldy weapon, man. Try again."

The doctor matched Harkins's own ascerbic tone. "Vampire bats."

"Funny."

"Ice pick, awl, God knows. She looks like a sieve. But the ice pick's out because it looks like whatever it was had more than one prong. I can tell better when I have the body back at the morgue."

Harkins crouched down again. "The face . . . Shine that torch over here, will you?" he called to one of the men combing over the steps. There were three or four torches in use, up and down the steps like giant fireflies. One swiveled over to shine on the woman's face. "Under the blood it looks like makeup, greasepaint of some sort. Black one side, white the other. Weird." Harkins rose, dusted his trousers by slapping his gloves against them. "Time?" he snapped.

Elaborately, the doctor took out his turnip watch and said, "Precisely one fifty-nine."

Harkins threw down his cigar, ground it under his heel. "You know goddamned well what I mean."

The doctor clicked his bag shut. "I don't work for you, remember. I'd say she'd been at least two hours gone, maybe three. I'm just a country doctor; you called *me*. So be civil."

As if civility were a term only in the lexicon of country doctors, Harkins turned to Constable Smithies: "I want blocks put up at both ends of these steps with notices to keep clear. And get those people out of here." Down on Grape Lane, ghostly faces were still appearing and disappearing as they had done ever since Harkins and then the other police cars had showed up. More and more villagers were tumbling out of bed to see what all the ruckus was. Harkins managed to ask the next simple question in the most withering of tones: "Her name was Temple, you said?"

Smithies tried to make himself small, difficult for such a big man. "Yes, sir. They tell me she was staying at the Fox Deceiv'd, the pub down by the seawall."

"Stranger to town?"

"I suppose so."

"You suppose so. Well, what's a stranger doing in that weird get-up? Does Rackmoor often get such visitors?" Smithies might have been personally responsible for the turning up of the woman in black and white.

"It's a costume, sir . . ."

"You don't say so." Harkins lit another cigar.

". . . because of Twelfth Night. There was a costume party up at Old House. She must have been going to it. Or coming back."

"Where the hell's Old House?"

Smithies pointed up the Angel steps, jabbing his finger as if to make it pass the church. "If you're from these parts, you must know it, sir. That's the Old Fox Deceiv'd Manor House."

"I thought you just said that was the name of the pub."

"It is, sir. Only the pub half belongs to the Colonel, and he named it after the house. So we just call one Old House and the other the Fox to keep them straight. Kitty's place used to be the Cod and Lobster, see. But the Colonel, Colonel Crael, he's that crazy over fox hunting—"

"I don't care if it used to be called my Aunt Fanny, what's—wait a minute. Are you talking about Sir Titus Crael? *That* Colonel Crael?"

"That's him, sir."

"You mean she"—he pointed to the place where the body was in the process of being carried down the steps in a rubber sheet—"she was a guest of his?"

"I guess so, sir."

Under his breath, Harkins muttered something, looking down at the chalked-off place as if he wished he could get her back here again.

Inspector Harkins had little respect for his superiors, whether in Pitlochary, Leeds, or London. He certainly had no respect for his *inferiors*, assuming they were down there because that's where they deserved to be.

But one thing he did respect: privilege. The Craels had as much as anyone in Yorkshire.

And now he was at war with himself: on the one hand he'd simply like to dump the body back where he'd found it and give London the headache.

But on the other, he was Ian Harkins.

· II ·

Morning in York

Melrose Plant rested his paper on his knee and turned over the hourglass.

"Where'd you get that contraption?" Lady Agatha Ardry was separated from her nephew by a splotch of Axminster carpet and a tiered cake-plate. She had been sitting for the last hour like a baby whale on the Queen Anne couch, shoving in fairy cakes and brandy snaps and calling it her "elevenses."

Fairy cakes at eleven in the morning? Melrose shuddered, but answered her question. "In an antique shop near the Shambles." He pushed his gold-rimmed glasses back on his elegant nose and returned to his newspaper.

"Well?" She held her teacup with little finger extended. It was, he noted, somewhere around her third or fourth cup.

"Well, what?" He turned the page, looking for a cross-word puzzle to break the tedium.

"*Why* have you been sitting there turning it over every minute?"

Melrose Plant looked at her over the rims of his spectacles. "It's an hourglass, dear Agatha. Were I to turn it over every minute it would defeat its purpose."

"Don't be cryptic. Aren't you having any of this lovely tea Teddy had done for us?"

"Teddy will never notice I didn't eat." Teddy. Any woman who permitted herself to be called *Teddy* deserved Agatha for a fortnight's visit. He wondered what the *Teddy* stood for: Theodore, from the look of her. She was a very large woman with red hair like a burning bush. This morning she was out doing the shops.

"You still haven't answered my question about the hourglass. Why did you turn it over? There's a perfectly good clock on the mantel." She squinted her eyes at it. "Wonder how much Teddy gave for it? Looks Italian."

She'd have the entire room appraised and priced inside of ten minutes, thought Melrose. "It used to be that pews had curtains, and parsons kept hourglasses on the pulpits. If there were to be further oratory from that quarter, the parson would turn over the hourglass. If one were bored by all of the sermonizing, one could draw the curtain. It is my understanding that Lord Byron, while visiting some friends in Yorkshire, attended church with them and immediately drew the curtain."

Agatha chewed this over, both literally and figuratively, while she ate a fairy cake with awful blue-y icing. After one of her infrequent silences, she said, "Melrose, do you remember that strange Uncle Davidson? The one on your dear mother's side of the family? Lady Marjorie's?"

"I remember the name of my mother, certainly. As to this uncle, what of him?"

"He was quite *mad*, everyone knew that. He talked very strangely, and I sometimes wonder . . ." She was stripping another fairy cake of its little paper coverlet. "It's just that you say and do the oddest things. *Now* here you are thinking of going off to some rubbishy little fishing village by the *sea* —"

"Fishing villages generally are." He remembered she had called it a "*quaint* little fishing village" before she discovered the invitation to visit did not include her.

She shuddered. "The North Sea, and in dead winter! Now, if it were Scarborough in summer, wouldn't that be jolly?"

Decidedly *un*jolly, thought Melrose. Scarborough in summer would be boardwalks and bathers and Agatha sticking to him like a barnacle. Melrose yawned and turned another page of the *York Mail*. "Well, there it is, then."

"I still do not understand why you are even *thinking* of going."

"Because I have been invited, dear Aunt. Which is why

one ordinarily goes places." Of course, the arrow fell wide:
Agatha had invited *herself* to Teddy's when she found Melrose was motoring to Yorkshire. Well, he thought he could
hardly refuse to take her as far as York; it was straight on his
way. Nor did he truly mind the stopover, for York was a
wonderful place. There was the Minster with its golden
pulpitum; the crooked Shambles with its closely tilting
shops and cottages. And he had even discovered a nice little
tucked-away men's club yesterday where he could relax in a
cracked leather armchair until rigor mortis set in. This
morning he had taken a walk part way round the walls.
Beautiful old York —

"... only a baronet."

Melrose roused himself from his reflections on the walls
and the gates of the city. "What?"

"This Sir Titus Crael. He's only a baronet. Whereas
you —"

"Whereas *I* am only a commoner. There are lots of us.
We are popping up all over Britain. I heard, though it
might be mere rumor, we have London surrounded and
have already captured the whole of Cornwall. Though we
might give it back." He snapped his newspaper.

"Oh, do stop being silly, Melrose. You know exactly what
I mean. No one will let you off with being just plain Melrose
Plant. Instead of the Earl of Caverness, I mean. *And* twelfth
Viscount Ardry, and grandson of —"

She was gearing up like a monkey-grinder and would be
cranking out the whole lot of titles, tunelessly, if he didn't
interrupt: "I am afraid they will *have* to let me off, since I
have let myself off. Funny how the old world keeps turning
without my title."

"I *still* don't see why you pretended to give it up. You're
not political. Your father might have been, but you're not.
You're not running for anything."

Only the door, thought Melrose. She *would* keep on

about it, but he had no intention of telling her. He leaned back and stared at the ceiling, thinking of his father, whom he had very much loved and admired. Except for all of that hunting tomfoolery. It was the hunting, he supposed which had made him such a friend of Titus Crael, whom Melrose hadn't seen in thirty years. His only memory of Sir Titus was of that day Melrose had gone cubbing, and of a tall, imposing figure standing next to him, the dead fox in his hands. They were going through that ghastly initiation, the ritual of blooding. Melrose found his ten-year-old face being wiped with the blood of the fox.

Where had it been? He could not remember. Somewhere in the Shires? Rutland, maybe? Or even up here on the Yorkshire moors. He could only remember drops of blood on the snow. Hunting had never appealed to him after that. . . .

"Quite a decent old house this," said Agatha, interrupting his reverie once again. "Bring a lot on today's market, I should think. That's an Adam ceiling."

Melrose had been studying its delicate pastels and white moldings. "A copy." Ceilings were his métier. He knew each ceiling in his own home, Ardry End, inch by inch. It came from staring up at them when his aunt was over to tea.

"The plates are Crown Derby. And that table's a very nice Sheraton," said Agatha.

Melrose watched her small eyes travel the length and breadth of the room, raking in Staffordshire figures, papier-mâché, cameo glass — the cash-register of her mind adding it all up. In her previous incarnation she had probably been an auctioneer.

"And did you see the size of that *ring* Teddy was wearing this morning? What sort of stone do you suppose it was?"

Melrose turned back to the front page of his paper. "A gallstone."

"You really do hate it, don't you, Melrose, when someone

has more than you." She looked at the cake-plate. "Let's have that butler in; there aren't any more brandy snaps." She plucked at the bellpull. Then she settled back, fluffing up the cushions. "I'd no idea Teddy'd done so well by her marriage. I believe her things are quite as fine as the ones at Ardry End."

"You mean by the late Mr. Harries-Stubbs's death."

"How cold-blooded of you, Melrose. But, then, I might expect you to take that line about marriage."

He refused to engage in any discussion of marriage. He was beginning to despair of ever finding that elusive She with whom to share himself and Ardry End. It was Ardry End, of course, that Agatha worried over. She liked to probe, was always dragging old names, old memories of women he had known like dead bodies across his path to see if she could trip him up, make him disclose some secret amour to which she was not privy and which might cut her out, as his only relative, of Ardry End — its real Adam ceilings, its early Georgian, its Meissen and Baccarat. What had ever given her the impression she had a right to this inheritance, Melrose couldn't imagine. And, although she was over sixty and Melrose only forty-one, it did not seem to occur to her he'd outlast her. Wishful thinking, no doubt.

"Is Vivian Rivington ever coming back from Italy, I wonder?"

It was another of her sidesaddle questions.

But Melrose did not answer because his eye was riveted on an item on the front page of the *York Mail*.

There was murder in Rackmoor.

According to the account, a body of a woman clad in some sort of mummer's costume had been found sprawled in a backwater street. Yorkshire constabulary sure to make an arrest soon. (Meaning they had no idea what was going on.) Murdered woman supposedly a relative of Sir Titus Crael, M.P. and M.F.H. — one of Yorkshire's wealthiest and most influential citizens.

A relation of Sir Titus — now Melrose found himself in a real quandary. To be barging in at this bleak hour of the Craels' lives, invited or not . . . perhaps he should just pack up and go back to Northants and send his apologies. . . . Northants, Agatha, and general malaise. There was no malaise in Rackmoor, he bet, at the moment.

There was blood on the snow. . . .

"What's the matter with you, Melrose? You're sitting there all white as death."

Fortunately, he was saved from comment by the entrance of Miles, the Harries-Stubbs butler, to whom Agatha said, "I'd like some more tea and one or two of those brandy snaps. But do ask Cook to see the cream's fresher. Just tell her to whip up some more."

Miles looked at her out of bulletproof eyes. Agatha always managed to depopularize herself with servants very quickly.

"Yes, madam," was his stony answer. In warmer tones, he addressed Melrose: "And you, my lord. Is there anything you'd be requiring?"

"The telephone," said Melrose. "I mean — would you mind ringing up this number for me and seeing if this party is there?" He tore a leaf from his memorandum book and handed it to the butler.

"Certainly, my lord."

"Who are you calling, Melrose?"

" 'Spirits from the vasty deep,' " he said, trying to shove the newspaper down between the arm and cushion of the chair. If she knew a murder had been done in the very place to which he was going, she'd be right beside him, tramping along and stamping out whatever poor clues there were. Agatha fancied herself a mystery writer. She had never got over what she called "her solution" to those murders in their own village.

The butler swanned into the room. "I've got —" (quick look at Agatha) "— your party on the line."

"Thank you. I'll just take it in the other room." Butlers were amazing. Melrose thought of his own butler, Ruthven. They could read minds even where there were no minds to read. He looked at Agatha and left the room.

Yes, certainly, Sir Titus was still wanting Melrose to come, perhaps more now than ever. Police all over the house, all over Rackmoor. There was even talk about calling in Scotland Yard. Titus Crael laughed, but without much conviction. The way they were questioning Julian, you'd have thought he was, well, a *suspect*.

"Look, dear boy," said Titus Crael. "You might be some help, you know. I'm a bit worried."

"About what, Sir Titus?"

"I don't know, to tell the truth. It's all very confusing. She was — well, we'll talk when you get here."

Melrose tried to remember Julian Crael, but couldn't. He didn't think they had ever met, not even as children. But he agreed to come as planned and to be of what help he could.

"Who were you talking to?" asked Agatha when he returned.

"Sir Titus Crael. Fixing up when I'd arrive. I make it about a two-hour trip." When the butler reappeared to apportion out tea and confections and lethal looks for Agatha, Melrose said, "Would you toss my things into my bag, Miles? I'll be leaving shortly." Miles nodded and left.

"Do you mean to say you're leaving now?" The brandy snap was poised aloft, like a small plane. Melrose nodded. "All across the North York *Moors* in winter!"

"That 'bourn from whom no traveller returns.'" Not a bad idea, perhaps.

She stared at him. "About your Uncle Davidson, now, I remember . . ."

Melrose Plant turned over the hourglass.

· III ·

Afternoon in Islington

Detective Chief Inspector Richard Jury was awakened from a dream of tiny men attempting to pin him to the ground, Gulliver-wise, by the rude ringing of his telephone. Sleepily, he tested his arms for ropes, and finding them disengaged, lifted the receiver.

Oiled with sarcasm, the voice of Superintendent Racer slipped over the wire: "It's gone one and you're still getting your beauty sleep, Jury? The WPC's will go wild. Have mercy, man."

Jury yawned. It was no use reminding his Chief Superintendent that Jury had had next to no sleep in the last forty-eight hours. And it didn't need Freud to put a name to the Lilliputian men who had pinioned him in his dream, either. "You wanted something, sir?"

"No, Jury, I didn't really want anything," said Racer with elaborate calm. "I called for a bit of a natter. Jury, you're in the frame, damnit!"

Jury knew that he was on call. But he was third down; there were at least two men ahead of him. He heaved himself up in his bed and rubbed his hair astringently, trying to wake up his scalp and hoping to get through to his brain in the process. "Wasn't Roper ahead of me?"

"He's unavailable!" snapped Racer.

That was impossible, thought Jury; Roper was on twelve-hour call, at least. Had Racer even tried to get ahold of him?

"The Yorkshire police called in. They want someone up there. Pronto."

Jury's heart sank. Yorkshire. "Are you sure — ?"

". . . village called Rackmoor." Jury heard papers rattling as Racer cut him off. "Fishing village on the North Sea." Racer said this with evident delight.

Jury shut his eyes. Last year at this time it had been Northamptonshire. That was wintry enough. He had noth-

ing against Yorkshire in spring, Yorkshire in summer, Yorkshire in autumn. But not January. Was he to be driven
farther and farther north by Racer, like a team of huskies?
He looked out of his bedroom window and saw flakes of
snow. Just a few, scattering like leftovers from another
winter. Closing his eyes again, he saw the Yorkshire moors —
the great, level, vast expanses covered with smooth crusts of
snow. He saw (or rather, heard) himself walking — *crunch,
crunch, crunch* — across the moors. And then he brought
his mind's eye back like a camera's lens and saw himself dark
and tiny in all that whiteness and tracks like birdprints. He
smiled. Jury was obsessively fond of unbroken expanses of
snow. He liked to muck it about.

The receiver squawked; his eyes snapped open. He must
have dozed off. "Yes, sir?"

"I said, get down to the office. Make it snappy. There's
been a murder up there and they want us. Wiggins can fill
you in."

"When did it happen?"

"Two days ago. Nights, that is."

Jury groaned. "That means they've moved the body.
That means —"

"Stop whining, Jury. A policeman's life is full of grief."

A half-hour later, Richard Jury stepped out into what
might possibly be a day of weak sunshine. He checked the
row of metal mailboxes just outside the front door, found
only circulars in his, stuffed them back in the box, and went
down the stone steps. The little park across the street was
delicately awash in pale sunshine, its pallid greens and dull
golds like a faded canvas.

Once at the gate, he remembered he had a small gift for
Mrs. Wasserman and retraced his steps, going back up the
short walk and then down the four steps which led to her
basement apartment. He knocked, but tentatively, not want-

ing to frighten her. Silence within, as she was probably debating whether to answer. A curtain to his left flicked back, and through the double iron grilling of the window he saw her eye and nose. Mrs. Wasserman was far advanced in paranoia. Islington for her was the Warsaw Ghetto. He waved. The curtain dropped. The chain clanged back and the door opened. Her ample bosom and broad smile appeared.

"Mr. Jury!"

"Hello, Mrs. Wasserman. I brought you something." Jury handed over a small package from the pocket of his Burberry.

Her face was alight as she opened it and then held up the whistle.

"It's a police whistle," said Jury. "I thought maybe you might feel a little safer about going to market or Camden Passage with that round your neck. One blow on that and you'd have every bobby for a mile running down Islington High Street to your side." Hell of an exaggeration, but he knew she'd never have occasion to use it. It was an old one he'd found in an antique shop near the Passage.

Jury had often watched Mrs. Wasserman from his window, as she went up the walk dressed in her black coat and flat black hat and flowered shopping bag. She'd stop inside the gate, look both ways. Outside the gate, both ways again. Down the pavement, look to the sides and behind. . . .

Over the years she'd asked him a few times — very meekly — to accompany her to the High Street or the Angel. To alleviate her embarrassment, he would say he was going that way anyway, and on the odd days when he wasn't at New Scotland Yard, his life was so loosely structured that he might as well have been going her way as not. He looked at her now as she took tentative pipes at the whistle, childishly pleased. He towered over her, the short, rather corpulent woman, her black hair in a bun drawn back as tight as a satin cap. The navy blue dress was pinned with a filigree brooch. He wondered what her youth had been like before the war. She must have been very, very pretty once.

That's what he had in common with her — the war. Both his own father and mother had gone in it. His father at Dunkirk, and his mother in the last blitz of London. When he was seven years old, their home had collapsed around the two of them like a house of cards. In the darkness he had searched for her through the night until he had seen her under the charred remains of beams and bricks, seen her arm, her hand lying against the rubble, thrown out from underneath as it might have been thrown out from under a dark coverlet in her sleep. For seven years after that he had been handed round from aunts to cousins and back again until he had, at fourteen, simply lit out on his own.

He could never glimpse a woman's hand after that, an arm lying against the dark cloth of a chair or the wood of a dining table — just the hand and arm, not the face, not the body — without that piercing numbness, as if his mind had been cauterized. This image, which should have been in the ordinary way of events absolutely hideous, was instead endowed with what he supposed Yeats must have meant by "a terrible beauty." That porcelain hand against the blackness of a smoking London building appeared in his dreams like a lantern in the dark, a light in the forest.

"Inspector Jury," said Mrs. Wasserman, bringing him back from that burning building, "I can't thank you enough. It's so nice of you." She clutched his arm as if it were a spar from a sinking ship. "My brother, Rudy. You know, the one I write to, the one who lives in Prague. Do they let them have their mail, do you think, uncensored?" Jury shook his head; he didn't know. "Ah, who knows? But I tell him not to worry about me. So much he worries. I tell him there's a policeman who lives here. No, not just a policeman. A true Englishman. God bless you."

He tried to smile but could only swallow hard, looking back and off at the sun-painted park. "Thank you, Mrs.

Wasserman." He did smile then and raised his hand to his head in a brief salute.

Walking through Camden Passage towards the Angel, he felt almost lightheaded. She had saved some part of his day. Jury, despite his twenty years with Scotland Yard and seeing, as he had, the dregs of humanity, had never been reduced to mere cynicism.

A true Englishman.

To Jury, it was still the ultimate compliment.

2.

"It's on the coast. Fishing village — or was once — near Whitby. More of a tourist place now, in summer, at least." Detective Sergeant Alfred Wiggins took out a small table-cloth of a handkerchief and blew his nose. Then he tossed his head back and applied drops with a tiny dropper, sniffing hugely after each application. Wiggins had managed to turn hypochondria into an art or even a sport.

"Still got that cold, Sergeant?" The question was so rhetorical even Wiggins didn't bother to answer. "Can't the Yorkshire people handle this murder? They're no fools."

"Tha sah is na jus the murrer."

Jury had, over the years, learned to interpret Sergeant Wiggins's secret language of the sick room. He so often had a cloth to his face or a lozenge in his mouth his messages were runic. "What do you mean, 'not just the murder'?"

Wiggins stoppered up the little bottle and tilted his head forward to hurry the draining process. "There's complications, they say. The victim, name of Gemma Temple, according to someone in Rackmoor, was actually somebody else."

Jury wondered how he could scale the warts off that message to see if some pointer would emerge. "Do you think you could explain that?"

"Yes, sir. What they meant was, there's some question

about who the woman actually is. She'd been in Rackmoor only four days, staying at a pub. Said her name was Gemma Temple. But according to this family named Crael, she was really some relation of theirs. Incognito, something like that." Wiggins flipped through his notes. "Dillys March. That was the name the Craels gave her. Did a moonlight flit, oh, fifteen years ago. And then just resurfaced. And got herself murdered."

"They aren't *sure* who she is?" asked Jury. Wiggins shook his head. "Well, but surely this Temple woman can be traced —"

"The Yorkshire police know she came from London, sir. Kentish Town was her last address. I don't know much more than that."

"The body?"

"In the mortuary in Pitlochary. That's about twenty miles from Rackmoor."

"*And* everything cleaned up and dusted. Probably hoovered the spot."

Wiggins's laugh was more of a giggle.

"Why the hell do I always seem to get these cases cold? Suspects?"

Wiggins shook his head. "Nothing much said there, except some crazy painter-type was mouthing off about murder in the pub on the same night. Saying something about Rasputin."

Jury looked up from his cup of tea. "Rasputin? What's he got to do with it?"

"Some Russian or other. Talked about superior types doing murder."

Jury thought a moment. "Raskolnikov?"

"They all sound alike, those Russians."

Jury checked his watch. "Have you got us a train?"

"Yes, sir. Not till five from Victoria, I'm afraid. We'll be met in York."

Rackmoor Fog

THE car heater of the little Ford Escort *thunked* despairingly, blasting out heat on the floor but nowhere else, so that Jury's feet were hot and his nose cold.

The North York Moors stretched endlessly to the right and left, white and frozen. Far off, the horizon loomed in near-translucent shades of gray. They had passed some dry walls, but mostly the land was unenclosed and uncultivated waste. No roads nor railways, no farms, no hedges, no walls nor steadings. The moors stretched away like another country.

For sixty miles they had driven straight as a shot from York, stopping at Pitlochary to give Jury a chance to see the body of the murdered woman and to talk to the doctor who had performed the autopsy. Jury and Wiggins had managed a few hours of sleep, and now it was early morning, the earliest morning Jury thought he had ever seen.

They were now crossing Fylingdales Moor where the geodesic domes of the U.S. Navy's early warning system rose incongruously in the distance. Coming towards the car, straggling along the side of the road, were a half-dozen moorjocks, the black-faced sheep of the moors. Thick rolls of curly wool scaled with frost, all supported by spindly black legs. They had long, black, and (Jury thought) sad faces. As the car passed the sheep, Jury wound down the window. The last in line had stopped to scratch itself against an ancient cross and looked curiously after the car.

Jury thought of the body of the young woman he had just seen lying on a slab in the Pitlochary morgue room and wished himself out there in the vast indifference of Nature.

"My God, sir, close that window, will you?" This plaintive wail came from Wiggins, who was doing the driving.

Jury rolled up the window and settled back and stared out at the desolate, forsaken landscape, the untrammeled expanses of snow, and he sighed.

* * *

Rackmoor lay in the hollowed-out cleft of the rocks, the North Sea beyond and the moors behind. It looked secretive, almost guilty.

They were forced to pull into a parking lot strategically placed at the top of the village. A hundred yards down Rackmoor's plunging High Street, an articulated lorry had got itself wedged, its cab stuck round the crazy jackknife turn, its trailer up the narrow street.

Jury looked down at the sea and the red-tiled roofs huddled in uneven tiers along the cliffside. Out on the gray horizon a ship hovered, stuck in the morning. The village was smoky with fog and morning fires, monochromatic except for the dull red-brown of the rooftops. Jury felt, as he had on the moors, as if he were caught up in some loop of time, going nowhere.

"Well, I guess there's nothing for it but to walk," said Wiggins, sniffing unhappily at the sea air. There must be better climates than this, his nose seemed to say.

As they passed the Bell, a pub on their left, they could hear the shouts of the driver, who was leaning out of the cab, yelling at a clutch of villagers. Jury wondered what faith in the laws of gravity had ever got the lorry even a short way down the High Street in the first place. Squeezing between the cab and a fishmonger's — he had come out, white-aproned, to find himself cheek to jowl with the lorry — they rounded this heart-stopping turn and went right. The road leveled off for the length of a block of shops: newsagent's with stiles of postcards which not many tourists would be buying in January; greengrocer's where an iron-haired woman was setting out swedes and giving Jury and Wiggins a businesslike stare; a little building on the right where a gray brindled cat slept in the window — the Rackmoor Gallery. And next, a small shop showing frocks as plain and brown as the cobbles underfoot.

A second and (Jury was sure) essential carpark had been

formed from a plateau on their right. The next turn left was another steep drop. At the end of it Jury could just glimpse the sea like a picture placed at the end of a green tunnel in a sort of trompe l'oeil effect. Off to left and right were little courts and tiny alleys. One narrow lane called Bridge Walk had a few steps leading up; a small stream ran beside them. Pavements were staircases; rooftops looked down over other rooftops.

At the end of the High Street was a cove; this morning the waves were breaking far out, and though there was no sunlight, the sunless glare of the sea cast its own light upon rocks and standing pools. Small craft — cobles and other fishing boats — were beached at the land's edge and painted in startling colors: sapphire blue, aquamarine. Breakwaters made part of a seawall.

The sign of the Old Fox Deceiv'd swung from iron, whipped by a sharp wind. It showed a fox looking a bit battered from too many chases, but now lolling by bushes in the filtered sunlight, eating grapes. Peering out on the poor unfortunate creature from bushes and trees were hounds, probably a whole pack of them.

Jury and Wiggins walked around the cove and up to the pub. Parked in front of it was one of the nattiest little sports cars Jury had ever seen. A Lotus Elan.

Wiggins let out a low whistle. "Look at that, would you? Set me back a year's salary, that one would."

"Wonder how it got round the artic?" said Jury. "Probably sprouted wings."

Mrs. Meechem — "Kitty," she said to Jury, looking wonderingly up at him, either at his height, his smile, his identity card, or all three — led them back to a small dining room to the rear of the pub, separated from the saloon bar by a beamed doorway with a low lintel. Jury had to stoop to get under it.

A slim, youngish man rose from the table. He had to be

the owner of the Lotus. And considering he was here, he had also to be Detective Inspector Harkins of the Pitlochary C.I.D. There was, sitting beside him, a short, rotund little fellow who looked as if he wanted to sink out of sight.

"I'm Harkins." He shook Jury's hand, having carefully removed a pearl-gray glove. "Good of you to come lend a hand, and so quickly."

That, thought Jury, was a lie. Harkins did not look at all as if he thought it were good. One could hardly blame the provincial police if they were angry at having their authority usurped. But it was still a problem.

Harkins introduced the other man as Billy Sims. "He's Wakeman here."

"Wakeman? And what's that, Mr. Sims?"

Billy Sims mashed his cap between his hands and looked everywhere in the room except at Scotland Yard. "Ah be Wakeman these ten year. Colonel Crael, he pays me t'do it."

Harkins, clearly more from a desire to get the explanation over with rather than to help out, said, "It's an old tradition. The Wakeman was once responsible for the safety of the village. Not Rackmoor. I don't think they ever had one before Sir Titus got it into his head. But there used to be one in Ripin, I think. Billy found the body."

"I see. When did you come upon the woman?"

Billy Sims studied the floor at his feet as if the hideous vision might reappear on the boards. " 'Twas near midnight on the Angel steps . . ."

"Hear or see anything?"

He shook his head violently. "Ah, no, sir."

"It would be a help if you'd just go along with us to these steps —"

He honestly thought poor Billy might go down on his knees to clutch at Jury's coat. "Ah, if you please, sir, t'would be I'd rather not. Such a sight 'twas." Billy looked quite terrified.

"All right then. You've been very helpful."

Harkins looked as if couldn't agree less as they watched Billy Sims's departing back.

Jury tossed his coat over a chair and sat down. He noticed that Harkins had not removed his incredibly expensive camel's-hair coat. Harkins appeared to be rather unwilling to stay a moment longer than duty absolutely warranted.

"You've been to Pitlochary? Seen the body?" asked Harkins. Jury nodded. Harkins handed over a manila folder, labeled and very neat. "It's all there, Chief Inspector." The folder just missed being tossed on the table by a hair.

"Richard," said Jury. He passed over his packet of cigarettes. "Have one?"

Harkins shook his head, permitted Jury a thin-bladed smile and took a leather case from his coat pocket. "I smoke only these. Cuban, very good. Care for one?"

"Sure. Thanks." Jury lit them both and then opened the folder. He looked down at the pictures the photographer had taken. "Who does your camera work? It's extremely good."

"Local chap."

"Describe the scene, will you?"

There was a short silence. "It's all in the folder, Chief Inspector."

"Yes. I'm sure the report's very thorough. But hearing it would give me a better perspective on things. You've the advantage of me, see. You saw it all and I didn't."

" 'Advantage'? I hope that doesn't mean we'll be left to carry the can back." He faked a smile. There was no question that Harkins felt he was the Little Red Hen who baked the bread while this Jury was the turkey who'd come along to eat it.

Kitty Meechem brought in coffee and Jury was saved a reply. As the cups were passed round, Wiggins looked at Kitty rather mournfully and asked for tea. He must be coming down with something, he said; sea air never did agree with his sinuses.

Holding her tray against her breast like a bundle of love letters, Kitty said, "Ah, and it's not tea you'll be needin', sir. A buttered beer, that'd be just the thing." She flounced out, an attractive woman, Jury thought: middle-aged, plumpish, satin-brown curls.

"What's buttered beer?" whispered Wiggins.

"Don't know," said Jury. "But it could cure a dead horse, I'm sure."

"But I can't drink on duty, sir."

"Medicinal, Sergeant." Jury picked up the folder — since Harkins seemed ill-inclined to proceed on normal lines of communication — and spread out the glossy photographs. He studied one of them.

The photo showed part of a row of stone steps. There was a crude stone bench on the widest step; it was in an alcove in the wall that bounded the left side of the steps. Jury observed the position of the dead woman.

The body lay head-downwards, half-on and half-off the landing. The legs were jackknifed, the torso sprawled down two steps, the right arm thrown over the head and down a third step, the left arm pinned between torso and wall. The face was turned towards the high wall on the left. What he could see of it was smeared with blood and greasepaint — black, white and dark red indistinguishable in that light. The black mask which had covered her eyes dangled by its elastic. The white satin blouse was nearly phosphorescent in the camera's glare, and the boots reflected the light. Her black cape floated down the steps. The picture he was looking at showed her head first and upside down. Very dramatic. He only wished he could have seen the body *in situ*. Jury closed the folder.

He rested his chin on his hands and said to Harkins. "The pathologist — what's his name?"

"Dudley. He comes in to help out occasionally."

"He says he doesn't know what made these wounds. You have any ideas?"

Harkins looked off, seemed to be considering, and was about to speak when Kitty came in with Wiggins's medicinal drink. "There, sir; that'll fix you up." She plunked down the pewter mug.

Wiggins looked into it suspiciously. "What's in it?"

Kitty's laugh was a delight to hear in the otherwise chilly atmosphere. "Bit of sugar, butter, and an egg. An egg can solve anything, I always say."

She started off again and Jury said, "Kitty, I'll need to ask you a few questions later, if you don't mind. I understand Gemma Temple stayed here."

"She did indeed. I'll be here when you need me." Her hand wandered up to her hair.

When she'd gone, Jury turned back to Harkins. "We were talking about the weapon."

"Yes." Harkins dribbled cigar ash against the glass ashtray. "Double-pronged, Dudley says. It's the way the holes are spaced. There are at least four pairs of them. I wonder why the murderer chose such an unconventional weapon."

Jury smiled. "Just for the reason we're sitting here trying to figure out what it was. I'd like to see these Angel steps."

"We're at your service, Chief Inspector." Harkins rose, made small adjustments to himself as if he were a valuable figurine about to be moved from mantel to table.

Wiggins downed his beer. "Snappy stuff, that."

Jury wished he had an egg. An egg, Kitty said, would solve anything.

The three of them stood on a wide step just below the point that the Angel steps debouched onto Scroop Street to the left. Jury looked down and then up at the church. "Quite a climb."

If one were looking up toward Our Lady of the Veil, the

Angel steps were bounded by a high, stone wall on the left; on the right, the wall was only waist-high, presumably for the view of the North Sea over the roofs and chimney pots. Smoke twined upwards in mauve ribbons; herring-gulls perched on ledges and dotted the shingle down below.

Jury looked down, towards Grape Lane. "Were those gates shut?"

"Yes."

"Then the Angel steps wouldn't have much traffic at night."

"That's right."

"There are other ways down to the shops and pubs, then?"

Harkins nodded. "From Scroop Street you can go through Dagger Alley alongside of the Bell. It joins the High."

"The steps must have been built more for religious or aesthetic reasons than for practical ones." Jury looked at the pictures he had brought along. He looked from one to the blank space on the steps. All neatly mopped up now, he thought ruefully.

Wiggins, having gained a vestige of strength from Kitty's beer, was down on his knees, looking at the step. "Dried blood. What're these white streaks?" He ran his finger along the lefthand wall. The tiny white lines were barely perceptible.

"Her head hit it," said Harkins. "That's greasepaint. It was a costume party."

"Tell me about that, Ian," said Jury.

"Sir Titus Crael gives a Twelfth Night party every year. The Craels live up at Old House."

Wiggins got up, folded a jackknife he'd used for a bit of scraping. "She was from London, wasn't she?" Harkins nodded. "Well, it's not likely someone followed her here. The murderer must have known Rackmoor."

Jury was surprised. Wiggins was the most industrious of policemen and an efficient note-taker. But he seldom ventured deductions. "It's all this about the Angel steps. Had to be someone from around here who knew they wouldn't be much used."

"You're right, Wiggins." Jury looked down at the photos, shuffled them around. "Gemma Temple . . ." He shook his head.

"*If* that was her name." Harkins smiled bitterly, seeming almost glad to throw a spanner in the works.

"It's a question of identity," Harkins said. They were back in the Old Fox Deceiv'd. "According to Colonel Crael — Sir Titus, but he likes to be called 'Colonel' — Gemma Temple, or at least, the woman calling herself Gemma Temple, actually claimed to be Dillys March, who disappeared fifteen years ago when she was eighteen or nineteen. Hasn't been seen since. Unless it's now. Dillys March was the Craels' ward."

"'Claimed'? Couldn't Crael tell for certain?"

"Colonel Crael thought she *was* the March girl. But his son, Julian, says no. I should think it would be easy to establish, but it's not proving so. We got her roommate up here from London. Name's Josie Thwaite. Identified the body as Gemma Temple, but didn't know damn all about her. The Temple woman went to share digs with her about a year ago."

"Where does this Thwaite girl live, then?"

With elaborate patience, Harkins pointed to the folder. "Kentish Town. It's all in there."

"Go on."

"She did remember Gemma Temple mentioning a family named Rainey in Lewisham, I think it was. We're checking on them. Now: handwriting, some of Gemma Temple's, none of Dillys March's. Not a scrap, not a signature. Dental records: same thing. The Colonel says Lady Margaret — his dead wife — took care of all that sort of thing, he doesn't know what dentist she took Dillys to. Someone in London, he said."

"Then comb them. Dentists are thick on the ground, but there'd be a record somewhere. It's hard for me to believe someone could live that long and not leave behind proof she wasn't someone else."

Harkins answered testily: "Well, this one has done a bloody good job of it."

"Why did the March girl leave? What happened?"

"Just got in her car and took off."

That wasn't much of an answer, but Jury imagined it was the best he'd get. "How did the Temple woman get here? Car?"

Harkins nodded, touched a match to another of his Cuban cigars. "Her roommate's, Josie Thwaite's. We went over it. Didn't tell us anything."

"I take it Gemma Temple *looked* like Dillys March."

"Obviously." Harkins blew a series of smoke rings. "Allowing for the changes of fifteen years, she was a ringer." Harkins opened the folder, detached a small photo from a paper clip, and dropped it on the table, wordlessly.

Jury examined it. The snapshot showed a very pretty girl leaning — posing, really — against a stone wall. Dark, straight hair, chin-length and curling slightly under, bangs, dark eyes. She was dressed in riding habit. Her face was sharp, with tilted eyes and a foxy-pointed chin. And indeed her whole expression, the upturned corners of her mouth not a real smile at all, seemed foxy also. She looked exactly like the murdered woman, or, more precisely, as that woman might have looked alive and fifteen years younger. "I guess this is the ward, Dillys."

Harkins looked disappointed, as if Jury had cheated on a test. "What makes you say that?"

"Only because of the riding habit. Colonel Crael has a real passion for hunting, doesn't he? I'd assume his ward would have taken to it —" Jury stopped. Harkins looked openly hostile. He changed the subject: "So the father and son disagree?"

Harkins nodded and extracted from his vest pocket a small, silver nail clipper, as if there were nothing weightier to apply his mind to than a manicure.

"Tell me about this Colonel Crael." Blood out of stones.

"Rich. Very rich. The baronetcy was conferred upon his father. The Craels were in shipping, amongst other things. He's Master of Foxhounds. And he owns half of Rackmoor, from what I can judge. It's on the historic buildings listings, you know."

"The whole *village?*"

"That's right. Worth keeping, apparently."

"Who are Colonel Crael's heirs?"

"Heir. There's just one. Julian Crael, his son."

Wiggins had been sitting there with a fresh cup of tea, thinking and stirring. "The prodigal daughter," he murmured. Jury and Harkins both looked at him. "The last person the son'd want is the one that's been away for donkey's years and having people blubbering all over her return." He tapped his spoon against his cup and drank.

That drive across the moors must have aired out Wiggins's brain and loosened his tongue. This was his second pronouncement in the past hour. "You're quite right. She'd be the very last person," Jury said.

"It would surely account for the son's denying she *was* this March person," said Wiggins.

"Yes. Of course, he could be right. Her story sounds fishy to me." When he saw Harkins look up apprehensively — as if there were something else coming he hadn't thought of — Jury changed the subject. Looking again at the police photographs, he said: "There must have been a lot of blood. It's hard to believe some of it didn't splash on the murderer's clothes."

"We found a large piece of stained canvas. Spattered with blood."

Thanks for telling me, thought Jury glumly. "What sort of canvas?"

"Kind an artist uses. To stretch over frames. It might have come from Adrian Rees's place. Studio, whatever he calls it. And he did a lot of mouthing off about murder." Harkins slipped another piece of paper out of the folder and shoved it towards Jury. "I've done a list of names here for you. We must have interviewed nearly the whole damned village" — *the Little Red Hen again*, thought Jury — "and I've winnowed out most of them, got it down to the names here that you might want to talk with first. The Craels, naturally. And Adrian Rees is the last one we know of to have seen Gemma Temple alive. He passed her on Grape Lane just before she was killed."

Jury folded and pocketed the list. "I'll see him first, then, before the Craels."

Harkins nodded and drew on his gloves. "I hope you won't mind my getting back to Pitlochary. I'm expecting a report from London."

It was unusual — not to say unprofessional — for this provincial D.I. to take himself off, but Jury said nothing.

Having shrugged into his coat, Harkins dropped (Jury was sure) his pièce de résistance: "Oh, by the way, there's a bit of a complication. Lily Siddons — she's the young woman who runs the Bridge Walk Café — claims the murderer made a rather dreadful mistake."

"Mistake?"

"Lily Siddons claims *she* was the intended victim." Harkins smiled all round the table as if to let them know the code they had just finished breaking had all been misinformation in the first place. "I think it's all eyewash, frankly. Big for the limelight, she probably is. But the costume, she says, was her own, and that's where the killer made his mistake. I'll be on my way. It's a bit of a drive to Pitlochary. Hope I've been of some help."

Jury stared at the floor at his feet. "I'm most eternally grateful to you."

2.

As the exhaust of the Lotus Elan roared in Jury's ears, Kitty Meechem was readying up for the eleven A.M. trade, wiping the china beer pulls, polishing the dark counter. Jury decided he'd sooner talk to Kitty's satin curls than Harkins any day. "Which rooms did you give us, Kitty?"

She tossed the bar towel over her shoulder and tugged down her dress, giving Jury the advantage of a bit more cleavage. "Oh, indeed, I'll show you —"

"Never mind, I'm sure Sergeant Wiggins can find the rooms. Just tell him where. I'd like a bit of a chat with you."

She directed Wiggins through the door and up a dark and narrow staircase to the right of the public bar. "There's only the three rooms, you know. And the police don't want anyone using hers." No one, Jury thought with an inward smile, seemed to be taking *them* for police. "So you'll not be havin' trouble findin' the right rooms, Sergeant. First two at the top. They face the sea: plenty of nice sea air for you, Sergeant. You're looking a bit peaked."

Wiggins smiled bleakly.

"Have a lie-down," said Jury. "I'll dig you out later."

Wiggins looked grateful, picked up the two small suitcases inside the door, and left the room.

"You're not Dublin Irish, Kitty, are you?" Jury smiled. It was a smile which had melted harder hearts than Kitty Meechem's.

"Well, aren't you the clever one. And which part would you say?"

"The West Country. Sligo, maybe?"

She was astonished. "Quite right you are. You really are clever, Inspector, to tell the difference."

"No, I'm not." He held up the folder and tossed two 50p pieces on the counter. "Harkins wrote it down in here. Buy us a beer, Kitty."

She laughed. "I don't mind if I do."

"I'll have a Guinness. It's medicinal."

"Right you are. Me mother had to drink two pints every day, the doctor told her, to get her strength back."

"Why are you in Yorkshire, Kitty? Ireland's a grand country."

"Husband was a Yorkshire man. I met him when he was on holiday in Galway. We lived in Salthill for a bit. But he hated Ireland. Most English do, of course. It's the Troubles."

"It's been going on for two hundred years, Kitty."

She stood with her hands on her hips waiting for the foam to settle itself. "Do you know Bertie Makepiece, sir? Lives in Cross Keys cottage up on Scroop Street?" Jury shook his head. "It's the one nearest the Angel steps. Anyway, his mum went to Ireland a few months back. I look in on him, but it's more'n I can understand, going off like that and leaving the child to fend for himself. I give him a bit of work now and then. Sick gran, that's what she said." Kitty shook her head, plumped up their glasses, shoved Jury's over.

"Cheers," said Jury, raising his. "What happened the night of the murder, Kitty? Did you see Gemma Temple?"

"I did. Went up to my room around ten and she was in hers; called me in, she did, to have a look at her costume. Quite smashing, she was, all that white satin and black velvet. Black boots. Said she was about to put this grease-paint on her face. Half-white, half-black she was going to do it, and wear a black mask over her eyes . . ." Kitty paused and looked away. "She was an awful mess, I heard, when they found her."

Jury didn't comment on that. "You say this was at ten?" Kitty nodded.

"Ten or ten after, I'd say."

"And she was about to leave, after she'd put on the makeup?"

"That's what she said. She'd be leaving directly. And that's the last I ever saw of her, poor thing. Of course, I didn't know her well, but one can still feel pity for her."

"Yes. She was bound for the party, as far as you know?" Again, Kitty nodded. "Nobody, apparently, in the pub here saw her go out. Why's that?"

"La, and that doesn't surprise me a tall, a tall. Drunk as lords, weren't they? Anyway, she'd not have come through here. She'd have come down the stairs and straight out the door. I asked meself, Kitty, what was she doing on the Angel steps? You see, if she'd wanted to go to the manor house the easiest way, she'd go round to the seaside, up the Fox steps and along the seawall. We just call them the Fox steps so as not to get mixed up with the Angel steps." Jury nodded. "And from the seawall you'd reach a path that goes along the cliff to Old House."

"It's not the only way to get there, though?"

"Oh, no. You *could* go up the Angel steps all the way to Our Lady and along Psalter's Lane and up and through the wood. But whoever'd want to go that way? It's dark and creepy."

"Who'd she get friendly with while she was here — anyone?"

Kitty shook her head. "No one in here, except she did talk to Maud Brixenham a few times. Maud comes in regular at lunchtime. She lives in Lead Street. The other side of the dock. And then there was Adrian —" She hesitated.

"Adrian?"

"Adrian Rees. I think she talked to him once."

"Why'd you not want to mention it?"

"Oh . . ." Then she leaned over the bar, treating Jury to yet more cleavage. "I'd not be wantin' to get Adrian in trouble. But he *was* in here that very night going on about murder. About some character in a book. And the awful thing is Adrian was the last to see her alive. That Mr. Harkins was all over him."

"And what do you think?"

Kitty waved her hand. "Tush. Adrian couldn't kill anyone. He gets loud, he does, and throws himself about, but —" She shook her head and drank her beer.

"How about the Craels? Apparently, the woman was a friend or relation of theirs."

"I don't know about that, except that she did go up to Old House. You know Colonel Crael owns half this place. He bought it up when it was the Cod and Lobster and I was only barmaid. The Colonel's a real gentleman; everyone in Rackmoor likes him."

"What did Gemma Temple say about the Craels?"

"Nothing. She didn't talk to me. That Julian, the son. He's odd."

"Odd? How?"

"Keeps to himself. Never see him in the village hardly. Forty and never married."

She said it as if it summed up all possible behavior aberrations.

"I'm forty and not been married, Kitty."

She stared at him. "Well, that's a bit hard to believe. Don't fancy it, is that it?"

"Oh, I fancy it. You didn't know the Craels' ward, Dillys March, did you? You wouldn't have been here that long ago, I expect."

"No. I've heard about her though. Went off and got married, didn't she?"

She'd got marriage on the mind. "Not that we know. This costume, I understand, belonged to a girl named Lily Siddons —"

Kitty was nodding her head. "Lily, yes, sir, that's right. Lily gave it to her, loaned it to her, I don't know. And then Lily went with Maud Brixenham as —" Kitty pursed her lips. "Somebody out of Shakespeare, I can't remember."

"Is Lily Siddons a special friend of the Craels?"

"Aye. Her mother was Cook at Old House before she died. Mary Siddons."

"Daughter of the Craels' cook? Sir Titus must be very egalitarian —" Jury helped Kitty over her puzzlement. "I mean, to socialize with his servants' children?"

"It's not the same a tall a tall. Lily's special to him. She lived up there with her mother for a while when her da just took himself off."

"People certainly disappear around here, don't they? Did you see Lily the night of the murder?"

"I did. We always have a bit of a talk round closing time. She lives just across the way. That funny little house where the High and Grape Lane come together. I ran on over after closing —"

Jury took out his notebook. "What time was that?"

"Eleven twenty-five, it was. I saw her light on."

"I thought she went to the party."

"She left early. With Maud Brixenham and Maud's nephew — that's Les Aird. Lily didn't feel good, she said." When she saw Jury opening the folder, she added: "I know it's important because of when the Temple girl was killed."

Jury looked up at her. "You know the exact time she was killed?"

"O, la, sir. Everybody in Rackmoor knows. Stabbed a dozen times she was."

"How long does it take to get from here to the Angel steps, Kitty?"

Kitty smiled winningly. "And isn't that just what that Mr. Harkins asked? Ten minutes to get up there where she was killed. Now I couldn't have done that and got back to Lily's place at eleven twenty-five, could I?"

Jury smiled. "Both you and Lily have pretty good alibis, then." Kitty beamed, and he added: "Not airtight, of course. One or the other of you might have run like hell . . ."

Kitty felt safe enough to laugh. "Oh, come now, sir." She lowered her voice. "What was it killed her?"

"I thought you might tell me. You know everything else. Tell me, Kitty, who'd want to kill Lily Siddons?"

She looked shocked. "Lily, sir? What do you mean?"

"You were a friend of hers. Didn't she tell you she thought someone had mistaken Gemma Temple for her? In the costume?"

"My God. No, she never mentioned it."

"Did they look alike?"

"No, but in that costume . . . it'd be hard to tell, I mean, in the fog and the dark."

"Hmm. I think I'd better see this Temple woman's room." Jury drained his glass.

Through the door, she led Jury up the narrow stair and down the hall to a large airy room facing out on the sea-wall and the slate-gray waves beyond.

As Jury went over the room — through closets, behind furniture and mirrors — Kitty was saying that she seldom let the rooms. "Not much call for it in winter. Why, the first stranger I've seen in two months is a gentleman yesterday afternoon, sitting over there in the corner reading some French book and drinking Old Peculier — whoever drinks that anymore? Bitsy — that's the girl waits on tables here, when she works at all — says he was on his way to Old House and was having a look round the village. Bitsy chatted him up as long as she could. Anything to keep from working —"

Old Peculier and French literature. "What did this gentleman look like?"

"Kind of tall. Fair hair. Quite smashing eyes."

"Green?"

"Green is right. They fairly glitter. How'd you know?"

Melrose Plant. What the devil was *he* doing in Rackmoor?

3.

Melrose Plant was sitting at one end of the Craels' dining room table, which was dark and glassy as a moonlit tarn and seemed a quarter of a mile long. He was having a late breakfast of buttered eggs. He had overslept to an embarrassing degree and had asked Wood, the butler, if a cup of coffee were available. Although it was clear Colonel Crael was genuinely pleased to have him there, it was equally clear Julian was not. Yet, it was not Melrose himself that Julian seemed to resent, but the appearance of anyone new on the spot. That made it very hard going for Julian, given the intrusion of the police.

Wood assured Melrose that the Colonel had insisted breakfast be kept hot as long as necessary. Colonel Crael (Wood had informed him) had gone to kennels in Pitlochary. Julian Crael had gone for his morning walk.

Melrose was just as glad. He thought the Colonel a grand old man, but he did not like Julian. Among other things, he was suspicious of terribly handsome men, and Julian had more than his share in that department. Or was he, in early middle-age, simply jealous of youth? Yet, Julian was not really *youth*. He was probably no more than five or six years younger than Melrose. It was just that Julian *looked* eternally young. That, thought Melrose, was even more reprehensible.

As Melrose was dissecting his second smoked herring,

Olive Manning, the housekeeper, walked into the dining room, jingling. Melrose had thought that chatelaines went out with the Brontë sisters and Gothic novels. But here was one in truth, a host of keys suspended from the house-keeper's waist.

"Colonel Crael asked me to see if there was anything you needed and if you'd care to join him later for a ride?"

Hell's bells, thought Melrose. Served him right for telling the Colonel about his horse at Ardry End. "That's very kind of him. But I've this dicky knee, must have stretched a tendon when I was doing a bit of jumping last week." (Melrose always fell into this Old Boy idiom when he was lying. It was as if he had to invent a persona for the purpose.)

Beyond a brief nod of her head, Olive Manning's expression did not change, dicky knees not coming within her purview. But she did murmur something insincerely sympathetic. "I hope it will be better; otherwise, you'll miss the hunt."

"Oh, my. No, we wouldn't want *that*, would we?" He rose and pulled out a chair. "Join me for a cup of coffee?"

She looked uncertain, and not, he suspected, because of her position in the household — Olive Manning was treated almost as one of the family — but because she seemed to regard him with something like suspicion. He would have to pivot round the subject of the Twelfth Night party, which was what he wanted to question her about.

He did not like Olive Manning, either. He did not like her tight features, her narrow chin, constricted brow, mouth bunched like grapes. She seemed to register a perpetual and controlled anger with the world. The head of black hair was set on a body like a stalk and dressed in (the very finest, he was sure, of Liberty's) dark lawn. She sat down, declined coffee, and lapped her hands on the table. On her finger was a rose-pink topaz that could have choked a horse. Nobody at Old House was starving.

"Sir Titus says that you were Lady Margaret's closest . . . companion." He didn't want to say "maid" or "servant."

"Aye." The single syllable was soft; for a fleeting moment her mouth relaxed.

"I'm very sorry I didn't know her. My father, Lord Ardry, spoke of her . . . said she was the most beautiful woman he'd ever seen."

It was clearly the right line to take. Mrs. Manning very nearly smiled. "Indeed, I've yet to see a lovelier woman. Her hair, when she let it down, was like a wash of sunlight. The boys both got it, Julian and Rolfe." She looked away. "Rolfe is dead, too, as you know."

"Yes. Awful to have both of them, the mother and the son, die at the same time. A motor accident, the Colonel said."

She sighed. "Eighteen years ago, it was. Rolfe was only thirty-two." She turned a silver knife over and over as if she might lift it at any moment and plunge it into her own breast. Or into his. The tightfisted look had begun to resolve itself into something akin to suffering. He knew she had a son in a mental institution, but he was not going to broach that subject. He glanced at her sideways.

"Terrible. So there's only Julian left."

"Yes." She gave him a whiplash look. It was too near the subject she didn't want to discuss. Melrose stuck what was left of a cigar in his mouth and leaned back, hands clasped behind his head. He blew a smoke ring. "Do you like to hunt, Mrs. Manning?"

Safe ground. The face relaxed again. "I do, yes. I've hunted ever since I was a girl. And in this house it would be difficult *not* to do it." Light, so watery it might have come through frosted glass, touched her hair. At one time she might have been a handsome woman, before whatever fury which possessed her had taken hold.

"Julian doesn't much like it, though. That must not go down a treat with his father." Melrose smiled.

"No, Julian's —" Again, her glance veered off him like a slap and she turned to look through the long windows.

"Doesn't like parties, either, eh?" Melrose looked everywhere in the room except at her.

She stiffened up, sat back in her chair. "Julian is simply not a very sociable person. Not like —"

When she stopped he picked it up, quickly. " 'Not like' —?"

"I was thinking of Rolfe. Rolfe was more his father's son. And his mother's, if it came to that." Her tone was neutral, matter-of-fact. Whether she did or did not approve of Julian, he was left to guess.

Melrose decided to be more direct. "Well, it's a pity he's come under suspicion. Julian, I mean."

"I know who you mean, Lord Ardry. It's ridiculous, of course." She rose, wiped back the sides of her hair, which was twisted into a chignon at her neck. "I must make a few calls for Cook. How long will you be with us, Lord Ardry?"

"Oh, I don't know. I've just nipped up from York. Possibly another couple of days. Two or three." Or four or five. "And it's just plain Plant, Mrs. Manning. Not Lord Ardry."

She did not seem to question the oddity of the only son's not tricking himself out with the deceased father's title. "I see. If you'll excuse me, then."

Brilliant, he said to himself, wandering from the dining room into what Colonel Crael called his "snug." *Brilliant, the ease with which you extracted all that information from her. You might as well have been doing a root canal.* Disgusted with himself, Melrose flopped in a chair and crossed his legs. He put out the stub of the old cigar, lit a fresh one, looked round for some decanters, saw two that would have brought the price of a trip to Heaven, fetched himself a glass of port, sat back smoking and drinking and staring at the ceiling. Ceilings were decidedly his métier. This one was a wonder to behold. Angelica Kauffmann? Joseph Rose? He didn't know. Whoever it was had been a brilliant stuccoist and the ceiling was relaxing. It helped him think. He turned the conversation of the previous evening over in his mind like the leaves of a book.

"Blackmail?" Julian Crael had said to him. A frosty smile. "Why on earth would this Temple woman think she could blackmail me?"

Melrose smiled serenely. "Well, I don't know, old bean. What have you been up to?"

They had been in the drawing room, Julian standing by the fire under his dead mother's portrait. Melrose wondered if those ice-blue eyes could be melted even by flames. "I'm afraid there's nothing in my past that anyone'd pay good money to know."

"A life without blemish? Do you mean if someone called you and said, 'I know what you did,' you wouldn't run like hell?"

The chilly smile stayed in place, but no answer accompanied it.

"Good heavens," Melrose persisted, "even innocent I, whose days drift by like flotsam in a stream — even *I* can think of one or two little incidents I'd sooner not have anyone else remark on." Melrose smiled winningly.

"Then I suggest," said Julian, placing his glass on a table, "that you do not remark on them yourself." With that he excused himself and simply walked out of the room.

Melrose sighed, eyes on the ceiling. He was afraid Sir Titus Crael was going to be disappointed if he thought that Melrose — the disinterested party — was going to get Julian to tell all. The unbending Julian Melrose regarded as a

taciturn and charmless fellow. The sort from whom dogs
and children flee. But not women, he bet. Julian Crael had
not married, but Melrose would wager there wasn't a lass
from York to Edinburgh who wouldn't have walked through
water to Holy Island for a shot at Julian Crael. Those looks,
that money, that position, that — privilege!

Melrose thought (but very modestly; only a small voice
whispered it) *I should know*. Melrose had less looks, though.
Up now and prowling the room, he couldn't resist a passing
glance in an ornate mirror, whose gilt frame sported fro-
licking cherubs. Acceptable looks, but no match for Julian
Crael. Who would be? He thought of the portrait over the
mantel in the drawing room. He looks just like his mother.
Now he passed behind a library table on which were spread
out some papers, pens, books. He looked at the spines:
Whyte-Melville, *The Best of the Fun*, Jorrocks — all hunting stuff. Then he poured another glass of port, stoppered
up the Waterford decanter, resumed his seat and his ceiling-
staring.

Julian Crael had the perfect motive. It wasn't simply
the money which this Temple woman could have claimed
if she'd really been the ward. She would also have laid
claim to the old man's affections. She'd have been a constant thorn in the younger Crael's side . . .

Unfortunately, Julian Crael also had the perfect alibi.

That was what rankled. At the time of the murder Julian
was in his room. He had come in from his walk, bypassed
the party, gone straight to his room, and stayed there. *And*
he could prove it.

Melrose Plant shut his eyes, rubbed his hair, trying to
jog his brain to squeeze out an answer to this riddle.

He took his hands away, his fair hair now a froth of
cowlicks. He wasn't going to quail before some Carter
Dickson locked-room mystery.

Where was Jury?

4·

The gray brindled cat uncurled itself from its window ledge, looked at Jury, yawned through the glass and re-curled itself, doughnut-fashion. Stuck between glass and window molding was a small sign: OPEN. Another sign hung on the door: PLEASE COME IN. Jury and Wiggins went in.

A bell tinkled. From regions above, a rich baritone called down to wait just a moment. The owner of the voice then clattered downstairs. He was wearing jeans, a blue guernsey, a nautical cap (its shiny beak turned backwards), a leather apron streaked with magenta paint, and a cigar behind his ear.

"Mr. Rees? My name's Jury —"

"Chief Inspector, C.I.D., Scotland Yard. And Sergeant Wiggins. I know."

Jury pocketed his identification. "News travels fast, does it?"

Rees pulled the cigar stub from his ear, got it going again. "In Rackmoor, Chief Inspector, there's nothing else *to* travel. You're here to question me about this murder. Couldn't I just say I didn't do it and let it go at that?"

Jury smiled. "It won't take long, Mr. Rees."

"Oh, sure. That's probably what they said to Thomas More as he was stepping up to the block."

"To which he replied something like, 'Help me up. I won't need any help down.' "

Adrian looked astonished, more at Jury's having read it than More's having said it. "God, did he really say that?"

"Far as I know. I wasn't there, of course."

Adrian shook his head. "My God, they had flair back then. Why must we be such mewling kiddies in the face of death? Why so weak?"

"Raskolnikov's philosophy?"

"Oh, Christ." Adrian's fists gripped his hair. "Is that going to hound me to my dea— never mind."

Jury was running his eyes over the paintings which covered the walls of the long room in which they stood. "Wonderful work. I'm sure you didn't do the postcard-type of the Abbey down there at the end."

Adrian looked around. "Bloody right, I didn't. But I have to take stuff on consignment to make ends meet. Local artists, local color, local garbage. But it sells in summer."

"I suppose so. You like that one, Wiggins?"

Sergeant Wiggins had eased his way over to an oil of a decomposed nude. He cleared his throat. "Interesting."

"Look, I wonder, would you mind coming upstairs where I do my work and question me? I'm not trying to impress you with the Dedicated Artist bit, but the paint's drying on a canvas and I won't be able to mess it about if it does. Okay?"

"Sure." Jury plucked at Wiggins's shoulder. The sergeant had his head bent at an odd angle, surveying the nude — or nudes, as there seemed to be more than one — done in some sort of cubist style so that the varying parts of the anatomy were strangely placed. They also seemed to be engaged in revels which Jury did not care to contemplate at the moment.

Jury and Wiggins followed Adrian Rees up a small, enclosed staircase into a very large room, awash in gray light coming largely through the skylight. "It's why I bought the place," said Adrian. "Every house I've been in in Rackmoor is as dark as sin. It's the way the village is all crammed into these cliffs. The houses above shut the light out from the houses below. They've got to keep lights lit in some of the rooms in full daylight."

The room was bare except for the canvases stacked three and four deep all around the walls: landscapes, still lifes, paintings that looked like the painter had dipped fingers in a pot and flicked them at the canvas, and portraits. Certainly, Rees had talent. There was a traditional portrait of a woman in a long, green gown which testified to that. "That's lovely," said Jury.

"Stately home stuff. Boring." Adrian was hunkering down over a canvas. It was enormous, lying on the floor, tilted upwards and with a long receptacle, something like an aluminum pipe cut in two, to catch the paint drippings. He picked up a small bucket and poured; the cerise paint ran like a river of blood, trailing down the left side and running into the container at the bottom. Wiggins was fascinated.

"You just toss the colors on and let them get all mucked about together. That it?"

"That's it, Sergeant."

Wiggins took out his handkerchief and turned watery eyes on Jury. "Am I allergic to paint, do you think, sir?"

Jury really didn't like being Wiggins's apothecary. He sat down on one of the several available stools, all of them paint-splattered. "You saw Gemma Temple just before she was killed, Mr. Rees?"

Intent upon running one of the red streams off to the left, Adrian nodded, then said, "I was walking up Grape Lane. From the Fox."

"Exactly where on Grape Lane? Near the Angel steps?"

He nodded. "Just a bit after. I'd already passed them and she was coming down the other side." Adrian got up from where he'd been hunched over the canvas and tried to relight the cigar on which he'd been chewing, by snapping a match with his fingernail. "I'll tell you, she was a showstopper. At first I thought I'd had one too many. Well, I always have one too many. But that night I was without funds." He picked up a bucket of bright blue paint and poured it slowly down the canvas propped on the floor. He moved quickly to the other side and diverted the thin, blue stream with a large brush so that it crossed over the red paint, looped and came round again. "I only saw her across the pavement. And it was foggy. As usual."

"Are you saying you didn't get a good look?"

"No, that's not what I'm saying. I got a good look all right. I'll never forget it." He got up. "Come here a moment." Jury followed him to the other end of the room where Adrian pulled a covering away from a small canvas. The figure had not been fully painted in, but the background was impressive: darkness, mist, an aureole of light round a streetlamp, and the dim impression of a cloaked figure.

"You mean this is her, Gemma Temple?" Adrian nodded. "I wish you'd finish it; it might be of some help."

Adrian covered it up again. "I'd forgotten it was the Twelfth Night party. I don't go to those things, can't stand them. But don't tell the Colonel I said that. He's a real patron of the arts, and he's usually good for a no-interest loan. And a commission here and there." They were back with the large canvas now, and Adrian was positioning a small bucket of green paint. He said to Wiggins, who seemed enthralled by the whole process, "Sergeant, help out a bit will you? When this green gets to your side, turn it back."

Wiggins seemed honored. "Oh. Well, if Inspector Jury—"

Jury put out his hand for the notebook and Wiggins rolled up his sleeves and hunkered down. Jury shook his head and took out his pen. "Go on, Mr. Rees."

"I don't think she saw me. She stopped for a second under the lamp near the steps." He stood up, flung an imaginary cape over his shoulder. "Black cape, white shirt." He clamped a hand over half of his face. "Face was white on the left side, black on the right. And a black mask to boot—"

"But how did you know it was Gemma Temple?"

"I didn't. Not until I got back there a couple of hours later, rubbernecking with the rest of the villagers. I heard police sirens. Police sirens in *Rackmoor*? Couldn't believe it. At first I thought it was an ambulance. Though I've never seen one of those in the five years I've been here. Nobody dies, I think. Percy Blythe is proof of that. I looked out the window and saw something going on. So I pulled on my pants and went for a look."

"Did you see the body?"

"No. Who could? There were police crawling all over the Angel steps. But there was talk that it was one of the mummers, some woman in a black-and-white costume."

"And then what did you do?"

"Came back here. I was a bit nervous, couldn't sleep. So I started in on this."

"You'd talked to her, hadn't you? Once or twice in the pub?"

Adrian looked at him for a long moment, smoking. "Once or twice, yes. She told me nothing about herself, except she was from London — Kentish Town, I think she said — and that she was an old friend of the Craels."

"You know them well?"

"Yes. At least I know the Colonel well. I doubt anyone knows Julian well." Adrian dabbed his brush in ocher paint, smeared it farther toward a corner.

"And she didn't mention why she was visiting Rackmoor?"

Adrian shook his head. "Damned strange that is, too. Rackmoor in January is hardly the place for your hols, is it? I think she said she was a kind of an actress."

Jury thought for a moment. "Do you know Lily Siddons?"

He looked up, surprised. "Yes, of course. Runs the Bridge Walk Café."

"Can you think of any reason why anyone would want to kill her?"

That got him off his knees. "*Lily?* For God's sakes, *no.* Why do you ask?"

Jury didn't answer. He stood up, made a sign to Wiggins, who rose too from his position of contemplating the canvas. "Incidentally, Mr. Rees. Are you missing a piece of canvas that you know of?"

"Canvas? Well . . ." His eyes trailed off to a corner of the room in which were stacked paint pots, frames, canvas. "I haven't looked, really. Why?"

"Do you lock your shop up when you leave?"

"Christ, no. The idea of anyone stealing paintings is a bit . . ." He shrugged.

"Thanks. I'll be talking to you later."

"I'm sure you will." Adrian wiped his hands on a rag and led them downstairs.

As they walked back through the gallery, Wiggins stopped for another look at the nude. Or nudes.

"Do you like that one?" Rees asked. "It's called *Dartboard.*"

"Interesting," said Wiggins. "Looks like the center here's got tiny holes in it. Is it something to do with using women as targets, or sexual playthings, that sort of thing?" He blew his nose thoroughly, one nostril at a time.

Wiggins the Art Critic was a new persona to Jury.

"Good guess, but, no. Actually, it's because I got bored one night and stretched the canvas over cork and painted a dartboard on it. See —" They leaned closer. "You can just make out the rings under the flake white there. Only I couldn't get rid of the holes. It's rather a nice effect. Gives the nudes a kind of riddled look."

"Like they'd got the pox, or something."

"Hmm. I like that. That's very good. I'll call it *Pox Britannica* and raise the price fifty quid."

"If I were you, I'd toss a few more darts at that one's face. Give her more of a poxy look." Wiggins smiled and offered Adrian a cough drop.

5.

The home of Sir Titus Crael, Bart., was an Elizabethan manor house, overlooking the giant, knobbled cliffs of the North Sea. It looked as if it were built of the same magnesian limestone as the walls surrounding the city of York, and was washed to a continuous whiteness by rain. It rose from a thick layer of ground mist, looming through great spoons of fog.

Wiggins drove the police-issue Ford up the gravel drive and beside a large stable block, surprising a magnificent horse into rearing back. The elderly man on its back, tall, spare, and distinguished-looking, seemed in complete control of the horse, though, and dismounted. He walked over to the car.

"You're from Scotland Yard, aren't you? I'm Titus Crael." He held out a strong-fingered hand.

Jury and Wiggins got out.

"Don't bother with the car. Just leave it there. Forgive me for meeting you at the stables, not very formal, I s'pose, but *I'm* not very formal. Anyway, I just wanted a word with you before you went in. You don't mind talking out here, do you? Bracewood will turn a deaf ear."

Jury looked round for Bracewood, and then realized the Colonel was talking about the horse. Colonel Crael still had his leather-gloved hands through the reins and was leaning slightly against the horse, as some people do against others for support — physical or moral. "You don't mind, do you, Inspector? Sergeant?"

Jury assumed the Colonel meant to have the questioning done out here, and, though it was more damp than

cold, he knew Wiggins would be a mask of misery. He said,
"No, not really. I'll just have Sergeant Wiggins go in and
have a talk with the servants."

"By all means. Right through that door. Wood — my
butler — will show you about." He pointed to the formidable facade of the manor house as if it were no more than
the entrance to some clay-and-wattle cottage. "Cook will
give you tea, or something. You look cold."

Wiggins also looked grateful. He walked towards the
house.

"To tell the truth, Inspector Jury, I just wanted a word
with you about this mess before you talk to Julian. We
disagree so completely about that girl, I didn't want to go
into it again when he was around. We simply infuriate one
another." The Colonel twined his fingers through the reins
of the horse. "I'm certain this Gemma Temple was my
ward. Dillys March." He looked off over the mist-blanketed
stones into the trees, tall beeches rising specterlike, and
talked about Dillys March. He said she had come to them
when she was only eight years old, after an airplane crash
had carried off both mother and father. "They were great
friends of Lady Margaret —" The Colonel stumbled over
the name. "Margaret was my wife. There's a wonderful
picture inside. Adrian Rees did it, and from only a photograph. He really is very talented. It will appear to you as if
he glamorized her — but he didn't. She really was very
beautiful. . . ."

"You were talking about Dillys March."

"Yes. She was a kind of . . . adopted daughter, really. I
mean, we treated her like our own, though we never legally
adopted her."

"According to Inspector Harkins's report — your own
statement, sir — Dillys March was about to inherit money
from your late wife's estate. And then she suddenly left."

"It wasn't all that much." The Colonel shrugged off the

sum. "Only fifty thousand pounds. When she was twenty-one."

"And is that money still held in trust?"

"It reverted to the estate. Margaret left everything to Julian and Rolfe. And this fifty thousand pounds to Dillys. When Rolfe was killed —" He stopped.

"The money went to Julian, then."

"Yes." The Colonel swallowed, hard. "They were both killed, Margaret and Rolfe, in a motor accident."

Jury said nothing for a moment. "That must have been terrible, losing your wife and your son all at once." Sir Titus did not reply, just looked off through the trees. Then Jury asked: "Was Dillys March the sort of person who would have walked off and left an inheritance behind? And it would have been more than fifty thousand pounds, wouldn't it, eventually? She'd have got more from you."

"To answer both of your questions: No, she wasn't. And, yes, she would. I admit her leaving that way surprised us. But there *had* been incidents before. Dillys would simply drive off. I gave her a red Mini for her sixteenth birthday and she was always going off in it. Once for as much as a week. We brought her back from London."

"Was she promiscuous?"

"I . . . wouldn't say that, exactly."

Meaning she was. "When she left this last time: you didn't call the police?"

"Actually, it was the police called *us*. They'd found her car in London, apparently abandoned. Not a clue as to where she was."

"What happened then?"

"It was very . . . difficult. They quite naturally assumed that she'd left off her own bat, you know. But I suppose they'd also got to consider foul play. I had a chauffeur, Leo Manning. That's Olive's — my housekeeper's — son. It turned out there'd been something going on between Dillys

and Leo. And Leo was the last person to see her. She'd been
with him, apparently. And that brought him in for rather
a heavy dose of suspicion. His mother thinks it's what sent
him over the edge. Leo had a breakdown. He's in an institution. And Olive has always hated Dillys March."

"What reason did she give — Gemma Temple, that is —
for staying away so long?"

"Remorse. Shame. Her life had not been, I judge, too
savory. She took a room at the Fox Deceiv'd, she said, because she didn't know if she'd be welcome. But of course
she was. Look, Inspector. If this Gemma Temple or whoever she was an imposter, how in God's name would
she have carried it off? How could she have known all of
the things she *did* know — even little things — about Dillys's childhood, those sorts of things?"

"Collusion. Someone in Rackmoor, someone in your own
house, possibly, who knew a lot about Dillys March. Someone who might have wished to split the profits. Or out of
revenge, jealousy . . . there are other motives."

"But such a deception is *unthinkable*." He sighed. "I see
you agree with Julian."

"No, I don't agree with anyone at the moment. I don't
know enough. But such deceptions have been worked before, Colonel Crael. Now, who might have known her well
enough?"

"The only others besides Julian and me would be Olive
Manning, Wood the butler, and an old maid, Stevens. But
the thought of any of them . . . well . . . I suppose I *have*
talked a great deal about her to Maud Brixenham, a good
friend of mine. Lives in the village, on Lead Street. And
Adrian Rees, when he was doing Margaret's portrait. I used
to go down to his studio and watch. . . ." He rubbed his
hand down Bracewood's neck. "This house was quite a
different place when Margaret was alive. Always a lot of
people. And there were Rolfe and Julian. Rolfe was older

by fourteen years. They both looked like her; it was that spun-gold hair. The gold-dust twins, people would call them. Julian looks exactly like her; I only wish he were like her in other ways. I don't know who Julian's like, really. Rolfe was much more fun-loving. Perhaps *too* fun-loving. Women, you see. And then there was Dillys. Margaret simply transformed her from a rather puddinglike child into, well, someone very like herself. Dress, manner, that sort of thing. Oh, she wasn't beautiful like Margaret. Or even Julian, if it comes to that. Though Margaret wasn't necessarily what you might call *good* —" He looked off; his face clouded. "But Julian adored her. People who look like that . . . their sheer physical beauty — it seems to put them beyond the pale of common morality. Don't you agree?"

Jury studied the older man, his strong face, strong hands on the reins of the horse, iron-gray hair and mustache. "No, I don't."

The Colonel looked down at the mist-shrouded courtyard. They seemed to be floating there as the silence lengthened, their feet and the horse's hooves lost in a lake of mist. Finally, the older man looked up, smiled bleakly. "Aren't you going to ask me, 'Where were you on the night in question?' Inspector Harkins seemed to favor that question."

"I was coming to it," Jury said, smiling. "You had a Twelfth Night party, right? I suppose you were busy with your guests."

"That's a somewhat more polite way of putting it."

"I wasn't trying to be polite. I've read your statement, that's all."

"Ah. Well, I can only repeat my statement, then. Yes, I was in and out and busy with my guests. Can't say I have an alibi, though; I mean I can't account for myself completely during the times in question. Not" — and he looked squarely at Jury — "like Julian."

"I see. I think I should talk to Julian now." Jury looked

towards the front of Old House. "I can find my own way. If you were about to go for a ride?"

"If you're sure. Yes, I was. There's a hunt in three days' time and I was just going over to the kennels. Wood will find Julian for you, if he's back. Julian walks out a great deal, no matter the weather." He mounted up, rubbed the neck of the horse. "I'll be off, then. I'm always here if you need me."

"I expect I will. And there's one other thing. You have a visitor staying with you?"

Sir Titus looked surprised. "Why, yes, as a matter of fact. An old friend — well, rather, the son of an old friend, Lord Ardry. Fine person, loved the hunt, of course. *This* Lord Ardry — the son, I mean — just goes by the family name. Melrose Plant he calls himself."

Jury smiled. The Colonel made it sound like a pseud-onym.

"Anyway, he gave up the title — don't know why; took me long enough to get mine and I'm only a baronet. Hardly worth noting, eh? But Plant — now he's —"

"I know. I've met him. In Northamptonshire, as a matter of fact."

"Yes. Yes, that's right; he was telling me about it. Quite a nasty business, wasn't it?"

"Murder usually is."

The butler took Jury's coat, told him that Mr. Julian had not yet returned, but that, yes, he would certainly fetch Lord Ardry. Jury reflected as he looked the hall over — an imposing mixture of dark panels and Doric columns — that Plant might have given up the title, but everyone else seemed to be giving it back to him. He looked down at the black-and-white design of the marble floor and wished that his own thoughts would assemble themselves into such neat, geometric patterns. To his right was a gallery. He wandered through it, past the fan vaultings and the paintings. He wondered if the portrait of Lady Margaret Crael were in here. . . .

"Why are you standing there dreaming, Chief Inspector?"

Melrose Plant stood at the entrance to the Long Gallery, leisurely smoking a cigarette. He was far enough away that he had to raise his voice, and it echoed from the stuccoed ceiling, the scagliola columns and gilt mirrors. He was wearing a gray suit made up by some God-bespoke tailor.

Jury was delighted to see him. "Mr. Plant." He moved towards him, hand outstretched. "I can hardly believe it. Understand you're an old friend of the family."

"I was in York when I found out what happened. I always seem to be around just when you don't need me."

"On the contrary, Mr. Plant: you might be very useful. Being a friend of the family, having the run of the house, so to speak." Jury looked at him. "Navigating the waters."

"Ha. *That* would be a bit tricky. Julian Crael is a rather formidable iceberg. He spends a good deal of time walking the cliffside and the moors and generally being pale and interesting."

"Am I to take it you don't care much for Julian Crael?"

Melrose shrugged and smiled and changed the subject. "I've been following your career in the newspapers."

"That must have made for very light reading."

"Not at all. I knew you'd been put in charge of this case. I must admit I rather enjoyed that business in Long Piddleton — though that might seem a trifle macabre. Indeed, I enjoyed it almost as much as Agatha."

"How will I ever get on without her?" Jury looked quickly round. "She's not — ?"

"You're safe, Inspector. She's not. Now. Could I induce you to have dinner with me at the Fox Deceiv'd? I hear they've very good food there."

"Good idea. How about seven?"

"How about six? That's when it opens, and I've a taste for a Rackmoor Fog."

"What's that?"

"It's a little drink the publican concocted — Mrs. Meechem? — I daresay for the tourist trade. Gin, rum, brandy, whisky and sharks' teeth. Tell Sergeant Wiggins to have one. It'll cure anything, even the Black Death."

"Have you seen Wiggins, then?"

"Yes. He's in the kitchen exhorting the cook to confess."

"I'll go along there, then. See you at six. If I'm not there just have a double."

"Then you wouldn't see me at all." Melrose called after Jury's departing back, "You couldn't use, well, you know, a bit of help in the meantime, could you? Even a sounding board for some of your reflections? Try it out on the dog, that sort of thing?"

Jury thought for a moment. "Perhaps. As long as you're here, Mr. Plant, you could go along to the Makepiece cottage and see what you can find out. It's the nearest one to the Angel steps, up on Scroop Street. It's called Cross Keys and there's a chance they might have heard something."

Plant's face, Jury saw, was beaming as he made a brief note in his pocket-diary. The little notebook looked surprisingly like Jury's own.

In a kitchen the size of a rugby field Wiggins was hunched over his notebook, a pot of tea, and a plate of excellent-looking sandwiches. Across from him sat a plump, red-faced woman of indeterminate age, her brown hair drawn back in a neat bun.

"This is Mrs. Thetch, Chief Inspector. She's just been kind enough to give me tea."

Jury was hungry himself — it must have been the sea air — and picked up a sandwich. Minced chicken, very good.

"I'll just get you a cup, sir." Mrs. Thetch started up but Jury waved her down. "No, thanks. This is fine. Tell me, Mrs. Thetch, how long you've been with the Craels."

"Eighteen years, I was just telling the sergeant."

"You knew Lady Margaret, then."

"Yes, sir. But not very well. I came just before . . . you know." Her face wore an obligatory sad look. "I was vegetable cook for a few months; then after Mary Siddons died, poor thing, I stopped on as cook."

"This Mary Siddons. She had a daughter, Lily?"

"Yes, sir. We still see Lily. Terrible about her mother. Drowned, she did." Mrs. Thetch nodded her head towards the rear of the house and the cliffs. "No one ever knew why she'd be walking along that stretch of shingle so near to high tide. There's a long, narrow strip right at the bottom of the cliff that'll take you from Rackmoor as far as Runner's Bay. But you can only walk it when the tide's out. Lots of folks do. Poor Mary Siddons must have tried to walk it when the tide was coming in."

Wood appeared to tell Jury that Mr. Julian was waiting for him in the Bracewood Room. (Apparently, the Colonel named his rooms after horses.) The butler gave the voluble Mrs. Thetch a dark look and preceded Jury through the dining room.

As he followed Wood, Jury thought: one disappearance, two auto accident victims, one in a mental institution, one drowned. One murdered. Rackmoor, for all its bracing sea air, didn't seem the healthiest place in the British Isles.

6.

When he walked into the Bracewood Room, Jury knew he'd found the portrait of Lady Margaret Crael. It hung above the marble mantelpiece, dominating the room and the room's other occupant, Julian Crael. The woman in the picture was seated on a sofa or chaise longue, the back of which was a dark curve of wood. The painter might have surprised her, his subject, from behind, for it was the back of the sofa which presented itself to the viewer. The woman seated there was shown from the shoulder upwards and in profile. Her head was turned to the left, looking along the length of her arm, black-sleeved and outstretched along the mahogany frame. Across the sofa had been tossed a silky material — a Spanish shawl, perhaps, black fringed. One had to peer closely to pick out details of silk and fringe and wood, for the dark shawl melted into the black dress, the dress into the dark background, so that all was dark except for that pellucid profile and hair. The pale gold hair fell loosely about her shoulders, swept back from her face as if a breeze had blown through the room. The palm of her hand was turned upwards, slightly cupped, the fingers apart and a little extended, as if she were beckoning to someone — someone out there beyond the portrait's frame. Jury looked away.

"I'm Julian Crael," said the man beneath the portrait. And, seeing the direction of Jury's gaze, added. "That was my mother."

The identification of Julian Crael as the son was quite superfluous; anyone with eyes in his head would have known this was her son. Had Julian Crael been a woman, a girl, he might have been the twin of the seated woman. The pastel coloring, the deeply set blue eyes, the cornsilk hair — he looked himself as if he had stepped down from a painting.

"She's beautiful," said Jury. A banal comment, considering.

"It's a good likeness, too, considering Rees did it from a photograph. He's the local artist. Lowers himself occasionally to do portraits. Pays the rent, I suppose. She's been dead eighteen years." Crael drank off what was in the glass he was holding, and looked away, into empty air, over Jury's shoulder.

"I'm sorry. And I didn't introduce myself. Richard Jury, C.I.D. I wanted to ask you a few questions about Gemma Temple, Mr. Crael."

Julian had left the fireplace to replenish his drink. He held the decanter up in mute question. Jury declined the whisky. "What about her?" asked Julian, pouring. "You mean, why don't my father and I agree as to whether she was Dillys March? Why should we, since we agree on little else?" He hoisted his glass, gave Jury a chilly smile, and drank. And then he returned to his position by the mantel, his outstretched arm across it like the arm in the portrait above him. It was not, Jury was sure, a conscious pose.

"You're sure she wasn't Dillys March?"

"Absolutely. It was a swindle. Would have been, that is."

"Then you must have thought of collusion, Mr. Crael. This Gemma Temple certainly must have had information supplied her by someone who *did* know Dillys."

Julian smoked and turned his silver lighter round and round in the fingers of the hand still lying on the mantel. "I suppose so."

"Who, then, Mr. Crael?"

Julian dropped the lighter into his pocket and his arm from the mantel and turned his back to the fireplace, still smoking. "I've no idea."

"But you do agree that's the only answer, at least if she wasn't Dillys March." Jury wanted to draw this commitment from him, found it strange he seemed reluctant to make it. "Mr. Crael?"

Briefly, Julian nodded. "Yes."

"Tell me: why did Dillys leave as she did?" Julian smoked and shook his head. "Colonel Crael says she had gone off before."

He nodded. "Dillys was willful, selfish, spoilt. I suppose

they gave her anything she wanted to make up for the loss of her parents. Nothing she did would have surprised me."

A log disintegrated in the fireplace, spitting out sparks and tiny tongues of flame. Julian's eyes, like the blue-tipped flames, seemed to burn at Jury. He was struck anew by the beauty of the man's face and how out of place it seemed here. He belonged to another time and place, Arcadian, perhaps. "I take it you did not care much for Dillys March."

For a moment, Julian turned his face away and did not answer. Jury took the opportunity to pocket the matches with which he had lit his own cigarette and which had been lying in a cut-glass dish beside his chair. One never knew where matches might come from. Moreover, he wondered why the lowly packet was even in the room, consorting with two table lighters — one of green Murano glass, the other porcelain, along with Julian's own silver lighter.

"Shouldn't you be asking me things more pertinent, Inspector? Such as, where was I at the time of the murder?"

Jury smiled. It had been the father's question, also. "According to your statement, you were in your room."

"That's quite right. I dislike these Twelfth Night parties. My mother started it. She loved parties, and so does the Colonel. I don't. I am, indeed, rather antisocial." He seemed waiting for Jury to challenge this. "I'd like to show you something." Julian walked over to the French doors, opened one, and beckoned to Jury. They went out into the icy air of the terrace. Rime edged the balustrade to which Julian had backed up, the sea behind him, the waves sucking against the cliffside. Julian was looking up at the blank wall of the house. He pointed. "Those are my windows." Then he crossed the terrace to the left and pointed towards the village. "There's a path that connects up with these terrace steps. It's a nice walk along the cliffs. It joins up with more steps down to the seawall. The easiest way to the house is to come round by the Fox steps, up along the seawall, then to the path, *then* to the terrace. And that's the way people came and went." He walked back to Jury. "All night long, Inspector Jury." His eyes glittered for the first time with something like humor. "As to the inside. There are two doors to my rooms. Both face the landing where the musicians were playing all the evening long. Oh, true, they did take a bit of a break, but there was always someone out there. I went into my room at ten. The party had started already. I could not have come out without someone's seeing me. Even if that were remotely possible, I surely could not have gone out and come *back* without someone's seeing me."

"And you couldn't even have scaled the wall," Jury said. They were back in the drawing room now, Jury sitting in the same chair and bending matches down one by one in the book he had taken from his pocket.

Julian, once again by the fireplace, spread his hands in mock-helplessness; he looked very amused.

"Do you often stay at the Sawry Hotel, Mr. Crael?"

"What — ?"

"The Sawry. It's quite exclusive. In Mayfair, isn't it?"

A moment of bewilderment, and Julian regained his icy insouciance. "Our family use it. I go up to London occasionally. Like all the rest of the world. Why do you ask that?"

Jury held up the matches, cover out.

Julian stared at the book of matches, looked away.

"Gemma Temple came from London."

"Well, good God, Inspector. So does Adrian Rees. So does Maud Brixenham. And Olive Manning just got back from London. Half the world's in London." He drank his whisky.

Charming evasion. Jury changed the subject again. "Tell me about Lily Siddons."

Julian had just picked up his glass and now set it down again, hard. "What in God's name has she to do with it?"

"Don't know. That's why I'm asking. Wasn't there a dinner party here the night before?"

"Ah, yes. Miss Temple's *debut*. Father invited Lily. Along with Rees and Maud Brixenham. But I still don't understand —"

"The costume. The costume Gemma Temple was wearing really belonged to Lily Siddons. There was, apparently, some swapping."

Julian stared. "Are you telling me the murderer meant to kill *Lily*?" Jury didn't answer, just looked at him. Julian snorted, shook his head like a hound baffled by a fouled line. "To tell the truth I wasn't paying much attention to their conversation and really don't remember anything about costumes. Oh, yes, this Temple woman decried the fact she hadn't one. I left round about then. You'll have to ask my father. Or Maud. Or Lily herself, why don't you ask her?"

"I certainly shall. Lily Siddons used to live here, didn't she? When her mother was cook?"

"Yes, as a child for a few years."

Jury thought for a moment. "You know, I sometimes feel murders are done in the past, in a manner of speaking. That what was really meant was to kill someone a long time ago — and it's taken all this time of dragging the feeling around — like a dead body, really. Until one finally manages to get on with it. And dumps the corpse in the present. On the Angel steps. Somewhere." He stopped because of the look on Julian's face: it was ashen, blighted, stricken. It lasted for only a couple of seconds, but it was sharp enough to convince Jury that Julian had been about to admit something — to step over a precipice, and had then quickly drawn back his foot.

All Julian said was, "Is Papa pairing me off with Lily, then? I expect he might. He's always had a soft spot for her. No matter she was the cook's girl."

"I imagine he'd like you to marry. You must be supremely

eligible. Titled, rich, handsome, intelligent — how have you escaped?"

"I'm glad you've got it in the right order. The title's not much. Only a baronetcy. Our guest, Mr. Plant, seems to have given away far more than I'll ever have. I'll be Sir Julian one of these days." He seemed to take no pleasure in it. "As to Lily. Yes, my father's very fond of Lily. She takes him back. In some small way she helps to create the illusion that it's not all over."

"Then does Lily Siddons come in for any money, Mr. Crael?"

Julian frowned. "Probably. Why?"

"Simply that anyone who did have a claim on your father's capital, either literal or emotional, might have some reason for wanting Dillys March out of the way for good and all."

Julian could only stare. Then he laughed. "Ye gods. First Lily is victim and now murderess? The idea of her wielding that knife — preposterous. To say nothing of its being a roundabout way of collecting on her inheritance," he added dryly.

"Why preposterous? A woman could have done it."

"She's so imminently *sensible*. Works like a demon at her restaurant. And she doesn't have the —" He seemed searching for a word to describe her lack. "She hasn't the passion to do murder. Lily's a bit of an iceberg. The original Snow Queen." Jury held back a smile. "I guess she's attractive enough. Pale skin, blond hair. Yes, I suppose she is." He seemed newly digesting this information, as if he'd just made the discovery. "The Colonel's very democratic, isn't he?"

"Who do you think might have done it, Mr. Crael?"

He gave a short laugh. "No one. Oh, let's see now. There's Adrian Rees. He's certainly a fiery sort. Always getting up to stuff. Barroom brawls. Living up to his image."

"You don't like him?"

"I don't care about him one way or the other."

That indifference, thought Jury, which appeared to extend to most things and most people, was too studied to be real.

"Rees might be capable of collusion with someone else, of course. He needs money for his gallery, I know that. Father's loaned him quite a bit."

"Did he know enough about Dillys March to prime Gemma Temple?"

"I don't know. The Colonel certainly confides in people. Maud Brixenham, for example. If I'm not altogether blind, she would like to become Lady Crael. Papa's quite present-able looking. Fifteen, twenty years older than Maud but doesn't look it. And, after all, she's fifty-five, so what's the difference?" Jury smiled at this small-boy way of looking at passionless old age. "The Colonel's very active. It's all that damned hunting, I suppose."

"Has your father shown an inclination in her direction?"

"He confides, Inspector. But not in me." Julian threw Jury a sardonic glance. "No, old Maud would not want Dillys coming back and laying claim, as you put it, to my father's affections. Nor would old Olive Manning. I think she blames my father for letting the sordid affair go on between Leo and Dillys. Her son is in some mental institution. But to give the devil her due — Dillys, that is — Leo Manning was round the bend long before he came here. Father hired him as chauffeur as a favor to Olive. He was no damned good, either as chauffeur or as person. But, of course, his mother doesn't believe that. No, it was all Dillys's fault. All *our* fault, I gather. Papa pays the bills for Leo Manning. He's a generous man. There are probably annuities in that will of his all up your arm." Julian looked at Jury. "No, Inspector. He would not disinherit me for Dillys March. Of course, he might leave it all to the Kennel Club or the Destitute Huntsmen's organization." He smoked and was silent for a moment. "Perhaps this Gemma Temple simply meant to pick up Dillys March's fifty thousand pounds and leave."

"Or stay."

"She *couldn't* have got away with it. Never."

"She seems to have made a good beginning."

"But to make an end would have been impossible. It's one thing to get through forty-eight hours of posing as someone else. But to play-act that out over a long period — ?" Julian shook his head in disbelief.

"Dillys March was, I take it, not universally liked."

"Quite correct."

"But she was only eighteen. When she left here."

"Chronologically."

"What were her relations with men?"

"She probably had one with any man she came in contact with. She liked to cause trouble, to make sparks fly."

"Yet the question remains: if this woman was *not* Dillys March, well, where is *she?* Why hasn't Dillys ever come back?"

Julian looked down, studying the rug, as if some pattern might emerge there. "I thought perhaps, you know, she might be dead."

Winter, with that remark, seemed to settle in the room. Jury had the oddest sensation of snow driven into corners, ice formed on sills, rime on mirrors. Of gray, unfiltered light hanging like lead. From where he sat he could see the long, bleak windows facing the terrace. Fog pressed against them. The mantle of depression to which he was never wholly a stranger wrapped him in even heavier folds.

7.

"All shipshape and Bristol fashion!"

Bertie switched off the Hoover and saluted the small statue of the Virgin which stood on the mantel over the electric log. Bertie's notion of religion leaned heavily towards the concept of salvation through duty, not grace.

"Come along, Arnold." Smartly he turned on his heel, picking up the Hoover and throwing one arm across his chest with the hand like a blade on the neck of the vacuum. "Hip, hip!" He marched it to the closet in the tiny, dark hallway.

Arnold always watched the hoovering closely and sometimes rooted things like old sweet wrappers out from under chairs. Bertie marched back to the parlor for a look round. "That ought to satisfy Frog Eyes."

Arnold's bark was as smart as Bertie's salute. The name "Frog Eyes" always elicited a hostile response.

Frog Eyes — or Miss Frother-Guy, as she was known to the village — was one of several women who had appointed themselves Bertie's guardians in the absence of his mum. There were also Miss Cavendish, the librarian, and Rose Honeybun, the vicar's wife. They took turns looking in on Bertie. Of the three, Miss Frother-Guy was the most disliked, largely because of her clear antipathy towards Arnold, whom she regarded as wholly unsuitable as a companion for the motherless boy.

The feeling was mutual. As far as Arnold was concerned, Miss Frother-Guy didn't go down a treat, either. Arnold would plant himself four-square in front of her and subject her to ruthless stares.

Miss Frother-Guy had a thin-lipped, peevish little face that reminded Bertie of one of those sharp-nosed mice in the Roly-Poly-Pudding story. Miss Cavendish, on the other hand, was not quite so sharp but was annoyingly dusty. Bertie always found trails of grime, either from muddy boots or bits of fluff deposited in the folds of her clothing. He put it down to the constant dusting of shelves in the Rackmoor Lending Library. Codfish (Miss Cavendish) did not seem to enjoy the charge she had been given by Miss

Frother-Guy, and would do little more than poke her head in Bertie's front door, her pale eyes darting here and there like little silverfish. She did not stay to tea.

Rose Honeybun was the best of the lot, and she *did* stay to tea, and supplied most of it, since her Christian duties were released largely through supplying Bertie with cakes and Bath buns. Although she was the vicar's wife, she had a certain salacious interest in the sexual side of Rackmoor and a kind of raw bonhomie, which made her better company. She liked to sit at the table downing cup after cup of tea and smoking cigarettes and trying to pry out of Bertie whatever chunks of gossip she could, as if she were searching for plums in the tart. Also, she liked Arnold and brought him bones. These he promptly hid.

Bertie was sorry it was Miss Frother-Guy who had jailer's duty today, rather than Mrs. Honeybun. He wouldn't have minded a good natter about the murder.

Among the three of them it was like a relay-race, with Bertie the stick handed from one to the other. It was Frog Eyes who was causing the most trouble; it was she who kept wanting to get the "authorities" in. His mother had been gone for six weeks, now close to two months. Frog Eyes was certain more "suitable" arrangements could be made. He recoiled at the thought. He held her off — he held them all off — with assurances that he had heard from his mum, but had misplaced the letters, and that she was still nursing a dying gran in Northern Ireland.

The letter he did *not* want them to see was the one his mum *had* written. He took it out of the dresser less and less often these days but still often enough that light was beginning to show through the creases of the paper worn thin by folding it into smaller and smaller squares. Unfolded now, it looked like a little leaded-glass window. Bertie did not understand its contents; her motive confused him, what motive there was.

He was not immobilized by her absence. He and Arnold carried on in the way they always had. Even when his mother had been around it was Bertie who really took care of the house, who cleaned, cooked meals, got himself off to school. His mother mostly daydreamed about London or sat eating Cadbury Fruit & Nut bars and reading thrillers.

So it wasn't that he really needed her to take care of him. But he could still feel the sense of privation, especially when he saw other boys with their mums. It was almost the way a boy might look longingly at a two-wheeler and think, Everybody else has one, why can't I?

For a while after she had left, he would forget she was no longer living there, and he would set out the usual three places for tea instead of just two. Then he and Arnold would eat their tea and stare out of their separate windows until Arnold would get bored with this and yawn and jump down from his chair and want to be let out. Sometimes they would walk in the drizzle together, Bertie hoping the rain would fertilize his mind, would implant some ingenious explanation for the absence of his mum which would hold off Frog Eyes and Codfish. He would stand looking out to sea while Arnold took one of his death-defying walks along the cliffs — narrow ways which were never paths, but which Arnold loved to go down (perhaps rooting out nesting birds, Bertie thought); Bertie would stand and wait for Arnold to come back and seem to search the waves breaking way out for some answer. It was during one of these vigils when he had come up with the Belfast idea. Frog Eyes, nor Codfish would want to go sticking their long noses into the affairs of Northern Ireland. Who would?

Bertie knew there were "homes" and he certainly knew there were police stations. Those were the only "authorities" he assumed would be at all interested in his case. So when Inspector Harkins came knocking at his door, he got all whoozy and thought for the first time in his life he might faint. If that detective hadn't come to lead him away to a "home" then he must have come about the cheques.

But he hadn't come about either. He had come about a murder.

8.

But it was neither Frog Eyes nor the police to whom Bertie opened the door this afternoon. It was to Melrose Plant. In an effort of concentration, Bertie screwed up his eyes and drew his mouth back, disclosing one missing tooth and others in a poor state of repair. A lock of brown hair stood up at the crown of his head like a small flag. There was a darned hole in the knee of his mud-colored breeches and his cardigan was misbuttoned, leaving a small wave of brown wool on his shoulder, which made him look slightly hunchbacked.

All in all, thought Melrose, the caramel-colored terrier with the luminous brown eyes was distinctly the handsomer of the two. Melrose stood in his velvet-collared coat, his silver-headed walking stick against his shoulder. "Would you get your father, please, there's a good lad?"

Bertie squinted. "Me dad's dead."

"Oh. Sorry. Well, may I have a word with your mother, then?"

A brief silence. "Mum's away. There's only me and Arnold."

"Well, perhaps this Arnold wouldn't mind a word with me. Scotland Yard asked me to stop by," Melrose was happy to add.

The boy gasped. "You from the Yard?"

"Not exactly. Let's say I'm helping out. My name is Melrose Plant." He was searching the air behind the lad for somebody bigger. "And your name is — ?"

"Bertie Makepiece." He held the door wide. Melrose saw

that behind the boy the house was silent and what rooms
he could see — a triangle of a parlor, a bit of a kitchen —
were empty. Two unpleasant-looking aspidistras flanked the
narrow hallway. Somewhere a clock was ticking.

"This here's Arnold."

Melrose looked down. "This is a dog."

"I know."

Melrose tried to smile, all the while silently cursing Jury.
He wondered now how to jolly the lad along.

There were certain things Melrose had always tried to
avoid — children and animals among them — and was always nonplussed when they seemed to regard him with
interest, as if he might do something awfully clever, be
good for a sweet or a bone or something. He did occasionally carry sweets and biscuits in his pockets for impromptu
meetings on trains (for example), but only by way of getting
rid of these invaders of his privacy. Why was he surprised
when it worked just the opposite effect, often involving him
in interminably wrought, baroque tales about their schools
or their nannies or their hated little sisters? You would
think if you kindly produced a sweet and said to the re-
cipient, "I hear Auntie calling, hop along now," the other
would take the hint. Not so. They only produced even
stickier smiles or thumping tail waggings and stuck you up
for another prize. He sometimes wondered if he were kidding himself.

"Well, well, this is a pleasant little cottage," said Melrose
with a heartiness he certainly didn't feel. He would get
Jury for this. Melrose had neither children, dogs (unless
he counted Mindy, who had followed him home and hung
about thereafter), nor aspidistra at Ardry End. Yet this
house seemed awash with all three, and all seemingly together, as if they had grouped themselves to sit for a portrait with him.

Now the lad was smiling in a silly way and when he

looked at the dark line of the dog's mouth he thought he detected a smile there too, as if they were expecting him to do something rather jolly.

"Come on in the kitchen. I thought you was Frog — Miss Frother-Guy."

Melrose followed him into the spotless kitchen, tossing his coat over the banister and planting his stick in the aspidistra.

Two places were laid for tea. Arnold slunk under the table and lay there, head on paw, looking bleakly up at Melrose. Melrose was not quite sure how the Yard would go about extracting information from one so young as Bertie. Should he pick him up and shake him, for instance? He settled on what he hoped was a tone both friendly and authoritative. "Apparently, your cottage here is the closest one to the Angel steps. Where the body was found. We thought perhaps you might have seen something."

"Stabbed a dozen times, that's what I heard. Summat bloody, she was."

Melrose would have preferred a little less relish in his tone. "An exaggeration. The question is: *Did* you see or hear anything at all?"

"No." Even the one syllable was weighted with disappointment. He moved a bowl from the table to underneath it. "You needn't sulk, Arnold." To Melrose he said, "You're sitting in Arnold's chair, see."

"Oh. *I* could sit under the table."

"No need. Have a cuppa. I'm just wetting the tea."

Given his general lack of congress with people of this age, Melrose thought he should lose no chance to be instructive. "Don't you think your mother might prefer you to say 'allowing the leaves to steep.' "

Bertie shrugged, and the wide, white apron he had donned rose and fell on his chest. "I could do. But me mum ain't here, and it sounds awful mouthy. As long as them leaves is lying there getting wet, I might as well say so. Care for a bit of Madeira cake or a fruit scone, then?"

"No, thank you. But what about a Weetabix?"

Bertie had his arm down in the box. "These's for Arnold. He always gets two for his tea." He put two biscuits under the table by Arnold's bowl. But Arnold did not let his gaze waver from Melrose Plant for so much as a second. His look was not hostile, merely concentrated.

Melrose thought they had somehow strayed from the subject. "Chief Inspector Jury —"

Bertie's gaze was rapacious. "*That's* that Inspector from the Yard."

"Yes. Did you hear or see anything?"

Bertie held the teapot, swirling it round and round. "I didn't, no. Only now I think on it, there was a kind of screech, but it was probably a gull."

Or your imagination, thought Melrose. "What time was that?"

"Not too sure. Maybe eleven, or half after."

"Late for you to be up. Don't you have to get up early for school?"

"Wasn't no scule that day."

"You said your father's dead. Where's your mother?"

"Away." He held the teapot aloft. "Wonder whatever happened to Miss Frother-Guy? She looks in on me till Mum comes back."

"Oh. And when will that be?"

"Soon."

Melrose couldn't think of any proper questions. Arnold's stare was extremely disconcerting. He kind of toed the dog's nose to make him stop. But Arnold merely shifted his nose to his other paw. "Do you think there's anything peculiar going on in Rackmoor?" Jury liked to ask general questions like that. Get the reaction. Milk them for knowledge they didn't even know they had.

Bertie shrugged and sat. "No more'n usual."

"Well, good grief. What's *usual?*"

"Oh, I dunno." He plucked a bun from the plate and nibbled round it, mouse-wise. "Percy Blythe says . . . You met Percy?"

"No." Melrose watched Arnold munch his Weetabix, still with his brown eyes cast upward.

"Percy says this woman that got, you know" — and Bertie drew his forefinger across his neck — "Percy says she used to live here. A bad lot, name of March, Percy says. He says she lived up at Old House and there was no end of trouble because of her. She disappeared years ago and now Percy says she's come back. Like a curse. And he must be right for look what happened."

"Your friend Percy is ignoring the fact that March wasn't this woman's name."

Bertie shrugged and slowly stripped the fluted covering from a fairy cake. Melrose was uncomfortably reminded of Agatha, who had called him twice in the last twenty-four hours.

"Don't know about that," said Bertie. "Percy says when she lived up there she was always getting up to something. A bad lot. Percy says that's what's wrong with that Mr. Crael."

That surprised Melrose. "Do you mean the old one or the young one?"

"You know. That Julian. Don't he act summat queer, though? He never comes down to the village nor nothing. And he's out walkin' at night along them cliffs up there. Percy says he's come across him in t'fog and it give him a turn, it did."

"What's this Percy person doing running around on the moors at night?"

"H'earth-stopper. Works for the Colonel. For the hunt." Bertie drank off his tea, holding the cup with both hands.

"Percy says Mr. Crael's been funny-acting for years — ever since this girl went off. And now she's back. I mean, she was." Bertie drew his finger across his throat again.

"Percy, then, must have decided who did the dirty deed, he knows so much."

"Probably. He never said, though."

"I should love to meet this oracle." Melrose looked at his watch. It was still not five, and he might get one up on Jury, who had sent him on this wild-goose chase.

Bertie's eyes widened behind his thick lenses. "We could go round there now. I've time before I have to go to work. Percy lives down Scroop Street on Dark Street. That's the street round the corner from the library. He'd be through his tea by now and might like a bit of a chat. Talks a lot, he does." Bertie got up from the table, leaving his second cake unfinished.

While Melrose was mumbling his agreement to this plan, Bertie was already out at the coat closet wiggling into an oversized black overcoat. He looked doubtfully back into the kitchen, at the table with its dirty cup and plate. "I guess I can do the washing-up later."

"Leave Arnold to do it," said Melrose, putting on his own coat, and watching as Bertie did his buttons up wrong.

"Can't you get the buttons straight, for heaven's sakes?" Melrose set his stick aside and unbuttoned and rebuttoned Bertie's coat. It was much too large for him. He had pulled on a black stocking cap and now all that showed was his small white face and thick glasses. "Where do you get your clothes? At a jumble sale for seals?"

"There's more to life," said Bertie, looking carefully at Melrose's velvet collar and silver-headed stick, "than fancy duds. Let's go."

Going up Grape Lane, with Arnold in the lead, Bertie said, "You mustn't mind Percy's place. He's not too neat, not like us. And he's got lots of stuffed things sitting round.

It's a bit dirtier than it should be. Funny-looking things on the walls and in bowls and all. There's lots of strange sights in Rackmoor."

Watching Arnold sloping up the street through a dust of snow, and the small, black gnome beside him, Melrose said, "Do tell?"

9.

All he needed was an owl on his shoulder.

Percy Blythe sat behind a Jacobean monstrosity of a library table, amidst the dark, dusty and Gothic confusion of stuffed birds and fish, tallow candles, driftwood, fish-netting, Nailsea balls, rank bits of clothing, old newspaper and books. Although the papers and books lent an air of intense scholarship to the proceedings, Percy Blythe seemed engaged in nothing more studious than pushing a few bits of seashell round the desk. He was small, with peaked, Satanic ears and rimless spectacles. When Bertie introduced them, he looked without interest at Melrose over the tops of these spectacles. He was dressed — or overdressed — in jacket, sweater, and scarf and wore a knitted cap similar to Bertie's. He went back to pushing the seashells about.

"I do hope we haven't interrupted your meal," said Melrose, noticing the dark rind of a sandwich and a milk-incrusted glass — both looking several days old — sitting on the edge of the table. Percy Blythe merely bent his face more firmly over his shells. "A most interesting room, Mr. Blythe. *Most* interesting."

That raising no response, Melrose looked round to see what else offered conversational possibilities. Since there was no electricity laid on, it was difficult to sort out the various stuffed, glass-globed, and otherwise encased objects for more particular comment. In their frosted covers, weak flames spurted, throwing ominous shapes along the walls.

It was the narrowest terraced house Melrose had ever seen, in Dark Street, which was more a mews than a street. It turned into Scroop Street at the one end. Its only other means of coming and going was Dagger Alley, nothing more than a crude stone walk between the Bell and a warehouse on the High.

"You are quite a collector, sir," said Melrose, feeling somewhat at a loss to explain his presence here. Bertie was no help, nor did Bertie seem at all out of place. He was examining some sort of a sea-urchin-like mess on a shelf. Arnold had immediately taken possession of an old piece of quilt tossed in a corner. There was the tiny scraping sound of the shells being rearranged on the desk. The movement sent several papers fluttering to the floor, but Percy Blythe seemed all unaware of the spillage around him — banks of papers like sand drifts about to slide away; ruined columns of books on tables, sills, and floor.

Never had Melrose seen anyone less inclined to meet the demands of even the most rudimentary social intercourse.

"I told him," said Bertie, "that you had all kinds of stuff. What's this here?" Bertie held up a kind of bonelike thing. But Bertie was apparently indifferent to Percy Blythe's silences, for he merely returned the object to the shelf and went to scrutinizing a planked fish.

Melrose shifted his silver-headed stick from one hand to the other and leaned that way for a bit. All of this verbal inactivity might have been the less disconcerting had they been invited to sit, had they been asked at least to remove their coats, but Percy Blythe seemed as indisposed to do that as he was to engage in any other of the social graces. So they still stood, fully accoutered, except for Arnold, sound asleep on a blanket. Bertie was quite at home, passing one object after another through his hands, humming. Only Melrose seemed to be cast adrift to sink or swim in Percy Blythe's monumental sea of silence. He cleared his throat and tried again:

"Mr. Blythe, I'm visiting at Old House; I'm a friend of Sir Titus Crael." This merely earned him a darkling glance before the head bent once again over the shells.

"You remember, Percy, how you was telling me how queer that Julian Crael was." Bertie was holding a bowl with water and a dark object floating in it. "What's this here? It looks alive."

Melrose seriously doubted it. But he picked up on Bertie's indirect reference to the crime. "It's really quite appalling to think that such a ghastly murder could occur in this little fishing village." No answer. Melrose plodded on: "Indeed, you were probably as shocked by this gruesome crime as were the other inhabitants of Rackmoor." No sign did Percy Blythe give of shock. "You, yourself . . ." said Melrose, switching his walking stick back to the other side and leaning that way for a while, ". . . must have been surprised to imagine such a beastly thing could occur in your own village." One crabbed finger pushed the shells about, knocking one to the floor, which he didn't bother to retrieve. "It might interest you to know, Mr. Blythe, that there was quite an awful series of crimes in my own village in Northamptonshire just about this time last year. And Chief Inspector Jury was the officer in charge there too. I expect he'll be coming along to ask you a few questions."

"D'ya think I could have that shell you promised me, Percy?"

There was a vague, fluttery movement of the arm beneath the shawl.

"Perhaps you remember something of the night of the murder?" Melrose prompted. Percy Blythe merely looked up at Melrose over his spectacles, shook his head, and returned to scrutinizing the shells. Perhaps the man, thought Melrose, was simply pathologically shy. Perhaps he felt comfortable only with stuffed or otherwise preserved objects.

"Ah, sure you do, Percy," Bertie said. "You remember you was telling me how you said you wasn't surprised. When that woman come to town you thought trouble'd follow after."

This earned Bertie a venomous glance, as if warning him off from dragging Percy Blythe into this witless conversation.

But Melrose quickly picked up on the point: "Why did you think that, Mr. Blythe?" There was, of course, no answer, and Melrose felt as if he were slowly being washed out to sea along with the shells and other flotsam and jetsam. Funny, he had always thought of himself as an engaging, if not a brilliant, conversationalist. Let Jury do it, he sighed, pulling on his gloves. He rather relished the confrontation; he hoped Jury would permit him to come along. "Well, I expect we'd best be off. I've got to meet someone."

"And I got to go to work, Percy. Be seeing you. *Hop it, Arnold!*"

Melrose jumped as a cat, frightened awake by Bertie's command, catapulted from a high shelf. Melrose had presumed it to be stuffed. He turned toward the door.

"Ask Evelyn," said Percy Blythe.

Melrose turned. But Percy Blythe was transferring shells to pockets and gave no sign at all of having delivered this cryptic message.

10.

The girl who opened the door had a face too thin for conventional beauty, but a fragile blondness, transparent, like glass. It was already dark at five o'clock and mist layered the air between the girl and Jury. An oil lamp behind her fuzzed the outline of the dress she wore, low-necked and white, full and formless. It fit her like a cloud, made her ghostly. Jury thought all she needed was a tallow in her hand to make him think he'd been dropped into some revenge tragedy.

"Miss Siddons?" Jury handed over his card. "I'm Richard Jury. C.I.D. I hope I haven't come at a bad time. I need to ask you a few questions."

"Oh." She bunched the dress in at the waist as if its very looseness were somehow embarrassing. "I'm just fitting this dress. I haven't a form and, well, I'm using myself. Not that there's much fit to it. Come on in." He did so and she shut the door behind him. "I'll just take it off, if you don't mind."

He could see there were pins in the dress, around the neck and defining the shoulders. "You're sewing it?"

"Not for myself. For one of the women in the village. I do occasionally, in the winter, when there's not much business at the café. The Bridge Walk is my place."

Jury nodded. "I know. The dress, though. It suits you." She had an unusual face, now that he could see it better. Triangular, with amber eyes. Her skin had the sheen of pearls.

Her hand came up to the neckline of the dress, apparently noticing the drift of Jury's gaze. "I'll only be a minute. Really," she said anxiously, as if more than a minute might find them all sliding out to sea. He nodded and she rushed from the room and up the stairs.

Jury looked over the sitting room, stuffed with flowered chintz chairs and bric-a-brac. Little ornaments and pictures seemed to overflow every corner — shelves, mantels, tables; they held cups and saucers, fluted pitchers, small china boxes. There was even, to his surprise, a crystal floating on a bed of black velvet. He picked it up, turned it round, peered into its depths but got no fortune back. He replaced it on its velvet bed. There were trinkets with painted greetings from Bognor Regis, Tunbridge, Southend-on-Sea — all of those once-fashionable resorts where ladies with parasols and fans promenaded, now replaced by amusement piers and fat children with sandbuckets. There were pictures too on the tables and around the walls, some of these apparently taken at those same resorts. One showed a young woman on a pier in the outmoded dress of the fifties catching at the brim of her hat. It must have been a windy day; a sea-breeze had sent her skirts flying, and she was also catching at these modestly, with the other hand. For a snapshot, it was very good, much the best of the pictures on the table, fresh, alive, and the girl quite lovely. But when he looked at it again he wondered why she had been placed so poorly in the camera's lens, mashed up against the left-hand edge of the picture. He returned that picture to its place and looked over the others, crowded on the table in square and oval frames. Most of them were of the same woman taken at different places, different times. One had been taken at Old House; he recognized the stable yard. He assumed the woman must be Lily Siddons's mother.

"That's my mother." Her voice came from behind him, confirming it. "She's dead now. She died young."

Jury looked around. "*The Duchess of Malfi?*"

"What?"

"I thought you were quoting from the play."

She tilted her head a bit and her amber eyes caught the light from the fire. "I don't know it."

"It was spoken by her brother. The duchess's, I mean. 'Cover her face; she died young.' " Jury replaced the picture carefully as if he might shatter the life of the woman in it again. "The brother, Ferdinand, was mad." He felt oppressed; anxiety knotted his stomach; he did not know why.

"Like Julian Crael, you mean?" She wrapped her arms round herself, covering her breasts in that unconscious movement women used to ward off violation.

"Julian Crael?"

"He was always odd." Lily sat down on a small, chintz-covered sofa. "Would you like some coffee?"

Jury shook his head. "Odd in what way?"

She shrugged her shoulders, as if dismissing Julian Crael. And then she said, "Did he kill her?"

The blandness of her tone, as much as the question, surprised Jury. "Why do you say that?"

"Because he's capable of it, I suppose."

Jury smiled slightly. "We're *all* capable of it. Given the right circumstances."

She shook her head. "I don't believe that." With her cat's eyes, she regarded Jury coolly. "Could you? Murder somebody?"

"Yes. I expect so. But you were speaking of Julian."

She pushed her fair hair, which was held back from her face by two tortoiseshell combs, away from her shoulders. "I've never liked him. I suppose you know I lived in that house for a long time, all the while I was growing up. Until my mother . . . died." Her eyes trailed from his face over to the little pie-crust table on which were grouped the pictures.

"Colonel Crael told me. He's fond of you."

"He's the only one of them who's really decent. A gentleman."

"Not Julian?"

"Julian." A slight gesture of her hand dismissed that possibility. "Definitely not Julian."

Jury wondered if there were some thwarted romance in the background. Somehow, he doubted it. "You went to a dinner party at Old House the night before the murder."

"Yes. The Colonel invited me up to dinner. I thought at first —" She paused. "I thought at first she —" Lily Siddons appeared distracted, or meditative, running her hand across her brow, as if chasing some vagrant shadow of a thought.

"What?"

"Didn't Colonel Crael tell you she looked exactly like his ward? The girl who left fifteen years ago. Didn't he tell you about Dillys?"

"You tell me."

Lily looked down at the hands locked in her lap and said, as if she were reading a history from a book: "They took her in after her parents died. When she was around eight or nine. I was only a baby then. She was five years older, but we more or less grew up together. She liked to lord it over me. I was only Cook's girl, see. In games I was always the handmaiden and she the duchess. Lady Margaret spoiled her to death. Of course, we went to different schools. Dillys and Julian both went to the public school and I had to go to comprehensive. That was when we were older. She always kept telling me no matter how much I put myself about, I'd never be . . . as if I *thought* . . ."

"And how did you feel when you first saw Gemma Temple, then?"

"I was afraid she'd come back." She looked him straight in the eye. "If you want someone with motive, yes, I had one. After my father left us — Mummy and me — we had to live there. I suppose it was very decent of the Craels having me in, giving me a roof. But Dillys. She was like a fallen tree across my path. I couldn't move her; I couldn't get round her." Lily stopped and looked into the fire.

"When the Colonel told you she was a distant cousin, did you believe it?"

She looked surprised. "Why shouldn't I have done? If it was Dillys, why would they have lied?"

"But didn't you think it extremely odd that Dillys March went off the way she did, leaving all that money she was to inherit?"

"Are you telling me it *was* Dillys?"

"No. I'm just asking. Inspector Harkins says you told him you think that the person who killed Gemma Temple really meant to kill you. That's very strange, Miss Siddons. Would you mind explaining it?"

"Someone *has* been trying to kill me." She leaned back with an exhausted sigh and turned her face to the fire. The flames gilded her pale skin, lit up her amber eyes, made bands of gold down her silk-stockinged legs. The legs, Jury noticed, were very good. But he was not so much aroused sexually as he was mystified by her, here in this habitat. She was like a rare species of butterfly drifted out of its territory. A Clouded Yellow in a cold climate.

"The first time was when I was riding. It was back in October and I'd taken out Red Run — that's the horse the Colonel lets me ride. I jumped a wall near Tan Howe and just barely missed a big hay rake which had been left on the other side. A few more inches and I'd have gone down on the tines. It was up-ended."

"Could anyone have known where your ride would take you, though? Even assuming the hay rake had been left there purposely?"

"That's just the point. I'd been practicing jumping Red Run at just that place because during the hunt he'd refused that wall several times and I was trying to get him over the fear. Of course, *then* I thought it was all accidental. But I told the Colonel and he said he'd make sure the farmer never left it there again. He was very upset."

"When was the next time?"

"Three or four weeks later. In November. It was the brakes on my car. They failed. I keep it in the lot at the top of the hill. You know, the first one." Jury nodded. "I don't use it at all in the village, except this one day I had to load up at the café. Some cakes and pies I was taking to a church fete in Pitlochary. When I got in the car I remembered I needed some things in Whitby, so instead of driving down the hill then, I drove the other way. Thank God. You've seen that hill. I'd have ended through the wall of the Bell. You see, it wasn't really until this . . . thing happened to Gemma Temple that I figured it out. Those other times weren't accidents. People knew I was taking the car down that day."

"Who knew?"

Impatiently, she said: "Lots. Kitty Meechem and I talked about it in the Fox. Adrian was there. The Craels knew; I'd mentioned it in front of them." Her face was tallow-white in the gloom. The only light was from the fire.

"So you think it was the costume?" She nodded. "Why was Gemma Temple wearing your costume?"

"At dinner the night before the Colonel said that Gemma hadn't a costume and could I lend her something? Then Maud suggested we — Maud and I — go as Sebastian and Viola out of *Twelfth Night*. Well, it seemed appropriate. So I let her wear mine."

"Why didn't *she* go along as Viola with Mrs. Brixenham?"

Lily shrugged. "With her being a stranger, she didn't really know Maud."

"Why didn't she go when you did? Kitty Meechem says she didn't leave the Fox until ten after ten."

Lily laughed. "That's obvious. I'm sure she wanted to make an entrance, all by herself." Her tone was bitter. "Actress! Jumped-up little shop girl's more like it."

"Then all of these people at dinner the evening before knew you wouldn't be wearing the black and white costume."

Lily shook her head. "No. Only Maud and the Colonel. The others weren't in the room at the moment we discussed it. Anyway, at the party I got a little sick. I think it must have been the fish paste sandwiches; they've never agreed with me. Or maybe it was the punch. It's deadly the way they make it at Old House. I didn't see but a few people there. The only people I can be *sure* weren't trying to kill me are the Colonel and Maud. They knew I'd switched costumes."

Which might conceivably have eliminated them if it were really Lily Siddons who was the intended victim.

"If I hadn't given her my costume, she might still be . . . I feel guilty."

Jury took out his notebook. "You told Inspector Harkins you got back to the cottage here around ten fifteen."

"That's right. Maud stayed with me for a bit to make sure I hadn't got a bad case of food poisoning. Then she left. I got into my robe and read for a while, until about eleven."

"Adrian Rees saw Gemma Temple walking along Grape Lane a little after. About eleven fifteen, just before the Fox closed. Near the Angel steps."

Lily was staring into the fire and nodded slightly. "I know."

"Had she been here?"

Her head whipped round at that. "Here? Why would she have been *here*?"

Jury didn't answer. He looked at her, his face impassive. "She'd been someplace between the time she left the Fox — Kitty Meechem says ten past ten — and when Rees saw her. She was not on her way to the party, apparently."

"Why do you say that?"

"Because she went up the Angel steps."

"Well, people do use those steps."

"Not in winter, do they? Not with the sign warning them off. She must have met someone there." Jury waited, but Lily said nothing. "And Kitty Meechem stopped here to see you just after the pub closed. That'd be around eleven thirty or even earlier. About eleven twenty-five, she said."

Lily rolled her head back and forth on the chintz cover of the couch, wearily. "I don't know. I suppose so. I wasn't looking at the time."

"It's important. Unless you could move quicker than lightning, you could hardly have got to the Angel steps and back in ten minutes."

She looked at him, her eyes darkening to the color of cornelian. "You don't believe me, do you? That someone's trying to kill *me*?"

"It's not that. I certainly think *you* believe it. But what would be the motive? Money? Revenge? Jealousy?"

"I've no money. And as far as I know, I certainly haven't done anything to anyone. Jealousy — of what?"

"Men. We could start there."

"You mean a jealous lover, something like that?" She laughed, but not happily. "In Rackmoor that's not likely."

"Did you ever feel the Colonel thought you and Julian might . . . ?" He stopped when the color flared up in her cheeks.

"Julian? Me and *Julian?* That's daft! The Craels don't marry the daughters of *servants.*"

"What happened to your father, Lily?"

"He went off when I was very little. I hardly remember him at all." She reached over to the small table, plucked the crystal from the velvet. "I like to look in this. Percy Blythe gave it to me. In the summer I take it to the café, pretend I can tell fortunes, can see things. Well, the tourists love it. Give me your hand." Jury extended his right hand, which she took and held. "You've a wide palm; you're very tolerant. A long thumb — that's strength of purpose. Straight fingers. Sympathetic. It's a very good hand." Then she dropped it as if it weren't good at all, and her eyes strayed to the little pie-crust table studded with all the pictures. Her hand went to the one of the woman on the pier.

"You were very fond of your mother, weren't you?"

"Yes."

"I don't like bringing this up; it must be painful . . ." He dealt in pain, he felt; dealt it out in little slices like cards off a deck. "That day she drowned." Lily did not look up. "Why would your mother have taken such a dangerous path when the tide was about to come in?" Lily shook her head. Clearly, she was near tears.

"Was it an accident?"

Lily's head was bent over the picture and she was crying.

Jury slid to the edge of his chair, took the picture from her hands, and replaced it with his handkerchief. "I'm sorry, Lily. I'll be going now."

Jury walked out of the cottage and around the little cove to the Old Fox Deceiv'd. The blue and green cobles bobbed in the dark water like strange flowers.

He had the picture in his pocket.

11.

"Give me a Rackmoor Fog," said Melrose Plant.

Kitty turned to Jury: "What about you, sir? Care to try one?"

"From what I've heard, it'd be worth my job. Just whisky, please, Kitty." Wiggins was already eating a plate of fish, chips, and peas.

She moved off and Jury turned to Melrose. "Well, Mr. Plant, and how did your inquiries go on?"

Melrose glared at him. "Arnold was most forthcoming. Far more, I must say, than Percy Blythe."

"Percy Blythe? That name is not familiar. Who's he?" Jury stole a chip from Wiggins's plate.

"You must find out for yourself, Inspector; you must come along and question him."

"I could do, of course, if he knows something. Was he on Harkins's list, Wiggins?"

Around a mouthful of cod and peas, Wiggins said, "Yes, sir."

"I'm surprised he's on *anyone's* list."

Kitty brought their drinks. The Rackmoor Fog was in a large rummer — a cloudy-looking brew from the top of which misty tendrils escaped.

Wiggins stabbed his fork toward it. "What's that stuff coming out the top?"

"Fog." Melrose brought the concoction to his lips, drank, made a face. "And barnacles and a shark's fin."

"Doesn't look very healthy to me," Wiggins said, eyeing it and then returning to his safer tea. Jury watched wonderingly as his sergeant spooned sugar into it with no regard at all for the tooth fairy.

"Do you know what runic message passed his parched and warty lips just as we were leaving?"

"Percy Blythe's, you mean?"

"Yes. 'Ask Evelyn.' "

"Who's she?" Plant shook his head. "Wiggins? Was there an Evelyn Somebody on that list?" Wiggins shook his head also. "Where's this Blythe chap live?"

"In Dark Street."

Wiggins speared a piece of fish as if it were still running underwater. "Now you mention it, I do recall a name like that from Harkins's notes, but I don't think this Blythe had anything important to say."

"No kidding," Melrose said, his voice heavy with sarcasm.

"We'll go round there after our meal."

"Goody," said Melrose.

"I mean Sergeant Wiggins and I'll go round."

"Could you do without me, sir? I've got all these notes I want to get together from questioning people up at Old House. Must be reams of them."

"That's right. Let Sergeant Wiggins do up his notes. Remember, I've been to Percy Blythe's. Why, I very nearly discovered him." Melrose tried on his winning smile, didn't think that was working, and changed it to a sad look.

"Oh, very well, Mr. Plant. Mind you don't interrupt my questioning, though."

"I wouldn't *dream* of it, Chief Inspector. And really it's a meeting I'd hate to miss." Melrose looked owlish.

"Thought you'd left the force, Mr. Plant. Very well, then. But let's have something to eat; I'm famished. Kitty does a very good steak and kidney pie, I hear."

"Has she any wine, do you think? Château de Meechem, 1982. Aged in the cask." Melrose looked round the saloon bar of the Fox Deceiv'd and said, "I wonder if Surtees decorated this place. Look at all those hunting prints." When Melrose and Jury surveyed the room, several pairs of eyes stared back. A great deal of celebrity had attached itself to Jury. When he had walked in heads swiveled as if on oiled castors, eyes squared off, talk ceased. Quickly, they looked away, the regulars feigning disinterest in their table. "I expect the entire field to rush through, giving chase, yelling 'Wind 'em, wind 'em,' or some such rot. I feel like I'm back in the middle of *Tom Jones*."

Over in the corner, near the kitchen door, Kitty seemed to be having an argument with Bertie Makepiece who was white-aproned and carrying a tray under his arm. "Who's the lad?" Jury asked.

"Bertie Makepiece." Melrose looked at the door between the saloon bar and the rear dining room. "And that's Arnold, in case you've not met." Arnold was lying across the sill of the door.

Kitty made her way to their table. "Excuse me, Mr. Jury." She pushed locks of light brown hair back from her high forehead and looked very red-faced. "Bertie is raising a fuss. I do give the lad work here, only when there's people for dinner. I *know* he's but twelve, and he shouldn't be working in a public house but I don't let him serve at the bar nor carry spiritous liquors — well, perhaps just the odd bottle of wine. The thing is, you see, his mum's left and the child does need the money. He wants to wait on your table awful bad and you being the police and all —"

Jury interrupted. "The child labor laws are hereby rescinded." He smiled.

Melrose watched Kitty Meechem grip the back of the empty chair, probably to keep from melting at Jury's feet when he smiled at her.

✷   ✷   ✷

"Veal and kidney pie, please," said Jury, giving his order to Bertie. They were the only occupants of the small dining room where a fire burned brightly and copper and pewter gleamed on the walls.

Melrose opted for the mixed grill. "And we'll have a bottle of your best wine, Copperfield. You wouldn't have a wine list, would you? I notice you're not wearing your key tonight."

"No list, sir. But there's lots of bottles down in the cellar that looks dusty enough they ought to be used up. Not," Bertie assured Melrose suavely, "that nothing's wrong with them. But another year or two won't do them no good."

"Well, if you can find a bottle of Côte de Nuit, 'sixty-four, bring it along. Mind you don't shake it; just dust it off a bit."

"I'll hoover it for you." Bertie dashed off, tray held high.

"That's the lad whose mother's gone missing. Where is she, then?"

"No idea. Belfast, he says." Melrose snapped a snowy-white, tablecloth-sized napkin across his lap. "The linen's clean, at least. More hunting prints, I see. Did you know Sir Titus owns half this place? Why do you think it's called The Old Fox Deceiv'd? He's titular head of the whole village, I hear. Someone told me he wanted to rename it 'Foxmoor.' But they wouldn't let him. Obsessed with hunting, that old gentleman is."

"How did you leave Lady Ardry, Mr. Plant?"

"With the greatest difficulty, I assure you. She was on my coattails till the last."

Jury smiled. "I've missed her."

"No one else ever has. She's in York. I keep getting daily bulletins about what she and this Teddy-creature are doing. If she knew *you* were here, she'd come rolling across the North York moors like a big snowball."

Bertie brought the first course. "Here's your starters, sir."

He plopped the two small plates on the table. "No smoked salmon, sorry," he said to Melrose, and continued *sotto voce*, as if they'd raided a secret hoard, "but Kitty found this nice piece of fresh fish from Whitby and sauced it up for you." He whisked off, stopping to admonish Arnold, who was lying quietly in the doorway watching Melrose.

Melrose poked suspiciously under the sauce. "Plaice, I'll bet. Wonder how this sauce will mix with the Rackmoor Fog? I wish Kitty Meechem would give me the recipe. I could serve up a few to Agatha and leave her behind the Minster. Have you noticed how that dog keeps staring at me? I suppose you won't tell me, but who have you lined up as chief suspect?"

"No one."

Melrose sighed. "I supposed you wouldn't tell me."

Jury shook his head and began on the fish. "It's the truth. No one."

"Julian Crael would appear to have the strongest motive."

"That's what Inspector Harkins thinks."

"How disturbing. I'd hate to think what he does."

"Why's that? He's an astute chap."

"A dandy and a martinet, far as I'm concerned. And, frankly, he seems to be wondering just why I — a stranger — am staying with the Craels. The Wandering Moors Murderer, that's what he's got me down for. Ah, here's the wine." Melrose rubbed his hands together.

Bertie was back, tray under one arm, bottle of wine grasped in the other hand. "Have a look, sir. I'm sure you'll approve." He thrust the label up to Melrose's face for inspection. "It's not that whatever-it-was you asked for, but it's got a nice color to it. Red."

"Red. Yes. But it's a nineteen sixty-six. No nineteen sixty-four, I take it?"

Bertie pursed his mouth. "Fresher," he said with authority. "I'll just yank out this here cork." With the bottle between his legs, Bertie applied the corkscrew. When he had disengaged the cork, he dropped it on the table where it rolled around. "Cork, sir."

"It does look like one, yes."

"Well, ain't you supposed to smell it, sir?"

"Ah, yes. Stupid of me." Melrose ran the cork under his nose. "Rich bouquet."

Bertie held the bottle to his chest, raptly attentive. "Thought you'd like it sir. Have a taste." Carefully throttling the bottle neck, he poured out a portion into Melrose's glass. "Just roll that round on your tongue."

Melrose did as instructed. "Excellent. A bit young, but excellent nonetheless." He extracted a note from his wallet, stuffed it in Bertie's pocket. "Clearly, you come from a long line of sommeliers."

Bertie beamed. "Leave it breathe, that's the ticket." He whisked off, tray afloat on his upstretched hand.

"The wine ritual had a certain *élan*, wouldn't you say?"

"I thought it was swell," said Jury. "But tell me why you think Crael's the guilty party. You've had more opportunity to observe him than I."

"I didn't *say* I thought it was Crael. I merely said he's got the strongest motive. It could cut rather deeply into his inheritance if this Dillys March should reappear. They seemed to have regarded her almost as a daughter. The Colonel and Lady Margaret, that is."

"Would still do — were she to turn up. If the woman who came to Rackmoor were not Dillys March, but Gemma Temple, then someone must have given the Temple woman a great deal of information. So the last person to do that would be Julian Crael."

Melrose was thoughtful. "I see what you mean. But why are you so eager to defend Julian Crael?"

"I don't defend him. I'm merely stating an hypothesis. You don't like him, obviously."

"I find him cold, hardhearted, and secretive."

"Secretive?"

"Antisocial." Melrose poked a chop around his plate and then took a bite. "Unlike Sir Titus. He'd be having the whole county to tea if he could. Well, I don't mean to be unkind . . . it occurs to me that to say something unkind about the Colonel makes one feel guilty. Anyway, Julian lives a hermitlike existence. Doesn't go in for the hunting, hates parties. Didn't even go to the Twelfth Night party. And doesn't seem to get along with the old man at all. Flaming rows they've had about this Gemma Temple or Dillys March or whoever she is. Was. Well, not flaming, exactly. Julian doesn't flame, does he? He just ices over. Colonel Crael was all for having her up to Old House, bag and baggage. Julian swears she's an impostor. But how could she hope to pass herself off as the March girl?"

"It might not be so difficult as you'd think. Not with inside help and a man as easy to convince as the Colonel. Julian would be the only problem, really."

They ate in companionable silence for a while. Then Melrose said, "Old House reminds me of Poe's Usher. Unsuspecting I drive up in my carriage at midnight —" Melrose held up his two hands as if framing a picture. "The manor house against the black sky, illuminated only by the pale disc of a full moon. Knarled oaks reflected in the dark tarn. The fissure running down the wall. And Roderick — that'd be Julian — glooming away at the pianoforte, lit by candelabra . . ."

"That the way it happened?"

"Not exactly."

"The house seems pretty substantial to me."

"Well, Julian doesn't. He's more like the ghost of himself. Like fog. I get the feeling I could run my hand through him."

"I found him to be rather melancholy, but not especially wraithlike."

"Have you no imagination?"

"Not really. I'm just a plodding policeman. But your analogy is interesting: Roderick Usher." Jury remembered Lily Siddons's remark. "Is it that you find Julian a trifle mad?"

"A 'trifle' mad? What a curious way of putting it. Losing one's mind is surely like losing one's virginity. Lose a little, lose a lot."

"However you want to say it, then. Unbalanced, psychotic — ?"

"Capable of murder, do you mean?"

Jury's gesture was dismissive. "It doesn't take madness to commit murder. Murder's a rather mundane act. I'm only trying to understand these people."

"There's something about the whole family that throws me off balance. The Craels, past and present." Melrose stuck his fork in a grilled tomato. "That house echoes with the past. They live in the past."

Jury swirled the dregs of his wine. "Don't we all?" He looked away. "Do they talk about it so much, then?"

"No. They *talk* about the present. But they're thinking about the past. It's as if one eye were permanently fixed on the portraits of the dead. Especially that one of Lady Margaret. *There's* a woman I'd liked to have known."

Jury smiled. "Do you expect — as in the case of the Lady Madeleine — to hear scrabblings on the coffin lid?"

"Really, you are a ghoul. No, I don't expect that. But one does feel her presence."

"And does one feel the presence of Dillys March also?"

"Not so much. Perhaps she was too young to leave that much of a permanent stamp upon things. But as part of the pervasive gloom — yes, I guess so. And Julian lives like a monk, might as well be in a monastery for all he goes about. He walks and he thinks."

"What does he think about?"

"Julian does not open his heart to me, Inspector. If he has one."

The image of Julian Crael leaning against the mantel came back to Jury. "Oh, he has one, I think."

"It certainly has not been melted by any of the county ladies."

Bertie was back with the sweet, a plum tart. Jury said to him as he cleared their plates away, "Tell me, Bertie. How long's your mother been gone?"

"Upwards of three months, sir."

"A long time to be alone."

Jury looked at him, but it was impossible to read the expression in his eyes, masked as they were by the thick lenses of his glasses. And the rest of his small, rather pinched face was quite blank. Perhaps it was a lark, to be left on one's own at twelve and not have one's mum to be nattering at one all the time. A lark, that is, if you knew she was coming back.

"It's odd your mother didn't arrange for anyone to take care of you."

"Oh, but she did, sir," was Bertie's quick reply. "Cod — I mean, Miss Cavendish. And Miss Frother-Guy. Religious they are about it. Always around."

Jury hid a smile. It was clear what Bertie thought of the policing. "She went to Ireland, did she?"

"*Northern* Ireland," said Bertie, pointedly. "It's her old gran. I think she kind of thought of her gran as her own mum. When her gran got sick she had to go."

"Yes. But to leave you alone —"

"I ain't alone. There's Arnold. And, like I said, Miss Cavendish —"

"Where in Northern Ireland does her gran live?"

"Belfast," was the crisp reply. Then a darting glance as he added: "The Bogside." Off he went.

"Bogside," said Jury, smiling at his plum tart.

"He gets credits for resourcefulness, certainly. People do have a way of disappearing around here. It's like the Bermuda Triangle."

"Mary Siddons, for instance. Lily Siddons's mother, who was supposed to have drowned by accident."

"Yes, I heard about that. The Colonel is worried about Lily's having turned inward. Her mother drowned not long after Lady Margaret and Rolfe Crael were killed in that motor accident. It mustn't have been a very happy time, all round, for the Craels."

"Rackmoor does not seem a very happy place, take it all together."

Melrose insisted on paying for the meal and Jury excused himself to have a few words with Kitty. Putting on his coat, Melrose said to Bertie, "The excellence of the food was only exceeded by the superior service. I've not had better at Simpson's." Bertie was flailing the table with his napkin, decrumbing it. Arnold, seeing a flutter of activity sat up, ears pricked.

Melrose stuffed a five-pound note in Bertie's pocket, saying, "There, Copperfield. That'll help you out of Salem House."

12.

Percy Blythe was still sitting at the library table when Melrose peered in through the window. And as far as Melrose could tell, he was also still sorting through the seashells.

"Well, Inspector, shall we go in. I just hope you can get a word in edgewise."

Jury only smiled.

Nor did Jury wait for introductions. Once inside, he simply strode across the room, darker, surely by three shades since last Melrose had seen it, stuck out his hand and said, "Hullo, Percy. My name's Jury. I'm with Scotland Yard."

Melrose smirked as Jury's hand hung, unshaken, stuck in

midair. It did not appear to disconcert the inspector, however, who merely withdrew it, shoved a stack of books from a stool, dragged it over to the library table and sat down, hitching his feet in the rungs. Melrose was himself dusting off a window ledge so he would have a place to sit. Grudgingly, he admired Jury's gall. But what was that he had just taken out of his pocket and tossed on Percy's table?

"Have some, Percy."

Curious, Melrose crept over to the shelves and pretended to be examining the black, dead-looking blob in the bowl of water. He looked over at the table as Percy Blythe picked up what Jury had thrown down, and now was strangling it with his teeth, or his gums, whichever he had. Tobacco? Melrose looked at Jury. Chief Inspector Jury chewing tobacco? But there he was, chomping away. They were both of them chomping away. Now Percy Blythe was toeing a spittoon closer to Jury. The dead blob moved. Melrose looked down and quickly replaced the bowl.

"Hear you're a thatcher, Percy," said Jury. "A lost art that is. You're from Swaledale, aren't you?"

Melrose watched Percy Blythe gum the tobacco, his face working like an accordion, collapsing and stretching, collapsing and stretching.

"Swardill, aye. Ah be thatcher and hedger forty year."

"Don't see much of it any more."

"Pssh! Woant trouble theirsen t'do it proper. They chiggles t'branches, nor cuts away t'leirs. No on does it t'right way na more. They cracks t' bark and t'heads die; they drive t'gibs too close." He shook his head sadly. "Hedger and thatcher and besom-maker, ah was t'best in Swardill, ah was. There be me flayin' spade on t'wall." He hooked his thumb over his shoulder towards some tools, hung on the wall like pictures, all neatly arranged. "Cud bray t'hazel sticks faster'n spit, and cut spelks, too. Cud tie threaves o' ling, verra near a fieldful in a day."

Melrose stared across the sea urchin at Jury, who was

chomping merrily away, apparently transported by all of this, his chin in his hands, elbows on desk.

"Ah made t'black thack roofs they'n lasten fifty year. Ah was besom-maker, too, ah was. Hand me mah besom needle." This was directed at Melrose, as if commanding him to be of some use rather than standing about like a stick.

"Besom needle?"

"On t'wall." Percy Blythe jabbed his finger impatiently toward the tools. Melrose moved over to the spot and the odd tools hanging there. He had never seen any like them. They were carefully labeled. *Easing knife. Twister.* And what in hell was a "whittling hook"? He found the besom needle and separated it from its nail. It was a long rodlike thing with a looped handle, something a giant might stitch with.

Percy Blythe neglected to thank him for his trouble when he handed it over. "Yes, one of t'best, if ah do say it, ah was. An me Dad afore me, best mower ever was. Oncet he mew tree acre in a day. 'E cud mow and 'e cud wap fast as he walked. An' 'e cud walk cross t'field wid sixpence on t'blade. Teached me t'stob, 'e did. Ah stob an' ah stob an' ah stob all t'day long when ah was t'lad. Got to walk up to t'corn, ya knoow. 'E use t'say, Go by t'sway. O, 'twas a grand sight 'twas, t'see t'field a corn stooked. 'Twas owd Bob Fishpool, gallock-'anded, 'e were, near as good as me Dad. Mew, stooked and nagged it afore 'e went t'bed. They'll coom nae mair, t'ones like that."

Melrose felt the darkling glance flung his way as if to say it were his breed which had risen to trample other and better men than he would ever be.

"A bit a gale beer for yer, lad?" said Percy Blythe to Jury. "Or mebbe a wee bit a' botchet?" He creaked up, not waiting for Jury's answer, and took a jug down from the shelf. "D'ya niver get 'lowance time in the po-lice?" He giggled as if he thought that were rich. Jury laughed and drank what he was poured.

Melrose wondered what it was; since he hadn't been included in the festivities, he guessed he would never know.

"Delicious," said Jury, wiping his hand across his mouth. "Never had any."

"No one makes it na more. Ya floats t'toast and yeast on t'top."

Melrose was just as glad he'd been left out.

Percy Blythe hooked his thumb over his shoulder and said, "Guesst ya coom aboot thet gurhl. T'dead one."

"That's right, Percy. Do you know anything that might help?"

"Mebbe do, mebbe don't." Silence.

"Bertie Makepiece seems to think you knew this woman years ago."

"Ah'd nowt say ah didn't. Seen 'er in the Ould Fox an' thowt 'twas a ghost. Fifteen year it be since her up and left."

"You're talking about Dillys March?"

"Aye. A bad 'un, she be."

"Bad? In what way?"

But Percy Blythe merely shut his eyes against the sins of youth and went back to drinking.

"You told Mr. Plant here to see someone named Evelyn."

Percy Blythe swiveled his head in Melrose's direction and gave him a look like a fist in the face. "Well, you did, you know," said Melrose across a fossilized starfish. "Not two hours ago. You said to ask her about this March girl."

Percy Blythe spat. "Not *her*, ya crazy fool! *Him*. Tom Evelyn." He turned back to Jury as if he were the only one with any sense. " 'E be huntsman. T'Colonel's pack, the Pitlochary. Tom lives up t'kennels, Pitlochary-way."

"He knew Dillys March."

But Percy Blythe wouldn't expound on the subject. He just drank his beer.

"Did you know Lily Siddons's mother, Mary?"

"'Er as was Cook up t'Ould House. Ah knew 'er. Drownded. Sad, 'twas." He shook his head.

"And Lily. You know her, too."

"Ah do. She come 'ere and we look at t'crystal. Ah taught 'er all she knoows. Summer folk like their fort'oons told. But Lily —" He tapped his head. "Ah think sees things."

"What things?"

Inscrutably, he shook his head.

Melrose, under close surveillance by the rough-looking cat, which had only one eye, was inspecting Percy Blythe's assortment of tools. He decided the cat had a face like the flaying spade.

"Percy," Jury said, "do you think maybe Lily might know something about someone in Rackmoor, something that might be dangerous?"

"Ah don't know, man. Cud be." A long silence fell as Percy Blythe set to fingering his seashells again. Melrose was vastly relieved to see Jury rise.

"I guess we've taken up enough of your time. We'll be off. Thanks for all your help, Percy."

"Ya coom back, lad, fer another bit a'gale beer."

Melrose noticed he had not been included in that invitation.

Outside, Jury blew on his hands. "Garrulous chap, isn't he?"

Melrose regarded Jury out of the corner of his eye. "Black twist, hedging, flaying spades. You hadn't even *heard* of the man until I told you about him. How in hell did you know all that?"

"Simple. I asked Kitty before we left the Fox." Jury looked at his watch "Well, I guess I'll pick up Wiggins. There's one more person I have to see: Maud Brixenham."

"I've met her. Puts me in mind of an antelope."

"Care to come along?"

"No. I think I'll write up my notes."

Wiggins was none too happy about being dragged from the warmth of his room in the Fox to go walking round in the fog.

As they left the pub, he was telling Jury that although several of the servants had vague recollections of Dillys March, they also had cast-iron alibis for the night of the murder. "Except for Olive Manning, that is. She went upstairs about the same time Julian Crael did, somewhere around ten o'clock, she says. And as her room's in the other wing, well, she could easily have slipped out and no one been the wiser. And she's very bitter about Dillys March, about all the trouble she caused her son, Leo."

"Yes, I know. I'll have to talk to Mrs. Manning." They were on the other side of the cove and Jury said, "Where's Lead Street?"

Wiggins pointed up a narrow little crescent of a street, scarcely wide enough to admit two walking abreast. "Just there, sir. Converted fishermen's cottages."

"How goddamned chic," Jury said.

13.

Maud Brixenham walked through life scattering veils and pins.

Or so it seemed to Jury as he watched the gray tulle scarf drift like a wave to the floor as her angular body moved between couch and credenza. He wondered if it had been draped there to conceal the signs of aging — the veins in the neck, the tiny lines.

"Sherry?" she asked, over her shoulder.

Jury and Wiggins, both seated on the couch, declined.

"I'll just have one if you don't mind." Her voice floated

back to them like her scarf. She was pouring from a bottle which Jury could not see. He observed the handkerchief which had dropped from pocket or sleeve as she bent to replace the bottle, and the porcupinelike bristle of hairpins sticking out from the brown bun wound loosely at the base of her neck. The hairpins seemed to hold little in place, for small licks of hair stuck out from around the bun like chicken feathers.

Maud Brixenham returned to sit opposite them, her hand held beneath her sherry glass like a small plate. She sighed. "I suppose you've come about that odd young woman."

Jury smiled slightly. Not "unhappy" nor "poor" young woman. Maud Brixenham didn't waste time feigning sympathy. She drank some of the sherry and set the fluted glass on the table. Jury noticed it was very pale for sherry. Was it gin? "Odd in what way, Miss Brixenham?"

"Actually, I was being polite. 'Conniving' is what I meant."

" 'Conniving'?"

"Why, yes. That whole Dillys March act."

" 'Act'?"

She just looked at him. "Do you always play Little Sir Echo, Inspector? You're worse than my psychiatrist, and he's a treat. Very well, I'll pretend you know nothing about it and elucidate. This Temple woman turns up at Old House, announces herself as Titus's long-lost ward, and more or less plumps herself down in the midst of the gilt and crystal expecting to be drawn to the family bosom." She waved a deprecating hand and picked up her glass.

"You didn't believe the story?"

"Not for a moment. Do you?" She took a cigarette from the japanned box and plugged it into a foot-long onyx holder. Her fingers were much-beringed.

"But Sir Titus did."

"Although he is my dearest friend, I must admit to his

being rather gullible. The thing is he quite doted on the girl when she was a child and you know he's horribly disappointed he's got no grandchildren. Julian will never give him any, it seems."

"You're fond of Sir Titus?"

His answer came in the two bright spots which flared up in her large, squarish face. Maud Brixenham was no beauty, but she had quality. The Colonel would have appreciated it; it was the sort of horse-breeding which runs to winners.

"You went to this Twelfth Night party, did you?"

"Yes. Nearly everyone in Rackmoor goes. It's an annual event. A lavish costume party — but, of course, you know that. She was wearing that costume when she was killed. It was striking, the black and white. Lily thought it up. Awfully original, and very strange, rather like a Picasso drawing, you know, where one gets that distorted half-and-half effect. . . . Well, I went as Sebastian. I thought that would be appropriate. And Lily went as Viola. I must say she made a handsomer twin than I, but then she's quite a handsome young woman. Les — that's my nephew — went as himself. He's always in costume. Cowboy hat, boots, fringed jacket or jean suit. T-shirts with awful pictures on them like tongues sticking out or inscrutable messages like *Frizday*. I simply refuse to ask him what it means. Do you know what it means?"

"Frisbee," said Wiggins. They both looked at him. "You know, that plastic plate-thing they toss about."

Wiggins could be a mine of incidental information, Jury had found.

"How very clever of you, Sergeant." She looked ceilingward. "He's up there now. I can't think why the music isn't playing."

"You were telling us about the party, Miss Brixenham."

"Oh, yes, sorry. Well, there must have been forty or fifty people there. Enormous buffet. It started sometime after nine, I believe. Most of the guests were in the Bracewood Room — Titus names the rooms after his horses, isn't that quaint? — but there were people all over the house, really. There were even the musicians he got in to play up on the landing. It looks a bit like a minstrel gallery, you know. And they certainly resembled minstrels. Strolled about some of the time. In costume, too. And he had it catered by . . . oh, I don't know who. Waiters running about all over. And *such* costumes the villagers got up to. There was Miss Cavendish from the library looking completely out of character as Madame DuBarry. Can you imagine? Then the Steeds, a young couple that live in Scroop Street, as Henry the Eighth and one of the wives, I can't remember which. Tedious combination. And the Honeybuns —"

"What time did you arrive?"

"About nine-thirty. I'm not absolutely sure. Les might remember. No, he wouldn't. He can't remember anything. Lily might. We stopped and picked her up."

"And what time did you leave?"

"Quite soon after. Not much after ten, I'd say. Lily didn't feel at all well; she'd eaten something that didn't agree with her. I came back with her and stayed for a bit."

"Did you see Gemma Temple that night?"

"Why, no. As I told Inspector Hawkins —"

"Harkins."

"Yes. Gemma Temple never arrived." She looked from Jury to Wiggins as if she'd just thought of something. "It occurs to me that it would have been a good night to do someone in. Nearly everyone in the village would be up at Old House. Except perhaps the regulars at the Fox and the Bell. Hard to drag them out."

"Which way did you and Miss Siddons — and Les, is it? — return to her cottage?"

"Lily and I. Les went off through the woods, I think. At any rate, Lily and I came by way of the seawall. It's a bit longer, but that other path, the one Les took, is so dark and creepy. . . ." She shuddered slightly and reached for her drink.

"So you weren't near the Angel steps?"

"No."

"And did you pass anyone on your way here?"

"No."

There was a brief silence while they regarded one another coolly and Maud drank off what was left of the water-clear sherry.

"You did talk with Miss Temple in the Fox Deceiv'd?"

"Yes, I did. I spend a good deal of time at the Fox, actually. Many a blighted hour when I can't seem to put words on paper, when the writing's not going well. Also I like to soak up the local atmosphere. I wish I were a mystery writer, let me tell you. I could jolly well do something with this whole affair."

Wiggins looked up from his notebook, startled into speech. "You're a writer, miss?" His glance round the room then was the one he might have cast round Merlin's cave. "What sorts of things do you write, then?"

"Oh, the usual tripe: flesh-pots of Europe, white slavery, bosom-rippers — all short on character, long on four-letter words. Rosalind van Renseleer. That's my pen-name."

"I've seen your books — haven't you, sir?"

Jury hadn't, but he smiled and nodded. "What did you and Miss Temple talk about in the Fox?"

"Nothing significant. She certainly didn't look like Rackmoor, I'll tell you. Fake fur coat down to her ankles nearly. Very Carnaby Street. Fashion boots which wouldn't do a thing for you in this weather. She talked about London and the awful weather here and the sea, that sort of thing. If you want to know more, I suggest you see Adrian Rees." Casually, Maud Brixenham picked a bit of lint from her blouse.

"Rees?"

"The thing is, I saw them together one night." Pointedly, she looked at Jury. "Walking up the High. On the way, I presume, to his place."

Jury said nothing.

"It was the night before Titus's little dinner party. Funny, he gave no sign he knew her. It was a small party. Just Titus, Lily Siddons, Adrian, and this Temple person. We were in the Bracewood Room. I recall Miss Temple was sitting before the fire. Julian and I were standing about with our sherry. I believe that's when Lily came in. She seemed terribly shocked, I mean by this Temple woman's presence. She just froze in the doorway, staring at her."

"She was struck by the resemblance to Dillys March, is that it?"

"Struck by it? She was utterly shocked. Her face went as white as her dress. Well, apparently the resemblance *was* striking. But to say the woman really was this Dillys March . . ." She shrugged. "Julian agrees with me, of course. The whole thing is preposterous."

"Did she give any indication to you, I mean in the pub, that she was familiar with Rackmoor? Used to live here?"

"None. But I'm sure she was saving that tidbit. Playing it, as Les would say, cool. She didn't strike me as the type to get herself killed. Not smart enough."

That was certainly a fresh way of looking at it, thought Jury. "I don't quite understand."

"Well, she seemed more the sort to carry out someone else's plans rather than instigate her own. Which has nothing to do with whether one gets murdered, does it?"

"What exactly did she say?"

"That she was on holiday. And had friends in Rackmoor. The Craels, of all people. I shouldn't have connected her with them. Not their sort."

"And did she go into any detail about her relationship with them?"

"No. But she said she'd known them a long time. As a child, she said. There wasn't anything else really."

"Exactly what route did you take through the village, I mean after coming down along the seawall?"

"Mind if I have another sherry to help this along? I just seem to be bone dry tonight. The writing's not going well." Up she sprang, cascading several loose pins from her hair and the leather thong belt which had been loosely tied round her India-print shirtwaist. At the cabinet once again she kept the bottle out of view and came back holding her palm upwards beneath the base of the brimful glass. Wiggins got out his inhaler as if politely joining her in this libation.

"We came down the Fox steps, you know, the ones that go up to the seawall, and passed the pub and then to Lily's cottage. As I said before, I stayed with her for a bit, to see she wasn't going to be in need of —"

A crash — not a crash, exactly; more a Klaxon call — pulled their three heads up. What was at first a deafening clamor finally separated itself into just-barely discernible instruments: electric guitars, drums, bass. Voices twanged rhythmically, but no words were recognizable, even as loud as the music was.

"Told you," said Maud. Without getting up, she reached to the bookcase against which leaned a long pole, kept there, apparently for the purpose to which she now put it. *Thump, thump, thump,* she banged on the ceiling. The clamor diminished.

"What a treat. The Grateful Dead. I will join them if he doesn't soon go back to the States."

"Is that your nephew? He's an American?"

"One look would tell you. He's my sister's boy. He's from Michigan or Cincinnati or one of those places, and she thought it would broaden his horizons if he could spend his Christmas hols in England. Now he's here and his holiday is supposed to be over, but I can't pry him loose. Think he's

got some girl or other up in that new government housing project. And, of course, he's not eager to go back to
school, nor is my sister eager to have him back. Can't imagine why." She gave the ceiling a few more whacks with
the stick. The noise lessened some more. "Since he's been
here I am sure I have suffered a temporary threshold shift.
I understand that the human ear can tolerate only fifteen
minutes of sound at a level of one hundred and fifteen deci-
bels. The average rock concert — to which I am treated
daily — is somewhere around one hundred and forty. The
threshold of pain." She gave them a toothy smile as the song
came to its raucous end and the music stopped. There was
the clumping of heavy boots on the staircase.

Wiggins, prone to catching anything, including deafness,
testily drew his hands away from his ears.

A young lad of about sixteen canted into the room as if a
heavy rain were at his back, pushing him on. Cowboy hat,
jeans, boots, fringed jacket, dark glasses, all like separate
stars fixed here and there, combined like an odd constella-
tion in the midnight sky, so that he seemed to be more than
just the sum of these parts.

"My nephew, Les Aird. This is Chief Inspector Jury of
Scotland Yard."

Jury remembered himself at sixteen doing just what Les
Aird was doing now: trying hard not to be impressed. Had
Jury ever really been this age? All he could scare up was the
memory of an amorphous blob of a youngster, dull and ill-
defined.

Les Aird was searching for some posture encompassing
both respect and ennui. The gum stopped working and the
glasses got adjusted and the throat got cleared and the hands
got stuck in the jeans pockets. Playing for time. Finally he
settled for simply sticking out his hand, snapping his chin
in a curt, serious nod, and saying, "Hey, it's cool."

There was no lack of respect in the tone or the greeting.

It matched some brigadier general's "What ho, old chap!" Les's had simply come from the sixteen-year-old storehouse of nonchalance.

"I'd like to ask you a few questions, Les."

Murder can both excite and unnerve and Jury heard the slight crack in Les Aird's voice as he said, "Okay, ask away." He sat down on the settee next to his aunt, on the edge of it, Jury noticed, leaning forward, one arm across his blue-jeaned leg, and the other elbow jutting out, with the hand on the hip. "Shoot."

It could have been a literal invitation. The gum started working at an even faster clip.

"It's about the murdered woman. Had you ever seen her during the time she came here?"

"Yeah. One foxy lady, man." He smiled and danced his eyebrows up and down above the glasses.

"Did you make any attempt to talk to her at all?"

"Say what?" The blank look was almost blinding.

"Did you talk to her, Les?"

"Uh-uh."

"But you had seen her," Jury said.

"Here and there."

"On the night she was murdered?"

"No." "Yes."

They spoke together, Les Aird and Maud Brixenham. Maud looked exceedingly surprised.

"I did, Aunt Maud."

"You didn't tell me that."

Les shrugged. "Didn't know it then."

"You didn't tell Inspector Harkins, either, Les."

"Didn't know it *then*, either. I mean that it was *her*. All he said was this lady got blown away. He never described her. How was I to know the one I saw was *her*? It was after we left the party, maybe around ten-thirty, quarter of, I saw her. With all those people in costume, I guessed she was just another one on her way up to the manor house. I don't dig it, man. But the spread was okay. Food to the max. Real bad. But after I saw all the bunny-rabbits, I booked."

Jury blinked. "Bunny-rabbits?"

"Musta been half-a-dozen rabbits running around. Crazy."

Maud explained: "Three of the villagers decided to come as Flopsy, Mopsy, and Cottontail."

"Which way did you take back to the village?"

"That path that comes out near the church and Psalter's Lane."

"Then where?"

"Then I went down that part of the Angel steps to Scroop Street. Arn was groovin' along so I walked with him down Scroop Street and through Dagger Alley to the High. I mean it was weird, man, to see that face come at you out of this wall of fog. Vampire time. Face was half black, half white." Les drew an imaginary line from his forehead down the bridge of his nose, blocking off the left side of his face. "Even Arn barked. And it takes a lot to make Arn bark."

"And this was on the High Street?"

"Yeah. I thought maybe she was coming out of the Bell."

"And where did she go from there? Up Dagger Alley?"

"Couldn't say, man. Either there or on down the High."

"And that was, you think, around ten-thirty?"

"Near as I can say."

"It took you a half-an-hour to get from Old House to the High?"

Les looked a little uncomfortable as he nodded. "Yeah. I, ah, missed a turning and had to double back."

Jury did not press the point; probably Les had stopped for the odd cigarette or two along the way; he doubted there was a more serious construction to put upon the time lapse. But he certainly wondered at the time lapse as far as the Temple woman was concerned.

"You saw her roughly at ten-thirty. Adrian Rees saw her just before the Fox Deceiv'd closed, around eleven-fifteen.

Where was she during those forty-five minutes?" The question was put more to himself than to Les, but Les answered,

"Beats me. I booked, man. Up the hill to Strawberry Flats. To see my girl."

"Who lives at that end of town, Wiggins? Let's see the map." There was Adrian Rees, of course. A good bet, that.

Wiggins took out and unfolded the map of the village supplied him by Harkins. "There's Percy Blythe. Lives in Dark Street. The Steeds live across from the library; that's down at the end of Scroop Street. Most of the houses are empty this time of year."

Jury leaned over and studied the map. Never had he seen such a web of narrow streets. No, not a web; spiders were far more symmetrical with their web-making than were the streets of Rackmoor. Dark Street was a cul-de-sac with no means of egress to any other streets except Scroop Street. Dagger Alley was a blade-thin walkway between the Bell and an empty warehouse.

"Well, thanks, Les. Let me know if you remember anything else."

"Later days." Les jabbed his dark glasses back on his nose.

Maud Brixenham followed Jury and Wiggins to the door, trailing after her a bit of paper which had come unstuck from her shoe and a tiny button which had finally given itself up to the pull of gravity. Jury wondered how Maud Brixenham could possibly get away with murder: she'd leave a trail of clues all the way from Rackmoor to Scarborough.

Out in the fog, Jury turned to her and said, "Thanks, Miss Brixenham."

"Don't get lost in the fog."

Jury smiled. "I don't think Rackmoor's quite big enough to get lost in."

"Don't you believe it. Used to be a smuggler's haunt. Easy to hide in, these twisting little streets."

Jury thought he detected a certain reluctance to leave on

Wiggins's part. "Did you have some more questions, Sergeant Wiggins?"

"I was just wondering," Wiggins said to Maud Brixenham. "Is it difficult writing?"

Jury sighed and lit a cigarette. Was Wiggins trying to find his true self in Rackmoor?

14.

The depression and anxiety which had gripped him when he had been talking to Lily Siddons washed over Jury like a dark wave when he awoke the next morning and turned his face to the window, knowing he would see nothing but the gray fog sealing off the room. Sadness hunched on his chest, like an incubus-dream.

He forced himself up and over to the window, looked out through sea-fret and minimal light to what he could see of the water, the color of pewter. He could barely make out the small green and blue cobles.

Jury got his clothes on, sat back down on the bed again with one shoe in his hand. He stared at the carpet, a fugue-like pattern of winding stems and leaves, faded almost into the gray background. He did not like this case; feelings which he had stashed away on the high shelves of his mind kept threatening to tumble down.

He tied his other shoelace, got up, walked over to the cheval glass, looked in it and for the hundredth, no, thousandth time, wondered why he had become a policeman and why he remained one. He wondered, too, if he were acting in unconscious collaboration with Superintendent Racer to keep that superintendency which he should have had long ago at arm's length. He thought, looking in the mirror, that he looked like a cop, or somebody's idea of one: big, square, dark-suited. Substantial. A cop or the Bank of England.

As often happened when he was depressed he studied his clothes with scrupulous attention to detail, as if, for example, the removal of a handkerchief from one pocket to the other would transform him from a frog to a prince.

It didn't. Why was he wearing this old blue tie? The hell with it. He yanked off the stupid blue tie, took off the jacket, pulled on a heavy sweater, over which he could wear his windcheater. From the four-poster bed he took an Irish walking hat and stuffed that on his head. Why was he doing this, vainly stopping here in front of this mirror, fidgeting with his clothes like a debutante changing frocks before the ball? Now he looked like he only needed a couple of hounds and a blackthorn stick for a walk across the moors.

An image surfaced in his mind and quickly disappeared, like something floating on the edge of a pool, just out of range, reflecting briefly, sinking. Like the name on the tip of the tongue, the elusive face, the dream-image that rises and sinks again. It was looking in this mirror which had brought it to mind. He went back over everything he had done, standing here, but the thing refused to surface again. He was sure that if he could find it, that small detail, he would have a very important piece of the puzzle.

He kept looking at himself; he sighed. Was he even clever enough to be a cop? he wondered, turning to go down to breakfast.

Breakfast was a slightly more cheerful affair than dressing had been, even with Wiggins washing down two-toned pills with orange juice. But he had the grace this morning, at least, not to trot out descriptions of the various coughs and chills and drafts which had kept him tossing and turning all the night long. Indeed, Wiggins seemed chipper. He complimented Kitty's breakfast of smoked herring, buttered eggs, fried bread and grilled tomatoes.

"Inspector Harkins called this morning — had some information to give you about Gemma Temple. It had to do with the Raineys, a family she lived with for eight or nine years."

"Could they vouch for her being Gemma Temple?"

"Yes and no."

"Meaning?"

"She didn't come there until she was eighteen or nineteen. Came as *au pair* and general dogsbody. They live in Lewisham." Wiggins read from his notebook: "Number four, Kingsway Close."

"But they must have asked for references; they got her to take care of their kids."

"Oh, she had references, but when Harkins checked them, he found out they were fake."

"What about the picture of Dillys March? Couldn't they tell anything from that?"

"Said it looked the spit of Gemma, yes. Of course, they could identify Gemma from the pictures taken at the morgue. It was Gemma, all right."

"But was it Dillys? Did Harkins get any further with the dental records?"

"He didn't say. This Olive Manning, I think you should speak to her, she's that bitter about Dillys March. Strong motive, if you ask me."

"Strong motive, maybe. But it's rather unlikely that Dillys March actually caused Leo Manning's breakdown. I don't think people drive other people mad, do you?"

Wiggins seemed to be thinking. "Well, there was what Charles Boyer did to Ingrid Bergman. I saw that on telly just the other night."

Jury pretended he didn't hear that. "Did Olive Manning seem to believe this was the March girl returned to the fold?"

"Definitely not."

"Then would she have a reason for killing her?"

"Well, no. But she could be lying about its not being Dillys."

"Hmm. Look at this, Wiggins." Jury produced the picture he had taken from Lily's collection. "Mary Siddons, Lily's mother."

Wiggins picked it up. "Drowned, didn't she?"

"Supposedly accidental; I'm sure it was suicide. As long as she lived here she knew damned well you can't walk that dangerous stretch below the cliff at high tide. But the picture is what I'm interested in. It's been cut." Jury had removed it from its small frame. "On the left, there, look. I wondered why the woman in it was so far up against the edge of the picture. Cut, but why?"

"Trimmed, to fit in the frame?"

"More likely someone's been cut out of it."

Wiggins looked again. "The father, maybe? He went off and left them high and dry."

Jury shrugged, repocketed the picture. Wiggins took out his nose drops.

Jury tilted back his chair and surveyed the row of hunting prints on the wall. "I've been thinking about that costume. Could there have been some motive in Lily's giving that costume to Gemma Temple? Lily Siddons feared someone was trying to kill her. It's happened twice before, two attempts. What if she simply decided to let Dillys March take her place?"

Applying the minuscule dropper to his right nostril, Wiggins answered, "Isbuhuffy." He sniffed in the drops.

Although Jury had pretty well mastered Wiggins's words coming through clouds of handkerchiefs and medicines, this particular phrase in the Wiggins's lexicon was lost on Jury. "Translate, please."

"Sorry, sir. It's this damned wet that's getting to my sinuses. I was just saying, it's a bit 'iffy,' isn't it? I mean, Lily Siddons isn't even positive — or at least wasn't before this murder of the Temple woman — that someone *was* trying to kill her. Just to have her wear that costume in the hopes the murderer would mistake the Temple woman for Lily herself, well, that's awful uncertain. And what would she have against this Gemma Temple?"

"Nothing against Gemma Temple. A hell of a lot against Dillys March. She hated her. Probably mutual. Though I must agree with you. It would be a damned uncertain way of ridding herself of an enemy."

"And what would she have to gain, except revenge?"

"Eventually, money from Colonel Crael. I can't believe she doesn't come in for a sizable sum, and that's easy enough to check out. If Dillys March were to turn up now, she'd be cutting a wide swathe across that will, I'd think." Jury leaned across the table. "Let's take a brief look at those people who would probably lose out if Dillys March were to come back. Motive and opportunity: how much does each have?

"Julian Crael: by far the strongest motive I can see. But a cast-iron alibi."

"Makes you wonder, right there," said Wiggins, folding his napkin carefully.

"Except it could be just as he says it is. Then there's Adrian Rees. Ample opportunity: he was walking up Grape Lane and saw her. But motive is awfully thin, there. I should imagine the Colonel's patronage would continue, though possibly in somewhat diminished form.

"Then, Maud Brixenham: both motive and opportunity. The Colonel, if he's interested in marrying; the return of the prodigal daughter (as you put it) might take up a lot of his emotional capital.

"Lily Siddons: motive, yes. But opportunity — very little. She's pretty well out of it unless she could run like hell from her cottage, murder the woman, and get back again all in ten minutes. It takes that much time to get there in the first place. This is further complicated by the fact that someone may be trying to kill *her*.

"Kitty Meechem —"

"Oh, surely not, sir!" Wiggins looked down at the ample breakfast he'd just enjoyed as if he couldn't believe it'd been served up by a murderess.

"Want some more eggs, Wiggins?"

"Oh, no thank you. I'm quite stuffed." He patted his stomach.

Jury threw some coins on the table, a tip for the rather slow-moving waitress named Biddie or Bitsy who had spent a great deal of time in arranging and rearranging the cutlery on the other tables and staring at the two of them until Kitty had finally collared her. "Let's go, then."

Jury splayed his arms and leaned out over the seawall where the tide had left its bright litter of shingle and shells and partially beached little boats. The morning was brighter, the horizon gauzelike, the sun misty. The whole of the tiny village, with its brown-red roofs staggering upward looked wonderfully precarious, as if it might tumble down at any moment like a child's building blocks.

"When Maud Brixenham described that dinner party . . . Look in your notes for that, will you?"

Wiggins took out his notebook. Jury had often marveled at how he could cram so much into such a small space, perhaps because the sergeant's writing was so crabbed. He found the part and read: " 'It was a small party. Just Titus, Lily Siddons, Adrian and this Temple woman. We were in the Bracewood Room' . . . that's the room, sir, where you were talking with Julian Crael . . . 'and Gemma Temple was sitting in front of the fire. Julian and I were standing about with our sherry . . .' "

Jury looked out to sea, not minding the boredom which Wiggins's notes often aroused in him. His exasperation with

Wiggins's editorializing and often painful longeurs was diminished by the fact that for absolute precision Wiggins couldn't be beaten. Here the lengthy report was compounded by the Brixenham's woman's love for detail. Wiggins's voice droned on, painting in, practically, the very textures of the materials, the paintings on the walls. Trollope, watch by his side, couldn't have outwritten Wiggins. Jury merely waited for the part he wanted and watched the pallid sunlight weaving in and out of clouds to cast an uneven pattern of light and shadow across the shingle like dull, flocked gold. A petrel flashed toward the sea.

" '. . . and then the door opened and Lily walked in. She just froze there, in the doorway, staring at the Temple girl.' "

" 'She was struck by the resemblance to Dillys March, is that it?' That's you speaking, sir. And then Miss Brixenham answered, 'Struck by it? She was utterly shocked. Her face went as white as her dress.' "

"That's what I can't understand," Jury said. "She reacted as if she thought it surely was Dillys March and clearly registered something less than pleasure. But she didn't appear to question it: that cover-up story of the Colonel's, about the cousin. Would you have believed that, had you been Lily Siddons?"

"No, I guess not. Why would this cousin never have turned up before?"

"And this whole costume business." Jury turned his back to the wall, took out a fresh packet of cigarettes, and slowly tore the tab from its top. Wiggins, as if in some comradely communion with his superior, took out a fresh box of cough drops.

"Assume for the moment that Lily really believed this so-called Gemma Temple *was* Dillys. She hated her. She was always playing second fiddle to her as a child. Why give over her costume to Dillys March?"

"As a favor to Colonel Crael?"

"Maybe. But why not just toss together another costume for Miss Temple? I think she's lying."

"Oh, well, sir." Wiggins's face was almost torn by his wolfish grin. "They're probably *all* lying, if it comes to that." He popped a cough drop into his mouth, said round it, "In your list, you never mentioned the Colonel. Do you think he's right out of it, then? And I honestly can't see how *Kitty* could've had a motive."

Jury laughed. "That worries you doesn't it? Well, it's not likely. But you can bet the Colonel's leaving his part ownership of the Fox to her. Though it's hard to see how that could be directly related to killing Gemma Temple. Anyway, Kitty's alibi is the same as Lily's. They were together. And as for the Colonel himself — ample opportunity, but absolutely no motive I can see."

"You didn't include Olive Manning. She'd both motive and opportunity."

Jury smiled. "You seem to favor her, Wiggins. You keep coming round to her."

"The thing is, she *knew* Dillys March well, didn't she? If there's any question of collusion, she'd be a very likely person to have found this Gemma Temple person, seen how much she looked like Dillys, and brought her to Old House."

"Yes. You're right there."

"Your instincts are good, sir. Which one of them do you think is guilty?"

"I haven't met the Manning woman, yet, of course, but . . ."

"Of the others, though?"

It was what had depressed him this morning. The thing which had diverted his thoughts into the channel of this phantom promotion, the superintendency which he had been so modestly brushing aside, telling himself he didn't need the money, the prestige, the ego-trip. He wondered now if what he didn't need was to be in an even worse position, to be faced with even more of the same, the dilemma which now confronted him. He did not know how to answer Wiggins's question. As he looked out over the gull-marked shingle, the dull gold of the horizon, he finally said, "None of them."

His feelings were playing hell with his objectivity.

15.

The gray brindled cat slipped from the sill and walked toward the back of the Rackmoor Gallery, pregnant with ownership. Jury had disturbed its nap by framing his face with his hands and putting it up against the window.

When he walked in, he nearly stepped on an envelope which must have been shoved under the door. He picked it up. The flap had come unstuck and he could see a pound note had slipped out, one of several. The envelope, cheap stationery, was addressed to *B. Makepiece*, and had been mailed months before. Jury was interested in the return address, what there was of it. *R.V.H. London S.W. 1.* He was studying it when Adrian Rees appeared, wearing his paint-smeared apron and carrying a small bowl which he set on the hardwood floor. The cat went over to it.

"I'd say, Come in, but you already are." Rees yawned.

Jury held out the envelope. "I found this on the floor."

Adrian looked at it, color spreading up his neck. "Oh, I see. It's just a bit of a loan. From Bertie." When Jury just looked at him, he went on. "For Christ's sakes, what do you think? I'm blackmailing him? Bertie's the only one in Rackmoor who can be depended on for a spot of cash."

"I would imagine he's quite a good manager. Could I have the envelope, if you don't want it?"

Adrian looked down at it, extracted the notes, and handed it back to Jury. "Is the Fox out of its letterhead again?" He leered. Then he frowned. "Hell, I know it's terrible borrowing from a boy. But I'm a bit desperate for money — not the best thing to say in the circumstances." He sighed and idly wiped a brush back and forth across his apron.

"What do you think of his story?"

"Whose?"

"Bertie's. About his mother going off to Ireland."

Adrian smiled. "It's hard to believe that one would go to such lengths to tend a sick old granny."

"Did you know his mother?"

"Roberta? Saw her about, is all. Puff of wind would have blown her away, at least in the brains department. But the old wowsers in the town seem to have swallowed it. Codfish and Frog-Eyes, that lot. You must admit for pure resourcefulness it's quite good. Who'd scarper off to Belfast to check up? That what you came about?"

"No. It was about Gemma Temple I came. Your relationship was somewhat closer than you allowed."

For a long moment, he was silent, wiping the brush back and forth. Then he shrugged and said, "Someone saw us, I suppose?" Jury nodded and waited. "Well, I should hardly call it a 'relationship.' It was only the one time."

"A lot can happen in one time." It always surprised Jury, this way some people had of doing it by numbers. He thought back over the last years, of the women he had known. A lot could happen in the one time, certainly. "Why didn't you tell me, Mr. Rees? I could have so easily found out. And did. Another thing: did you see Gemma Temple the night she was murdered — I mean, *before* you saw her in Grape Lane?"

"What? No, absolutely not! Anyone says I did is lying."

"She was seen on the High Street. Near here."

"I don't know anything about that. As for not telling you about the other business: I already had all the suspicion I needed attached to me, thank you very much. I was the last person to see the Temple girl, and that right after all that stupid mouthing off in the Fox about Raskolnikov and murder."

"You don't think I attached any importance to that, really, do you? That sort of crime might be convincing in the hands of Dostoyevsky, but I've never run into it on the streets of London."

"Well, why didn't you tell me that? Perhaps then I'd have admitted to knowing the Temple woman."

"It's not a trade-off, for God's sake. Now would you please tell me about Gemma Temple?"

"Oh, very well," said Adrian, truculently. "She'd seen me in here once and a couple of times in the Fox. And I, of course, had noticed her. Who wouldn't? She was quite good-looking and something new to turn one's thoughts to. One night just after closing she walked out of the pub and I followed her. She was walking along the seawall in the direction of Old House. I caught her up and we chatted a bit and I suggested she come back to my place for a drink. Not very clever but it's all I could think of, Rackmoor not being the Sodom and Gomorrah of all England. Anyway, we came back here."

"Then what?"

"Then what 'what'? You know what. The scenario is pretty well fixed."

"It didn't need much persuasion, is that it?"

"Inspector, it didn't need *any* persuasion. And I don't regard myself as all that magnetic, either."

Jury thought he was being overly modest. Adrian Rees exuded sexuality, masculinity, intensified by the exotic touch of his being a painter. "Which night was this?"

"Two nights before the murder." Adrian smiled grimly.

"What did she tell you about herself?"

"Absolutely nothing, and that's the truth. No more than I told you before. She walked about with a drink in her hand looking at my paintings and making idiotic, I suppose obligatory, comments about them. And she talked about the village, which she found a trifle dull. There wasn't that much talk, after all." Adrian smiled roguishly.

"And she didn't mention having lived here once?"

Adrian shook his head. "And when she turns up the next night at that little dinner party, *I* was the one who stammered and blushed. You'd think she'd never seen me before that evening. I'd no idea she was some sort of cousin of the Crael family."

"How much did you know about Dillys March?"

"You mean the Craels' ward, the one who disappeared?" Jury nodded. "Only what the Colonel told me about her. About her and Lady Margaret and his son, Rolfe. I was up there and he was down here when I was doing Lady Margaret's portrait. . . . What are you saying, exactly?"

Jury didn't answer that. "You're quite sure you had never seen Gemma Temple before she came to Rackmoor?"

Adrian looked furious. "Bloody hell! Of course, I'm sure!"

Jury smiled briefly. "Don't be overly indignant. You didn't tell me the truth before, you know." He looked off into the dark environs in the rear where the cat was washing himself. "Did you finish that picture, the one of Gemma Temple? I'd like to see it."

"No, but I shall. I'd just been working at it when you came."

Jury looked down. "With a dry brush?"

The anger which had started to drain from Adrian's face returned. "My *God* but you do notice everything, don't you?"

"That's what they pay me for. I'll see you later."

16.

The bell tinkled over the door of the Bridge Walk Café when Jury walked in. The dining room was small, with a low-beamed ceiling, whitewashed walls, small tables with ladder-back chairs. A large sideboard with stacks of blue and white china. Very clean and attractive and empty of customers. Business would hardly be expected to be very good in mid-winter.

Lily Siddons appeared, her pale hair tied back in a kerchief, and with an apron on. Jury supposed this was the kitchen entrance. "Oh. Good morning."

He touched his hat and was a bit surprised to feel its tweedy floppiness. He'd almost forgot he'd put it on this morning. "Miss Siddons, would you mind if I asked you a few more questions?"

She wiped her hands down her apron. "No. No, I wouldn't mind, if *you* wouldn't mind coming back to the kitchen so I could get on with my work."

Inside the kitchen, he saw she had been chopping up vegetables. Jury pulled out a chair and sat down. She was working at a large table in the center of the room, an enormous butcher's block table. "I wanted to ask you about your mother."

For a moment she was silent. Then she said, "I don't see the point." She picked up a cup of coffee, now cold, apparently. She poured it down the sink and turned her back to Jury.

He waited for her to turn round again, tracing his finger through some flour which remained on the table, probably from the loaves of bread left to rise in bowls under towels. Lining the walls near the big stove were copper bowls. A row of small, high windows overlooked the stream which ran below and under the bridge. Bands of morning sunlight cut across the window sills, made rhomboids of light on the floor, and sparked the bottoms of the copper bowls.

"You do all this yourself?"

Turning back to the chopping block, she nodded, and picked up the knife. "In winter, yes. In summer, I have help. We've a lot of people on holiday here." Jury had never seen such swift chopping. She held the tip of the big knife down with her right fingers and with her left hand lifted the hilt and brought it down in short, swift, rhythmical movements. The knife cut the carrots into ever smaller bits as she chopped, swept it back, chopped, swept. "You're very deft with that knife." Jury fished for a cigarette in his shirt pocket, slapped his pockets for matches.

"The trick is that the blade should never completely leave the board." She wasn't looking at him when she added, "And I suppose you're meaning to suggest that I could cut up a person like a carrot, is that it?"

"Was she killed with a knife? First I knew it."

Lily stopped, angry, hand on hip. "May I please have my picture back? The one you took last night?"

Jury reached in his pocket. "Sorry, Lily. I took it off by mistake."

She started in on the vegetables again. "I doubt you do anything by mistake."

He put the picture, framed again, on the table. "Your father doesn't sound a very steady type, to go off and leave the both of you the way he did." Lily didn't answer. "It's odd her marrying someone she must have known so little, too. How long were they married?"

The knife stopped. "You're trying to say something rather nasty, aren't you? Like maybe he got her pregnant and she had to marry him."

"Did he?"

"No." She emphasized the single syllable by using the knife to sweep all of the vegetables into a stainless steel bowl.

"After you were born, your mother stopped on at Old House as cook."

Lily wiped her hands down her apron. "Mr. Jury, you *know* all this. Why do you keep *asking*?"

To see if it'll come out different, thought Jury. He was

watching her face closely. What he said was, "Because there's got to be a reason in all of this for her suicide and these threats to your life, Lily." Quickly and sadly, she looked down at the bowl in her hands. She said nothing. "Could it be because of your mother?"

Startled, she looked up at him. "What do you mean?"

"Something that happened when she was alive? Or something she left behind? I'm not sure just what I do mean."

Lily turned away, furiously shaking her head and slamming the knife and the bowl down on the counter of the sink.

Jury persisted. "Could it be something you don't even know about, but someone thinks you do? Could it be you're a threat to someone?"

"Threat? That's silly."

"What about to the Craels?"

She whirled round to face him and her skin was as white as the flour on the table. "Me a threat? *Me?*" She flattened her hands against the outmoded gingham apron as if proving her identity. "I was only Cook's girl. 'Cook's girl' is what they used to call me. Not Lily, just 'Cook's girl.'" Two bright spots came into her cheeks as if she'd just pinched them to bring the color up. "I even thought it was my name. Mum told me someone asked me on the street what my name was and I said, 'Cook's girl.' She thought it was ever so funny."

"But you obviously didn't."

Her back was turned to him now and her head lowered. Jury was sure she was crying when he saw her hand swiftly go up to her face and drop away. She ran water in the sink and tossed it on her face and pulled down a kitchen towel. Then she turned back and went on. "The only one who was decent was the Colonel. *He* at least knew my name. And he was the only one who defended Mum when—" She stopped, looked off. "Dillys hated me, but he never knew that. The only reason we were so much together is that the Colonel liked us both. He always wanted a daughter, I think. And he's not a snob, he's not like the others were — Lady Margaret, Julian, Rolfe, too, though he was a bit more fun-loving, I guess. The Colonel used to take me looking for butterflies. It was beautiful then." She turned and looked out of the little window where the weak and wintry sunlight was gilding the branches.

Was she seeing, Jury wondered, summer? That enormous house with its velvet lawns and behind it the purple carpet of the sea and before it the rising moorlands, thick with heather? Looking at her now, her profile feathered in light, he felt he could move inside her head, run through the grass, see the swishing of the net. "You said Colonel Crael was the only one who defended your mother. Defended her from what?"

Lily came to sit down across from him. She seemed very tired. "It was Lady Margaret. Some jewelry, some emeralds or diamonds — I don't know — came up missing. She said it was Mum who took them. All of those years my mother worked there . . . She began as vegetable cook. And suddenly she'd take it into her mind to *steal?*" Then she turned away from Jury again, presenting only her profile, sitting on a high stool, legs crossed, hands cupping elbows. It was as though she had simply removed herself, like an astral body, leaving behind this marble pose.

"It doesn't seem like much of a reason for suicide, though, does it?"

Slowly, she turned her head and Jury saw her amber eyes had clouded over, darkened to the color of cornelian, as they had in the firelight. Her voice was level but it was clear that she was very angry. "And do you know all the reasons for suicide, then?"

"No. But one has to be very, very depressed. To be unjustly accused — and you certainly seem sure she was —

that would result more in self-righteous anger than in sui-
cidal depression. Do *you* believe she'd have killed herself
for such a reason?"

Evasively, she answered, "I was only eleven when she
died."

"Yes. But do you believe it?"

"I don't know." Her face, her voice were stony.

"What did you do then? After she died?"

"I went to my Aunt Hilda in Pitlochary. I hated it. She
didn't want me. But she liked to think of herself as a God-
fearing Christian; well, it was her duty to take me in."

"I'm rather surprised the Craels didn't take you. He's so
fond of you."

"Good God, Inspector. I was only a servant's child. Fond-
ness doesn't extend quite *that* far. And even if *he* would,
the others wouldn't have stood for it. Julian, Olive Manning, Dillys. *She* had him wrapped round her finger, and
she wasn't even flesh and blood. But he did see to it that I
got extra money, clothes, and made sure I went to school.
He paid Aunt, I'm sure. I think she'd have had me out
waitressing or something when I was working age if it
hadn't been for that."

"This cousin, Gemma Temple, suddenly appearing. It
would seem she might have been able to wrap Colonel Crael
round her little finger, too."

"I don't know what you mean."

"Don't you?"

Jury was sure she was lying.

17.

The Rackmoor lending library was a long, narrow room,
the first floor of what had been a small terraced cottage that
looked from the outside very like its neighbors. The down-

stairs had been converted, the walls removed so that now what had probably once been receiving room, dining room, parlor, and kitchen were all one. The counter at the front looked like it had been taken from an old pub. On it was a sign demanding SILENCE even before the book-borrower had got his bearings. The bookshelves of varying heights, the threadbare carpet, the little, mismatched lamps on the tables scattered about all contributed to the appearance that the room had been done from the leavings of a jumble sale.

There was something of the jumble-sale look about Miss Cavendish herself: an old brown skirt which nearly reached the ankles, sagging olive cardigan sweater, brown hair in a bun like a pincushion. She appeared to be remonstrating with some school-aged children when Jury walked in. When she saw Jury and moved off toward the front, the children bent their shining heads together once again and proceeded to giggle and whisper. Aside from them, there was one other person, a stout woman passing slowly along one of the shelves.

The library certainly seemed to be Miss Cavendish's métier. Her eyes, regarding Jury over the tops of half-glasses attached to a narrow grosgrain ribbon, looked weak, as if she'd spent too many late nights reading. Her sallow complexion was marked by many moles like a foxed-page book. And when she moved, she seemed to whisper and creak as if her pages were loosening, though the sound was probably from a stiff petticoat.

Jury produced his I.D. "There were a few questions I wanted to ask you, Miss."

"I rather suspected that's who you might be." She looked him up and down with a satisfied smack of unrouged lips. "But I don't see how I can help. I live at the other end of the village from where she was . . . so brutally killed. I've told the other policeman that."

"Yes, I know. Actually, it's another matter I've come

about." Miss Cavendish raised her brows, astonished that there could be another matter. "It's to do with Mrs. Make-piece, Bertie's mother. We understand you've been looking in on Bertie."

"Aye. Roberta — that's Bertie's mother — asked me to look in on the lad. Rose Honeybun and Laetitia Frother-Guy have been doing so, too. Look here, it's not a police matter, now is it? I should certainly hope we're not to be held accountable for his welfare." Jury opened his mouth to reply, but she hurried on in her own defense. "It's certainly nothing to do with us. Laetitia Frother-Guy contacted the social services people *tout de suite* and they came round to the Makepiece cottage, but everything seemed to be going along smoothly enough and, of course, Roberta's taken herself off before, don't think she hasn't. Well, shocking, I call it. Absolutely shocking, sick relative or no, and, frankly, I even wonder about that. According to the boy she's gone to Belfast, though that wasn't what she told *me*. And it's not the first time she's asked me to have a look in when she's just decided to have herself a little holiday; this must be the fourth or fifth time. You know what I mean, *affaires d'amour* more than sick grans, that's my notion of what she's getting up to. I will admit it's the longest she's ever been gone. Never should have had children, that's what I told my *confrère*, Rose Honeybun. Her sort should be satisfied with a budgie if it's company they want. That child's had to take care of himself near all his born days, and does it better than ever *she* could. Do you know he's done nearly all the washing up and cooking and shopping ever since he was in infant's school? But of course he needs guidance, doesn't he? Should be living *en famille*. But I've never seen a child so self-sufficient. I must admit I find his manner a bit off-putting, never know what's going on in that little head, he's a bit of an *enfant terrible*, I'd say, and that dog of his does do my nerves a turn. A *bête noir*, if ever there was one. You'd think it could read your mind, and the way it *looks* at one, well —"

"Where did Mrs. Makepiece tell you she was going?" Jury stemmed the flow.

"London. Yes, London, I'm quite sure. That's why I was so surprised when the boy told me the gran — the sick one — lived in Belfast and she'd gone there. Of all places." Visions of black-bereted Irish Nationalists no doubt assaulted her eye.

"Didn't you wonder, then, why she said she was going to London?"

"Yes, I did. But as I said, Roberta Makepiece was always having her little holiday. And quite shirty she'd get, too, if you so much as blinked at her over her little *affaires de coeur*. The husband died when he was rather young, you know, and I'm not sure but what living with Roberta hadn't something —"

"So you did wonder that she went to Belfast?"

"I suppose I simply thought she'd got to go to London to get a train or whatever to get to the boat. Or to Heathrow."

Jury thought for a moment. From Yorkshire that would certainly be a waste of both time and money. If she'd wanted to go to Northern Ireland she'd have gone up to Scotland and taken the ferry from Stranraer.

"Inspector, why are the police asking me these questions? I told you *I* was merely trying to help out."

"I was merely concerned about him. He seems so young to be staying there alone."

She seemed to take this as implicit criticism. "Don't you think I know it? Shocking, for a mother to do such a thing. I was saying to Rose and Laetitia just the other day we should have the social services people do something. But they seemed satisfied nothing should be done at this time. Well, I ask you. It's been upwards of three months now and that mother still not back? The boy should be placed in a home."

Jury's inward eye turned upon long, barren rooms, rows of iron cots. He tried to picture Bertie within those institutional walls. He could not.

Outside the library's window a small dog with a ruff of fur round its neck was tied, an incongruous blue bow stuck in the neck fur. Probably waiting for the stout lady who was roving among the stacks to return and claim him.

"I don't know that would be the best solution for Bertie," Jury said. "Besides, whatever would happen to Arnold? They're mates."

"Well, I *hardly* consider a *dog* sufficient company for a *child. Bête noir*, as I said." She sniffed.

Jury looked at the counter: the SILENCE sign must have killed Miss Cavendish. "Yes. Oh, well, *delenda est Carthago.* Good day, Miss Cavendish."

She blinked and stared as he turned away.

Outside on Scroop Street he wondered why he had told her Carthage should be destroyed. Probably because it was the only thing he could dredge up at the moment. Jury loved Virgil.

He walked along Scroop Street and peered in at Bertie's window, saw no sign of either him or Arnold and everything seemed quiet and dark within. The big apron hung from a peg by the kitchen counter. Bertie must be in school.

When he reached the Angel steps he decided to walk up to Psalter's Lane and approach Old House by way of the path through the woods. At the top of the steps, just below the church, he turned and looked down. Even in dead winter Rackmoor was beautifully unreal. The whole village lay before him, carved into the cliffside, stairsteps of houses, winding streets, tiny blue and green boats the only bright spots on the monochromatic grays of stone, sky, and sea.

But there were really two views, not just one: far off to his right Jury could see the beginnings of the North York Moors, miles and miles of unbroken reaches of snow.

He wished he could think of some excuse to walk across them.

18.

Like a migrating bird, Sergeant Wiggins always managed to fly to the warmth; thus, Jury found him near the kitchen hearth with a pot of tea, seated across from Olive Manning.

She did not lend warmth to the setting, however. She presented to Jury a cool, dry hand and a cooler smile. She gave the impression of someone uncomfortable in her clothes, as if they were ill-made (which they certainly weren't) or made for someone else. Sitting in her dark dress, from the belt of which hung a set of keys, Olive Manning seemed to be all angles: elbows, cheekbones, straight, sharp nose. Her voice was sharp, too, with the ring of metal in it. The obligatory smile vanished after she first greeted Jury, and her expression became as set and immobile as the face on a coin. Her eyes were a tarnished silver, her mouth thin. A haze of gray had settled over her once-dark hair like the bloom on stale chocolate.

Jury drew up a chair, declined the proffered cup of tea. "Mrs. Manning, I don't want to make you go back over everything you've told Sergeant Wiggins, here. What I'm most interested in is whether you thought this young lady was Dillys March."

Decidedly, she shook her head. "Definitely not."

"How can you be so sure, when Sir Titus fully believes she was?" Jury had little doubt that Olive Manning was sure about everything she thought and felt.

She smiled slightly. "I'd say that was wishful thinking, Inspector Jury. You realize, of course, that Julian agrees with *my* view of the matter." Jury nodded. "There is, certainly, a superficial resemblance —"

"Much more than superficial, surely. From the pictures I've seen of the March girl, I'd say Gemma Temple was a dead ringer."

"That's true. Only, those pictures of Dillys are fifteen years old, aren't they? And it's not merely the girl's looks. There are other things. Gestures, speech —"

"Not quite to the manor born?"

"If you want to put it that way. I found her a bit vulgar. Breeding is breeding, after all."

"Couldn't some of it get roughed up a bit in fifteen years?" She didn't answer. "Your son, Mrs. Manning, is, regrettably, in an institution, I believe?"

The steely eyes charged up with something, but all she said was, "Yes."

"From what I hear, you hold Dillys March largely responsible for his breakdown."

Her face, her posture were resolute. But she was twisting her beringed fingers as if she were trying to keep them from his throat. "Well, since you've heard all the gossip, there's no need for me to embroider, is there, Chief Inspector?"

"There's every reason, if that's all it is — gossip. What happened between Dillys and your son?"

"All the while that Leo was here — it was a year, and he served as the Colonel's chauffeur — the girl was after him."

"Did she get him?"

There was a silence. "She led him a merry chase. It wouldn't have been so bad if he'd been the only one. He was one of many."

"Was she so very attractive?"

Olive Manning smirked. "Really, Inspector. One doesn't have to be attractive, one only has to —" She looked at Jury as if he should know. "And she very nearly got him discharged a month after he was here. And then there was that hideous police inquiry, everyone thinking that Leo had something to do . . ." She stopped, grew very pale. The anger which she must have had the devil's own time controlling seemed to surge up. "The poor boy couldn't take the strain of it; he was genuinely in love with her."

Jury put that down to a mother's sentiment, although there seemed little enough of that in Olive Manning.

"You were the one who saw Dillys March leave that night, fifteen years ago, weren't you? Tell me about it."

"I don't sleep well, I never have, and I was up. I don't know what drew me to the window; perhaps the car door slamming. I looked out and saw her by the garage door, looking down, searching for her keys, I suppose. Then she got into that red car of hers and drove off. *Tore* down the drive. She always drove that way."

"And that's the last time you saw her?" She nodded. Jury changed the subject. "You just visited your sister in London, didn't you, two weeks before Christmas?"

"Yes. I stay there when I go to visit Leo . . . that policeman, that Inspector Harkins or one of his men had to go talking to Leo. Really, it's disgraceful. Can't the poor boy be left alone? He's perfectly innocent of anything. . . ."

Jury was surprised to see her near tears, but thought that perhaps the son was the one thing that could arouse her feelings. "They talked to him, yes. I don't think there was any way Leo could be much help to them. He remembered — little." According to Harkins's report, he remembered nothing at all. "It's Colonel Crael who's paying for that particular home where Leo is, isn't it?"

She looked up sharply. "The Colonel has always been a responsible person. I think he realizes where the fault lay, there."

"But it would be unfortunate, wouldn't it, if Dillys March were to come back and maybe change his mind on that score?" Olive Manning glared at him, opened her mouth, shut it. "I'd like a word with your sister, Mrs. Manning. Perhaps you could give me her address?"

"Why? What does she have to do with it? Do you think I'm lying about that visit?"

"No. Not when all it would take to confirm it would be a telephone call. What's her address, please?"

She was flustered. Her hands seemed to beat in air like small wings. "I can't see why you need to talk to her. It's Fanny Merchent. The Victor Merchents. They live in Ebury Street, number nineteen. It's near Victoria."

"Thank you, Mrs. Manning." Jury got up and Wiggins rose with him. "I may need to talk with you again."

Olive Manning did not reply, nor did she turn her head as they left the kitchen.

"Have you seen Mr. Plant this morning, Wood?"

"No, sir. He's not been down, sir, at least not to my knowledge."

"Would you tell him, when you see him, I've gone to London?" Jury smiled. "And also tell him not to be forever stopping a-bed."

The butler's tiny smile seemed one of complicity, as if they — Wood and Jury — were well acquainted with the ways of the gentry.

As they crossed the black-and-white marble of the hall-way, Jury said to Wiggins, "While you round up a car, I'm going to see Tom Evelyn. I won't be in London long — a day at the most. But I want to talk to some of these people."

"Inspector Harkins might take that as meaning he's been derelict in his duties, mightn't he? As if it's a kind of slur on him?" Wiggins smiled.

"It doesn't matter. Anything I do he'd take that way. I'll drop you in Pitlochary, though, and you can explain the matter to him."

"That's kind of you, sir," said Wiggins, with a perfectly straight face, only partially obscured by his inhaler.

19.

Melrose Plant *was* in bed, or rather on it, but not in the way Jury meant.

He was lying fully clothed, staring up at the elaborately painted ceiling of miniaturized scenes of gods and goddesses and cupids. He was smiling; he was thinking of Julian Craels' rooms — three doors down from his own room.

Melrose had just taken the picture he was turning round in his hands from those very rooms. It made him, actually, quite happy.

First Melrose had made quite sure that Julian would be going for his morning walk by offering to accompany him. Julian had given him the same look he might have used had Melrose offered to share his bath water. Walking for an hour on the moors (as Julian said he intended to do) when one could be sitting by a warm fire drinking Cockburn's Very Superior Port seemed to Melrose the act of a madman, but it would give him an opportunity to undertake his search.

They did not like one another, that was clear. Similarities of age, rank, wealth, position created no bond between them. And Melrose felt guilty: he had really wanted to get something from Julian — an impression, if nothing more — which would alleviate the Colonel's anxiety. Deny it as he might, Melrose felt the elder Crael was very worried about the younger — alibi or no alibi.

Blood out of stones. That was about as far as he'd got with Julian Crael, though he could hardly blame the man, he supposed. Now, with Jury, it was more like St. Peter striking the rock: all *he* had to do was walk into Percy

Blythe's cottage and fountains of conversation had gushed forth.

Thus Melrose had decided that if he couldn't get information one way, he'd try another, and so he had. Perhaps searching a gentleman's rooms was not a gentlemanly act. But neither was murder.

He had gone to Julian's rooms, not sure what sort of evidence he was looking for. Nor had he thought he'd be lucky enough to find it. But he had.

The house had been very quiet. The Colonel was out slopping around in the kennels in Pitlochary. Olive Manning was in Whitby, and the servants were doing nothing, as servants will.

So Melrose had the house virtually to himself. And he was wise enough to leave the door to Julian's room wide open in the unlikely chance someone *should* walk by; that way it would not look as if he were snooping. He could just make up any old story about borrowing a book or some such rot. Julian had a marvelous library of old books on Yorkshire.

Melrose quietly searched everything — every drawer, every shelf, every closet. It hadn't taken long, for the rooms were spartan, almost dreary with their moss-colored draperies and heavy Tudor furniture.

Melrose parted the draperies and looked out of the long windows which faced the sea to assure himself Crael hadn't decided to make an early and sudden return. It was a morning of weak sunlight and not so much fog, so that he could see for a little distance along the cliff walk. No sign of Julian Crael.

There were two rooms, a bedroom and a small study or library. He began with the bedroom. On a chest of drawers were the usual gentleman's accoutrements, including a Victorian fitted box, a dressing case holding silver-backed hairbrushes (which Melrose picked up and envied). There were keys, a bottle of lime water, a photograph of Lady Margaret. The drawers disclosed nothing of interest. In the closet hung few but very good, exquisitely tailored suits, a robe, a hacking jacket. He had seen Julian take one of the horses out once very early in the morning; yet he would not participate in the hunt itself.

Melrose returned to the library, where a handsome davenport sat in a recess in a wall of bookcases. He pulled out the writing-slope above, found nothing but writing accessories — no personal papers beyond a few bills from a tailor in London. Systematically, he went through each drawer and found precious little: stationery, pens, and in one drawer, some loose snapshots. These he examined. They were largely views of the manor house and the moors, taken, he thought, some time ago. He closed the drawers and began looking over the bookcases. They seemed in perfect order, nothing shelved behind them, no secret panels, hidden documents.

There was an arrangement of small, framed photographs along the shelves. They were snapshots, really, a dozen or more set up on two of the shelves. They had that sort of brown tint which bespeaks age. He recognized in several of them Julian in his younger days, recognized the elegant Lady Margaret (here on the arm of her husband), knew that the black-haired girl had to be Dillys March, since Melrose had seen the pictures the Colonel had brought out for the police.

There must have been a half-dozen of Dillys, more even, if he counted the ones in which she appeared with others. There was one of Dillys and Lady Margaret, taken when she was little more than a child — ten or eleven, perhaps, snapped in the garden. Another of her, Julian and a young man who must have been the brother, Rolfe. They were all up on horseback. Rolfe looked a man beside the other two, snapped at an awkward age. He was good-looking, but not a patch on Julian for sheer physical beauty, except for that golden hair, which was his mother's. Then there were two of Dillys and Julian, taken a bit later, both posed like sticks on the steps of Old House. Three more were of Dillys alone. In one she was again on horseback. In the other two she was leaning against a rail fence, looking coy, her head tilted, her eyes looking up from the shadows of bangs and lashes. She might have been in her late teens there, wearing the same light silk frock she wore on the steps of the house.

All told, seven pictures of Dillys March. More of her than of anyone else, and yet Julian Crael professed not to like her at all.

Melrose did not know what, now, brought unbidden to his mind an old trick of his mother's. When she had more photographs than frames, or when she had wanted to supplant an older, tireder picture with a fresher one, she had simply slipped out the cardboard backing, and put the new in front of the old. Starting with the photos of Dillys and Julian he pulled down the velvet backing and found nothing but the piece of cardboard. He repeated this process through four other pictures. On the fifth, the one of Dillys leaning against the fence, he found another snapshot; it was of Dillys in a park somewhere. Could it be Regent's Park? Hyde Park?

But this girl was no longer a girl; she was a woman. Dillys March? or was it Gemma Temple? Melrose had not seen the pictures of Gemma Temple, but if the likeness were as great as he had heard . . .

In the sixth frame he found another picture behind the first. Here she stood in front of a building, leaning against an iron railing. The building was indistinguishable from hundreds of brick buildings on city streets. He would have liked to go through all the other pictures, but he was afraid Julian might be returning; Melrose had been in the study a good half-hour as it was.

He opened the desk drawer, the one in which he had found the loose snapshots, took two of them and slid them in behind the pictures of Dillys. It was taking a chance, of course, but if Julian merely checked the frames to make sure there were two pictures, he might not bother to take the back ones out to examine. It was worth it, certainly. Jury would have to see these pictures.

Back in his own room, lying on his bed, he knew he had found what he wanted. Whether the woman was Dillys March or Gemma Temple was to him at this moment almost irrelevant. Whoever she was, she shouldn't be turning up in London. Or in a picture frame in Julian Crael's rooms.

20.

"Dillys March? 'Twas a long time ago ah knew her. What's she got to do with it?"

Tom Evelyn, huntsman for the Pitlochary hounds, had been in the process of carrying what looked like buckets of porridge out to the kennels when Jury approached him. "Did you see this Gemma Temple when she was in Rackmoor?" Evelyn shook his head. "There was a very strong resemblance between Gemma Temple and Dillys March."

His eyes widened and his eyes were very blue. He was nearly forty but he looked less than thirty. In another ten or fifteen years, Tom Evelyn would look much as he did now — straight, spare, dark, taller then he actually was because of the way he carried himself. And fifteen years before he had probably still looked much the same man, one who would appeal to any woman who liked men, and perhaps to a few who didn't.

"Yer not tellin' me this murdered woman was Dillys March, now, are you?"

"No. But we would like to know about Dillys March from anyone who knew her."

Evelyn rolled down his sleeves, slowly buttoned up a leather vest. "She was trouble, ah can tell you that, man."

"For whom?"

"Just about any man she'd a mind for."

"You?"

His blue eyes looked off into the distance, across the courtyard which surrounded the kennels. He was embarrassed, Jury thought, but showed it little. Jury wondered if the woodenness — the straight bearing, the carved features — came from his dealing with animals more than people. And undoubtedly liking them more than people, too. A slight flush had tinged his permanently sunburned face. "She would ha' been if ah'd let her. Ah been huntsman for this pack over ten years. Before that, ah was whip. Ah wasn't about to throw that away on the likes o' her."

His tone was not merely contemptuous; it was venomous. Evelyn was not the sort of man to show his feelings; if Dillys March could arouse them in such a way after fifteen years, she must have been trouble indeed. The man had a great deal of pride which Jury tried to tread by carefully. "You might have wanted to leave her alone but did *she* leave *you* alone?"

Evelyn hunkered down, stirred the porridge, thick enough to stand a spoon in. From the kennels fifty feet off hounds were setting up a terrible racket for their food. "She got me sacked, she did. For a while."

"What happened?"

"Once, only the once ah was stupid. Young, see. Well, Dillys comes up to the kennels —ah was second whip then. She was with the Colonel. She stayed after he left, and . . ." He shrugged, letting Jury fill in that part of the story. "She wanted to keep it up, but ah was scared. My God, the Colonel's ward! But she was nothin', nothin' like them. Ah don't care where she come from and ah don't care where she's gone to. Dillys March was trash."

"Where do you think she went? And didn't you think it very strange, her leaving that way?"

"Ah don't get paid, man, to think about things like that."

"What about Olive Manning's son, Leo? There was something going on there, I hear."

Evelyn's laugh was sharp, like a signal to hounds. "Of course. Any man, like ah said. Olive Manning could have killed her —" Evelyn threw Jury a swift glance. "You know what ah mean. It broke Olive's heart when Leo was sent to hospital."

"You don't really believe, though, that the girl could turn an otherwise sane man into a psychotic?"

Evelyn didn't answer. He reached down to pick up the buckets of white, glutinous stuff.

"I think it odd that she'd overlook the one right under her nose, the one who would surely be, from her point of view, the best catch."

"Ah don't understand. Rolfe Crael was interested in *women*, not little girls." Evelyn smiled and the smile was surprisingly warm. "But Ah'm sure *she* tried."

"I didn't mean Rolfe. I meant Julian."

"What makes you think she wasn't after him, too?"

"Nothing, really, except he certainly had a strong aversion to her."

Again, that sharp laugh. "That's daft. Julian was crazy about her. Anyone could see that."

21.

There was the barest whisper of a knock on Melrose's door. He stuffed the photos under his pillow and said, "Come in."

Wood presented his mummified self and said, "Begging your pardon, sir. But there's a call for you. And Colonel

Crael would like a word with you, sir, when you come down. He's in the Red Run Room. His snug, sir."

Melrose took note of the flicker of disapproval on Wood's face: a gentleman napping fully clothed at midday on the counterpane, and with his shoes on? His own butler, Ruthven, would have hidden that look. He thanked Wood as he swung his legs from the bed. "Have you a magnifying glass about somewhere, Wood? I need to do some close work."

"Colonel Crael often uses one for his butterfly collection. I'll find it for you."

"I'll be right down. And could you scare me up some tea and toast? Is it Inspector Jury calling, by any chance?"

"No, sir. Inspector Jury wanted me to tell you he's gone to London. It's Lady Ardry ringing up."

Oh, God! thought Melrose. And Jury gone to London. What was he to do with these pictures? "Sergeant Wiggins, did he go with Inspector Jury?"

"I can't say really. They left the house together, though. I'll just have Cook do your tea, sir." Before Wood made his straight-backed exit, he added reflectively. "Very busy man, Inspector Jury."

Agatha sounded, to his dismay, as if she were in the next room.

Which was where she said she would be within twenty-four hours. Dear Teddy had been invited, also, by Sir Titus. They would both motor along.

She had invited herself, of course. Melrose knew he could neither reason with her, insult her, nor threaten her. She was impervious to all treatment of that sort. He could, of course, bludgeon her to death, only she was in York and he was here. All he could do, then, was trick her.

"*How* very pleasant," he said to her, his eyes screwed shut in pain. "Only, just listen, Agatha. If you could simply stay there for another couple of days, I'll be driving through."

He lowered his voice. "There's something very important Jury wants you to do *in York*; he especially asked for your help." Jury would kill him.

Thrilled silence. It fairly trilled across the telephone wires. She reminded him that she was always willing to help the police. Had he forgotten how helpful she had been in Northants?

Melrose finally replaced the telephone receiver with no idea at all of what he was going to have her do in York. He would think of something.

But the phone at least gave him a small inspiration. As Wood whispered like a black swan across his line of vision, Melrose asked him if there were a London directory about. Wood said he would find one and bring it along with the magnifying glass.

"I've just had a very nice chat with your aunt," said Sir Titus Crael, slapping shut his Whyte-Melville book. "And here's your tea. Sleeping late, eh?"

With a smile pasted on his face, Melrose smoothly accepted the cup. "It was most awfully kind of you to invite her here, Colonel Crael. Really terribly decent."

"I'm just sorry you didn't mention she was so near, Melrose. She's just in York. That's only a few hours away."

Don't I know it? thought Melrose. He polished his gold-rimmed spectacles, stuffed his handkerchief back in his pocket, and surveyed the ruins of Rackmoor. One simply didn't have Agatha coming to a village so prized, so valuable it had had a preservation order slapped on it. It would be rather like planting a cow on the steps of Castle Howard. His eye traveled the room, as his mind slogged through years of Agatha and he wondered why she had to be his last remaining relative. "Do you think that this is the best time, though, Colonel, for a visit?"

Sir Titus seemed surprised. "But she said she was such a

good friend of Inspector Jury. Said they'd actually worked together on a case in your own village in Northants. You didn't mention that, Melrose."

Melrose laughed weakly. "I felt you had enough on your platter with all of this business. . . ." His voice trailed off as his eye flitted here and there, wanting inspiration. He could tell Colonel Crael she'd suddenly caught cold or died or something. Melrose's eye fell on a series of hunting prints, mates, it appeared, of the ones in the Old Fox Deceiv'd.

"You did tell her about the hunt, Sir Titus?"

"Hmm? The hunt? Well, no, I didn't. Why?"

Melrose clapped his hand to his forehead. "Oh, dear. Well, that *is* too bad. Agatha has a violent allergy to horses."

Sir Titus looked at Melrose with his mouth open. Melrose might as well have said his aunt had some social disease.

"Yes. If she so much as comes within breathing distance of horses, she has an attack." He shrugged. "When I tell her there's to be a hunt in three days' time, I'm afraid she'll change her mind. These allergies are tricky things."

He had seen Agatha up on Bouncer once. Where Bouncer began and Agatha left off was impossible to tell from the rear. Bouncer had very soon rid himself of her.

As all the world should do. Melrose sighed and drank his sherry.

Back in his room Melrose ran the magnifying glass over the second picture, the one taken in front of the railing of a building.

At first he thought the whitish blob behind the woman was her own white dress reflected in the window. But the magnifying glass showed it up as a white-jacketed figure. A waiter, possibly. On the glass behind her, curving down below her right shoulder were the letters *A C E*. A word in itself — or part of a word? He ran the glass over the amorphous shapes suspended inside the window. Lanterns. Quite possibly those paper lanterns often serving as the tawdriest sort of decor in Oriental restaurants. That would explain the white jackets. The building, what he could see of it, had the warehouse look of such restaurants. *A C E* — it could be anything. Melrose grabbed up the London directory, turned to the restaurant listings in the Yellow Pages and was immediately discouraged. There must have been a hundred or more Chinese or otherwise Oriental restaurants. Then, running down the list, his eye fell upon one common denominator for some of them. The word *Palace*. He looked again at the picture. That could, possibly, account for the *A C E.*

He started in again on the list of restaurants, noting down every one which ended with the word *Palace*, beginning with China Palace. When he was finished, he'd accumulated nearly twenty of them, but that was better than a hundred, certainly.

Melrose slapped the directory shut and debated the problem. He supposed, since Jury and Wiggins weren't here, he should hand the pictures over to Harkins. But Harkins, the last he had heard, was in Leeds with the Chief Constable.

The hell with it: he could kill three birds with one stone by going to London himself — leave the evidence off at New Scotland Yard, help Jury out by finding the whatever-Palace Restaurant, and stop off in York and do something very cunning to get Agatha off his back. (Not very cunning, considering Agatha.) He checked his watch: not yet one. He could be in York for a late lunch or early tea by two, and in London by nine-thirty or ten at the latest. The way he drove.

He was extremely pleased with himself. Three birds with one stone.

Or two birds and one turkey.

22.

The Sherry Club was a sedate, cream-washed, flat-fronted building near the Shambles and in the shadow of York Minster. It had made an earnest endeavor to dissociate itself from anything commercial; its only identification was a small, brass plaque to the right of the oak doors. It had retained the air and function of a men's club, but did allow ladies in its dining room, as long (one felt) as they were discreet about their sex, and moved silently.

It was no place to meet Agatha.

Melrose was simply irritated to death at having to waste a precious hour or two having tea with his aunt, but he knew she was more malleable once stuffed with food. And he supposed this meeting was a small enough price to pay to keep her out of Rackmoor. Not to mention the Teddy-creature.

He had requested a table near one of the long windows facing the street. Not that he was eager for that first glimpse of his aunt, but in spite of his instructions she was liable to march on by, since the Sherry did so little to make its presence known. Here he could rap on the window if he had to.

Deliberately, he had arrived early, so that he could look over the patrons before she got here. There were few people in the room at this late-lunch hour. At a rear table were a man and two women; they wouldn't do. The only others were a tiny, birdlike gentleman who was eating muffins, and another who seemed a more likely prospect: black-suited, bowler-hatted, umbrellaed like a Guards officer. His face was stiff and hawklike. The bowler hat lay on the table; the tightly furled umbrella (surely never unwound) was hitched over a chair. He was reading a newspaper.

Melrose motioned the waiter over. "That gentleman,

there, looks very familiar to me; I believe we were at Harrow together many years ago. The Honorable John Carruthers-White, isn't it?"

The waiter followed the direction of Melrose's glance. "Oh, no, sir. That's Mr. Todd, sir. He comes in regular for his lunch, as it's so near the Minster."

"I'll be dashed!" said Melrose, looking dumbfounded. "He's the very image of Carruthers-White. The Minster? And what does Mr. Todd do at the Minster?"

"He's in charge of the tours, sir." The waiter flicked his white napkin across the table at some nonexistent crumbs and said, "Very popular is the Minster."

York Minster might have been the latest appearance of a new rock group. "Yes, I understand it is. And does Mr. Todd conduct these tours in the winter months? Now?"

The waiter did not seem at all curious as to why Mr. Todd, who was not Carruthers-White, was still arousing Melrose's interest. "Oh, yes. There's one or two tours this afternoon. Round about three o'clock, I think."

He might be leaving soon, then. Drat Agatha; she was late. "Bring tea for two, would you, please?"

The waiter whisked off. It was only a few minutes before he was back with the tea, setting out pot and cups and cakes. Melrose saw his aunt. She was standing gawking up at the Sherry Club, managing, as usual, to look out of place, like an émigré from another solar system. The hat she was wearing helped the illusion along: it was a violent combination of purple and blue, topped with a long, green feather. She disappeared.

She reappeared in the dining room, led to his table by the waiter. Melrose glanced over at Todd to make sure he was not preparing to leave now that Agatha had just arrived. No, he seemed quite settled in behind his paper and with his pot of coffee.

"Well, Melrose, I see you've started without me." She

plucked back the lid of the silver pot, peered in, and then examined the selection of sandwiches and cakes. She poked her finger at each tier of the plate, mouthing the contents *sotto voce.* "Hmph. No fairy cakes."

"The better places don't do fairy cakes, Agatha. You don't get them in Fortnum's, now, do you? You'll have to make do with the pastries."

She removed from herself a tatty fox fur piece and settled in to eat. "Did you drag me here from Teddy's just to talk about cakes, Melrose? Have you been drinking again?"

No, but he wished he'd fortified himself with several large brandies before trying to talk to her. It was like swimming upstream into shoals of minnows. She drank off her first cup of tea, polished off a fish-paste sandwich, and then settled down to the real business of eating.

Melrose buttered a fruit scone. He did not like scones plugged up with bits of fruit, really. "I — we — have something we want you to do. But you must keep very mum about it."

"What is it? And how is Jury? And why isn't he here? Pity they're always sending him to these out-of-the-way places. Isn't he good enough to do the job in London?"

"You know perfectly well he's good enough. He's one of the Murder Squad. He apologizes for the murder's not being done somewhere more fashionable, like Belgravia or Mayfair. Anyway, I thought you admired Jury so much."

"Oh, *admire.* That's a bit strong. He's a good enough chap, I expect." She topped a scone with clotted cream.

It was clear she was smarting under Jury's absence from this scene. "Agatha, there's a gentleman sitting over there behind you to the left — No! Don't turn round or you'll attract his attention."

Elaborately, she did not turn. Having finished her scone, she started nibbling on a rock cake, decided she didn't want it, and, like a bad-mannered child, put it back and took a fruit tart. "What about him?"

"I believe he's following me. I can't be certain, of course, but — No! Don't look! Jury thinks he must be an *agent provocateur.*"

Agatha's curiosity, he knew, would have killed off the entire cat population of York. Melrose moved his silver about and went on. "There's something that I — ah, Jury, that is — would like you and Mrs. Harries-Stubbs to do for us —"

"Teddy? What is it, then?"

"Whilst I was staying there I was, I hate to admit it, very careless . . ." She smiled happily at this hoped-for fall from grace. "A claim check was lost. It was in my wallet, and I can't think how it could have fallen out. But I know it was lost in the house somewhere, for I missed it right after I left."

"What's this claim check for?"

Melrose debated several possible answers, finally settling on "The Lost Luggage at Victoria." Weren't people always leaving things in the Lost Luggage?

"And what's this Todd person to do with it?"

"Mr. Todd is also interested in the claim check." Melrose lit a cigarette casually as if he were not, for all the world, being pursued by secret agents.

Her eyes bulged. "Is he dangerous?"

"I shouldn't think so; after all he doesn't know it's in Teddy's house, does he?" Melrose smiled brightly. That should ensure they hang about the house searching before Mr. Todd descended upon them. "You and Teddy must turn that house upside down. It's so small it could easily go unnoticed."

"What if the servants have swept it up?"

Melrose studied the tip of his cigarette. "Search the dustbins, then."

As she seemed to balk at this, he put his hand over hers. It was a gesture so uncharacteristic of him she looked at it as if a fish might have landed on the table. "Agatha, this is deuced important. You won't let me — us — down, now will you?"

Brushing some crumbs from her scone onto Melrose's sleeve, she said, "Well, I expect if it's for old times' sake . . ." Apparently it didn't occur to her that if Jury needed a search done he had the entire Yorkshire constabulary at his disposal. "When will I see him? To report?"

Blackmail, probably. Perhaps he could induce Jury to stop off on the way back from London. Surely, he would be just as eager to keep Agatha out of Rackmoor as Melrose was himself. Hell, no. He wouldn't be bothered. Jury would manage to ingratiate himself and ignore her simultaneously and she'd never be the wiser. Where did he get his style, anyway? Glumly, Melrose thought once again of Percy Blythe. "Jury'll be coming back with me. Tomorrow, the next day, the day after, maybe." Or never. It was doubtful that Agatha would visit the Minster, but he'd better touch that base too. "Mr. Todd works at the Minster, incidentally. That's his cover. Tour guide."

"Really? But what's this Todd person to do with the Craels, anyway?"

Melrose could have stopped here the rest of the afternoon constructing a whole history of Todd and the Craels, but he wanted to get to London. In any event, he saw that Mr. Todd was gathering up his newspaper and umbrella. If Melrose wanted to be followed, he'd better be quick off the mark. In a low voice he said to Agatha, busy with a brandy snap, "If we leave now, we might just ditch him, Agatha."

Grumpily, she answered. "Well, I've not finished my tea, but if we must . . ."

He hooked his hand beneath her arm and pulled her up.

At the bottom of the steps to the Sherry Club, Melrose delayed a little by dropping his car keys. He observed the door opening behind them and Mr. Todd appeared. "Not quick enough, I guess," he whispered. "Pretend you don't notice him. He'll have to walk on, you know; he can't stop here staring at the sky, can he?"

And, just as Melrose predicted, Mr. Todd started off up the street at a jaunty pace.

"Clever, isn't he?" said Agatha. "Never know he was following you at all." Now it was her own hand placed comfortingly on her nephew's arm. "Remember this, Melrose: if anything should happen to you, Ardry End is in safe hands."

Looking down now at the pudgy hand clamped on his arm, Melrose took that as gospel truth. She was wearing two of his mother's rings.

"That's decent of you, dear Aunt." He tipped his hat.

And the three of them — Melrose, Agatha and Mr. Todd — stepped off in their different directions.

· V ·

Limehouse Blues

1.

Jury stopped off at his flat to pick up his mail, which consisted of bills, circulars, and a letter from his cousin in the Potteries. She was — she never stopped reminding him — more like a sister to him than a cousin. But the reminder always seemed to be aimed not at her sisterly obligations, but at his brotherly ones.

He ripped open the envelope and read the letter as he walked up the two flights of stairs to his flat. As usual, she was going crazy with Alec (her alcoholic husband), her kids, too little money, too much work. Jury looked at the postmark. The letter had lain weeping in his mailbox for three days.

Had he been gone only three days? Tiredly, he stretched. It felt more like he'd been walking the moors for three weeks. He switched on his desk lamp, surveyed the mess — the sitting room awash in books in various stages of being read, the old coffee cups — and took up the telephone and positioned it in his lap. He rested his head on the back of the single easy chair and thought about his cousin. Granted, the husband was not much good. But she had chosen him, hadn't she? Don't we choose our lives, at least somewhat? Why then must the people we live with always be taking us by surprise, things we stumble over like furniture in the dark — *who put* you *there?*

Reluctantly, he picked up the telephone, knowing it would be a good quarter-hour of counting over her troubles. It turned out to be more like a half-hour, with all the crying. At the end of it all, Jury told her to take a vacation, to hire a housekeeper and go off for a week, to Blackpool or somewhere, and that he'd send her the money to do it. When she hung up she seemed almost happy. He knew he was really doing it more for her parents than for her. They had been so decent to him after the war, taking him out of that home to live with them. They were dead now. And he was thinking, too, of her kids. If she was at the raw-nerve stage, they would have to pay for it. Their faces rose in his mind like a row of polished coins. And that made him think of Bertie Makepiece. He was certain Bertie's mother was in London. Jury took the envelope Adrian had given him out of his pocket and studied that return address: *R. V. H., S.W. 1.* He dismissed the initials as being those of the correspondent: the return address was insufficient for that. A business establishment, probably. He tapped the envelope against his thumb and thought for a while. Could the letter *H* possibly stand for "Hotel"? It would be easy enough to check it out down at the Yard.

As he was writing a short note to his cousin, there was a light tapping on the door, apology sounding in the very knuckles.

"Oh, Inspector Jury." It was Mrs. Wasserman. She was still wearing her black coat and hat and clutching her purse tightly to her breast. She always wore black. Mrs. Wasserman was in perpetual mourning. "Forgive me, I bet you just got in, but you know what happened?"

"Come on in, Mrs. Wasserman."

Gingerly, she stepped inside, checking the corners for intruders. "I'm just on my way out to visit my friend, Mrs. Eton, you know the one. Anyway, today, earlier, I was followed all the way from Camden Passage. There was this man —"

The streets, for Mrs. Wasserman, were full of dangers. They leapt at her like slavering dogs behind ironwork fences. Jury wondered if the streets made her think of that limbo of ground which lay between the train she was once herded from and the camp. The fear which had begun there had rooted firmly in her mind and could not be confined to its proper time and place.

"What'd he look like?" asked Jury. Knowing it would be useless to allay her fears by denial that she had been followed, he took out his small notebook, clicked his ballpoint pen into place.

Immediately, she looked relieved. She only wanted to be taken seriously. "Short —" Her hand sprang out to measure off air. "Kind of skinny and a face like a skeleton, narrow eyes — mean, you know. He had on a brown hat and coat."

Watching her watching him, Jury took it all down. "He shouldn't be hard to find; we keep tabs on all the dips that work the Passage." Mrs. Wasserman always loved to go there and look through the stalls for bargains which she never found. "Did you buy anything? Show any money?"

"Only this —" she clicked open her bag and drew out a small, tissue-wrapped ring. Predictably, it was a mourning ring, the tiny braid of hair wound inside. It was rather pretty, though. "I paid for it with a ten-pound note."

"Well, you know these pickpockets and purse-snatchers. They see folding money and think they've hit on El Dorado." Jury pocketed his notebook. "Don't worry, we'll get him. Ever seen him before?" Vigorously, she shook her head. "Camden Passage attracts lots of nickel-and-dime crooks. Fairly harmless, they are."

"It's not safe to go in the streets any more, Mr. Jury." Her small, ringed fingers clutched her purse to her. "Nothing's safe." Her eyes were like black worry-beads.

The fear which must have begun when she was young and pretty had metasticized and spread to everything, Jury thought. She would always be a prisoner.

"Never mind, Mrs. Wasserman. I'll tell you, though. If I were you I'd get myself one of those money-belts. So you won't need to carry a purse with you when you go there. They make them so you can put them inside your skirt band. It's simple. Or you could get one on a garter and wear it round your leg. Of course, then when you reached for your money you might have other problems besides purse-snatchers." He winked.

She whooped with laughter. "*My* legs, Inspector? Varicose veins, I've got. I've been thinking of having them tied, even. My legs I'm not worrying about anyone wanting a peek at!"

Jury smiled. "Did you take along that whistle I gave you? Did you carry it with you?"

She blushed and looked down. "I admit I forgot it. So good you were to give it to me, too."

"Oh, well, not to worry. Take it next time. I have to go out, too. Are you going to the Angel?"

"Yes. Yes, I am. In Chalk Farm Mrs. Eton lives."

Josie Thwaite lived in Kentish Town. "Well, you're in luck, Mrs. Wasserman. I'm going to Kentish Town, and that's only a tube stop away. So you get a police escort."

"Oh, Mr. Jury, that would be indeed wonderful." Her grip on the black purse relaxed.

2.

The eyes which peered at him through the chainlocked door were a soft, vulnerable brown. Jury assumed they belonged to Josie Thwaite.

"Miss Thwaite? I'm Inspector Jury of —"

Her indrawn breath cut him off. "Have you come about the L-plates, then?"

"No. I wanted to ask you a few questions about your friend, Gemma Temple."

"Oh, sorry." The door shut slightly as she drew back the chain. Then she opened it wide, scooping black hair away from her shoulder. The white jumper she wore emphasized the thin shoulders. She was thin all over, Jury saw, when she stepped back and motioned him in. Her walk was a little stoop-shouldered. Everything about her was apologetic

— her posture, her look, her voice. The air stirred with sadness.

But not, apparently, about her roommate. There she was quite matter-of-fact. "See, Gemma borrowed my car. It's because she'd just gotten her L-plates and she wanted to go on this holiday, only she wouldn't say where, except that she was afraid of getting stopped, and her only with the L-plates." Realizing that she was keeping Jury standing, she said, "Oh, sorry," and waved him to a squarish lump of lounge chair. The cover prickled his skin. "So it was my car they found at this place —"

"Rackmoor. In Yorkshire."

"Yes, that's right. There was a policeman from Yorkshire, he was here only two days ago. You're not the first."

Jury smiled. It sounded like a confession to the loss of virginity. He took the picture Harkins had given him from his pocket. "Is this Gemma Temple?"

"Yes, it does look like her. Sun's in her face, though. But, yes, that's Gemma."

Jury took back the snapshot. "You said that you didn't know much about her past, only that she'd mentioned a family named Rainey."

"That's right. I think she went to see them a couple of times whilst she was living with me."

"How did you find Gemma?"

"Through an advert. I needed someone to split the cost of the flat." She looked about her wanly. "Though it's not all that big, just this room and a bedroom, but it's better," she assured him, "than a bed-sit, you've got to admit."

"Much better than mine. Cigarette?" He handed over his packet.

It was obvious she didn't smoke much, the way she looked at the packet as if it were some sort of exotic bird. Finally, she pinched one out carefully and just as carefully leaned forward, holding her hair back, out of the way of Jury's match. Then she leaned back and blew tentative puffs into the air, holding the cigarette between thumb and forefinger. She relaxed then, as if she'd just gone down on opium, crossed her legs, and swung her foot in its furry slipper. The impression of a little girl playing around with her mother's makeup and fags was overpowering.

"So she answered your ad . . ."

"Um."

"Tell me, did you like Gemma? Did you get along okay?"

She looked at him, looked away. "Well, we didn't have any real set-to's, if that's what you mean. But I didn't like her all that much. And she was, you know, vague about herself. I should have got references, shouldn't I?" She looked at Jury, wide-eyed and apologetic, as if he might castigate her for being stupid.

"Hindsight is always wonderful, Josie. I've solved a hundred cases with it. Do you think Gemma Temple *had* any references to give? Or was she pretty much a floater?"

She leaned forward and lowered her voice a little, as if her mum might find her out here behind the barn, smoking and telling dirty secrets. "Floater's too nice, I'd say. She brought men here. And not the same one twice, either, far as I know. I'd lie in bed in there and hear them. . . ." Josie leaned back with a look on her face not of outrage at this invasion of her home, but of perplexity, as if wondering what they'd been doing. She went on: "Thing is, Gemma said she was an actress. I think once she might have got this little bitty part in one of those theatres that's just a loft and they put down the chairs before each performance. Not much, know what I mean? Anyway. Gemma didn't really *work*. But she got money from time to time. . . ."

"You're saying she worked the streets, that it?"

Josie nodded, went back to concentrating on the tip of her cigarette, as if trying to get the hang of it.

"She never said anything at all about her past?"

She shook her head.

"Why did you give her the loan of your car, if you didn't trust her?"

She got defensive. "Well, hers was ever so much better, wasn't it? And she wrote me out something like a receipt. Said if anything happened to mine, I was to have hers. It's the yellow one out there now, but I expect they'll take it away." Her tone said she was sadder to see the car go than to see Gemma go.

"How'd she get the money for the car in the first place?"

Josie's smile was lopsided. "You tell me, then we'll both know. From one of those men, I don't wonder."

"Did you ever actually meet any of them?"

"Only on the stairs, like, when I was going to work. Once, in here. In the middle of the day, mind you." It was always more sinful in the middle of the day. "Always a different one. No, I was just on my way to asking her to find another place."

"But you never knew their names? No one I could ask about her?"

Genuinely sad, she regarded Jury. "Gee, I'm sorry. I never got one of their names."

"That's not your fault, is it?" Jury got up. "Where do you work?"

"In the launderette just down the street." She stood with her face against the doorframe, looking up at him, almost as if she were sorry to see him go. Wrapping her sweatered arms around her she said, "Well, good-bye. You don't think they'll do anything to me about the car, do you? I mean, letting her drive it and all?"

He handed her his card. "No one's going to do anything to you, Josie. Just give me a call if anyone comes round. But I doubt anyone will. You didn't commit any crime, after all."

Her enormous relief was palpable. She smiled and her small, white teeth nearly glittered in the dark. It gave him an odd sense of exhilaration, knowing she had this one lovely feature, something to get by on. "Good night, then, Josie."

Dead end, he thought, outside the block of flats. He looked up and down the street and saw the Three Tuns on the corner, debated whether to have a beer or to go along to the Chalk Farm stop and wait for Mrs. Wasserman, whom he had promised to pick up. It was 10:15, too early for that. A drink might help him sleep. He flicked his cigarette into the gutter and that was when he saw the small car, a sickly yellow in the ghostly glow of the street lamp.

You horse's ass, he said to himself, staring at the L-plate. All that time talking about the plates, and he hadn't even tumbled to it.

3.

Melrose Plant had no idea how he was going to eat his way through six more Chinese restaurants. The ones in Soho and Kensington had earned him heartburn for his labors and he had been wrong in thinking that buying a meal would buy him information. Uncomprehending looks from the waiters (who also pretended not to understand English) had been his reward when he had produced the picture of Gemma Temple. It was after eleven, but he couldn't sleep until he'd made one final try. So he unbent himself from the tube at the Aldgate East stop and headed for Limehouse.

He found the Sun Palace restaurant on a grim side street where the sun probably never shone. It was not very large, outfitted with a plate-glass window and the iron railing against which Gemma Temple had been posing. Flaking gold paint spelled out a curve of letters: SUN PALACE.

It was closed.

Sighing, Melrose looked around, saw no one, started up the street in hopes he might find someone who knew the restaurant.

" 'Allo, love," she said, but without much enthusiasm. "Slumming?"

The young lady was attractive enough — exactly how young was difficult to determine in the pool of light cast by the street lamp, which turned her lipstick black and gave her whole face a leaden look. She was sitting on the steps leading up to a scarred door of a building so narrow there was room only for the fanlighted door and a window no wider than a wound. The building was cramped between a lock-up shop and another, similar house to its right, which looked as if it might have been this house's other half some years back. Together they would have made one ordinary brownstone. The two houses were mirror-images of one another and he half-expected to see the girl's duplicate sitting on the steps next door.

Melrose stopped and leaned against the low, peeling stone post against which she rested her back, her one leg bent at the knee on the same step, the other on the step below, showing off jeans tight as a wet suit, culminating in bare ankles and stiletto heels. Topping this, quite informally, was a cardigan with sleeves pushed up and neckline down. This was accomplished by the top four buttons having been undone and the ends of the sweater tucked in to make a low V. Her clothes were so pasted to her body she could have swum the channel merely by kicking off the shoes and adding a swimming cap. The cap would have been a pity, though, for it would have hidden a mop of Shirley Temple curls. They were silky, brown, natural, her own. He could tell that. They were like something left around from childhood, something she hadn't been able to tame or to burn out of her from the past. It was strange. The curls seemed to reduce the rest of her, the whole act, the whole sexual aura, to a shambles, while the little girl rose, like a phoenix, out of the ashes of Limehouse.

"Me name's Betsy," she said, rising, dusting her bottom, turning up the steps. He stood there for a while as she swayed up the steps; seeing he was not following, she waved her arm impatiently. "C'mon, then, mate."

Melrose followed her.

Beyond the door was a long, blank hallway, fitted out with old linoleum, overblown roses on a gray background. A bulb covered with a fly-blown shade hung from the ceiling on a long cord. He wondered if the doors going off to the left and right held other Betsys. One door opened and a tangled mop of red hair hung out, took in the action, and pulled itself back in.

Betsy led him into the first room on the left, the one with the high, narrow window. She had a view of a warehouse. The room was monopolized, as might be expected, by an enormous bed, the grandeur of which took Melrose's breath away. It was a magnificent period piece, Tudor or Renaissance, a four-poster with marquetry inlays. Besides the bed there were a dressing table, triple-mirrored, covered in flaking pale green paint, a chest of dubious heritage, and a single painted wooden chair. Up and down the dingy wallpaper, little knotted bouquets crept like faded reminders of flowergirls.

With one hand she shut the door, with the other she automatically reached toward him — to remove something, no doubt. "Whyn't you take off your glasses? Smashing eyes you've got. Green as a bottle of Abbot's."

He doubted that was part of the routine; he imagined compliments were hardly necessary. She smiled a little and further contributed to the childish image: her teeth were small and one was missing.

When he brushed her hand away (knowing the removal

of the glasses would only be a preliminary to the removal of other things), she shrugged and turned away. "Suit yourself." She flopped on the bed, began tugging at the jeans. She was scowling. Not at him, but at the jeans painted to her body. Clearly, she had to lie down in order to get them off at all. " 'Ere, 'elp me off wi' these bleedin' pants, love." She had got them down far enough that he could see the flowered bikini underneath.

"Do you think we could talk, Betsy?"

"Talk?" She stopped tugging and looked at him as if the idea were new and rather novel. " 'Bout what?" She continued wiggling impatiently. She needed help with the jeans, like John Wayne getting his boots off. Melrose wondered how she ever managed it by herself and then supposed she never had to.

"I'm looking for somebody."

Indifferently, she shrugged, gave up on the pants and started on the sweater buttons. "Ain't we all?"

Her metaphorical interpretation of his literal statement startled him utterly. He took out his cigarette case, and offered it. "Cigarette?"

She shook her curls, bent over the buttons of the cardigan, which she was undoing with childish concentration, her small brows knotted. Short of violence, it was apparently impossible to stop Betsy once she got going. But he was more interested in information than he was in Betsy. He had found in his life only a few fascinating women — intelligent, intriguing. The others were, at best, endearing — like Betsy, nearly done now with her buttons, the Shirley Temple curls bobbing, as she began to struggle out of the sweater, which was hard for her because she was straitjacketed by the jeans. Underneath the sweater was a wispy bra, flowered like the panties. One of the straps was attached to the cup with a tiny safety pin. It made him feel desolate, he did not know why.

When her hands reached behind her back to unhook the bra, he said, "Hold it, Betsy!"

Her gamin face looked up at him. "You queer, or what? Just like to watch? You some kind of vayer?"

He assumed she meant *voyeur*. "Probably." Melrose extracted both the snapshot he had taken from Julian Crael's room and a ten-pound note from his billfold. Both of these he passed across to her. "All I want, truly, is a bit of information."

She looked from him to the money. She smiled, showing the broken tooth. "My, ain't we the nob. Here now, how come you dress so posh?" Then as she was stuffing the bill into her bra, her eyes narrowed. "Crickey. You police?" She struggled wildly with her jeans, trying to drag them back up.

"No. Look at the picture, there. Do you ever remember seeing her going into or coming out of the Sun Palace down the street?"

She shook her curls, peered more closely at the snapshot. "Fancy frock, ihn't? Looks pricey."

"The clothes are expensive, but the lady is not."

"She in the trade?"

Melrose rested his elbow on his knee, smoking. "It wouldn't surprise me."

Absently, Betsy rolled a curl round her finger, making even more of a corkscrew of it. "Looks a bit la-de-da, if you ask me."

"That's probably just the clothes, Betsy."

Her eyes came up to meet his. "That's nice, the way you say my name."

"How many ways are there to say it?"

She shrugged. "Most of 'em never say it atall." She lay back, the sweater still off, unconscious of the bra straps slipping off and spreading her breasts. Losing interest in the picture, she looked all ready to tell him about her hard life.

He forestalled that: "Perhaps someone else here — I presume there *are* others?"

"Ain't you a caution?" she said without smiling, and hooking the strap back up, and swinging the legs, repacked in the jeans, off the bed. "Want I should ask?"

"I'd certainly appreciate it. Show the picture round. Someone might recognize her."

Betsy yawned. He added, "For whoever can find out about her, who she is and where she lived — there's fifty pounds in it."

That got her on her feet like a shot. "Fifty quid? Gawd. Be back in a tic." Coyly she flounced her hip. "Don't you go way now."

But he hardly had time to go away. In five minutes there was gabbling at the door. Three others stood there, all taller than Betsy: the redhead, an African with long purple earrings, and a very fat one who wouldn't see forty again. All wore kimono-type wrappers, as if they'd just finished with the chorus line. And all started talking at once. But it was the fat one who managed to take over.

"I seen her," she said, her breath heaving as she sat down on the bed, one fat thigh drawn up. Melrose saw a stocking rolled and held below the knee with a garter. "I can't say's I know her, but I seen her."

"Where?"

The fat woman drew a strand of bleached hair through her berry lips and chewed, her expression gravely concerned. "I been thinkin'."

That, thought Melrose, must be a job in itself. She snapped her pudgy fingers. "It was at the Sun —" and she clapped her hand over her mouth. Then she simpered. "Do I get the fifty quid if I can tell you who *does* know her?"

"Twenty-five," said Melrose. "The person who can tell me about her gets the other twenty-five. That's fair."

Not to the black girl and the redhead. Somehow they

seemed to feel mere association with the fat one should gain them some reward. He gave them each a five-pound note and they brightened. The other, the fat one, took her twenty-five and stuffed it in the rolled stocking. "It's Jane Yang knows her. She works at the restaurant. That's where I seen this one. Waitressing in the Sun Palace. She mighta been on the block too, I don't know. But Jane Yang can tell you."

Melrose got up. "Thanks very much. Who can I say told me about Miss Yang?"

"Just say Fat Bertha. She'll know."

"Fat Bertha. All right, thanks." The girls were all lounging about the door. To Betsy he said, "Is that your bed?" He picked up his silver-knobbed walking stick, adjusted his coat.

She looked puzzled. "Well I was just all over it, wasn't I? Yes, it's mine."

"I mean, do you own it?"

"No. The landlady does."

Melrose could imagine what the landlady did for a living. "Think she'd sell it?"

"Sure, she'd sell her own gran if she had one."

"What do you think she'd ask for it?"

"Why, you want it? Fifty, sixty quid she offered it me for."

"No, I don't want it. But if you can raise the fifty, buy it, Betsy." He took out a card and wrote a name on the back and handed it to her. "Then ring up this gentleman and ask him to come and value it. I don't know, but I'd say you could get a thousand, easy."

Her large eyes grew larger. "You kiddin' me?" He shook his head. "Gawd." As he ran the gamut at the door, she threw her arms around him and kissed him. The others giggled.

4.

The ringing of the telephone overlapped in Jury's dream with the mournful wail of the Whitby Bull and when his eyes finally came unglued and he looked toward the window, he wondered why it wasn't blanketed with fog. He groped for the telephone beside his bed.

"London is lucky." Chief Superintendent Racer's voice slid down the wire. "You're back. The question is, *why* are you back and why aren't you down here, giving me a report? If it weren't for Sergeant Wiggins, who, along with the sense to blow his nose, also has the sense to report in, I wouldn't know where the hell you were, Jury."

Jury's bedside alarm said 7:50. Racer in the office that early? Jury picked the clock up and shook it. "I've got to go to Lewisham, sir —"

"You can bloody well go to Lewisham on your way to hell, Jury, there'll be plenty of time for a stop-off. I want to see you within the hour. Get your socks on." The phone went dead.

5.

Fiona Clingmore was a pale blonde who favored black. Today, it was a tight black jumper tucked into a tight black skirt. She served as Racer's secretary and general dogsbody; Jury hoped she wasn't serving as anything else.

Fiona belonged to the '40s. She was like a character from a dated play who had stumbled onto a modern stage. Whenever he looked at her — at the outmoded hairdo, the mouth re-formed with red lipstick, the pillbox hats she liked — Jury was swamped by feelings of nostalgia which he could not fully explain. A few times he had taken Fiona out for a meal and wondered if it were not in the faint hope that some sense of the past would rub off on him. Although she pretended, whenever he mentioned the war, to have no living memory of it, he suspected that she was older than he. Once when she had taken out her wallet, he had seen stuck amongst the credit cards and other pictures, an old snapshot of a good-looking young man in R.A.F. uniform. He asked her if this was the "Joe" she kept referring to and she had blushed and said the picture was of a friend of her mum's. Much too old he would have been for Fiona.

Jury wondered if Fiona weren't really living in two worlds, after all. That if these clothes she now wore, instead of being the latest new-old thing from a Carnaby Street boutique, weren't instead the *real* thing: costumes dragged from old trunks that others would have packed in years ago.

"How's the job, Fiona?" Jury asked, lighting her cigarette.

"I've been chased round desks by better men than that one, haven't I?"

"I'm sure you have." Jury took the envelope from his pocket and handed it to her, saying, "Find out what those initials mean, will you, love. I think it might be a hotel in S.W. 1. If it is, it should be easy."

"Anything for you, dearie," said Fiona, handing him a cream-colored envelope.

"What's this?"

Fiona, now employed with the elaborate job of filing her nails, shrugged. "Well, I don't know, do I, love? One of the PC's on duty downstairs brought it up. Said a gentleman brought it in late last night, some nob in a swell car who thinks it's public parking outside the door, and nearly got himself nicked. Told him to push off. . . ."

Jury had torn open the envelope, pulled out the single sheet of notepaper, and retrieved a snapshot which had fallen to the floor. He paid no attention to Fiona's chatter as he read:

Dear Inspector Jury,
Hope the enclosed will interest you — I found it in Julian
Crael's room. I also hope you don't mind my keeping the
other for purposes of identification. You and Wiggins had
apparently departed for London before I could catch you,
but that gave me a chance to stop in York and see Agatha:
you will be happy to know she's working for you. Makes
an excellent Mole. I will be at the Connaught and thought
we could meet later and return to Rackmoor together. I've
a very fast car.

PLANT

He studied the snapshot. It certainly looked like a picture of Gemma Temple — or Dillys March? — but it was
a very recent picture, not something torn from a photo
album of years ago. He assumed Plant had asked himself
the same question: What was it doing in Crael's room?

"Sounds a right muddle," said Chief Superintendent
Racer, after Jury had filled him in on the Rackmoor case.
The comment was not intended as an extension of sympathy, but rather implied the muddle was Jury's fault. "So
why the hell aren't you up in this godforsaken village sorting it out? Why are you down here flatfooting it all over
London?"

"I told you. I need to make some inquiries —"

Racer looked around him, arms extended, mock-aghast.
"Funny. I could have *sworn* we had a whole police force
somewhere around here, all sorts of people who can make
inquiries." The expression changed, the brow settling in its
usual hard lines. "If somebody had to come down here, why
didn't you send Wiggins?"

Jury searched for a reason. "I needed him there. There
was something he could do better than I."

Racer guffawed. "Wiggins can't do anything better than

anybody. Not even *you*, Jury." Racer flashed a kind of cutthroat smile, as if he hadn't meant the slight, which, of course, he had.

Jury's tone was all innocence as he asked, "Then why do you keep assigning him to me? You must think it's the blind leading the blind." Although Jury was always promising himself he wouldn't engage in any sort of sparring match with Racer, it was usually a promise he broke.

"He needs his training, doesn't he, man? I suppose you think one of your mates should have to suffer Sergeant Wiggins, is that it? Always the other chap, isn't it?"

Racer's illogic was as impeccable as the cut of his Savile Row suit. "It's no good being a loner, Jury. A policeman's got to be on the team. You know my policy is two men on an inquiry. How the bloody hell would the country get on if the P.M. went hightailing it all over the place, instead of sending one of her underlings?"

"I didn't know you held me in such esteem." Jury smiled.

"Very funny." Race spat out a shred of tobacco. "That's not what I mean, but you do put yourself about, don't you? Too bad you haven't more ambition."

Jury suspected what was prompting this talk of "ambition." "Has the subject of my promotion come up again?"

"The A.C. did mention it, yes." His tone was grudging.

Jury did not even bother to smile. When Racer rose from his desk, his thumbs hooked in the little pockets of his vest, Jury knew it was lecture time. The Summing Up. Jury's whole career laid out in little, presented in Racer's florid and cliché-ridden style. He started in now, walking round his desk, the red carnation in his buttonhole bobbing a little with each springy step. As Racer recounted — endlessly, it seemed — Jury's weaknesses, Jury looked out of the window over the smoky chimney pots and between highsided buildings like a tunnel at the end of which lay a tiny bit of the Thames. The sky above was dove gray and a few flakes of snow mashed against the window.

". . . pack it in unless you go up before the selection board, Jury." He stopped in his circling of the room to give Jury a thin-lipped smile. "Cold feet, that it?"

Jury didn't rise to that particular bait. "I intend to. Sometime."

"Sometime? *Sometime?* Why not now? When I was in your position . . ."

He droned on. Jury could only assume all of this avuncular talk was Racer's way of discussing Racer's own rather illustrious career, managing to polish it here and there by comparing his own ascent with Jury's. Racer liked to think that Jury was afraid of failure; whereas, Jury hadn't gone before the selection board simply because of his own ambivalence about the promotion to superintendent.

It was almost an annual ritual, some years, semiannual, this talk of Jury's career. In some perverse way he almost enjoyed Racer's attitude. Jury was fascinated by the over-wrought meanings lavished on the subject by Racer, who loved to talk about it. The delicate balance which Racer kept between the talk and the action was a marvel of fancy footwork. It was like watching a man climbing a filigree fence, searching out ever more toe- and fingerholes. Since the Assistant Commissioner was always bringing up Jury's future, Racer had to keep finding fresh reasons for denying it. Why he did so was much too complicated for simple vindictiveness. Jury wondered sometimes if Racer saw him as his younger self, as the *tabula rasa* on which Racer could write his own failures and thereby disown them.

Racer was still talking as he walked round the room. Over the top of his tartan vest blossomed a tie like a rare flower into which was stuck a sapphire stick pin — all of this mere gilding to his suit. Where did he get his money? Jury thought he recalled talk of the wife having private means. Racer came to a halt in front of a painting — one of the two bad ones he had acquired from the government cache. It was a wretched study of Westminster Bridge. With his back turned to Jury he meticulously ran down the list of Jury's cases, lingering over the details of one which Jury had botched many years ago. That was his way: he dwelled upon Jury's failures as if they were paintings he could scrutinize at leisure and in detail.

". . . so I'd appreciate a report in. You just pick up the phone and dial." Racer's finger made little circles in the air. "Simple. You won't get far as superintendent if you can't play on the team, Jury."

Jury left Racer's bracing presence to find Fiona Clingmore adjusting her black hat. Her black coat lay beside her on the desk. "Got that name for you." She picked up a pad, tore off a paper from it, and handed it to Jury. "Royal Victoria Hotel. In Victoria, it is."

"You're wonderful, Fiona. I'd take you to lunch, only I've got to see some people."

She motioned him closer with a conspiratorial wink and a crooking of her finger. *Sotto voce* she said, "Expect I shouldn't be talking about this, but the A.C. and your super had a real set-to the other day about you."

"How flattering."

"You're to be superintendent, you know."

"I wouldn't count on it." Jury took a sip of bitter coffee from Fiona's cup and set it back.

"This time's different. Everyone knows you should have got it long ago, don't they? Disgraceful, I call it, the way he keeps getting in your way." She hitched her thumb toward Racer's door. "I've heard lots of talk about it." She snapped her purse shut with a decided little click, lay it and her arm on the black coat. "Indeed, I've even heard some say you should be Commander. Funny, though . . ."

"What's funny?"

She shrugged. "You don't seem to care all that much."

Jury looked at her arm, clothed half way down in the

black jumper sleeve, the skin white against the dark wool of the coat.

"Maybe I don't," was all he said.

6.

The Raineys lived in a tiny maisonette in the euphemistically named Kingsman's Close in Lewisham. Lewisham itself was a fairly straightforward rundown and riotous place. But Jury had always loved that section of London across the Thames which took him through Greenwich and Blackheath, its expanses of green grass and trees. And in the winter, snow.

A sickly trail of ivy leeched its way up around the front door, which was answered, finally, by a sticky-faced boy of six or seven. "Me mum ain't home," he announced, and shut the door.

Jury knocked again, and heard a voice call, "Gerrard! Who was that?" There was then some commotion and presently the door was yanked open by a youngish woman who used her free hand to wallop the child. "You bad boy."

"Inspector Jury, madam. C.I.D." She looked at his I.D. as if she were starved for reading matter. "I'd like to see Mrs. Rainey."

"Well, I'm one of them," she said, blowing out her cheeks and wiping her brown hair back from her forehead. "But I expect it's Ma you want. My mother-in-law, Gwen. But Gwen's out for the day. Gone to the films. Come on in." Wiping her raw, red hands on her apron, she held the door wide as she used her other hand to smack her son's fingers away from his nose, which he had been picking all the while he had been staring up at Jury.

"Ma told me another policeman was here the day before yesterday." Rather desperately, she looked around the small, crowded sitting room, with an eye to locating a seat for

Jury. A large basket of laundry occupied the couch. A cat had jumped from the basket and come to snake its way round their several legs. Gerrard kicked it and got another slap. Jury imagined this was the common mode of communication between mother and son.

"We could go into the kitchen, couldn't we? It's just a madhouse out here when the twins wake up."

They were behind the couch, sleeping in a playpen. Gerrard was doing his best to wake them by beating the sofa cushions with a stick. "Stop that, you bad boy." His mother cuffed him on the ear. "Come along, then," she said to Jury, in a friendly voice. She was probably happy for any diversion.

Jury started after her to the kitchen, Gerrard bringing up the rear, yelling at the top of his lungs, "Mum! You was to give me my marmite and bread!"

Jury grabbed him by his overall suspenders. "You're under arrest, old chap."

The boy yelled and giggled in turn. The younger Mrs. Rainey turned and gave Jury a stupidly grateful look for taking over the child. He supposed she could do with a bit of help.

If the sitting room was a shambles, the kitchen was a jewel of cleanliness and order, probably the woman's only refuge. Sitting on the counter were a cut Swiss roll, a jar of marmite, and slices of bread, set out for the boy's lunch. As she went about pouring the tea to the tune of Gerrard's whines, Jury spread some marmite on the bread. Never the one to stand on polite ceremony, he shoved the slice into the boy's mouth. Gerrard choked and giggled again, thinking it a great lark to be thus manhandled by a stranger and a policeman to boot.

Mrs. Rainey pressed a mug of milky tea into Jury's hand. "My name's Angela, by the way. It's Gemma you've come about, isn't it? That other policeman was here and he asked Ma an awful lot of questions."

"Yes. I'm sorry to bother you again, but I thought just possibly your mother-in-law or perhaps you might have remembered something else that would be helpful."

Angela Rainey shook her head. "Really, there just doesn't seem to be anything. Believe me, we've talked and talked about it. Do you know, Gwen said that it wasn't until this happened that she realized how *little* she actually knew about Gemma Temple. I didn't know much either, and I think I knew her better than Ma. See, Gemma and me were about the same age. I lived next door. Next door, I mean, when we all lived in Dulwich years back."

Gerrard was demanding "choc in my milk!" and his mother went to the fridge and took out a bottle and a small tin of Hershey's.

"Didn't Gemma Temple ever talk about her life before she came to the Raineys as au pair, then?"

Angela shook her head as she slapped Gerrard's hand away from the Swiss roll. "Said she was raised by an old auntie, and she was dead. Said she'd been in a home after that for a while. But we can't remember the name. *If* she really was. . . ."

Gerrard, who had been maintaining a fairly constant noise level either with whining or humming, saw he was getting little for his troubles, gave up, and went to sleep. His chin fell forward on his chest.

"She was how old when she came to live with the Raineys?"

Angela calculated. "Round nineteen, I'd say."

"What about her birthday?"

"Birthday?"

"Yes. Didn't she ever celebrate it?"

"Funny. I can't say she ever did. Funny, I never even remember Gemma *had* a birthday."

"Never any mention of other relatives?"

"No. Said she was an orphan."

"But even orphans have a past of sorts."

"Not Gemma. Believe me, I was that curious too. Gemma was very secretive."

"Was there anything at all about her that was memorable? I mean, habits, nervous mannerisms, likes and dislikes, that sort of thing?"

Angela looked at Jury over the rim of her cup. "Only men. Men seemed to be her chief 'like.' Do you think maybe it was something deep in her past that got her . . . killed?"

"It could be, yes. Do you — did you — still see her?"

"Yes. She'd come round maybe once or twice a year. She was just here about a month ago. We had a nice chat. Gemma fancied herself an actress and she even managed a tiny part in some play. That was back in the summer. Last I ever saw of her. Poor Gem."

"These men. Did you know any of them?" Angela shook her head. "Another thing: Did she drive?" Angela looked puzzled. "Drive a car, I mean."

"Oh. Now you mention it, no, she didn't. Funny about that. All the while she was here, she never learned to drive. But didn't they find her car, or something?"

"Yes."

Angela glanced at the counter and slammed down her tea cup. "Look at that, would you! Where's my Swiss roll gone to?"

Gerrard, mouth lost in chocolate crumbs, was pretending to be asleep and trying not to smile.

To the tune of a loud slap and a louder scream, Jury said good-bye and left the house.

7.

Victor Merchent sat in vest and suspenders alternately scratching his stomach and his dog as if one were an extension of the other. The dog lolled lazily on the tile hearth before the imitation log. Around Victor Merchent's feet, which were shoved into carpet slippers, lay the scattered pages of the *Times*. He himself was deep into a racing form.

Fanny Merchent sat squarely in the center of the couch. She seemed more receptive than her husband to this interruption of the daily routine. Probably welcomed it, thought Jury, since Victor must figure prominently in that routine.

The parlor on Ebury Street was like Victor — overstuffed. The pieces ran from the worst of period to the worst of modern; there was none of the usual English chintzy-charm. And Mrs. Merchent was a bric-a-brac person, too. Presents from Brighton, Weston-super-Mare, Blackpool, and other middle-class watering places lined shelves and sills. The sentimental relics of a lifetime spilled over onto tables and desks: seashells, framed snaps, memory books. Small porcelain figurines graced the fireplace mantel above the sleeping dog.

"You were asking, Inspector, about my sister's boy. Olive was here just before Christmas. Carries her cross like a true Christian."

Jury's makeshift excuse for being here at all was that he needed additional information about Olive Manning's son, Leo, and any interest in the mother was purely peripheral.

Victor Merchent looked up from his racing form. "Ain't she always here round Christmas?" His lower lip protruded and his mouth downturned in testimony to his feelings about Olive's visits.

"Just never you mind, Vic. When I look at some of *your* family."

"Well, they ain't bleedin' livin' here on the cheap, are they, my girl?" He snapped the paper. "And where's my tea?"

"Be a bit patient, can't you?"

"I like my tea at the regular time." Bleakly, he regarded Jury.

"You were just saying, Inspector . . . ?"

"Your sister's son is in an institution?"

Before the poor woman could answer, her husband cut in with, "Mental. Daft, that one is." He drew a circle round a spot on his head.

"That's unkind, Vic. He *is* your nephew."

"*By* marriage." And his look made it clear anything mental was definitely on her family's side.

To Jury, she said: "Tragic, it was. The boy had a kind of nervous breakdown a long time ago. Olive comes down here several times a year to see him. Terrible expensive, the place is, but she'd have it no other way. Leo gets the very best treatment."

"It must put quite a strain on Mrs. Manning's purse-strings."

That was Victor's cue to cut in again: "On *our* purse-strings. Mrs. Olive-bloody-high-and-mighty-Manning comes here to eat our food and drink our whisky." Victor's eye strayed to a cabinet near the window. "Would you like a wee nip, Inspector?" He held up thumb and forefinger to show his wife how "wee" the nip would be. This unexpected gesture of friendliness Jury knew was designed to procure a drop for Victor himself. If Jury refused, Victor would only continue to toss up whatever obstacles he could to Jury's questions.

"Thanks, don't mind if I do. Just a small one."

Victor smiled broadly. "Well, then, I'll just join you. Man can't drink alone, I always say." He rose and walked to the cabinet and opened the little door beneath. "Mother, what about you? Glass of sherry, perhaps?"

With a face locked into disapproval of these early-afternoon libations, she shook her head. Victor Merchent became quite hearty and encouraging as he returned with bottle and glasses. "Fire away, Inspector Jury. You was saying about Leo . . . ?" Jury took the glass Victor pressed into his hand.

"How did Mrs. Manning feel about the Craels? I mean, at the time?"

"I'm not sure I take your meaning," said Fanny.

"Let's begin back with their ward — you might remember the girl. Dillys March. She ran away, apparently, about fifteen years ago."

Fanny gave a loud hoot. "Her! Indeed I *do* remember that name. Olive *hated* the girl. You see, Olive blamed her for what happened to Leo."

"So who's this Dillys March when she's at home?" asked Victor, looking morosely into his already-empty glass, and at the bottle, as if he wondered if he dared.

"Oh, *you* remember, Vic. Olive talked about nothing else when Leo first had his trouble."

"I don't pay no mind to that woman's natter. Far as I'm concerned, Leo's been funny in the head for all his life." He returned to his racing form.

"But she might have held the Craels generally responsible?" suggested Jury.

"I think she did. She thought they never should have taken the girl in." It must suddenly have occurred to Fanny Merchent that these questions had, oddly, to do with Olive, not Leo. Jury saw the question in her eyes before it was out of her mouth. "Why can't you find all this out from Olive?" asked Fanny, stiffening in her chair.

"I would do, of course, Mrs. Merchent." Jury's smile was at its disarming best. "Only I'm in London and she's in Yorkshire. And you see, I happened to be in Victoria and recalled she said she'd been visiting her sister. . . ." Jury shrugged. He thought if policemen really lived such a strolling, aimless, boulevardier existence, they wouldn't get much done.

Still, his "just happening by" seemed to satisfy Fanny, who was not disinclined to talk about the whole sorry business. "I see. Well, as I was saying, Olive was most upset about the Craels keeping this Dillys. She said the girl'd caused nothing but trouble ever since she'd got there and was that glad when she took herself off. Though Sir Titus Crael was heartbroken over it. Poor man. He'd lost his wife and son earlier, you know."

Jury nodded. "What sort of trouble did Dillys cause, according to your sister."

"Men, wasn't it? Young as she was, too. And she was deceptive. 'Little sneak,' Olive always said."

"Was she jealous of the girl's position in the house?"

Fanny Merchent did not deny this. "I don't know. But Olive is a funny sort of person —"

Victor snorted. "Funny's the word. All that lolly and she comes along here to live off us. Snooty she is to me. Why, I'd like to know? She's only the bleedin' housekeeper, ihn't she?" As if in defiance of Olive Manning, he poured himself another drink.

"That's no call to be nasty to her. As much grief as she's got —"

"Grief! I'll show you grief, my girl. Just look at what's been done to me. . . ."

Before Victor could begin on his downward path into self-pity, Jury said, "Nothing happened while Mrs. Manning was here that seemed to upset her, did it? Or make a change in her behavior?" Jury expected a negative answer to this, and was very surprised when Fanny Merchent said,

"Yes, there was something. It was after that phone call. You remember, Vic, you answered once. That was the second one." She reached over and flicked the paper with her fingernail to get his attention. He didn't answer. His eyes were fixed on the bottle as if a genie might vaporize out of its top.

"What phone call was that?"

She looked darkly from her husband to the whisky bottle and turned to Jury. "It was some woman called. I didn't recognize the voice, and I was surprised someone'd be asking for Olive. Olive don't know anybody round here, not that I know of. At first I thought it was the hospital, but I knew it wasn't from the way she acted. Took the phone into another room after a bit and closed the door." Fanny Merchent sniffed her disapproval of secrets kept from sisters. "All keyed up she was, after. For two weeks she was like that. Tense, kind of, but excited, you know. And she started going out then. Not to the hospital, for I usually went with her when she went there. She went somewhere else and every day, more or less at the same time. Just put me off when I asked, said she was going shopping. Wouldn't let me come along."

"You said there were two phone calls."

"That's right. Vic answered the second one. He just said it was someone ringing up Olive, and what'd Olive think this was, a B-and-B or something, expecting him to answer the telephone and all."

Victor Merchent held the bottle which had all the while been resting in his lap and poured himself another drink. He had given up including Jury in this ritual once Jury had served his purpose. "Bleedin' hotel she thought the place was. Bleedin' hotel." Then his expression changed. He looked surprised into cleverness. Like a senile old man getting crystal visions of the long ago, he stared vacantly into space. "That was it, then. An hotel. It was somebody calling from an hotel because when I said Olive ain't here, she said to tell her to call the Sawry Hotel."

His wife clucked her tongue. "You never told me, Vic."

Hastily, he said, "You never ast, did you?" and drank off his whisky.

8.

Jane Yang was an exquisite, delicately formed girl in a turquoise dress with a high collar. Her black hair was cut straight across and down like a helmet. When Melrose walked into the Sun Palace, she was behind the counter, working the cash register.

It was not yet noon, but the small, cramped restaurant was still crowded. Sullen-looking waiters streamed by with trays of silver-domed food, slapping in and out of the kitchen's swinging door. It couldn't have been the ambiance which accounted for the restaurant's popularity, so it must have been the food. The air was redolent with mysterious, spicy mixtures.

Melrose took up a place in line behind the half-dozen customers queued to pay their bills. When his turn came he handed over twenty pounds and the snapshot. "You're Jane Yang? Fat Bertha told me you might know the woman in this picture here."

Miss Yang looked confused. Should she be mixing this bit of business with the bill-paying customers? But she held on to the twenty pounds.

Behind Melrose, a burly man sighed. "Move it along mate. This ain't Kew Gardens flower show." The toothpick in his mouth moved acrobatically.

"Could you wait over there?" said Miss Yang, apologetically. "Very busy."

Ignoring the giant sighs all down the line, Melrose produced the twin of the twenty. "Very rich."

She looked utterly startled by all of this money suddenly floating her way, at the same time looking at Melrose's chesterfield and taking the bill from the man with the dancing toothpick.

With her shoulder she motioned Melrose behind the counter and signaled a tiny woman, old, her brown face creased with wrinkles like a Chinese tea egg. Jane Yang's beckoning finger brought the old woman shuffling over to listen without expression to the girl's spurt of Chinese — probably directions about the cashier's post.

The girl led Melrose to a corner near the kitchen, plucked

the second twenty from his fingers, then folded both of the notes to a neat square which she slid between two of the small, black frogs which served as closures down the length of the turquoise dress. He wondered why women seemed to think this was the last place a man would look.

She had the picture in her hand. "I know her, yes. She waitress here, oh, three week, I think it was." And she held up three fingers as if teaching Melrose a new language.

"What was her name?"

"Gemma. Gemma Temple."

"And then what happened to her? After she left here, I mean?"

"She meet a man. I guess she go living with him."

"Did she meet him here? When she was working?"

Jane Yang shook her head and the satiny helmet of hair swirled on her shoulders. "Somewhere — I forget — in London. Maybe train station? She go off one day to visit friend. Look —" She spread her hands. "We was not very close, you know. She not tell me much about private life."

Melrose nodded. "So you don't know who this man was? She must have told you something, since you know she went off with him."

Again, the black hair swirled. "No. I just saw him."

"*Saw* him?"

"Yes. He come to restaurant. Very posh, he was." She looked Melrose up and down. "Like you." She smiled. "The Prince." To Melrose's questioning eyebrow, she said, "I mean, that what she call him: The Prince. It was joke. But he did look . . ." She seemed searching for words and her eye fell on a painting above the cash register which was totally out of keeping with the dragony decorations of the Sun Palace. It was a print of the Millais painting done for Pears' Soap. "Like him. I mean, when the Prince was little, yes, he would look like that."

The description couldn't have fit Julian Crael more aptly.

The beautiful child, dressed in green velvet, golden curls tumbling: it was just what Julian might have looked like in that far-off age.

"He came here to see her?"

She nodded. "He come here *with* her. She stop work here, see. I guess she want to show him off to other girls. The Prince embarrassed, though. The gentleman used to another life."

Melrose smiled at the way she said it, so succinctly and so perceptively.

"Did she tell you where she was going?"

Her porcelain skin wrinkled slightly in concentration. "There was something. She tell me he live at fancy hotel. . . ." She shook her head. "I cannot remember name."

At that moment, a small man, who made a twin-set with the little old woman, stomped out of the kitchen and, seeing Jane socializing, let loose with a spate of Chinese, gesturing wildly toward the register. The line had diminished and increased several times since they'd been talking, never disappearing altogether. Off to their right the door to the kitchen slapped open and whooshed shut continuously. The noise in there was even worse than the din of the customers' chat. They must have been killing chickens in the kitchen, thought Melrose.

"Sorry," she said, turning to Melrose. "Papa very angry I leave cashbox. I must go."

Melrose brought out a card case, extracted his gold pen, and wrote both the number of his hotel and of Old House on it. "Look, if you should remember anything at all about this Gemma Temple, about her life, her family —"

Jane Yang shook her head. "She got none. I think she raised in home. That all she tell me."

"And you can't remember the hotel where he was staying?"

They were back at the register now, the girl relieving Mama. "If I do remember, I call." She shrugged her turquoise shoulders and smiled a smile that made the porcelain mask of her face open like a lotus on a blue lake. She was really quite beautiful, but so fragile-looking a man might be afraid of handling her. "Sorry," she said once more, shrugging.

He turned away. When he had his hand on the door, he heard, over the crowd, "Mister!" She was waving him back, smiling brightly. When he got back to the counter, she said, "That's it! The hotel. *Sawry*. The Sawry Hotel."

She pronounced it just as she had *sorry*, erasing the *r* slightly. Melrose grinned. He would have produced the money-clip again, but the darkling looks of the bill-payers up and down the line were at this point congealing into one collective rain cloud. He thought they might all fall on him together, so he walked out of the restaurant.

Once outside, he started whistling "Limehouse Blues."

9.

The Sawry Hotel was a well-kept London secret, closely guarded by those discriminating patrons who realized what would happen if the secret were to get out. It was not cheap; neither, though, was it outrageously expensive. Money seemed not to be the issue, as if excellence could not be measured in terms of pounds and pence.

As the door smacked softly shut behind him, Melrose Plant was washed with a wave of nostalgia. It was more than thirty years since his father and mother had brought him here as a child during one snow-bedazzled Christmas holiday, and it had not changed one whit. The Sawry held tenaciously to its past. Melrose approved. He kept his own home as it had been when his parents were alive. He had only added a few pieces; he had removed none. To him the past was perfect as it stood, preserved beneath the glass bell of Ardry End.

It was another reason he had never married: no matter how much she would have insisted on keeping him and the house intact, eventually she'd have had to start moving the furniture around.

A blue, gold and rose Persian runner led straight to an Adam staircase that swept upward as if it were suspended, floating in space. Discreetly placed off the foyer was the desk attended by a gentleman in the Sawry's customary uniform — black suit and white gloves.

"May I be of assistance, sir?"

"Ah, yes," said Melrose. "I'm calling on Mr. Crael. I wonder could you ring him up and tell him Mr. Carruthers-Todd is here. Thank you."

The clerk, whose expression ordinarily wouldn't have been changed by a dish of cold water in the face, registered surprise. "Oh, I'm very sorry, sir. But Mr. Crael isn't staying with us."

Melrose's feigned surprise was far weightier even than the clerk's. "Surely, you must be mistaken. Why, I've a letter from Mr. Crael telling me he'd be visiting the Sawry on the eleventh. . . ." Melrose made a great show of slapping pockets as if he were looking for the letter.

The clerk smiled slightly. "I'm sorry, Mr. Carruthers-Todd. Could you possibly be mistaken as to the date?"

Melrose Carruthers-Todd drew himself up and offered the clerk a rather frosty look. The clear implication was that the Carruthers-Todds were seldom, if ever, mistaken about anything. "It was the eleventh; I distinctly remember." His tone suggested that the clerk had better produce Mr. Crael in no short order and in good condition or there'd be trouble.

He knew that establishments such as the Sawry did not give out information freely about their guests. But having put the clerk in the unfortunate position of now having to prove that Mr. Crael wasn't indeed tied up in the broom closet, Melrose watched as the clerk brought out the guest register.

"As you see, sir, Mr. Crael *was* staying with us on that date in *December. Not* January, sir." The clerk managed not to appear too self-satisfied, as he turned the register round.

"Drat!" said Melrose. He sighed deeply. "Then I suppose that Miss March isn't here either?"

The clerk raised a puzzled eyebrow. "Miss March? I don't believe I remember anyone by that name."

"Temple," said Melrose, snapping his fingers. "Miss Temple is the one I mean. Friend of Mr. Crael."

"Ah, yes. No, sir, she isn't with us either now, sir."

"Ummm. Guess she left the same time he did." Melrose tried not to turn this into a question. The clerk nodded, beginning to look a trifle weary with the absent-minded Mr. Carruthers-Todd. "Well, blast and damn. I suppose that means poor old Benderby won't get a chance to see them either. He'll be *most* put out by this whole mix-up." Melrose took from his pocket a small, gold pencil and his little notebook. "Look here, give this to him, will you, when he comes round. There's a good chap."

The clerk was clearly puzzled. "I'm sorry sir, give this to *whom?*"

"Benderby. He'll probably be round asking after Crael. Well, I told him to meet us both here and he's going to be deuced put out by it all. Eustace Benderby. Name's on the front there." Melrose glowered at the clerk as if the man's schooling must have given him a great deal of trouble; he couldn't even read the direction on the note.

The clerk slipped the note in one of the cubbyholes kept for mail. "I shall certainly do that, sir."

Melrose mumbled distractedly and marched out.

And once on the street, he started whistling again "Limehouse Blues."

10.

The clerk's confusion deepened visibly when Chief Inspector Richard Jury turned up two hours later.

"There isn't any trouble, is there, Chief Inspector?"

That sort of "trouble" was alien to the Sawry. "No, I don't think so. I'm inquiring about one of your guests." Jury pulled out the picture of Dillys March, taken when she was young. "Ever seen this woman?"

The clerk took the picture in his gloved hand and looked at it for some moments before he said, "There is something familiar about her. But I can't be sure. It's rather an old picture, isn't it?"

"Yes, it is. I've a newer one." Jury produced the picture which Melrose Plant had given Wiggins. "What about her?"

"Oh, yes. She was a good friend of . . . one of our guests."

The Sawry took upon itself the responsibility for its guests' well-being; there would be no unnecessary divulging of information, certainly no gossip. The place was like a sanctuary or a safehouse. It was as if the mahogany and glass were firmly shut against the ugly facts of the world beyond.

"A friend of Julian Crael?"

He looked relieved. If the police already knew of the connection, then perhaps it wasn't a breach of trust to confirm it. "Yes, that's right." He was not, however, about to embellish unless he had to.

"How often did she come here?"

He thought for a moment. "A number of times. Off and on, for about a year. Visiting Mr. Crael."

"Her name?"

The clerk looked decidedly puzzled. "Temple. Miss Temple." He brought out the guest register again. "It was only last month — December. Here." He turned the book round for Jury's inspection. "December the tenth. A Miss Temple.

I believe she left the evening of the same day Mr. Crael left."

"Had she any visitors?" Jury helped him out by describing Olive Manning. The clerk shook his head. "Telephone calls?"

"None that I know of, but I can check."

"Please do. And let me know." Jury handed him his card and turned to leave, when the clerk stopped him.

"There is one thing, sir. Another gentleman was here a short time ago — a Mr. Carruthers-Todd — just this afternoon, inquiring after Mr. Crael and Miss Temple. And he left a message —" The clerk plucked it from its cubbyhole.

"And what did Mr. Carruthers-Todd look like?"

"Quite well-off, I'd say. And well-spoken." Having dispensed with the important points, he went on: "Not quite as tall as you, fair hair. Very green eyes. The message was left for —" and the clerk looked down. "A Mr. Benderby. Eustace Benderby."

"I'm Benderby," said Jury, putting out his hand for the note.

11.

The Royal Victoria Hotel did not live up to its name. It was wedged between two other buildings, one called the Arab Star, where a peeling sign brandished a scimitar and star. From its portals emerged two young men, black-mustached and talking with their hands.

Inside a small room with a cottage-style door sat a girl who was more interested in applying lip rouge than in greeting prospective customers. Finally, she came forward, her purple-hooded eyes drifting over him. She blew a bubble and tucked it back in. He showed his I.D. "I'm looking for a woman who might have stayed here. Her name is Roberta Makepiece."

"Can't say I remember no one like that. They come, they

go." She made the most of arranging her breasts under the blue twin-set. Another bubble appeared close to Jury's chin. Then she said, "Dotty might know."

"Who's Dotty?"

"Owner-manager."

"And *where's* Dotty?"

"Manchester. Went off with her fella." Her lashes worked. Thick with mascara, they had beaded the skin under her eyes.

"And when will Dotty be back?"

"I don't know, do I?"

"Then I can't ask Dotty, can I?"

The sarcasm fell wide. "Well, you could ask Mary, I s'pose. If this person worked here, Mary'd know."

"Where is this Mary?"

She had a small purse-mirror out now and was inspecting the mouth again, bored with Jury now that he was interested only in Mary. "Mary Riordan. Round there —" and she waved vaguely. "Setting up tables in the dining room, I expect."

There were two of them in the dining room, the one named Mary and another bucolic lass, bovine, her hair in two spare brown braids, her complexion biscuit-colored. She moved about lethargically placing napkins and cutlery.

Mary was, fortunately, less dim-looking. She had a soft, breathy, Irish voice to go with her very blue eyes. "Roberta Makepiece? Well, now . . . aye. I remember now. Though she didn't work here long." Mary clasped her metal tray to her bosom like armour plate. "Went off with some fella."

The Royal Victoria seemed to cater for lovers. "You don't know where?" Jury's heart sank and then surfaced when Mary nodded and said:

"I might do. See, I got a letter from her . . . well, it was money she'd borrowed and was giving back. There was an address. Could you just be waiting a bit and I'll run up and get it?"

"I'll wait all day, love, if need be." He smiled. He could have kissed Mary; she was, indeed, growing prettier and more pink-cheeked by the moment.

Jury's smile sent her walking backwards into the door-jamb. Blushing, she turned and hurried out, still carrying the tray. In her absence he reread Plant's note. It was short enough:

Call me at the Connaught. If you're still speaking.

PLANT

The girl with the braids, whose progress round the tables was less than brisk, snuffled adenoidally. Jury was reminded of Sergeant Wiggins.

Mary returned, a letter in her hand. "I found it. But her name's not Makepiece any more. It's Cory. Here's the address." She held the note out to Jury. It was a flat in Wanstead.

"Must of got married," said Mary.

Jury smiled. "Or something. Thank you, Mary. You don't know how much you've helped out. Is there a public telephone? I need to call someone."

Mary's blue eyes glimmered up at him. It was plain to see she was only too glad to help out Scotland Yard as she led Jury to the telephone.

12.

The look she gave him, up and down, could have stripped varnish off a chair.

"Roberta Makepiece?"

Above the chain lock, her jaw stopped working over the gum which she had been slowly chewing. "My name's Cory. Mrs. Cory. You've got the wrong place." As she started to shut the door, Jury put his hand against it.

"C.I.D., Mrs. Cory. Chief Inspector Richard Jury." He shoved the plasticined I.D. toward her face.

"Whatever — ?" Her eyes widened. "Joey? Is it Joey?" But her voice was more relieved than anxious. It made Jury wonder about love and loyalty.

"If I could just come in . . . ? It won't take long."

The door closed a bit while she rattled back the chain and then held the door wide, motioning him in with a curt nod. "I was only just on my way out to the shops."

"It won't take long. Could we sit down?"

She shrugged. "Suit yourself." Jury sat on the edge of a shiny, imitation-leather chair. She took a seat on the white, fake-fur couch. Everything in the flat — the furnishings, the curtains, the clothes she wore looked cheap and new and clean, as if the lives lived here had sprung suddenly and fully staged from the stones of Wanstead. The flat was like a model-display in some department store window, complete with mannequin. Roberta Makepiece had a gaunt, wooden prettiness — uninviting and unbending. The steps with which she had retreated to the white couch were small and mincing, restricted by her tight, calf-length skirt. Above it she wore a striped jumper molded around small, pointy breasts. Her face was made thinner by the deadweight of looped curls held up around her head by little tortoiseshell combs and cemented there with hair spray. Jury wondered what Cory found appealing in all of this constriction. To have her around would be like always having a sore throat. He also guessed she wasn't really Mrs. Cory; she would be, like the furniture, easily disposable.

With a brightly varnished thumb and forefinger she took the gum from her mouth and dropped it in an enormous glass ashtray where it lay sadly, the only thing in the room that looked used.

Her bag and her coat rested beside her on the white couch. That she had been on her way out was apparently the truth. He doubted she often told it.

Why had he seen it, in his mind's eye, so differently? A blowsy, pretty woman in a wrapper, an unmade bed, snaps of Bertie stuck here and there round a mirrored dressing table. There wasn't a sign of him here, not in a photo, not in her face.

"Well? What's this all about, then?" The bright red fingers went up to her hair, making sure its shellacked perfection remained undisturbed by this awkward intrusion into her life.

"I'm here about your son, Mrs. Cory."

She looked away quickly, plucked the gum up out of the ashtray. "I haven't" — she popped it in her mouth — "got any son. I don't know what you're talking about."

Jury felt himself grow cold, his fingers stiffening around the edge of the chair arm. "I'm talking about Bertie. Bertie Makepiece." He said it, he felt idiotically, as if the name might jangle some chord of memory. *Oh, him*, she would say, snapping her fingers.

What she started to say was that she didn't know, but his expression must have been fearful, for she said instead: "Look here, what's Scotland Yard to do with this? Why are police coming round? Have you got something to do with social services, or something?" Her tone grew more urgent. "I suppose you're going to make me go back?"

"I'm not here officially. I'm just interested. I met Bertie while I was working on a case and thought the story he told of your absence peculiar. Bertie claims his mother — you — had to go to tend a sick grandmother. In Northern Ireland. Seems you're in London, though, doesn't it?"

"Northern *Ireland?* I never said nothing about Ireland!

I've got an old gran lives there, but I never said I was going there." Bertie, she seemed to feel, was now culpable. "*Imagine!*"

"Bertie's been telling people the old gran lives in Northern Ireland. On the Bogside." In spite of himself, Jury smiled. But she merely looked blank. Had he meant to surprise in her some humor, some shared laughter over her son's ingenuity? To find something of the mother in her yet?

"He always made up stories. He was a great one for making things up. . . ." Her voice trailed away as she plucked the fur of the couch.

"Bertie? He strikes me as just the opposite. Serious, level-headed, a good manager." If anyone was living a fantasy life, it was the mother, not the son. Looking around the room once more he thought what a thin fantasy it was, too.

"Yes, he is. A better manager than me. Bertie could do it all and often did when I was working. Cooking, washing up, cleaning. He even got so's he could send that old dog to the shops. He's still there, ain't he? Arnold?"

She might have been inquiring after some childhood acquaintance. Jury nodded. Her tone became belligerent and she leaned toward him, hands tightly clasped about her knees. "You listen, now. Bert gets money, I see to that. I told him just to go ahead and cash the pension cheques —"

"He'd have to sign them to do that. That's forgery."

"Well, anyway. Look, you've got to understand. I did write to him a few times. I *did* explain things to him, I mean how I couldn't stand living in that place. I *didn't* just go off and leave him high and dry."

You could have fooled me, thought Jury. "So you told Miss Cavendish and one or two others to look in. You told Miss Cavendish you were going to London, is that right?"

Eagerly, she nodded, as if now that they were on the same wavelength, it didn't look so bad to him, did it? "Look, I admit I'm not much of a mother." Grimly, she smiled, as if the admission wiped the slate clean. "But let me tell you, I was never one wanted kids. I got married too young. Only eighteen . . ."

And so it began, like the celebration of an old mass which had lost all meaning, the justification of her behavior: tedious and familiar to Jury, who had heard the story, or stories like it, so many times before.

The hardships of her life in that little fishing village. A failed marriage to a no-good bastard. Struggle, struggle, struggle with money. The lack of advantages, the lack of prospects, and she was still young, wasn't she? And Rackmoor itself. The sheer bone-aching boredom of it, up there in the North, no city lights, no entertainment, nothing. Her meeting with Joey Cory. Handsome, made her laugh, had money. But he didn't want her if it meant a kid around. No kids, he said.

"See all this? New, it is. Cory buys everything new. Something gets beat up, dirty, we just throw it out and buy new." Her tight, bowlike smile was triumphant, as if she'd found a way to beat the house.

A disposable life. Jury could see the days peeling away from this room like the pages of a calendar, still blank, nothing entered. He rose from his chair. "And what does he do with you when you get beat up and dirty?"

Rage drew her up from the couch, her thin face like a cold, white flame. The slap across his face made him flinch, but hardly hurt. Her hand was so weightless it was more the hysterical brush of a bird's wing.

And she had merely frightened herself, after all, catching the offending hand with the other. He saw now how thin the hands were, thin and blue-veined. He wondered at her gauntness, those formerly rounded and pleasant lines planed now into angles. There were hollows under the cheekbones.

"You've no right to come here, saying things like that,"

she flared up again. "And now I suppose you're going straight to social services and tell them? I'm not going back to Rackmoor, I can tell you that. If I've got to keep him, he'll have to come here and —" She drew a hand across her forehead as if it ached. Obviously, the thought of Cory stopped that idea.

"I'm not going to tell them," Jury said. "I don't want them to find you."

She blinked and stared at him in the expanding silence. But she didn't look relieved. Her brows drew together. It was as if life had merely formed itself into a new puzzle, a harder one, its design cut up in even tinier bits of grass and sky, its colors muted, more difficult to fit.

Jury thought of the life Bertie would have with her, mashed under her oppressive frustration of having to carry him, a lumpy bit of luggage, in her aching hand. Anyone, anything, nearly, would be better company than she: loneliness, deprivation, need, loss — all would be better company. More dependable, more palpable even, something you could reach out and touch. But Roberta Makepiece seemed incapable of being touched any longer. She stood there now — they were at the door — in her straight dark clothes against that white background like an angry slash some artist had drawn against his composition, hating it.

"What you'll do is this," said Jury. "You're going to write three letters. One to Bertie — to him you'll tell the truth. Just what you told me. Be careful that you don't lie, pretty it up, give him any hope. Except the one hope: that he'll never, under any circumstances, have to go to a Home. That you'll help him, temporarily, with the lie he's been forced to tell. That's the purpose of the second letter: you'll tell Miss Cavendish what Bertie's told people. You're in Northern Ireland, in Belfast, taking care of poor old granny. Make it good and sad and a lingering death. Indeed, so lingering, you're not sure if you'll get back in the foreseeable future. That means you'll need someone in Rackmoor to look after Bertie. And that's the third letter: Kitty Meechem. I'd say Kitty is the perfect person —"

"*Kitty!* You mean her as runs the Fox Deceiv'd? Listen, I'm not having my boy living in no pub —"

Jury was not even angered by the oddity of that "my boy," by the strangely twisted morality, since he half-suspected that what motivated Roberta Makepiece now was a very real sense of impending loss.

"It's a perfectly respectable business and Kitty's a great person. She's very fond of Bertie. And Arnold, too. Of course, there's always Frog Eyes and Codfish, if you'd rather —"

That surprised a smile in her, which she quickly hid. "Not them, not hardly. But look here —"

Jury overrode any objection: "Then take those letters and put them in an envelope and send them to that old gran for posting from Ireland. That at least will give us something to be going on with until the whole thing can be sorted out —" He did not want to say "legally." It would have had, for her, such a ring of finality. It was strange. Cold as she was, made colder still by this ice-white room — cold, calculating, self-centered — still, he sensed a fear in her that she might really lose what she had already thrown away.

"And if I don't?" There was only the pretense of a challenge in the tone.

"Then I'll be back. Good-bye, Mrs. Cory."

But she plucked at his sleeve as he opened the door. "Just you wait —" She didn't seem to want him to leave, yet she didn't seem to know why she wanted him to stay. For one more moment she held him there by saying: "Robert. His name's really Robert."

"What?" Jury was confused.

Vaguely she smiled, her mind seeming to shift through

an old album. "He's called Bertie for short. But his name's Robert. Named him after me, I did."

It pierced Jury like a tiny arrow that she had, at one time, found some need to tie the child to her. Roberta and Robert.

A long way back in their interview, his anger toward her had died. "I'll remember that." He smiled. His smile coaxed a smile in return from Roberta Makepiece. "Goodbye."

The door shut behind him.

He walked back down the street towards the tube stop. The block was deserted except for a mangy-looking orange cat washing itself on a stoop. The fur looked intractable beneath the tongue; still the cat kept at it. A wind sprang up and pasted a page from a newspaper against Jury's leg. It blew off again, shunted by the wind, now against a tree, now catching an iron railing, like some old distracted pensioner seeking out its own door, not finding it.

He walked on down the street, the paper blowing farther and farther, and wondered why he had come, felt he had accomplished little. Yet, some person he had internalized seemed to approve his act. He remembered a teacher he had had when he was very small, a teacher whom he had loved with a child's passion, putting her hand on his head and smiling down at him and commending him for having wiped a chalky blackboard especially clean.

13.

When Jury walked into the George at six o'clock, he saw Jimi Haggis sitting at the bar, long legs hooked round the stool, spearing a piece of cold veal-and-ham pie.

"Hello, Jimi," said Jury, taking the stool beside him.

"Richard! Hey, man." Jimi clapped him on the shoulder and went back to his pickled onion, chasing it with his fork.

Jimi was on the Drug Squad and Jury suspected one reason he liked it was, with the sort of assignments he got, he could wear his hair long and his shirt unbuttoned. He wiped a crumb of pastry from his drooping mustache.

They sat in companionable silence for a few moments. The pub was filling up with the after-work regulars and a lot of casuals. An especially plummy-looking young lady nestled herself onto the stool to Jimi's right.

"Excuse me, sweetheart," said Jimi, taking advantage of the way she was arranging herself to reach in front of her for the mustard pot. He managed to brush her breast and Jury saw her reflected brows pull together in mild anger when she looked at Jimi. Then, seeing Jury watching her, she looked off and then back. Jury smiled at her as if they shared a secret. Through the smoke of her cigarette, she returned what looked like more than a smile.

Jimi was dotting his pie all over with mustard and saying, "What I can't understand is, here I am, with an old lady and three kiddies, two in nappies. Here I am —" And he spread his arms, again managing to brush the breast beside him and murmur, "*Sorry, love* — young, sexy, handsome, a free spirit, at least I feel like one. And there *you* are — big, solid, dependable as a safehouse — your eyes remind me of the London silver vaults, you know that? — anyway there you are, no responsibilities and the women melt at your feet. Here comes one now." Jimi poked his fork toward the barmaid, Polly.

" 'Allo, love," she said to Jury, managing to ignore Jimi. "What'll it be?"

"Best bitter and one of those Scotch eggs, Polly." Between Jury and Jimi sat a cake stand with a high plastic dome. Polly plucked off the dome by its button and rolled an egg onto a little plate. She leaned across the bar, enhancing her cleavage. "Where you been, dear? This one's in here every day, nearly. Don't he do no work?"

Jimi scowled at her low, frilled neckline.

"He's working right now."

Polly saw the direction of Jimi's eyes and waved her hand at Jury, winked, and moved off down the bar.

"That's what I mean," said Jimi. "I don't get it."

"I don't either."

"You have to admit I got a certain appeal." He paused, as if his whole sense of identity were tied to Jury's reassuring nod. "Last night, let me tell you, I had one with a pair like —" He held his hands palm up and moved them as if weighing fruit, then grabbed the dome housing the pyramid of Scotch eggs and rested his forehead against the plastic.

Jury shook his head. Jimi was one of the best men they had, probably the best on the Drug Squad, though he was younger than most of them, some ten years younger than Jury himself. He exuded supreme self-confidence on the job; off, it was something else again. He needed every last crutch he could find, Jury being the one to bear the most weight.

"That redhead you used to go round with," said Jimi. "What happened to her?"

Maggie was a snapshot in his desk drawer. That's where he'd buried her. But he still exhumed the body now and then. "She married somebody else. An Australian."

Jimi looked at him in genuine disbelief. "Married someone *else*? And an Aussie to boot? Christ. Hasn't there been anyone —"

"Why don't we drop it, Jimi?" He looked at the girl beside Jimi. She was dressed in burgundy and her arm lay like silk along the dark mahogany.

"Okay, man, okay." Jimi held up his hands, then went back to his meal. "Hear you're getting that long-overdue promotion."

"Not bloody likely, as the flowergirl said." Jury didn't feel like talking anymore about either women or promotions; he flung some coins on the bar and got up. "I'm meeting someone, Jimi. I'll see you later."

All the way across the room he felt the velvet look of the girl in burgundy.

The door swished open and Melrose Plant walked in, searched the crowd, saw Jury, and pushed his way through what was by now quite a crush.

"Benderby, old chap!" said Melrose.

Jury kicked out a chair. "Sit down, Mr. Plant. Benderby and I thank you for your notes. And the picture. Come on, now, how'd you do it?"

"Give Scotland Yard my methods? Why on earth should I? I'm for getting a drink. Want another of those?" Plant pointed at Jury's glass with his silver-knobbed stick.

"Don't mind if I do. You can buy."

Melrose took the glass, put his stick on the table, and pushed back through the crowd. Jury hitched a chair closer under the table and put his feet on it. Dog-tired, he was. Idly he rolled the stick, picked it up, got curious and monkeyed around with the knob. He pulled on it. A sword-stick. Christ.

Back with the drinks, Melrose sat down and launched into an account of his night and day, beginning with the picture, which he passed over to Jury. "We know Crael knew her, then. But which one did he know? I mean, which one was she?"

"Gemma Temple," said Jury, pocketing the picture. "She drove up to Rackmoor in her roommate's car because her own had learner's plates. Gemma Temple was only just learning how to drive."

"And Dillys March was always driving that red car. For God's sake."

Jury nodded and they were both silent, looking into their beer. Jury leaned back and looked through the top of the leaded-glass window where the lamp came on. The apricot light of a rare, sunny-cold day had disappeared from the tulip-tracery of the glass and London was glooming over into early evening. But it did not produce a feeling of gloom in Jury, who could sense, even in the smoky pub the hint of snow outside. London in winter was for Jury the best of seasons. Streets soggy as old gloves; damp, rubbery smell of Wellingtons; mounted horses steaming in the palace grounds. He loved London, and the knowledge sometimes caught him unaware.

"The way I read it is that Julian Crael saw Gemma Temple somewhere and was overwhelmed by her resemblance to Dillys March. I believe Dillys meant far more to Julian than he ever admitted. So he and Gemma became lovers. Gemma saw a way to cut in on a fortune. He must have told her a great deal about himself, his family, his home — and Olive Manning. I think he was about to ditch Gemma, perhaps seeing how threadbare this fantasy was he was living. So Gemma got in touch with Olive and they worked out this little swindle."

"Wait a minute: Olive Manning denied right from the beginning the woman was Dillys March. It doesn't make sense, if she wanted the Colonel to believe Dillys had come back."

"True. I don't get that either. All I know is that she and Gemma were in the thing together. And if the thieves fell out, that's a damned good reason for murder —"

"There's a better, isn't there? Julian Crael's."

"I know he's your favorite suspect. But why would he *murder* her? Why not, instead, just tell his father the whole story? Julian knew the woman wasn't Dillys March. And don't forget that alibi of his —"

"You really don't think he did it, do you? You certainly keep defending him."

"I don't know *who* did it, I'll tell you that. And I'm not 'defending' him." Jury wondered if that were true. Why would he feel such empathy for a man so distant, cool, and — come on, be reasonable — with the strongest motive? Julian Crael was a weight on his mind, and he was probably rationalizing away Plant's perfectly justifiable suspicion.

Yet he thought of Julian, standing in the winter light of the drawing room, his arm across the mantel, under the picture of that silk-shawled, exquisite woman who had been his mother. And he felt the same chill sitting here in the noise of this smoke-filled pub as he had sitting there in the silence of that drawing room listening to Julian. "*I thought, you know, she might be dead.*" There was just that hint of question in the words as when the speaker does not himself understand what he has said, as if Julian expected something beyond him, something vast — the moors perhaps, or the sea — to give him back an answer.

Who might be dead? wondered Jury.

"You don't want him to be guilty." Plant's statement cut through his thoughts and made him realize that while he had been thinking he had been staring at the girl in burgundy still sitting at the bar.

Angry with himself, he finished off his pint quickly, and said, "It's nearly seven. We'd better be pushing off. It's a six-hour drive back to Rackmoor. I'd certainly like a word with Olive Manning." Plant's look was like an arrow. "Yes, I heard what you said. Whether I want or don't want someone to be guilty is beside the point. Remember, though, Crael has an alibi."

Plant still sat there, now sighting down the length of his walking stick. "Is that all? Alibis have had holes punched in them before."

14.

"Shall we stop and rout out Agatha? She will report only to you, remember. I wonder how she's getting on with the search for the claim check?"

From under his hat, Jury said, "I think I'll forgo that little pleasure, if you don't mind."

They were taking turns spelling one another on the driving and had made good time. Melrose had been driving since they'd stopped at an M1 cafe for a cup of coffee and a slice of dreadful pie. "You know," said Melrose, "the killer just might have mistaken Gemma Temple for Lily Siddons. But what in hell would the motive be?"

"The Colonel is very fond of Lily Siddons," Jury said, his voice muffled by his pulled-down hat. "As fond as ever he was of Dillys March. I think."

"Well, good God, he's fond of half the county. I hope we're not going to be finding corpses all over Yorkshire."

Jury didn't answer.

Melrose assumed he was dozing and drove the Jaguar up to ninety.

15.

Plant had excused himself discreetly and gone to his room, and Wood — unable to hide his surprise at the request — had gone to summon Olive Manning.

Everyone else in the house seemed to be asleep, for which Jury was just as glad; he wanted to create as little stir as possible.

Jury was standing in the Colonel's snug, the Red Run Room, when Olive Manning appeared. In her bathrobe, without her keys, and with her hair undone from its intricate coil, Olive Manning looked somewhat more human. Nor was she, Jury found to his relief, going to waste any time.

"Fanny always did talk too much," was the first thing she said. Like Jury, she preferred to stand to say it.

"How did Gemma Temple manage to find you, Mrs. Manning?"

"Through Julian, of course. He was extremely indiscreet. However, the whole thing worked to my advantage — *would* have, I should say, had someone not killed the woman."

" 'Someone'? Not you, Mrs. Manning?"

"Decidedly not I. Although it will be difficult to convince you of that, I'm sure."

"Your connection with Gemma Temple would certainly point in that direction. But let's back up: I mean, more specifically, how did Gemma Temple know you were visiting your sister?"

"She called here, first. Wood, or someone, told her I was visiting in London. She rang up there, told me she had something of great importance to impart about Dillys March. I was stunned. Who was this stranger who knew something about a girl missing for fifteen years? She was at the Sawry Hotel. Julian had just left that morning — I later found out. When I saw her —" Olive Manning shut her eyes. "The resemblance was absolutely uncanny. Well, of course, I thought it *was* Dillys. The woman was at least smart enough to know that the information she had about Dillys, about the past at Old House, simply wouldn't stand up to close scrutiny. Had it not been for that, I think she might have gone along there and tried it on her own. She needed a bit of teaching; she needed some smoothing out if she were to pass herself off as Dillys." Olive Manning said it with perfect equanimity, and no remorse.

"So you went along and did the smoothing."

"Yes."

"How could you hope to get this by Julian? He would never have allowed the woman to live here, impersonating his cousin —"

"*Live* here? Good Lord. Neither would I. She was to collect the fifty thousand and we were to divide it. That's all. Why would Julian allow it? 'Allow' might not be precisely the term, you know. Could he have convinced the Colonel she *wasn't* Dillys March? Gemma could have matched any story Julian might have told his father. And would very much have enjoyed that little bit of play-acting, too."

"Why not go the simpler route of blackmailing Julian, then?"

"For one thing, I don't think Julian would have paid up. He's very much the 'publish and be damned' sort, you know. For another, he couldn't have got his hands on that much money that quickly." She smiled slightly. "Poetic justice, you see. Dillys March was allowed by the Craels to ruin my son. I thought I deserved to see 'her' make Julian squirm."

A tender woman, thought Jury. "How did she meet Julian in the first place?"

"Accident. In a railway station — Victoria, I believe."

"At first you denied the possibility of her being Dillys. Was that to give added weight to your opinion when you finally came round to saying that perhaps she could be, after all?"

"Precisely, Inspector. I thought I shouldn't be too easily convinced at the outset."

"There were no proofs."

"I did have access to some papers. A copy of Dillys March's birth certificate, some other things. If it really had come to the point. But you don't know Colonel Crael very well if you think it would have. He'd have given her her 'inheritance,' never fear. Still, I could have had 'Dillys' produce something at the appropriate moment."

"The moment never came."

There was a long silence. She sighed. "Well, Inspector. Before you set the dogs on me, I would like to make a bargain with you."

That she was in no position to bargain didn't seem to occur to her. They might have been haggling over the price of the green velvet love seat on which she was now resting her hand. In the dim light of the frosted globe — the only lamp which Wood had turned on — the rose topaz ring on her finger glittered.

"What sort of bargain, Mrs. Manning?"

"You see, I'm admitting rather freely to — fraud, I guess you'd call it. And I'll give you no trouble on that score. However, I feel I've the right to try and clear my name of murder. I can't do that if you take me away."

Jury smiled slightly. "It's up to us to do that — clear you, that is — if it can be done."

She shook her head. "There would be no assurance of success. All I want, Inspector, is some four or five hours time. There's a hunt tomorrow — I should say *this* morning. If you could allow me some freedom of movement only until then —"

"In four or five hours you could be far away from here —"

She snorted. "Oh, come now, Inspector. I've no place I want to go. I've no life apart from Old House except my son, and how could I ever see him again if I should scarper?"

He liked the word on her tongue. Jury smiled. "What is it you intend to do? In this bargain, what will be *my* reward if I allow you those hours?"

"I think perhaps I can flush a fox out of covert for you, Inspector. Tomorrow, as the Colonel is fond of saying" — she smiled — "we get out the old red rag."

The Old Red Rag

AT 8:30 A.M., Melrose Plant, breakfastless, with only a draught from a mind-numbing stirrup cup to sustain body and soul, was picking himself up off the ground. He had already taken one fall a half-hour ago when his mount just barely missed clearing a wall. Now it had gone down jumping a beck and he was dusting himself off and remounting. It was as well his mind was numb, for so were his hands and feet. What feeling of gentlemanly obligation to his host had cured his dicky knee and dragged him from a warm bed into the cold, dark hour of six, Melrose couldn't imagine. A rare scenting day and rising glass, the Colonel had kept declaring with obnoxious regularity.

Melrose remounted. The scent and the glass could rise to heaven, for all he cared. He wasn't interested in hounds nor fox, but he was very curious about people. Here they were chasing across the moors, scarlet-coated, swallow-tailed, tweeded, galloping about as if there'd never been so much as a scratched face or a torn coat (plenty of both), not to speak of murder.

He surveyed what part of the field he could see — pinks and Melton coats, derbies, velvet caps on the women, stocks, boned boots, jeans and sweaters. A motley crew, all apparently having a spanking good time out here on this heathen moor in the wet and the fog and the snow. A band of hardy foot-followers crowned the hill in the distance like spectators at a cricket match. Only God knew where the huntsman was; Melrose hadn't seen him since they'd hacked to covert where Tom Evelyn had made his draw a half-hour ago.

Peering through the mist he thought he made out the Colonel, and since Evelyn was not in evidence, Melrose thought half the pack must have slipped aside on another fox, for Colonel Crael had lifted his hat and was giving the "view hallo."

The gray he was riding was enamored of it all, even if Melrose wasn't, and when hounds started throwing tongue, it set off again at a fresh gallop. Thank heavens it was open country, few fences and no wire. Melrose kept his head down as the gray took what seemed to be a double ditch. Now the tail hounds were away in the mist so that they were following with ears rather than eyes.

The gray flung itself over another ditch and Melrose expected to see the cold ground come up in his face at any moment. Over the sound of other hooves splintering the frosty ground, Melrose could hear hounds racketing away. When there was a clear patch in the fog he made out a cluster of horses and riders, all halted at a long stone wall. He assumed the Colonel had found and was just as glad of it. Now maybe they could go back and eat and be civilized. He broke his horse's gallop, trotted up, and dismounted where ten or a dozen riders were doing the same.

The wall before them seemed to jut up out of the mist, a purposeless boundary for all Melrose could see. Hounds were rioting, and that didn't mean a find, even to his untuned ear. Colonel Crael seemed to be warning them off, and the second whip was standing there looking much whiter than the cold allowed for.

Dear God! thought Melrose, when finally he saw her.

Olive Manning was lying across the wall, face down, like a huge rag doll, her legs hanging down one side, arms straight out and down the other. Blood was everywhere — running down the stone, staining the snow, smeared on breeches, black Melton coat, boots. It was as if she had tried, before she died, to hoist herself up and off the murderous stones. The fence would have made any horse and rider refuse it and look for a gate or some other way through it. It was not its height which precluded a jump, but the fact it was coped with knife-edged pieces of limestone, laid transversely. It would be like falling on spikes.

"Get Jury," said Melrose, to no one in particular.

2.

"I found her, Inspector Jury; that is, Jimmy and I did." Colonel Crael was leaning against the wall as if his legs wouldn't hold him.

Between the time the second whip had ridden to Cold Asby to telephone the Fox Deceiv'd, and Jury's arrival, Melrose Plant had done a good job of fending off the field and Tom Evelyn an equally good one of rounding up hounds.

There was no one now on the moor except for Jury, Wiggins, Colonel Crael, and the body of Olive Manning.

Jury was silently cursing himself all the while he was examining the body, waiting for Harkins and the Scenes of Crime man. Had he not given Olive Manning her several hours of freedom this wouldn't have happened. "When was the last time you saw her this morning?"

"I don't recall I *did* see her, Inspector. There must be some fifty hunt members turned out; it's a large field for this time of year. I wasn't really looking for Olive."

"How was it she got off by herself? She was *ahead* of hounds?"

"I honestly don't know. Perhaps she'd been following the first fox, Tom's fox."

"Tell me what happened, then."

"We were having a very fast gallop. Hounds must have gone for a half-hour or so without a check. Well, it's a good scenting day, so they held on and held straight for Dane Hole. After that the pack divided about a half-mile back near Kier Howe. It's the other side of Cold Asby. At any rate, I saw this fresh fox break from Badsby Hole. The second whip — that's Jimmy — raised a view and we were off. As we neared this damnable fence, I wondered, Why are they checking so suddenly? I thought the line had been crossed and the ground foiled, you know, sheep-trodden.

Sheep are worse than cattle sometimes; they can wipe out scent like a sponge —"

Jury interrupted: "Yes. Go on."

"Then hounds went down the fence. I thought they were searching out the gap — there is one some way farther on, and then . . . well . . . Jimmy had come up beside me just when they started rioting. We both reached . . . Olive at the same time. And a few moments later Evelyn came down the hill over there with hounds in full cry." The Colonel shrugged, looked off into the gray light. "That's all. Evelyn got hounds under control and packed them off."

Jury turned away from the remains of Olive Manning. "Sergeant Wiggins, take the jeep and Colonel Crael and get back to Old House and make sure no one leaves."

"That'll work a hardship on them, Inspector," said Crael. "Some of them have to hack all the way to Pitlochary, and I'm sure —"

"I don't give a bloody damn how far they have to hack."

3.

Dr. Dudley wiped his hands and shook his head. "Clever. But couldn't have happened."

"That's what I thought," said Jury, watching Harkins's men feather out much like hounds, spreading thin all along the stone wall. They were combing everything — ground, cracks, snow for evidence.

Harkins stood in his sheepskin-lined coat, smoking. "Clever is right." Harkins ran his gloved hand across the stones. "I shouldn't like to fall on that, not at all."

The doctor was packing up his bag. "Fall on it. But it won't kill you, though it'd do a bit of damage." He snapped his bag shut and got up. "Those stones will lacerate, but they can't go through you like a row of knives. The wounds weren't made by the stones, that's all."

"I'm afraid to ask," Jury said, looking at Dudley.

"Same thing, I'd say, as was used on the Temple woman."

"And since we still don't know what that was ..." Harkins went over to the spot where Olive Manning's horse had been found, simply standing, as if waiting for her to remount. The body had been moved at Jury's go-ahead and was being transported in its plastic cover to a waiting van, whose red light winked in the ghostly weather. The men from Pitlochary had reached the desolate murder-scene on an old dirt road which crept up from the Pitlochary-Whitby road and wound across Howl Moor. From there on it was rough going to where they were now. "So someone stabbed her, threw her over this wall to make it look as if the horse had thrown her, and then rode off. Clever, very. Except the someone was not so clever about the horse. It was standing on the wrong side of the fence." Harkins clipped the end of a hand-rolled cigar.

Jury looked at him. He wished Harkins were not quite so much of a martinet. He was a very good cop.

The doctor said, "It would have happened about four, five hours ago. I'll know better when I get her back to the morgue-room."

"Just before the hunt, then. It began around seven or seven-thirty, I understand."

"Hellish hour," said Harkins, looking round at the cold, bleak moor. "And a hellish spot to meet someone."

"Yes. But I guess we know why it was chosen," Jury said.

Jury nearly had to swim through a brown river of hounds, tails waving like flags, being herded into the rear of a waiting van by two of the hunt servants. Tom Evelyn came toward him on a glossy bay. Jury wondered how it was that some men fit their vocations so well. Scarlet-coated, leather-legged, up on that horse, Evelyn looked as if he'd been painted in place.

"I'd like you to stick around for a while, Tom."

Evelyn touched his fingers to his cap, but said nothing.

All across the grounds of Old House were scattered horse-carts, caravans, vans, trucks, cars, Land Rovers. Jury walked across the court, past the steaming horses, the men and women collected there in better or worse spirits, probably depending on how much of the stirrup cup they'd imbibed. Jury was starting up the stair when he heard a voice behind him:

"Inspector Jury. I've brought you something."

Lily Siddons sat atop Red Run, her chestnut mare, and looked simply smashing. She was a far cry from the aproned lass he'd seen in the Bridge Café kitchen. She was wearing neither the black Melton nor the plain tweed of the other women. Lily was dressed in a velvet jacket of hunter's green. It was hard to believe this was the same girl. Her amber eyes glinted even in this dull, morning light. Her cap was off, hitched to the bridle and her gold hair was blown by a small breeze. She was no longer "Cook's girl." This was her milieu. She looked elegant, composed, secure.

She looked, indeed, every inch a Crael.

He reached up for the silver cup she was handing down to him. "What is it?" Jury tried to smile, but found it hard going.

"Stirrup cup, something to take the chill off." Her eyes darkened as he had seen them do before when she was troubled. "Terrible. I'll tell the truth. I didn't like Olive Manning, and there's no point —" She shrugged slightly, moved Red Run off through the courtyard, the hooves echoing on the cobbles. Jury did not drink, just held the cup, as if transfixed. He watched her dismount there in the stables and wondered how in hell he could have been so blind.

As he watched her the fog seemed to lift, disperse, recede back into the trees. There was no sun visible, but there were clear tones. The sky was milky; the morning shone like old pewter. And the fragments of Lily Siddons's life flew, in his mind, into place like broken bits of a kaleidoscope to form a design.

The gold-dust twins: Julian and his brother Rolfe. Mary Siddons being discharged, summarily, by Lady Margaret. Rolfe, ladies' man (and seldom the proper lady) whisked away to Italy. And Mary Siddons's suicide.

The gold-dust twins. That incredible hair, which he'd noticed the first night when she stood with the light behind her. Lady Margaret's hair, passed on to Lily Siddons. Colonel Crael's granddaughter.

4.

Ian Harkins loosened his bindings, so to speak, unbuttoning that rich suede and sheepskin coat to reveal the slate blue suit beneath it. He settled back, crossing one silk-clad ankle over his knee, taking his ease in slow motion, keeping them all waiting.

They were in the Colonel's study — Jury, Harkins, the Colonel, and Wiggins. Jury had just filled Harkins in on what he had discovered in London and Harkins was none too happy that his own men — that he — hadn't discovered t. Since Jury had bested him (at least, that's the way Harkins clearly regarded it) on the London end, Jury had decided to let Harkins commence with the questioning in the Colonel's study.

Harkins refused the Colonel's offer of a good cigar in favor of one of his better ones, slipping the cellophane from it. He lit it with a silver lighter and went about drawing it to a red coal. Jury let him take his time, let him, as Les Aird might have put it, "get his act together." It must have been a tough act, for Jury also suspected that Harkins would have preferred not to tread on the toes of rank and privilege — in this case, the Colonel's toes. His options were slim, then; he would not want to appear the sycophant in front of Jury, by deferring to Sir Titus Crael. He was the type of person to go whole hog the other way, to be abusive. For Harkins, Jury imagined this was not a quantum leap. Jury only wished that Harkins's temper were less divided, for underneath he felt the man was a good policeman, shrewd and perceptive.

Looking at Harkins now, who sat there looking at the Colonel, he felt he was getting the real Inspector Harkins, Harkins whole, Harkins *en aspic*.

"Don't you wonder, Sir Titus," said Harkins, "why, if she was such a good horsewoman, she'd take that wall?"

The question seemed to disorient the Colonel. "What?"

"Why would Olive try to jump that wall?"

Jury smiled slightly. Harkins was apparently on a first-name basis with Death, if not with Jury.

"I don't know."

"Would you?" Harkins asked, with a slight lift of an eyebrow.

"No."

"Would *anyone?*"

Colonel Crael frowned. "I've never known any of the field to do so before, no."

"Neither" — Harkins sliced the ash from his cigar with his little finger — "did she." The Colonel looked at him, puzzled. "Oh, you must have suspected that, Sir Titus. She didn't fall over those stones. She was put there."

"Put — ?"

Harkins cut him off. "Where was your son this morning?"

Coming out of left field as it did, the question hit the Colonel like a fist in the face. "Well, I suppose Julian was in bed. Or out for his walk. Sometimes he leaves early —"

"Out for a walk on Howl Moor, perhaps?" Harkins crackled the slip of cellophane which had encased his cigar.

The noise was grating, a good accompaniment to his tone. The Colonel's color rose and he started to protest, but Harkins wouldn't give him the opportunity. "In the circumstances, Sir Titus, didn't you rather suspect your housekeeper had been murdered?"

"What do you mean?"

Harkins gave a snort of impatience at such dimness. "The murder of the Temple woman, of course. You say you went off on the line of a fresh fox, is that right?" The Colonel nodded. "You are far better acquainted with hunting etiquette than I, of course. But that strikes me as a breach of it." The Colonel again could only register puzzlement. "I mean, Sir Titus, that your huntsman was following the first fox. It's rather unusual for the Master to take off on the line of a second. That is not" — Harkins flashed a smile like a man showing a pass — "polite. No one would know that better than you." He picked a bit of lint from his silk sock. "And the second fox took you straight to the spot."

The Colonel got very red, started out of his chair, sat down again, said, "Are you suggesting, Inspector Harkins, that I *knew* Olive Manning would be lying dead over that wall?"

"The thought had occurred to me."

In the silence that followed, Wiggins started to open a fresh box of cough drops, looked at Harkins, and put them back and sucked away on the tag end of the old one already in his mouth. Jury broke into this silence, and suffered a black look from Harkins for doing it. "Colonel Crael, we know that Gemma Temple was not your ward, Dillys. Her whole story was lies. She came here with the intention of picking up that inheritance."

Harkins threw a scathing look in Jury's direction for giving out any information. In a way, Jury didn't blame him, but he felt the Colonel had to know.

Colonel Crael blinked his eyes slowly. Then he said,

"Very well. But I just don't see how she could have known so much about Dillys, about us."

"She was briefed." Jury almost hated to say it. "By Olive Manning."

The Colonel's face seemed to wither as he sat there. "Olive? *Olive?*"

"I'm afraid so. She always resented the fact that her son was driven over the brink by Dillys March, or so she thought. It was by way of revenge. And greed. So Olive Manning was dangerous to someone—"

"She knew who killed Gemma Temple." Harkins said it with all the authority of a *deus ex machina* suddenly dropped onto the stage to clear up the sorry mess wrought by the players.

"Perhaps," Jury said. "Or perhaps something else. . . ." He was thinking of the attempts made on Lily Siddons's life. But he did not want to make any bald statement about Lily and the relationship he suspected between her and the Crael family, so he skirted it. "That trip to Italy that your wife and son planned. Did it come about suddenly?"

"It's been such a long time. . . ."

"Did Lady Margaret want to get Rolfe away—from somebody? Some woman?"

"I don't see what you're driving at."

Neither did Harkins, who was looking very unhappy about the turn the questioning had taken.

"I mean Mary Siddons."

His surprise couldn't have been feigned. Jury was sure that if there had been something between Rolfe and Mary Siddons, the Colonel wasn't aware of it. But Jury bet Lady Margaret had been. "She was a pretty girl, a lovely girl, Mary Siddons." The Colonel was silent. "Isn't it just possible there was a love affair?" Jury could tell from the changing expressions on the old man's face that it was more than possible. It was probable.

"Dear heavens." The Colonel indrew his breath. "Margaret tried to sack the girl. It was just before she and Rolfe left on that trip. I always wondered why. I never believed Mary took anything. Well, I wouldn't have her go, I simply wouldn't, and I won the day on that point, but—"

Certainly lost it on others, thought Jury. "You had no notion of that liaison?"

"I think, Chief Inspector, it might be wise to get back to the business at hand." Harkins was frustrated.

"It is the business at hand, indirectly," said Jury. "Could Olive Manning have known about Rolfe and Mary, Colonel Crael?"

"Olive? Well, it's just possible. She certainly was close to Margaret."

"How old was Lily then?" He kept the question as casual as he could.

"Oh, I don't know. Ten or eleven, she must have been."

Mary Siddons had kept quiet for all those years. Bought off or frightened off, a husband found for her, and Rolfe too weak or too uncaring to stand up to his mother. But Mary Siddons must have tried one last time to attach him, and failed dismally. Rolfe got spirited away by his mother. Jury didn't know whether it was the presence of Ian Harkins or simply intuition which kept him from saying all of this aloud. But he didn't.

"What will happen now?" asked the Colonel.

"There'll be another inquest. Your son doesn't hunt, does he?"

The way Harkins snapped the question out startled even Jury. And the color drained out of the Colonel's face now the questions had come round to Julian once more. "No."

"Where was he this morning, then?"

"I couldn't say. You asked me that before, Inspector." His voice was weary.

"And he doesn't follow on foot?"

"No, he doesn't. Julian doesn't like hunting," answered the Colonel in a battered voice.

"But he does enjoy long walks. Knows Howl Moor pretty well, I expect."

"I don't like the implication of your questions, Inspector Harkins," snapped Colonel Crael.

Jury was tired of the bullying. "Anyone could have arranged to meet Olive Manning out there, anyone on foot or any member of the hunt. So walks across the moor don't prove much who killed her."

For that little speech he was rewarded by two very different sorts of looks.

After a moment's reflection, Colonel Crael said: "But wouldn't it be extremely difficult for the murderer to come upon Olive out there on Howl Moor by that wall?"

"Apparently not," snapped Harkins. "You did."

"I think the old man was rattled," said Harkins, as they stood in the long gallery. A woman came out of the dining room, looking upset. It was in there that Harkins's men were questioning the hunt members.

"Yes, I think he was, too," said Jury. "I certainly was."

Harkins smiled grimly. "That a compliment? Or don't you care for my methods?" He applied flame to a fresh cigar, then said, "Julian Crael is the one I'd really like to get my hands on. And I doubt very much he has an alibi this time."

"I think I'll question Julian Crael myself."

"I'd prefer to be there."

"Why don't you talk to him later. Just give me a few minutes —"

"Look, Jury, this is my bailiwick, after all —"

"*Your* bailiwick!" Jury forgot his vow never to tell off the men on provincial police forces. "You people call up London and ask for help. Okay, what you get is me. Bloody tough. But as long as I'm here it's *my* bailiwick. *I* say how this investigation is conducted."

Smoothly, Harkins said, "Calm down, calm down, Inspector Jury." His smile was irritatingly superior, and he touched his pigskin-gloved finger to his satiny mustache as if to erase the smile. "I'll see you later." Harkins turned and walked off down the gallery.

5.

In the Bracewood Room, Julian sat on the couch opposite Jury. He was leaning forward, hands clasped tightly, looking at the floor so that Jury could see only the crown of pale hair. It seemed vulnerable, the head of a young boy. "Cigarette?"

Julian shook his head, got up. "I could use a drink, though. You?"

"Why not? Just a small one, though." Considering the loneliness which Julian must have been living with all these years and the pain he was about to endure, Jury couldn't quite stick at making him drink alone, too.

Julian splashed whisky in two glasses, adding soda to his. "I feel sorry about Olive, knew her most of my life." He went to stand by the mantel. "Though you might not believe that."

"Why shouldn't I?"

"I rather have the impression that, in spite of my alibi, you still think I killed this Temple woman." His arm lay across the mantel and the dark material of the blazer he was wearing made him seem to match the pose of his mother in the portrait above him. He looked so very young. Though he was not that much younger than Jury, still Julian looked untouched.

Jury did not remark on his last statement. "Where were you during the morning?"

"Out for a ride. I came back about nine. And, no, I was not riding out on Howl Moor. That spot where the wall is is a bit distant for my before-breakfast ride."

"By yourself?"

Julian glared. "No, I had my horse with me."

"Did you see Olive Manning this morning?"

"No."

"I wanted to ask you about Dillys March."

"For the hundredth time, that woman was *not* Dillys March."

"I know." Jury took a sip of his whisky; it bit his tongue. "She was brought here to masquerade as Dillys by Olive Manning."

He seemed as baffled by this news as the Colonel had been. He had to retreat from his position by the mantel so as to sit down. "*Olive?* My God, but why —?"

"Money and revenge, presumably. She felt the Craels were responsible for what happened to Leo."

"I find it hard to believe she'd deceive my father in that way. How did you find out?"

"I went to the Sawry Hotel." Julian turned white. "Perhaps it was Miss Temple who left the matches, after all. Quite deliberately."

There was a long silence, broken only by a log disintegrating and sparking in the fireplace. "So you know about it," Julian said.

Out of his pocket, Jury took the picture which Melrose had found, outreached it to the small table beside Julian's chair. Julian looked at it for a long while, and then murmured, "Stupid of me." Wearily, he leaned his head back against the chair and said, "Stupid to keep the pictures. I won't bother asking how you came by it. It's an academic question, anyway. I suppose that ties it all up for you, doesn't it?"

"No. Was it in London you met her?"

"Victoria Station. I'd taken the train down . . . last year, it was. I went into the café for a cup of coffee and there she was, eating a bun, drinking a cup of tea. I couldn't believe it. To see this girl sitting there who could have been Dillys. One allows of course for the ravages of Time, as they say. But she was hardly ravaged." His smile was thin, quirky. "I'm not used to approaching women, really, but I screwed up my nerve and managed it. Inane conversation about the trains and the weather. I found her very friendly."

"Prostitutes have been known to be."

Julian flushed. "But she wasn't. I mean, not really."

Jury smiled. "Just a little round the edges?"

"Oh, have it your own way. She was really an out-of-work actress. And we've some proof of that, isn't that so?"

"Yes. So you knew Gemma Temple for upwards of a year. All of those trips to London . . ."

"An unwise, a dangerous liaison obviously. But I couldn't help myself. How many men have said that, I wonder? But it was like — getting something back. When Mother and Rolfe and then even Dillys went, I felt robbed. Not only desolate but, well, robbed, violated. As if this house had been ransacked and everything taken. I can't explain it. But seeing her, it was like . . . having things in the right place again." He fell silent.

It was really Julian, rar more than his father, who was trapped back there in the past. "You must have felt very deeply about Dillys to think you could resurrect her somehow in the person of Gemma Temple."

Julian shot him a glance. "The *idée fixe*, is that what you mean? A kind of madness?" He turned to stare up at the portrait of Lady Margaret. "I was her pet. Pet, *objet d'art* — she flashed me about like a perfectly cut gem. I was beautiful." There was contempt and bitterness rather than vanity and pride in the tone. "I was something to be pampered and polished and returned to the tissue-lined box when she was done with me, a flaxen-haired, sapphire-eyed doll. I don't think she thought, when I wasn't on public display, that I was *there*. It was as if I simply disappeared when there wasn't anyone around to see me. But I worshipped her, adored her. I'd lie awake at night waiting for her to come in, come back from a party. I'd steal over to the window to look down when I heard the car come in. If it was too dark to see, I'd listen. She wore dresses that rustled. Odd, how other women's dresses simply hung on them, silently. But I always knew it was she, because of the rustle." He leaned his head against the chair, shut his eyes. "Why did she have to die with *Rolfe?* It should have been me."

"But Dillys March. We were talking about her. Was she so much like your mother?"

"Not in looks, no. But in every other way, she reminded me of mother. She was my mother's protégée, her alter ego, almost."

"Your earlier statement — that you disliked Dillys — I take it was not precisely true."

Julian turned his head and smiled slightly. "And not precisely a lie, either." The firelight caught at a glaze in his eyes which might have been tears or a sabre's flash. "She was fascinating, Dillys was, but not nice at all. She would have loved today; she would have loved the hunt and the kill at the end, if I might speak metaphorically. Death fascinated her. I think she's the type who would have loved a suicide pact. Even at sixteen, even at *fourteen*, she had men and plenty of them."

"You told Gemma Temple a great deal about yourself, didn't you?"

"Yes. A great deal."

"Even about Olive Manning and her son."

"That got into the conversation at some point, yes. The story of my life. I don't often tell it."

"What about marriage, Mr. Crael?"

"Out of the question." He said it like the lid snapping shut on the box from which he took a cigarette.

"But Gemma Temple mightn't have thought so. She must have thought she'd landed a very big fish indeed."

"I think I can follow your line of thought, Inspector. Gemma Temple, knowing what she knew from me and with all the other details filled in by Olive Manning — Gemma came here with the notion of passing herself off as Dillys. And out of rage or vengeance or whatever, I killed her. Simple as that."

"No, sir. Not so simple. There's Olive Manning's death. Why would you kill Olive Manning when she would be the next best bet for the murderer of Gemma Temple? Thieves falling out?"

"My God, Inspector. Are you going to save me from the dock after all?"

"Please don't try that tone on me, as if you didn't care. You care about a lot of things, and more than's good for you, I think. Tell me what happened after the Temple woman got here."

"First I knew of it was when I walked in here — they were in this room — my father, Gemma, Olive Manning. Wood had just served sherry. I opened the door and found myself staring straight into her eyes." He looked at Jury. "This woman I had left — for the last time, I thought, amidst rather much tears and yelling because I wouldn't marry her — here she was. And she smiled," Julian said, conveying somehow that her smile had carried with it all the malice of the universe. "I think every word spoken that afternoon is etched into my mind with acid. 'Hello, Julian,' she said. She held her hands out to me. 'What in the hell are you doing here?' I said.

" 'I don't wonder you're shocked,' my father said. 'I couldn't believe it either.' He was so overjoyed he could hardly contain himself. 'She's come back — Dillys has.' "

Julian closed his eyes. "I almost blurted it out, then and there. But something in her eyes stopped me. The whole ruddy situation was so impossible, I had to laugh. The idea she could pass herself off as Dillys . . ."

"You killed her, didn't you?"

Wearily, Julian turned his head to regard Jury. "No. But I know you won't believe —"

Jury was shaking his head. "Not Gemma Temple. Dillys March."

Almost as suddenly as if fingers had pinched out a candle flame, daylight had faded from the room. Beyond their immediate half-circle of firelight, the room was dark. The dim outlines of chairs and tables seemed left over from some other life. For a long time Julian was silent, then he said, "How in hell did you figure that out?"

"I suspected it for some time. She didn't sound like the sort of person to walk away from a lot of money. But you just told me, yourself, really, a few minutes ago."

"How?"

"That account of your meeting at Victoria. After all, Dillys was supposed to have run away to London. That's where her car was found. Why didn't you assume this young lady, this 'dead ringer,' *was* Dillys? Because you knew she was dead."

"Christ," breathed Julian, closing his eyes again.

Jury picked up his glass, mixed him another whisky and soda, and brought the drink back. He stood over him for a moment. "Go on, tell me. Cigarette?" Absently, Julian accepted both cigarette and drink and then said:

"When we were younger, Dillys and I, we made a pact we'd never keep secrets from one another. We even sealed it in blood, by cutting our fingers — that was Dillys's idea; she was so very dramatic. She wanted us to mingle our blood. I nearly fainted. Literally. I've never been able to stand the sight of blood and Dillys thought that was terribly funny. . . . But I guess you don't want to hear all that —"

"Yes, I do. Go on."

He leaned back, the drink encircled by his fingers, like a psalm book pressed to his chest. "Dillys was jealous of Lily, that was perfectly clear, only she would rather die than admit it. The Colonel was very fond of Lily and Lily was really prettier than Dillys; but Dillys was beyond 'pretty,' if you know what I mean. In that way, she was like my mother. They both had a kind of — fire, I suppose you'd say. And not always an attractive one, either. Fiendish, sometimes. Mummy had the most terrible temper. Smashed things, screamed like a fishwife. Poor father, I used to think. Only it was exciting, in a way. . . .

"Dillys was clever, very convincing — she could make you believe almost anything. That story of Mary Siddons taking the jewelry, some ring or other, was an absolute falsehood. Mary would never have done anything like that. *If* anything was taken, Dillys took it, believe me. That business with Leo Manning is what brought it all to a head. He was a proper mess, poor fellow. Olive was either straight out lying or deluding herself when she said Dillys was responsible for his breakdown. Not that she wasn't capable of driving someone to the brink. And lord knows she didn't do him any *good*. But Leo was in awful shape when he came here. He seemed at times a mealymouthed sycophant, a modern Uriah Heep; other times I'd look at that smile and think it was sharp as a blade. He made me think of that fellow in the play who went about with a head in a hatbox. Just the sort of psyche Dillys would consider a challenge and love to mess about with, like sculptor's clay. Punch it this way, punch it that. Well, they were lovers. There was a summerhouse near the cliffs where they used to meet . . . that's where they were that night.

"I was taking a walk. No, I was *looking* for her. I saw a dim light in the summerhouse so I went a bit farther along the cliff path and looked in. There she was, stark. It all came at me in a rush then. I thought she'd been only teasing him; I didn't really think . . . You can't imagine what it did to me. That expression 'seeing red' is absolutely true. I felt as if I were staring into that window through a pane of blood. So I waited. I don't know how long I waited out there in the cold. I'll never forget the way the wind sounded coming off the sea and rattling the branches like sabres. The hatred simply washed over me like the sea, but not cold — more like a molten wave.

"Finally, she came out of the summerhouse, walking along the path to the main house. I can still hear her footsteps coming up the gravel, and she humming some stupid song as if nothing had happened when for me everything had. I stepped across her path, started screaming at her. Dillys only laughed.

" 'How long's it been going on?' I asked her.

" 'If it's any of your business — nearly as long as Leo's been here.'

" 'He won't be here much longer then. Not when I tell Father. And you might not either. He won't put up with this sort of thing.'

"And she really laughed at that. 'So tell, like some tittle-tattling schoolboy. But he'll believe me more than you. I'll just say it was Leo made all the advances. And he did, too. Very experienced along those lines, he is.'

"And then she told me in the most graphic detail possible everything they'd done over the year in all of their meetings. I was transfixed with rage. The ironic thing was that she was wearing this cloak that reached to the ground, hooded, and it gave her the look of a religious. I picked up a rock, the nearest thing to hand and crushed her skull with it. She crumpled. I stood there looking down at her for the longest time. I think I expected her to get up, just get up and dust herself off and laugh. Somehow I don't think I let it really seep in that she was truly dead." Julian sat forward, looking hard at Jury as if explaining a very complex legal point. "I felt I had to get her out of there. It wasn't fear, at least not then; that came later. It was that I had to get her out of my sight, out of my *mind*. Cancel the act, wipe it out. It was from myself I wanted to hide her more than from anyone else, more even than from the police. I wasn't even thinking of police.

"Below the cliff path at one point there was a place sort of back beneath the rocks with a hell of an undertow. Not even a diver would go down there, it was so dangerous. She'd disappear, the body would never be found. I was standing right above it. I just shoved her over. . . .

"I ran back to the house, went up to her room, threw some of her clothes in a suitcase and grabbed another one of those capes she liked so much. It covered me completely. When Olive looked out of her window, of course she thought it was Dillys getting into the car. I drove the car to that lot above Rackmoor, parked it there, one car among many. Then I walked back. No one saw me. No one missed me." He said it as if no one ever would again. "The next day, naturally, there was some upset about Dillys tearing off, but then Dillys did it often. I said I thought I'd motor to York for the day. I drove my car to the parking lot, picked up Dillys's, drove it to London and left it there, abandoned it. And took the train back to York and a bus to Pitlochary and walked back to Rackmoor that night and picked up my car." He looked up at Jury. "Believe me, I know how it sounds. Very cold-blooded, all planned out. The cloak, the car, the trip — but it wasn't then. It was frenetic; it felt completely haphazard. What feeling there was at all. I might have been moving under water, it was all so leaden. Only part of my mind was functioning. The rest felt . . . asleep. For a week after that I was sick, I mean, literally. It was like my whole system rejected what had happened like a transplanted heart. I just couldn't assimilate it. That night was something that shouldn't have been there, like a tree suddenly crashing across one's path, like — oh, Christ, I don't know how to explain it."

Jury got up again, took his empty glass, splashed whisky

in it. "You did a pretty good job, I'd say." He lit a cigarette and sat down. "And, of course, after the furor died down, Leo seemed the best suspect. Had they found a body."

"I never even thought of it. You're wondering would I have let him swing for it, if it came to that?"

"I don't wonder much."

"I bet you don't."

"Only now about Gemma Temple."

"Whom I didn't kill."

"You had one hell of a motive. She knew about Dillys, didn't she?" The ashen look of Julian's face told him the answer to that. "That's why you didn't come right out and denounce her, wasn't it?"

"I would have. I was on the verge of telling the Colonel the whole rotten story —"

"Only you didn't have to, as it turned out."

There was another long silence, and in the dim light Jury could make out the tear tracing its slow way down Julian's face. He looked up at the portrait of his mother. "She was trapped in that car, they told me. And Rolfe, God damn him, was drunk when they left. I always keep wondering. If I had been there, could I have saved her?"

Jury looked away from Julian. But not up at the picture. He looked toward the fog, implacable beyond the windows, moving and shifting as if it might find its proper form and give some ghostly knock.

"No," was all he said.

6.

"*Crime passionel?*" said Melrose Plant, his eyebrows up-lifted like wings, his whole bright face so surprised it might have taken off into the somber sky. "Julian *Crael?*"

"Not quite the cold fish we'd imagined, is he?"

They had their backs to the seawall as they stood on the

promenade looking down at the Old Fox Deceiv'd. Jury saw a window open and sweatered arms — Kitty's, probably — tossing out water from a pail. Life goes on, thought Jury. "You never did like him much, did you?"

"I guess not. What happens to him now?"

"I'm saying nothing about it just yet. I want to get this other business sorted out first. A fifteen-year-old crime of passion . . ." Jury shrugged.

"It must be awful to be so besotted with a woman you lose all sense of — perspective."

Jury smiled at Plant's way of putting it. "He's capable of violence, yes. But not necessarily premeditated violence."

"You certainly do defend him. Then who is it who's stepping over bodies on his or her way to the Crael fortune?"

"I don't know yet." Jury watched a cormorant searching out its breakfast. "Tell me, Mr. Plant. What do you think of Lily Siddons?"

"Lily Siddons? I don't know. Haven't had much to do with her. Seen her only a few times. I must admit, she's rather fascinating. Chameleonlike. You see her in the café with some scarf about her head pummeling bread dough and think nothing much. But when I saw her today, I *must* say . . ." Melrose pursed his lips in a silent whistle. "She rather looked, up on that horse . . ." He seemed to be searching for the proper words.

"To the manor born?"

"Now you mention it — yes."

"I think she was." Melrose stared at him. "Remember the other son, Rolfe? Suddenly spirited away by Lady Margaret. Rolfe, I think, was her father. I daresay Lady Margaret would have gone to some pains to keep that knowledge from her husband. Imagine how he'd feel about his own granddaughter — 'Cook's girl' or not. So the mother took him off to Italy."

"My god. But, Lily — she doesn't know?" said Melrose.

"Apparently not. It certainly provides a motive for some-one to kill her."

"Such as Julian Crael."

"Or Maud Brixenham or Adrian Rees. With that paint-er's eye of his, I'd be surprised if he hadn't put it together long ago."

"But how stupid. Why not kiss her instead of kill her? Marry her and make off with the swag that way?"

"Lily would have to agree to that. And she seems oddly — cool towards men."

"But why kill Olive Manning? Or did she know that Lily is a Crael?"

"My guess is she did. Olive was Lady Margaret's confi-dante. And I think she was very happy to keep the secret forever."

Plant shook his head. "It doesn't add up."

"No. But it will. After Julian ditched Gemma Temple, she had a double reason for the imposture: money and spite. It must have seemed almost fun to her. She needed more information and someone inside the house to keep bolstering the Colonel's belief in her if he wavered. It was clever of Olive to deny, at first, the woman was Dillys. And then after she was killed, well, pretty obviously, she had to keep denying it."

"Surely you agree that all of this gives Julian Crael more of a motive than he had before."

"He's also got an alibi. Believe me, Harkins checked it out."

"No, he doesn't." Melrose tossed it off as carelessly as if he were throwing crumbs to the gulls. "I've been chatting to the servants. Don't you remember all the extra help the Colonel hired?"

"Please don't tell me that Julian Crael was running about in a waiter's uniform, incognito —"

Plant shook his head impatiently. "Outside of his room,

up there on the landing was a section of the hall that looked, if you remember, kind of like a minstrel's gallery. The musicians were up there. In costume." Melrose smiled. "And they strolled about. Now, if Julian donned something, a cloak, anything to cover that hair of his, and mask and carried, oh, a dulcimer? Good Lord, I wouldn't even recognize my aunt if she were carrying a dulcimer. He didn't need to play the damned thing. All he needed was to get down those stairs. Or up them. What's one more musician in a funny costume. Why are you shaking your head?"

"Julian didn't once throw that alibi in my face when I was talking with him. He almost seemed to accept his guilt as a *fait accompli*. Or at least that *I'd* believe him guilty. And anyway, Julian's not —"

"If you say 'not the type to do murder,' Harkins will have to arrest me for assaulting a policeman."

"Harkins would stand you drinks." Jury was thoughtful. "I'll have to admit, what you say is a possibility — though, I think, a slim one."

"Well, I'm tired of Julian's 'perfect alibi.' Why is it so hard for you to believe that he's the guilty one?"

Jury looked down the steps. Sergeant Wiggins was approaching at a fast pace, taking them two at a time. "It's hard for me to think any of them did it, to tell the truth. Here comes Wiggins."

Sergeant Wiggins was out of breath. "Inspector, it's . . . Les Aird . . . Mrs. Brixenham . . . says he was . . . out on Howl Moor this morning . . . wants you to . . . come along and talk to him." Wiggins had to lean against the seawall following this exertion.

"You mean he saw something, Wiggins?"

Wiggins nodded, mopped his forehead with a handkerchief, put a pill under his tongue.

"Well, let's go along then to her cottage."

"Might I come, too, Inspector? I know it's police business, but . . ."

"After all your work, Mr. Plant, I don't see why not. And I'm sure you'll be a help talking to Les. After all, you're good at the Romance languages."

7.

"He's really *quite* upset about this," yelled Maud Brixenham over the din of the rock music. The three of them stood like trees shaken by thunder while ashtrays danced on the tables. Maud stove the ceiling with the broom handle. The uproar diminished to a kind of subroar, as if the train you thought was going to run you down veered off onto another track suddenly.

Melrose Plant, seeming quite at home, sat down and drew out his gold cigarette case, offered it round. Looking ceiling-ward as he tapped a cigarette on the case, he said. "Your nephew has quite conservative tastes, doesn't he? That's the Rolling Stones, I believe?"

Jury and Maud Brixenham stared at him as he lit his cigarette and then smiled at them.

"What happened this morning, Mrs. Brixenham?"

"I've never known Les to take any interest in the hunt. I was simply astounded when he said he'd been out there and seen — or thought he'd seen — those two people by the wall where she . . . Olive . . . was . . ." She fiddled with a button which was dangling by a thread. It came off in her hand.

"You follow the hunt on foot?"

"Yes. I don't ride. I hate hunting."

"I'd like to talk to Les. May we go upstairs?" She nodded. "Perhaps you could give Sergeant Wiggins some informa-tion as to your own movements."

Unhappily, she nodded again.

✻   ✻   ✻

"Hullo, Les," said Jury, when the door opened and Les Aird looked through a narrow crack with misgiving. "This is Mr. Plant. May we come in?"

Once they were in the room, Les went to the stereo, turned it down a decibel or two, and flung himself back on the bed. What bed could be seen from the wads of dirty clothes mounded here and there like tumuli. The faded, flower-sprigged wallpaper was scarcely visible beneath its lathering of posters: they were groups — rock groups, Jury assumed — but were they different groups? Or was it just one with continuous costume changes? The same ratio of clean-shaven to hairy faces, of blacks to whites, of floppy hats to Afros stared out from them.

At first, Jury thought the record was stuck; then he realized it was merely that the vocalists were hammering out the same phrase over and over again. His expression must have betrayed him, for Les said, in slightly vinegarish tones, "Guess you can't relate to these jams, right?"

Before Jury could answer, Melrose Plant said, "On the contrary, they've improved immensely ever since they got Ron Wood. May we sit down?"

Les Aird stared at Melrose, mouth open. Then he smiled broadly and said, "Yeah man. Mellow out." He swept a stew of unsavory socks from a chair. "You a cop?" He looked ready to discount whatever points Melrose had just got.

"*I?* Heavens no, would I lower myself?"

Les smiled again. "I didn't think you looked like one."

"I should hope not." Melrose took the easy chair; Jury had to fetch his own wooden one. Les lay on the bed, his small muscled arms walling in his chest, nearly obscuring the half-moon of curved letters spelling out *The Grateful Dead.*

"Cigarette?" Melrose extended his gold case.

Les looked tempted, but then shook his head firmly. "I don't smoke. Too young."

Jury noticed Les looking sidewise at him, clearly suspicious he might be reported on by Scotland Yard. Considering the reek of smoke in the room, Jury had a hard time keeping a straight face at Les's disclaimer.

"Well, so am I old chap, but I do it anyway." Melrose still held out the case and Les snatched one up as if suddenly overcome by reefer madness.

"Thanks, man." The music thumped on.

"Mind turning that down just a bit?" Jury asked.

Les looked at Jury as if that's what he might have expected from him and then grudgingly rose from the bed and padded over, stocking-footed, to the stereo.

Melrose Plant said, "You wouldn't happen to have 'The Wall' would you? Pink Floyd's not one of my favorites, but it's more music to be questioned by, perhaps."

"It's cool, man." Les hunkered down over his box of albums, fingering through them. "I thought I had that, but I don't. I got 'Atom Heart Mother,' though."

"It'll do," said Melrose. Jury stared at him. It was as if he'd come along for the concert.

"That other guy," said Les, changing discs, "he didn't look like a cop, either. Great threads."

"Inspector Harkins."

"Yeah. He acted really radical. You'd a thought *I'd* done it. I mean, I couldn't tell where his head was at."

"What happened this morning, Les?" Jury asked.

"Say what?"

Les had turned his face to Melrose, expression innocent.

"Inspector Jury wants to know about your walk on Howl Moor."

"Oh, that." Les blew a smoke ring and poked his cigarette through it, saying, "This is one strange place. Somebody's always getting blown away."

"Regular Dodge City," said Jury.

"Say what?"

Jury sighed. Les was obviously going to keep giving him those uncomprehending looks. Or perhaps Dodge City was before his time. Jury looked at Melrose Plant.

"You went up to Howl Moor, and then what happened?" asked Plant.

"Yeah. I went out around six-thirty, seven. Aunt Maud, she'd been after me to get out and see the hunt. Some fun, standing around freezing your balls off on the moors in the dark. Or near dark. Well, I got bored waiting around for the redcoats, so I just started walking around. I wound up by that wall, you know, the one where she was found. It was only half-light and I couldn't see for nothing in the fog but I could hear — not voices, exactly. More like whispers."

"What direction did you come from? How did you get to that part of the moor?"

"By way of the High. On the other side of the parking lot there's a path that goes across the main road, finally. Lots of people take it, Aunt Maud told me lots of the foot-followers took it. They all seem to know where the hunt's going by. Me, I could care less. But I guessed one morning of it wouldn't kill me."

"Why didn't you wait and go with your aunt?"

"Say what?" Les rounded his eyes at Jury.

"Why," asked Plant, "did you go by yourself?"

Casually, Les brushed a bit of ash from his cigarette. "Oh, I dunno." Nervously, he looked from the one to the other. "Okay, okay! See, I thought my girl was going to meet me there — she lives in Strawberry Flats, you know — those counsel houses off the Pitlochary Road. She never showed."

"Go on. You heard voices. Men's? Women's?"

"Dunno. They were too far away."

"It could have been others on foot, couldn't it?" suggested Jury. "Waiting for the hunt?"

Les swung his legs off the bed and hunched forward, warming to his subject, but also getting himself closer to

Plant's cigarettes. "I hear this sound, see. It's like something between a shout and a moan. Scared shit outta me. I looked all around, but like I said, you couldn't of seen an elephant beside you in that fog." He accepted another of Melrose's cigarettes, and when it was lit, puffed mightily as if trying to make up for all the ones he'd missed. "Listen, I booked, man. Christ, what a weird place. You feel a hand on your shoulder, you wonder if it's hooked to a body. Spook City. What the shit's goin' down, man? And that ain't *enough*, that other cop comes nosing around here early this morning after they found her and asks me a bunch of questions, and you know what he says? 'You might have been the last person to see Olive Manning alive.' Oh, boy, that's nice to hear. I'm out there on that shitass moor with a murderer?"

Maud Brixenham was having a sip of her watery-looking sherry and giving clipped answers to Wiggins's questions when Jury and Melrose Plant returned to the sitting room. "Poor boy," she said. "Truly unnerved him."

The music, once again being played at full volume, did not attest to that fact, thought Jury. Neither did Les Aird himself. It wouldn't be easy to unnerve Les.

"Did you go up to the moors by yourself, Miss Brixenham?" asked Jury.

"No. I walked up with the Steeds. Young couple on Scroop Street."

"Did you stay with them?"

She sighed. "No. Wish to the devil I *had*. But I did see Adrian Rees a bit later. I was that surprised, because he thinks hunting's quite dreadful. But there he was slogging along. Said he was after material for a painting, of all things. Why does he paint it if he hates it?" Maud shrugged her shoulders and sipped her sherry.

"Where were you when you saw him?"

"At Momsby Cross. Near Cold Asby. It's boggy there.

And there's that beck that runs through, but it's as good a place as any for a view."

"And where is that in relation to the wall?"

Her face was as pale as her colorless sherry. "Momsby Cross is, oh, about a quarter mile from there. But I'm not sure. Ask Adrian. It was in that direction he went —" She clapped her hand to her mouth in what seemed to Jury a stagey gesture. "But I don't mean he . . . well, he simply went off."

"And what time was this?"

"About seven-thirty, I think. Quite early."

"How well did you know Olive Manning, Miss Brixenham?"

She sighed. "Inspector Jury, I've just been through all of this with your sergeant *and* with the Yorkshire police. It was that Inspector Harkins again who came round."

"I realize that. But what with the raft of people they had to get through, questioning was necessarily cursory."

"*Cursory?* I certainly wouldn't have said so. I think that man in charge goes home nights and sticks pins in dolls."

"Inspector Harkins is thorough, yes," said Jury. She only looked at him. "It's just that there are a few people who have some special connection with the case —"

Maud sat up straight. "You mean by that, 'chief suspects,' don't you?"

"How well did you know Mrs. Manning?"

"Not very. I tried to be friendly, but found it rough going."

"You can't think why someone might want her dead?"

"Good God, no!"

All of this time she had been looking not at Jury but at Plant or Wiggins, as if they were the ones asking the questions.

"You said Adrian Rees was with you at Momsby Cross, and then went off. And this Mr. and Mrs. Steed. Where did they go?"

"Said they thought they'd walk round to Dane Hole. That's often where Tom Evelyn makes a draw. But I didn't feel like it. It's another half-mile to Dane Hole."

"Did you see Mr. Rees again, then, after he left you at Momsby Cross?"

"No."

"When did you hear about Olive Manning's death?"

"When Mr. Harkins came round this morning."

Jury got up and Plant and Wiggins rose too. "Thank you very much, Miss Brixenham."

She followed them to the door, her neckerchief fluttering to the floor on the way.

"Pink *Floyd?*" said Jury, stopping Melrose on the walk outside the house. "Where did *you* ever meet up with Pink Floyd, for God's sakes?"

Out of his pocket, Melrose drew a folded up copy of *New Musical Express* and handed it to Jury. "Really, Inspector, you'll never get anywhere in this game if all you read is Virgil." He checked his thin, gold watch. "I see it's past time for our tea. May I buy you gentlemen a Rackmoor Fog?"

8.

"Vampire-bats!" Bertie yelled, swooping through the kitchen, an old quilt upraised above his head, his elbows beating in and out, stirring the traces of smoke from the rashers that had burned because Bertie was more interested in flying than cooking. He shrilled in a high, piercing treble a sound he thought a bat might make.

Arnold stepped back a pace. If this was a new game, Arnold was not participating.

Bertie started walking on tiptoe, fluttering the quilt. "They thuck blood, thath what they do, old Arnold." His teeth were stuck out over his lower lip, making vampire-teeth. Bertie's screeching laugh would have raised the hackles of any other dog. Arnold yawned.

Sighing, Bertie threw off the quilt and inspected the burned rashers. They would have to settle for toast. He apportioned out the rashers thrice weekly: two for him, one for Arnold. Bertie was very budget-minded.

"Anyway," he said, pronging the bread with a toasting fork, "it's what it sounded like to me. A bunch of holes in her, she must've looked like a sieve." He held the toast over the fire and turned it carefully, then stuck it out for Arnold's inspection. "Brown and crispy. I think we'll have a boiled egg for tea." He set a small pan of water over the fire, added two eggs from a bowl on the shelf, pronged another piece of bread with the toasting fork. "Toast fingers and eggs." He hummed a little and thought. "I guess the holes was too big, though, and too far apart. . . ." He turned the bread and hummed some more while it toasted to a golden brown. Then he took that piece from the fork and started to prong another. He stopped and looked at the fork itself. Prongs. "Whatever it was only made two holes, didn't it, Arnold?"

Arnold's nose twitched. He was not interested in the toasting fork, he was interested in the toast and rashers.

Suddenly, Bertie's eyes widened, and he whispered, "*Arnold!*"

Arnold, who had been scratching under his collar, tensed. Bertie's tone suggested something worth attending to, as if a cat had sprung to the sill outside.

"Arnold! The swallowtail!"

9.

Melrose Plant and Sir Titus Crael were in the Bracewood Room that evening, having drinks. Julian was nowhere to be seen, out for a walk, perhaps, and Melrose was just as glad of it. He was, almost, beginning to feel sorry for him. Julian's responses since the morning had been especially lethargic; he seemed merely waiting for his life to wind up. But the sympathy did not change Melrose's mind. He still thought him guilty. Who had the better motive? Julian would never have let her get away with it. Perhaps what Gemma Temple had had in mind was a spot of blackmail: *I'll go away if you give me such-and-such.*

He was called back from these reflections by the voice of Colonel Crael, saying "I'm sorry, my boy, you've walked into all of this trouble."

Melrose went a little red. He was thinking of what hand he had had in "all this trouble." "It's I who should apologize, Sir Titus, for bothering you with my presence in the middle of it. I was planning on leaving today." That was a lie.

The Colonel made clucking sounds, waving the words away like smoke. "Not at all. Indeed, I'm awfully glad you're here. What's wrong with Julian, do you know? I can't believe he's in shock because of poor Olive. He never liked her much; well, she wasn't really a likable person . . . but I'm speaking ill of the dead." He took a drink of whisky and wiped his face all over with a huge handkerchief, like a farmer in the middle of a hot field. "God, I don't know. It's too much."

"It is indeed."

"Let's talk about something else, shall we?"

"When will you have your next hunt?"

"I don't know we *will* have another this season after what's happened."

"But there's lots of good hunting weather left. You can hunt here much longer than in Northants, can't you?"

"Oh, yes. Into April much of the time." He reached over and shook the red coat, which he had hung across a chair and turned to the fire.

Melrose wondered why he didn't have the servants perform this homely task of drying out the damp cloth. Maybe it was a small ritual the Colonel enjoyed doing himself.

Sir Titus said something about a small hole in the worn sleeve. He clucked sympathetically as if the coat would understand. "The old red rag. I'll have to send it along to the tailor in Jermyn Street. I'll have to make do with the swallowtail for a while. Though the Master doesn't ordinarily wear one. Oh, well, no sense standing on ceremony these days. Do you read Jorrocks?" he asked Melrose, who shook his head, his mind not on hunting but on the torn body of Olive Manning.

Quoted the Colonel: " 'I knows no more melancholic ceremony than takin' the string out of one's 'at and foldin' hup the old red rag at the end of the season — a rag unlike all other rags, the dearer and more hinterestin' the older and more worthless it becomes.' "

" 'Swallowtail?' " said Melrose suddenly, looking at the Colonel.

"I beg your pardon?"

"You said 'swallowtail.' "

"Why, yes, the coat I use when —"

But the Colonel broke off because Melrose Plant had shot out of his chair, spilling his drink, and then nearly run from the room.

10.

The gray brindled cat, face besotted with sleep, sat like a lump in the window of the gallery, apparently used by now to these interruptions of its naps, for it made no move, other than to turn itself in a sleepwalking way when Jury cupped his hands round his face and looked in. No one was about — business must be hell in winter. It was dark inside, but since the OPEN sign was stuck in the glass, Jury assumed

Rees was there and opened the door. The bell tinkled and the cat stretched, made several circles, and returned to its original doughnut-rolled position.

Jury let out a *hallo, anyone here?* and soon a clattering of boots came from the back stair. Adrian appeared in his paint-blobbed apron. The black hair falling over his forehead seemed slightly matted as if he'd been working up a real sweat. He wiped it back with his arm, his hand still clutching a camel-hair brush.

"Ah, Inspector Jury. I rather thought you'd be coming round. Let's go back to the kitchen, shall we?"

While Jury settled himself at a listing table crowded against the wall, the kitchen being hardly big enough to admit two upright bodies, Adrian shot open a window and pulled in a couple of bottles of cooling ale.

"None for me, thanks —"

Adrian returned one bottle to its dirty bit of snow. "I guess you're here about Olive Manning. Inspector Harkins almost had me convinced *I* killed her." Adrian flashed Jury a smile. "But not quite."

"You were following the hunt this morning. Why? You hate hunting, I hear."

"My, my, you *do* know my likes and dislikes. Where'd you hear it?"

"Little bird."

Adrian uncapped his ale, sat down, and tilted chair and bottle simultaneously. He wiped his hand across his mouth and said, "It's true. I think fox hunting is one of the stupidest sports there is. It's a sham sport, actually."

"Why did you go out this morning, then?"

"Because the Colonel wanted a picture. A large one, to put in the Long Gallery, of the Pitlochary Hunt. I was merely an observer."

"Maud Brixenham says you were with her at Momsby Cross. She said you went off in the direction of Cold Asby."

"So there's your little bird. Maud is not terribly fond of me."

"I wasn't aware of it. She's never said anything against you."

Adrian clattered the chair down and snorted. "Oh, come *on*, Inspector. She's too smart for that. Direct attack would not be Maud's way."

"What would she have against you?"

"I think she's jealous of anyone who has a stake in the Colonel. He likes me; he actually *admires* me —" Adrian smiled, dipped his head, tapped ash from his cigar.

"I don't see why that surprises you. You're very good, at least from what I've seen. Were you anywhere near that wall?"

"I'm not really sure. I don't know the moors all that well, not like those who follow hounds, certainly."

Jury took out an ordnance map, spread it on the table, pointed to Momsby Cross. "You and Maud were here." Jury ran his finger along the map. Dane Hole, Cold Asby, Momsby Cross. "The body was found here. That'd be about a quarter of a mile from Momsby Cross."

Adrian picked up the map, squinted at the lines, dots, and shadings, and shook his head. "Maybe that tumuli there . . . I think I might have passed that. But that doesn't seem to be specially near the wall."

Jury folded the map, stuck it in his back pocket. "And then you came back to the village?"

"Yes. First I heard of all this was when Inspector Harkins came knocking at my door several hours ago."

"About this picture: if you dislike hunting so much, why would you take that commission?"

"Art and morality, is that the lecture? Inspector, I'd take *any* commission. No scruples. If Scotland Yard wanted to commission me to do Identikits, I'd do it, believe me. And speaking of *that* —" Adrian creaked his chair forward, jammed the cigar in his mouth and got up. "Come on up-stairs."

Adrian flung back the cover from the canvas in the corner of the room, the picture he had been working on. "Done from memory, of course, but true, I think, to detail. And mood, I hope. Like it?"

Jury was stunned. The figure seemed shrouded not so much by the black cape, as by night and fog. Thin tendrils of it wrapped about the woman. She was as stiffly posed as if she had sat for the portrait, and Jury imagined it was not precisely as she had appeared to Adrian on the night of the twelfth. The form was elongated, long-limbed, the neck and hands etiolated; the face, black-masked, and rather frightening. The left side glimmered ghostlike; the right side was black and almost disappeared into the dark background. The play between light and shadow was wonderful. Fog made a silver aureole round the street lamp. It was, in its way, as affecting as the portrait of Lady Margaret.

Jury reached out to pick it up — the canvas was not very large — and said, "May I?"

"Of course."

He took it over to the lamp and studied it again. "It's remarkable. Only, I wish you'd finished it before. Did you show it to Harkins?"

Adrian was rooting through a jar of brushes; he threw them down and turned. "Good God! Philistines! All you can think of is murder."

"It does rather occupy my time, yes. Is this the Angel steps in the background?" Adrian nodded, wiping off the brushes. "It's a hell of a lot better than an Identikit, if this is really what you saw."

"I'm an artist, remember. Observation is my business."

The bell tinkled downstairs. Adrian looked at the floor, surprised. "Surely it can't be a customer. I've forgotten what they look like. It can't be you, you're here. Someone must have got lost in the fog."

"Why don't you go and see?"

Adrian took a swipe at straightening his hair and went downstairs.

All Jury heard from below were muted voices; he was still absorbed in the picture. He frowned.

Something was wrong. An image, obscure, opaque, floated in his mind. A face in a wave, a reflection in a pool. His mind jumped back to watching himself in front of the mirror in the Old Fox Deceiv'd. . . .

"Mr. Jury!" yelled Adrian up the stairs. "Come on down; you've a visitor."

Carefully he replaced the canvas on the easel, the image lost to him again. But something was still wrong.

Of all the people he hadn't expected to see it was Percy Blythe: much sweatered, heavy-coated, bundled nearly to his nose in scarves. He was wadding his knitted cap in his hands and darting quicksilver glances at the paintings on the walls.

"Hello, Percy. You wanted me?"

"Ah do." A darkling look fluttered toward Adrian Rees. "Alone."

Adrian excused himself with elaborate politeness, and once his footsteps had receded and Percy Blythe had made sure he was out of earshot, he said, "It's Bertie. The bairn's been in me heeam, thievin'."

"*Bertie?* Oh, surely not —"

"Seen 'im wit me own eyes." He pointed to his eyes, to make sure Jury knew he had two. "Coomin' up Dagger Alley, ah was 'n ah seen 'im 'n Arnold, coomin' outa me heeam. Ah hung back i' t'shadows."

"But weren't they just visiting, Percy? They go in when you're —" Seeing him shake his head, Jury stopped.

"Not t'goin' in ah mind, but t' coomin' out. An', oh, so sly they was, slippin' along like two eels —"

(The thought of Arnold as an eel nearly made Jury laugh aloud.)

"— wit t'murder weapon."

"*What?*"

"T'murder weapon, lad. Wot 'er was done killed wit. Ah cudda tol' ye wot killed 'er soon as ah knowed 'twas puncture wounds."

11.

Bertie did not like coming this way even in full daylight, certainly not at night.

He held the swallowtail prong-down and stepped carefully. He didn't want it putting his eye out in case he stumbled, which was a likelihood in the sea-roke and on this boggy ground. Roots of trees which he could not see well in the moving mist lay across his path like the feet of prehistoric monsters. A couple of times he nearly fell.

He was making his way to that part of the cliff between Old House and the seawall where there was a place (according to Percy Blythe) where you could send anything over and it wouldn't be seen again. That's where he intended to throw the swallowtail. Of course, *he* knew Percy hadn't had anything to do with the murder. But that wasn't to say the police wouldn't think so if they found this thing in his cottage. Someone must have walked in and taken it and then put it back.

Bertie knew he might be destroying evidence; he had seen enough American telly to know that. It had kept him for hours sitting over a cup of tea at his kitchen table, head in hands, debating. He had even forgot Arnold's Weetabix. Finally, he had managed to rationalize it. There was no proof the murder *had* been done with the swallowtail.

There were lots of things with prongs like that. The toasting fork, for instance. Lots of things.

Something hard hit his foot — a root, he supposed — and he nearly fell again. "Come along, old Arnold," he whispered, and wondered why he was whispering. There was no one to hear him. And he didn't have to tell Arnold to come along since Arnold was glued to his side. It was more to hear the sound of his own voice than anything else. To make sure Arnold wouldn't lag, he had a finger hooked in his collar. "Come along," he said again. He heard the Whitby Bull; in this silence it sounded as if the horn were right by his ear. Perhaps he was getting nearer the sea.

So that he would have a free hand to search the fog before him, he put the swallowtail in the coat of his slicker. He should have worn his black coat; this old yellow slicker wasn't nearly warm enough. And the torch he had was almost useless, its dim yellow glow more frightening than helpful, for it pointed up branches with skeletal arms, bushes like crouching beasts. He wished Percy Blythe hadn't made those silly jokes about Arnold's being a bargast. It wasn't funny. He wished he hadn't talked on about gabble ratchets, too. And the killing pits of the druids. It was all well and good to hear about that stuff between the safe walls of Percy Blythe's cottage; but it didn't go down a treat to think of it when you were out here, and maybe those other things were too. He should have gone by way of the seawall, but that might have meant meeting up with somebody on the High or in Grape Lane. He wished he could hear something except the sound of his own feet squelching over the boggy ground, or Arnold snuffling the wet undergrowth like a hound reeling in scent. Bertie yanked on his collar. Now he could hear the sucking sound of the waves and he walked on a bit faster, pulling at Arnold, who didn't need to be pulled. When he could hear the waves' collapse not far off, he was relieved; soon he would be rid —

Something moved.

Bertie swung round, beaming the torch full circle, shouting, "Who's there?"

But amongst the wind-whipped branches and in the mist it was difficult to tell what was stationary, what was not. With his back to the sea, off to his left he could make out the lights of Rackmoor village, those on the far side of the cove. Arnold growled, low and soft, as if lit by Bertie's own imagination, and then they turned and started again toward the cliff's edge. It was all this pondering on gabble ratchets and bargasts —

Something was coming up behind him. There was no doubt this time that he heard steps, or something plowing through the undergrowth. But since the trees themselves in the dark and fog took on almost human form, it was hard to tell if the something were human.

Arnold growled again, deep in his throat.

There was a rushing sound through the undergrowth, like wind sweeping down a corridor. Arnold was barking in earnest now and Bertie's scalp prickled with fear the same as if he'd been trapped in a tube station tunnel and the train coming at him. A bright light suddenly shone in his face, its Cyclops-eye blinding him. Bertie flung up his arm, but not before a hand reached out and knocked off his glasses.

Arnold was barking furiously. Bertie could just barely make him out, rushing at the dark blur — at whoever it was who had dashed the glasses to the ground and grabbed at his slicker, pulling it off the shoulders. Someone was after the swallowtail, he was sure of it.

Bertie heard more rushing and scuffling and Arnold's barking was near-hysterical and it was like two dogs going at each other's throats. Except from the other dog there was no sound, no voice, only heavy breathing. He was afraid to move without his glasses. Without his glasses he couldn't see anything clearly and he knew he was near the cliff's edge, for he could hear the heavy crash of the waves beneath him.

He knew how near he was when hands shoved him over.

It was a thatching tool, Percy Blythe told Jury, once they were inside his cottage. He pointed to the wall where the other tools were hung and labeled. The swallowtail was missing.

" 'E goes in me heeam t' get nowt or summat. Ah niver mind. But what'd Bertie 'n Arnold want in theirsen fer?" He described it to Jury as about a foot and a half long, pronged, and the prongs sharp as you wanted to make them.

Jury asked him who knew about it, and he said everyone, yes, even the Craels. "They been 'ere. T'owd one come t'talk about stoppin' h'earths or layin' 'edges. T'youngun coom too, onct, twict." No, he never locked his door, and Dark Street was empty this time of year. Anyone could have come along.

Despite the warmth of the little cottage and his two sweaters and windcheater, Jury felt something very cold move down his spine. Bertie was walking around with what was probably the murder weapon.

The drop might have been a few seconds or a few hours; all sense of time was lost to him in the black pool of his mind. His hands had found something against the cliffside, something like a thick stub — he couldn't see it; it might have been an old root, but it was stationary enough to hang onto.

The trouble was, he couldn't get any purchase with his feet, scrabble as he might against the rock, his toes searching out a toehold. But, the rock seemed to dip inward a bit, and his feet merely passed over lichen and then — nothing. So in the few moments he had hung there, his arms had already tired. His eyes were screwed shut; what good were his eyes anyway? His arms felt pulled from their sockets, nearly. There was a thundering in his ears, more than the waves. "Holy Mary, Mother of God . . ." he began. But that was all he could remember, all the rest of the words had sunk, fallen from his memory like the shale sliding down this forsaken cliff. Then he heard a scrabbling, a sound drawing nearer and labored breathing. There was that familiar wet-fur smell. He pasted his face against the rock, crying. At least Arnold hadn't been made a sieve out of too. And then, miraculously, he felt something beneath his feet. He was being buoyed up, just a little, just enough to take the hideous weight off his arms. It moved under him and with the relief to his muscles, the roaring died out in his ears and he could hear Arnold, panting hard, Arnold who knew the little narrow paths on these cliffs and could maneuver them like a mountain goat.

There must have been a ledge just beneath, something wide enough for Arnold, and a kind of path, too, perhaps something left over before part of the cliff had given way so many years ago and sent three houses toppling right into the sea. Mustn't think about that.

Somewhere between hanging and standing, Bertie shoved his face against the rocks, molded his body to the cold, hard cliff as if it were indeed some soft, human form, what a mum might have been if she hadn't gone off. But he would not think about that, either. And he forgot about blessing the Holy Mother, Jesus, the angel Gabriel, the stars, the sun, the moon.

He just blessed Arnold.

There was no one in the cottage on Scroop Street. The panes were black, the door shut. But it was unlocked so Jury went in, felt for the switch, saw the telephone on its little stand in the hall. He called Bertie's name a couple of times, but didn't expect an answer.

He dialed Old House and Wood answered. No, he hadn't seen Master Bertie, and, no, Mr. Plant wasn't there. He'd gone out less than an hour ago in a terrible hurry — and indeed, Wood thought he had been looking for Inspector Jury.

Nor had Kitty seen Bertie. She answered the phone at the Fox. When Wiggins came on the line, Jury told him what had happened, told him to ring up Harkins and have him bring enough men to scour the village, Howl Moor, the woods near Old House, and the cliffside, too.

"What's a swallowtail?" asked Wiggins. His voice was thick and scratchy. That meant he was coming down with something, God help them all. "Whyever did Bertie take it?"

"Who knows? Helping out police or playing detective or protecting Percy. Too much American telly. I want him found, *now*. I'm going up the Angel steps and through the woods. I don't fancy Bertie walking round with that thing."

"Is Arnold with him, sir?"

"I don't know, but isn't he always?"

"Not to worry, then," said Wiggins with a bleak attempt at humor.

A rock, a clod of earth — something loosened and fell down the cliffside. And Arnold's weight shifted a fraction. Bertie could hear the nails of his paws rasping across the stone and was sure they were both going over the side. Bertie pressed against the wet rocks and used the root to try and draw himself up a bit to take the weight off Arnold's back. The cold was bitter; he could hardly feel his fingers and he was hanging now by his crossed wrists.

Arnold barked. Bertie took that as a sign he had steadied himself and he brought his feet down again through that one inch of space and rested them on Arnold's back.

But then he heard a different sound, which came from above. There was a scraping along earth and rock and he realized that someone was making his way down, the same way he had heard Arnold coming.

Relief swept over him in a warm wave. Someone had heard Arnold barking, someone was coming to rescue —

Or was someone coming back to finish the job?

His blood barely had time to freeze up when he heard a voice very close to him say, and in a commanding tone rather than a friendly one, "Give me your hand."

The voice was unfamiliar and cold. Bertie sensed, rather than saw, an arm outreached toward him. Whoever it was could come no closer; whoever it was could not have had much room to stand nor a very good foothold, either.

"*Give me your hand!*"

The voice stabbed into him, and the terror he felt toward the cliffside turned round in him, and he clung to it now as if it were his own mother's body. A paroxysm of fear shuddered through him and he was afraid its very vibration would send him hurtling.

And then Arnold moved out from under him.

Bertie shot his hand out toward the voice, toward the other's breathing, aware only of that one more moment of life before the hand which closed round his own would drop him into the darkness forever.

It was just that: one more moment of life.

But then he heard other sounds coming from above him. Voices. Hounds. For one crazy moment, as the hand grasping his swung him down from his perch and another arm grabbed him round the shoulders, he wondered if the bloody fools were out riding to hounds.

"Bertie!"

That voice came from the top of the cliff and he knew it: it was Inspector Jury. He was being dragged upwards, hard going by the sound of the breathing from the turbid figure beside him. With one final lurch, he was swung up by his arm, set finally and firmly on solid ground.

Bertie could see nothing but vague lights and amorphous shapes, moving dream-wise across his vision. But he wasn't thinking of them.

"Arnold!" he yelled. The terrier barked and Bertie dropped on his knees and threw his arms round the dog's wet fur.

Someone was beside him, wiping the boy's face with a handkerchief. "Bertie, old chap." It was Inspector Jury. "Look, we found your glasses." He positioned them on Bertie's nose.

The scene sprang to life as if someone had raised a curtain. Bertie wondered if it was what you felt like if you were blind and could suddenly see again. In the night as black as jet the people stood out like white statues in a dark garden.

One of them stepped forward and he recognized Inspector Harkins, hands cupping a match as he lit a cigar. Jury was speaking to someone behind Bertie — not Harkins, but someone else. "It's a good thing you were out here."

Bertie turned to see Julian Crael standing behind him.

He stood just beyond the rim of light thrown by the electric torches. He was wiping his hands with a handkerchief. Across his shirtsleeve was a large tear. The coat, which he must have thrown on the ground so as not to impede his downward climb, he now picked up and put on.

"Quite a coincidence," said Harkins.

Julian said nothing.

As if the bitter pill were his own, Jury swallowed. It would be hard to take — to be accused of trying to kill the person you'd just saved.

"I think we'd better go back to the house and talk," said Harkins.

"I'm taking Bertie home," said Jury.

"We need to question the boy," Harkins snapped.

"I can do that once he's home. Not here." Harkins

turned away in disgust, and Jury pulled Wiggins aside. "Go with them to Old House and see Harkins doesn't lynch him, and then come along to Bertie's cottage."

Harkins gave some directions to two of his men to keep searching for the weapon and then set off with Julian.

"Mr. Crael!" Bertie broke from Jury's grasp, ran up to Julian, and threw his arms round his waist, as if Julian too were covered with rich, damp fur.

When he let go, Julian sketched a small salute in the air. "Anytime, sport."

Arnold barked and his tail swished once like a whip.

Close as he'll ever come to wagging it, thought Jury.

· VII ·

Simon Says

$\mathcal{S}$INCE Bertie had nearly fallen asleep on his feet, they'd put him to bed and Jury had insisted on staying with him, said he'd take a kip on the couch. Nobly, Wiggins had forgone his room at the Fox Deceiv'd and stayed also. And Melrose Plant, not wanting to miss out on anything, had awoken in the early hours of morning with a very painful shoulder from having slept in a chair.

Now they were all crowded round the oil-clothed kitchen table: Jury, Bertie, Melrose, Wiggins and Arnold. Melrose had given over the last chair to Arnold and he himself sat on a high stool.

Bertie had been over it and over it as they'd filled him with tea and toast fingers. No, he had seen nowt; no, he had heard nowt; no, he had smelled nowt to give him a clue as to who had pushed him.

As if bribery might charm memory, Jury shoved a couple of more rashers out onto Bertie's plate and some onto Arnold's too. "There must be *something*, Bertie."

"Well, but there ain't," said Bertie decisively, forking his rasher. "Who's payin' for these?" He held a rasher on the end of his fork.

"It's on me," said Melrose. "Sergeant Wiggins here knocked up that old shopkeeper in the wee hours."

Wiggins did not look at all well after his sleepless night. He was probing the yolk of an egg with a toast finger.

"Well, thanks, then. We do like rashers, me and Arnold."

"Someone followed you up there," said Jury. "Whoever it was must have thought you were going to take that thatching tool to Old House or to the police, and that you'd seen who'd taken it from Percy's cottage."

"But I didn't did I?"

"The murderer didn't know that. Why else would you have taken it?"

"To keep Percy from getting in trouble."

"That's very loyal of you," said Wiggins, through a mouthful of toast, "but it's tampering with evidence, lad." He pointed his fork at Bertie.

Bertie went a shade paler. "What'll they do to me?"

"Oh, give you a medal, probably," said Melrose, shifting uncomfortably on his stool. Then he sighed. "I just missed being spot-on with the goods again. I think I'd best retire from the force."

Jury smiled and drank his tea. "*I'm* the one should retire. Didn't even think of Percy's tools."

"Well, you weren't studying them like I was. They were all over the walls. Since there was nothing else for me to do that night . . ." It still rankled.

"It's old Arnold that deserves the medal," said Bertie.

"I agree," said Melrose Plant. "Maybe you could get him one of those ties you told me about. A Murder Squad tie. It'd look good on Arnold."

Bertie gave him a look. "I know who it *wasn't*, I can tell you. That Inspector Harkins's daft. It wasn't Mr. Crael."

Melrose stopped in the act of lighting his cigar and looked over the sputtering flame of his lighter at Bertie. "You mean because he crawled down there and then lugged you up. That, of course, would be most commendable, had he not shoved you over in the first place. Hearing all of us up there, he could hardly let you drop *then*."

Bertie shook his head. "It's because of Arnold."

"I must be dim," said Jury. "Explain that."

"Arnold *moved*. When Mr. Crael told me to let go, Arnold stopped barking and he moved out from under me. I *had* to let go then. Didn't have no choice, did I? You don't think he'd a done that if it'd been that same person that went for me and him with the swallowtail, do you? You don't think *Arnold's* dim, do you?"

"Decidedly not," said Melrose, opening the morning paper and searching for the crossword.

"Bertie's got a point there," said Jury.

Wiggins said, "But you can't always depend on a dog, can you?"

Jury looked at him, to see if he were joking. But Wiggins's expression as he spooned sugar into his tea was almost holy in its seriousness. Jury lit a cigarette. It tasted like old socks.

"You can on Arnold," said Bertie to Wiggins. "Smartest dog I ever did see. Bertie stuffed another toast finger in his mouth. "He can play 'Simon Says.' "

"How jolly," said Melrose, trying to figure out a six-letter word for *obfuscate*.

"Just watch. Arnold, Simon says do this." Bertie jumped up from his chair.

Arnold imitated the movement, rearing up his hind-quarters.

"See?" said Bertie. Then to Arnold: "Arnold. Simon says do this!" Gleefully, Bertie clapped his hand over one side of his face.

Arnold raised his paw up to his eye.

"Aw, come *on*, Arnold!"

"Well, he did it, didn't he?" said Melrose, fascinated, in spite of himself, by the dog's movements.

With a deprecating gesture, Bertie said, " 'Twas the wrong side."

Melrose clapped his own hand against his brow. "For heaven's sakes, you can't expect Arnold to figure out a mirror-image, can you?" Melrose rooted into the bottom of the Weetabix box and lined up two more by Arnold's empty plate.

Bertie was all nonchalance. "The dog shoulda knowed."

Wiggins giggled.

Jury stared.

Like a petrel splitting the water and ascending with his treasured catch, that elusive image at the bottom of the well of Jury's mind swam upward. An image of himself in the mirror, changing a handkerchief from one side to the other . . . another image . . . the hand of Les Aird going over his face to describe the strange look of the person in the fog . . . and more than anything, Adrian Rees. That picture. Yes, everyone had made the same mistake. And he had been the biggest fool of all. His mind traveled back over the description in the police report of the body of Gemma Temple . . . or maybe he had just resisted it, the answer which lurked, fugitive, at the bottom of his mind.

They were all looking at him.

Without even realizing it, he had stood up. "I've got a call to make. Wiggins, I want you to meet me in about fifteen minutes. Finish your breakfast." Absently, he pocketed his cigarettes.

Wiggins looked surprised. "Meet you, sir? Where? Is something wrong?"

"No. I want you to meet me at Adrian Rees's place in fifteen minutes.

2.

"What was that all about?" said Melrose Plant to everyone at large, Arnold included.

"Looked like he'd seen a ghost, or something," said Wiggins, drinking the last of his tea.

Melrose returned to the crossword puzzle. Perhaps it was frivolous, but he was done with detection, so he might as well return to a pastime to which he seemed more suited. *One could play music on her name.* A Shakespearean character. Five down. He chewed the pencil. Fifteen across was *Idiot.* A fitting entry, he felt.

Play music. *Piano.* No, Shakespeare had never named anyone *piano.* At this rate he would not finish in under fifteen minutes, his usual time. Oh, for God's sake, he thought. *Viola.* From *Twelfth Night.* Propitious, all things considered.

Viola and Sebastian, twins . . .

His mind started clicking over. For the next fifteen minutes, he thought about it, finally turned to Bertie and said, "May I borrow Arnold?"

3.

She came out of the fog, walking toward him on Grape Lane, hatless, a wind off the sea lifting her fair hair.

"Kitty just told me about Bertie," said Lily. "I was having coffee with her at the Fox just now. That's awful, awful." Tears shone in her eyes. "Whoever could do such a thing?"

She looked at him sadly, expectantly, and he was struck afresh by her pale beauty and the pathos of her life. He tried to answer, but his mouth was numb. Finally, he said, "We don't know."

"I'm just going to the café. Were you on your way there?"

"No. No, I'm going to the gallery."

"Please come by later for coffee; please do."

Jury thanked her and watched her walk away. Had it been just yesterday when he'd seen her up on that chestnut mare, elegant in green velvet. He still watched the spot where she had vanished, disappearing into the fog which closed round her like a glove.

4.

The gray brindled cat was trying to catch snowflakes hitting and melting on the windows of the Rackmoor Gallery by mashing its paws again and again on the glass. It kept up this frustrating pursuit even when the bell tinkled and Jury walked in.

It was darker inside than out, but not by much. Snow had started when Jury had left Bertie's cottage and now, with the fog, Rackmoor lay hunched in a dusk-dark gloom.

From the little kitchen at the rear came a clatter — a pan

dropped, perhaps — and then assorted obscenities, followed by some out-of-tune whistling.

"Mr. Rees!" called Jury.

Adrian appeared, the dim yellow light of the kitchen silhouetting him in the doorway. "Ah, Inspector! Just in time to share my humble breakfast of dried oatcake. That's what poor little Jane Eyre had to eat at that dreadful school. Well, actually, I'm doing eggs and rashers, but I always feel a bit Brontë-ish on days like this. What's the matter?"

"I'd like to see that painting again, the one you did of the Temple woman."

"A customer at last! How much will you give for it?" Adrian leered and led Jury upstairs.

The oil stood on the easel which Adrian had set up near a window to catch what weak light it could. The effect on Jury was the same; ghosts stalked his mind. "Are you sure this is the way she looked?"

Adrian sighed, drank round the spoon in his cup of coffee. "You keep asking me that. Yes, yes, and, again, *yes*."

"It wasn't Gemma Temple."

Jury turned and walked downstairs, leaving Adrian to stare openmouthed at the empty stairwell, then back at the picture.

Jury pulled the Irish walking cap from his pocket and shoved it on his head. The snow wasn't sticking; he wished it were. He wished, as he walked down the High, that there were great heaps of it — dry, white, untrammeled . . .

From behind him came a voice calling his name. He turned to see Wiggins running to catch up.

"What happened with Adrian Rees?" The sergeant was breathing hard and getting out his inhaler as they walked side by side.

"Nothing. I just wanted to see that painting."

"Painting? Which painting? I thought you were setting off to arrest him. You looked so —" Wiggins could not find words. He applied the inhaler to his nostril.

"One he did of Gemma Temple. Or, rather, thought he did. I'll explain —" They had turned into Bridge Walk, gone up the narrow little stairs when Jury stopped short, looking towards the bridge itself. "Who the hell's that?"

Wiggins squinted through the snow, which was getting heavier. "Looks to me like Mr. Plant. *And* Arnold."

5.

Melrose Plant was leaning against the wall of the Bridge Walk Café, smoking. He pointed to the tiny sign in the glass. CLOSED. "It opens at ten. We've a few minutes to go."

In a not unfriendly tone, Jury said, "What the hell are you doing here? And with Arnold?" Arnold on a leash? He couldn't believe it.

"Thought you'd never ask. Oh, it's so nice to get someplace before you do. Cigarette?" Jury shook his head. "Shall I launch into a long, tedious, though somewhat brilliant explanation now, or shouldn't we wait for a demonstration? But I see by the stony look on your face it should be now. Very well. Arnold —"

The windowshade in the door snapped up. The small sign was turned to OPEN and Lily peered out, smiling. She opened the door and said, "Sorry, I didn't know —" and then her eye fell on Arnold.

Arnold's eye fell, too, on Lily. Arnold growled.

It was not loud, but the growl through an almost-closed mouth seemed rooted in his stomach. It was steady and dangerous.

Lily took a step backward. She tried to laugh. "What on earth? Whatever's the matter with Arnold?"

Melrose looked at Jury and Jury nodded. Melrose tugged a little at the leash but Arnold stood, square, adamantine, unyielding. Now Jury knew the reason for the leash, which Melrose had wound several times around his wrist. He tugged at it. "Come along, old bean." At first there was no movement from Arnold, and then the terrier, with more self-control than Jury had ever witnessed in a human being, turned at Melrose's next tug and trotted off beside him down Bridge Walk.

A gentleman and his dog out for a morning stroll.

Lily had started to close the door but Wiggins put his foot in it, his thin hand splayed against the molding. "We'd like some morning coffee, Miss."

Jury nearly laughed. It was so seldom he heard something like humor from Sergeant Wiggins. And Wiggins must have been very surprised at this visit.

Halfway across the room, Lily stood stalk-straight, her face chalky.

"Your name is Lily Siddons," said Jury with chilly formality. There was, of course, no answer. "We're here to arrest you for the murders of Gemma Temple, Olive Manning, and the attempted murder of Bertie Makepiece. I must warn you that anything you say may be taken down and used in evidence against you in a court of law."

For a moment the whole room seemed white· with her silence. Only the hiss of snow against glass broke it. Wiggins had his notebook out.

Then she laughed. It was unnerving. She seemed to collapse with laughter, falling into a straight-backed chair. "And who's going to be your chief witness, Inspector?" She gulped down air. "That *dog?*"

The laugh seemed real, which was what struck Jury as awful. "No. Though he'd make a better one than most I've seen."

When she started out of her chair, Jury said, "Sit down."

"I need some water."

"Sergeant Wiggins will get it." On a refectory table near the side window were water and glasses. Wiggins poured her out a glass, brought it over.

As she sipped it, she looked at Jury over the rim. He had never known eyes to change as hers did. Pale, from the color of moonlight, to the Clouded Yellow of the butterfly, to cornelian. "You seem to forget," she said, "that some-one's been trying to kill *me*." Her voice was soft; her lips toyed with a smile.

"That was the cleverest part. To put yourself in the position of intended victim. Whoever would think of the victim as the murderer? But we only had your word for it, didn't we?"

Lily smiled with unnerving serenity. "I had no motive, did I? To say nothing of opportunity." She was up now, and Jury let her walk, wending her way through the tables, straightening a glass here, some cutlery there, as if Jury and Wiggins really had only stopped in for coffee. He could not have drunk it, in any case; his throat was tight, his mouth dry.

"You had the best motive of all. As Colonel Crael's granddaughter, you'd have got millions."

She looked up from a napkin she was refolding with perfect equanimity. "That's absurd."

He had to hand it to her. She didn't even flinch. "How long have you known it? Not long, I'd say. And Olive Manning knew it; she was Lady Margaret's confidante. Your mother killed herself over Rolfe Crael, didn't she? Rolfe going off like that, letting himself be spirited away. And the theft of that jewelry —"

So quickly and furiously did she yank the ring from her finger and throw it at him that Jury only knew it when it *pinged* on the floor. "He gave it to her! *Gave* it! It's got their initials and a date. Mummy's and — Rolfe Crael's!

Damn them to hell, they drove her to kill herself. And I've as much right as anyone to the money, the house, the position, the name. I'm *Lily Crael!*"

Jury grabbed her by the shoulders. She stood stock still beneath his hands and he thought she'd got back her control until the hand flew up and came down and the nails ripped like tiny knives across his face. He could feel the welling of blood. Wordlessly, he pushed her into a chair as Wiggins overturned his own chair in an effort to reach Jury. "It's okay." He took the handkerchief Wiggins held out.

She sat there silently. On the table, in the center, was the crystal which she brought here to amuse her customers, like a gypsy fortune-teller. It sat on its little ebony pedestal in a drapery of black velvet. She looked at it as if it could tell her her future.

Jury wadded the handkerchief against his face and went on. Wiggins retreated to the table next to them, his notebook open, watchful. "It was easy for you to get the thatching tool from Percy Blythe's cottage; you're friends."

She plucked a cigarette from a small china holder and held it to her lips. "I don't know what you're talking about."

"Yes, you do. I'll light that cigarette if you think you can keep it away from my face." He half-smiled, struck a match.

"You're a very clever policeman." She let her eyes trail over his face and said, "I'm sorry about that. Really sorry." Putting her chin in her cupped hand, she cried silently, tears rolling down her pale cheek. "It's true. I knew when I found a box of her things. The ring, that picture you took away with you. I'd cut his face out of it — Rolfe's. He was with her." She reached down and picked the ring up from the floor, sat looking at it, dropped it on the table. "I didn't wear it around the Colonel. My God! I even *look* like them! Why has no one ever seen it?" Her voice was high and wretched.

"You got Olive Manning to meet you by that wall. And you thought Bertie'd seen you take the swallowtail, didn't you?" She said nothing. "You must have sent Gemma Temple a note — something to get her to the Angel steps. Did you pretend it was Julian who wanted to meet her? Or Adrian Rees? My guess is, Adrian. That's why Les Aird saw her coming along the High. She didn't know Adrian was in the Fox because she didn't go through the bar. I imagine Maud Brixenham dropped a hint or two about their relationship." Lily's persistent silence was as much of an admission that he was not far off the mark as if she'd agreed to every word he'd said. "You might as well tell me, Lily. It's all over, you know."

"There's no way I could've got from my cottage and to the Angel steps in just a few minutes. Even *you* said that."

"You weren't in your cottage when she was killed. It wasn't Gemma Temple that Adrian saw in Grape Lane. It was you. Gemma Temple was already dead. You'd killed her between the time Les saw her and the time Adrian saw *you* walking along Grape Lane.

Her face was white, her voice raspy. "What do you mean?"

"What I said. She was killed *before* eleven fifteen. Not after, as we all were led to believe." Jury leaned toward her, unmindful of the lashing she had just given him. In her face he thought he saw the remnants of Lady Margaret's beauty slipping away. "Lily —"

It happened even more quickly than the lash of her nails. The upraised arm, the crystal within an inch of his head and the flying foot of Wiggins, who overturned everything — table, chairs, glasses, cutlery, and Jury himself — in an effort to keep her hand away from Jury's head.

"My God!" said Jury, pulling himself off the floor. "Where'd you learn *that?*"

"Karate, sir." Wiggins was breathing hard. "Good for the sinuses, I've found."

Jury was down on his knee beside Lily, who was lying unconscious on the stone floor. "She must have hit her head. Is there a doctor at all in Rackmoor? See if you can scare one up. I'll stay with her." Jury took his anorak and stuffed it under her head. "Have you got an aspirin, Wiggins? My head's killing me."

It was one thing he knew he could always count on. That Sergeant Wiggins would have aspirin.

From the window he watched Wiggins bolt up the street through a day steadily darkening, and looked through the gathering snow toward the little bridge across the stream. Its balustrades were mounded with snow.

Jury went back to the table, sat down, watched her face in the gloom. Pale as marble, as ashes. She moved slightly, made a small moaning sound. He wondered if he should give her brandy. Was there any? Better wait for the doctor. He sat there studying her face, in which he could see the traces, like smoke, of the face of Lady Margaret.

Jury put his head in his hands. *What a waste*, he thought.

6.

"Lily?" said Colonel Crael. "*Lily?* Of all people — you can't be serious!" He looked up at Jury standing in the center of the Bracewood Room as if Jury surely must have misunderstood, as if he'd mixed Lily up with someone else.

"I'm sorry, Colonel Crael."

There was a silence. "I'd like to see her, if I may."

"No. Not now, at least." Not ever, if Jury had anything to do with it. Maybe it would all come out, her relationship to the family. But Jury certainly wasn't going to bring it out now. For the Colonel to discover now, when there wasn't an earthly thing he could do about it, that Lily was his granddaughter — after all the losses the old man had suffered, it was just too much.

At least he could take some refuge in the knowledge that Julian was innocent. "Then Julian — well, thank God he's no longer in danger."

Julian, who was leaning against the mantel, looked at Jury, gave him a weird little smile.

When the Colonel had left, fortified by some whisky and the company of Melrose Plant, Julian said to Jury, "Unfortunately, I'm *not* out of danger, am I? But then I never was. I'm glad it's over."

Jury wondered how Julian himself would respond to the news that Lily Siddons was a Crael, was Rolfe's child. It would be for him an added burden of the blood ties from which Julian seemed to have suffered all of his life. Jury hoped he would never find out. "You know, Mr. Crael, I don't think the courts are going to be all that hard on you. A fifteen-year-old —" Jury shrugged. He didn't want to say *murder*. "And you did save Bertie's life."

"You sound almost apologetic, Inspector. Bertie's rather a brave lad, isn't he? It's too bad about his mother going off like that. I'll look in on him. Sometime. If I'm free."

He had added that out of his store of irony and in an attempt to recapture his old indifference, a habit of mind which had broken during the last twenty-four hours.

Julian tossed his cigarette in the fire and, wordlessly, put out his hand. Jury shook it.

At the door of the Bracewood Room, Julian turned and said, "I've decided not to register that complaint with Scotland Yard."

"What complaint's that?"

"Police brutality."

With the first genuine smile Jury had seen from him, Julian quietly shut the door.

"I don't know what to say, sir . . . my God . . ." Wiggins's voice came over the telephone, high-pitched and tight with anxiety.

Jury shut his eyes against the news. "How'd it happen?"

"She said she wanted tea and I said yes, but I'd have to go with her. Watching her like a hawk, I was — really. I didn't take my eyes off her —"

"Go on. What happened?"

"We were in the kitchen. She didn't plug in the kettle; I suppose I should have known from that. She put a pan of water on to boil. I was standing near her, by the stove. And before I knew it, she'd flung it at me — pan, water, the lot."

"Are you okay? Did it burn you badly?"

"No. It was painful at the time and of course I flung up my arms and it gave her just long enough to bolt. She got out the door and latched it. It was five minutes before I could break it open, but by then —"

She was gone. "Harkins there yet?"

"They came just before I rang you. I believe he's going to kill me, sir." This was delivered in such a matter-of-fact tone that Jury nearly laughed.

"Well, he'll probably need more men. And straightaway, tell someone to get up to the parking lot at the top of the village. See if her car's there."

"It's the first thing I did, sir. I figured that's what she'd make for, but apparently not. The car's there. There's only the one road out, and Harkins has that blocked off."

"There are plenty of ways out on foot. We'll have to cordon off the whole village." Jury said good-bye and started to hang up when the voice of Wiggins said, "Sir?"

"Yes?"

"I'm not trying to excuse myself. But she was so quick, sir. I mean, I've never seen anyone move so quick."

"It's okay, Wiggins. Could have happened to anyone. I know she's quick. I've watched her wield a knife."

Wiggins tried to laugh. "Better boiling water than a knife."

7.

All afternoon they combed the village, paying special attention to the empty warehouse beside the Bell and all of the cottages left vacant by the summer people. Jury recalled the words of Maud Brixenham: *Used to be a smugglers' haunt. Easy to hide in, these twisting little streets.*

Nothing could have been truer. Streets, alleys, cul-de-sacs, winding up and down and across like fretwork. A dozen or more men, including Melrose and Bertie, had been wandering in and around Rackmoor, questioning, looking.

It was Jury's opinion that Lily Siddons was in York by now or on her way to London.

It was nearly dark, now. Jury and Harkins were sitting in the Fox Deceiv'd bolting their food, their first since early morning. In a state of shock, Kity had still managed to put together two plates of cheese and bread and pickled onions.

"Rees and I made the same mistake," said Jury. "That picture he did showed the left side of her face as white. Of course it was, if you were looking at her. But Les Aird must have indicated the *right* side, because he saw Gemma Temple, not Lily. The police report said, 'the left side.' But you were looking at it, as I should have, as the *victim's* left side. So it was Lily Siddons that Adrian Rees passed in Grape Lane. She made sure someone saw her; she wanted to be certain we thought Gemma Temple was still alive when she knew Kitty would be around to supply her with an alibi."

"Mirror image," said Harkins, clearly pleased the police report had been accurate when no one else had. "Did she take the canvas to get Rees in trouble?"

"Maybe; I'm not sure. But I should have noticed the white paint on the left wall of the Angel steps. Gemma Temple had caused that smear when she'd sprawled upside-down. It was the left side of her face made that mark."

Harkins clipped the end of a cigar. "I must say Miss Siddons deserves points for pure damned nerve. Turning suspicion away from herself by inventing this mythical killer out to murder *her*."

"The brakes on the car, the hay rake. It was only her word, wasn't it? She made up two identical costumes. The only thing she couldn't know in advance was which side of her face Gemma Temple would put the white greasepaint on and which side the black. I wouldn't be surprised, even, if it never registered with her — that she made the same mistake I did. I guess we all do it. Although I don't think you'd have made that mistake. I think you'd have known immediately, had you seen that portrait of Adrian's."

Harkins was silent, studying the pigskin cigar case as if it were new to him. "I had the advantage though, didn't I? I saw the body; I saw the face; you didn't." He held out the case. "Cigar?"

Jury smiled. They seemed to have come full circle.

They were standing up to leave when Wiggins rushed into the Fox Deceiv'd to tell them Lily Siddons had been found.

8.

At least two dozen people — some police, a few villagers including Bertie, and Melrose Plant — were standing near the cliff's edge, at almost the exact spot were Bertie had gone over the night before. All were looking down.

Two of Harkins's men, ropes tied round their waists, were making their slow descent down the face of the cliff. But the same rocks' configuration which had prevented Bertie getting a toehold prevented their going down farther. There was no way down, not even for Arnold this time, on whose collar Bertie had a firm grip.

Lily Siddons was — or had been — walking along the narrow strands of shingle between Rackmoor and Runner's Bay, the same one her mother must have walked so many years ago. Jury could barely make her out down there, where she stood looking up. The water was already round her ankles and would soon be up to her knees and then —

She raised her arm. She could have been a bather on holiday, hallo-ing to friends back on shore.

Jury tossed off his coat and was halfway over the edge before anyone knew it, before Wiggins could yell: "My God! You can't get down there!"

From the people assembled at the top of the cliff came screams of protest, among them Harkins's and Plant's, who both yelled in their different idioms to *get back up, you goddamned fool!*

Only Bertie's yell was effective. "Get him, Arnold!"

Before Jury had gone another inch, he felt the terrier's mouth close round his forearm. It gave Plant, Harkins, and Wiggins just enough time to drag him back to the top.

"We don't need your stupid heroics, Richard!" Harkins threw Jury's coat round his shoulders.

"It wasn't that . . ." said Jury, wiping his hair away from his forehead as he looked, dazed, over the edge. What he saw was the collapse of the last wave over Lily's head and the arm outstretched against the dark waters of winter.

She might have been waving good-bye.

9.

They were saying good-bye to Bertie.

"The Chateau de Meechem was especially fine tonight, Copperfield," said Melrose Plant as he stuffed an incredibly large tip into Bertie's shirt pocket. "And the meal excellent, though the promised smoked salmon was once again noticeably absent."

Bertie snapped the towel he used for wiping tables and draped it over his arm. "Ain't salmon season, I expect."

"Bertie," said Jury. "I have an idea your mother will be in Northern Ireland for some time yet. At any rate, you should be hearing from her very soon. And so should Miss Cavendish. So if any of them — Frog Eyes, Codfish, any of them — come round with their questions, just tell them there'll be something in the post. And if that doesn't satisfy them, tell them to ring me up." He stuffed a card with a New Scotland Yard number into the same pocket Plant had just stuffed the money.

Bertie beamed and squinted in turns. "How'd you—" Then he apparently thought better of it, and simply started rubbing Arnold's head.

"Not to worry," said Jury, holding out his hand. "Good-bye, Bertie."

Bertie shook hands. "Ain't you stayin' overnight, then, sir?"

"No. I'm taking a late train from York. But call me sometime, will you? To let me know what happens?" Jury winked.

"You bet, sir. Shake hands, Arnold. Ain't you got no manners?"

Arnold held up his paw.

"Good-bye, Bertie," said Melrose Plant. "And may you never turn thirteen."

* * *

Outside, Jury and Plant strolled up along the seawall to look at the village for the last time.

"I don't think it was the money," said Jury. "I don't think she wanted the money, or the privilege that went with the Crael name. "I think she only wanted the family." Plant said nothing, and Jury turned to stare out at the dark waves rolling in. "Sometimes I feel it's like, I don't know, a false vocation. And now I'm about to be made superintendent. I feel as if I'm being asked to mete out justice, somehow. How do I do that? You look at someone like Julian Crael or someone like Lily and feel they're as much victims as the rest of us . . . yet she's supposed to have done all of this in cold blood?" He looked out to sea as if the sea might give her back. "It's not up to me to decide, is it? All I'm supposed to do is collar them and bring them in. Only sometimes I don't bring them in. I wonder about justice." For a moment he was silent, looking out to sea. "Wonder about being a superintendent, too."

Plant lit up a cigarette. "It's cool."

And they turned from the sea and walked back into the fogs of Rackmoor.